A GAME OF INCHES

A GAME OF INCHES

WEBB HUBBELL

BEAUFORT
BOOKS

A Game of Inches

Library of Congress Cataloging-in-Publication Data
/ Hubbell, Webb

ISBN

COVER DESIGN by Michael Short
INTERIOR DESIGN by Mark Karis

Author's Note

In 1899, the Sewanee Tigers of the University of the South reveled in a 12-0 season. Their opponents included the University of Georgia Bulldogs and the University of Tennessee Volunteers. In mid-season the team took an extended road trip, playing five teams in six days. Not only did the Tigers win all five games, each game was a shut out. During this remarkable feat they beat Texas, Texas A&M, Tulane, LSU, and Ole Miss—not a "weak sister" among them. Joe Paterno, former head coach of Penn State, said that this accomplishment by the "Iron Men of Sewanee" had to be one of the most staggering achievements in the history of football.

Today, the school is better known for its academic excellence as one of the southern Ivies. The Sewanee Tigers still play football, but not in the Southeastern Conference ("SEC"). Instead they play at the Division Three level in the Southern Athletic Association. Their opponents include Rhodes and Millsaps, not Auburn or North Carolina. In 2012, their record was 3-7. The Tigers don't play to thousands of screaming fans on national TV. They play to small crowds of students, parents, academics, alums, and the stray dogs who run around in the end zone. But the rules of the game are still the same; the scholar-athletes still risk serious injury every practice and game; and the individual effort isn't any less than in Division One.

Billy Hopper is a fictional character. He didn't attend Sewanee, wasn't awarded a Rhodes scholarship, and didn't play football for the Tigers. He is simply a compilation of characters I've known. The book is primarily set in Washington, DC. You might recognize some of the restaurants and neighborhoods I describe, but the characters and events in this novel have no connection to reality—they only exist in the imagination of this author and his readers.

PROLOGUE

ON THE MORNING of March 20, 2016, a drowsy Billy Hopper stretched his arm across the bed in his room at DC's Mayflower Hotel to discover a woman lying by his side. As his brain began to focus he realized he was covered in blood and that she was clearly dead. He flew out of the bed in horror, backing himself against a wall. His whole body shook as he tried to figure out what to do. He had no idea who she was. She was naked and had been stabbed multiple times. There was so much blood—gulping for air, he called the only man he knew he could trust. Needless to say, every TV or radio sports news show has focused on little else.

During the previous NFL season, Billy "Glide" Hopper had been the "go to" rookie wide receiver for the newest NFL football franchise, the Los Angeles Lobos. His story of coming from obscurity to rookie success was a sports publicist's dream until the events of March 20, which quickly became known as the "Mayflower Mutilation." At just 6 feet, barely 200 pounds, Hopper doesn't quite fit the image of a pro football player. Baby-faced with golden locks and deep tan, he looks more like a skier or a surfer. He has neither blazing speed nor a whopping wingspan, but he does have two things going for him on a field dominated by giant gladiators—a unique ability to elude pass defenders and hands of Gorilla Glue. During the first game of the season, Seattle's all-pro cornerback was overheard to say. "Coach, I can't cover that dude. He ain't fast, but he glides right by me." The nickname stuck.

Hopper played college football in obscurity at the University of the South in Sewanee, Tennessee. No one from Sewanee goes to the

Pros—even the football players are there for an education. He dreamed of a pro career, but not a single NFL scout looked at Billy or considered his 3673 receiving yards as a Tiger. After graduating with Honors in 2013, Hopper spent the next two years earning an MPhil at Oxford on a Rhodes scholarship. As there were no philosophy jobs waiting for him back in Tennessee, he decided to consult his old coach at Sewanee. Sure of Billy's talents, Coach Samko convinced Billy to attend an open tryout for the new LA franchise. The rest is history. In his rookie year, he had 111 receptions for 1773 yards and 18 touchdowns.

Hopper's phenomenal year propelled the first-year franchise Lobos to 4-12 in their first NFL season—a record much better than expected. The team won their last two games of the season including an upset of New England in the last week of the season, knocking the Patriots out of the playoffs. Billy caught three touchdown passes in that game—all highlight reel catches. He was unanimously elected the Associated Press offensive rookie-of-the-year.

These days all the controversy surrounding Hopper centers on how the sport of football continues to produce off-the-field violence and how it might have prompted Hopper to commit such a heinous crime. Faithful Patriot fans are ready enough to throw this southern kid under the bus, as are the police, politicians, the press, and most preachers. After all, the unidentified young woman was in his bed, he had been drinking at the banquet, and his fingerprints allegedly were found on the murder weapon—a room service steak knife.

He will surely be charged with murder. Speculation focuses more on the murdered woman—who was she? Not a soul has come forward to identify the body, despite law enforcement's repeated appeals for help.

As for Hopper, it seems everyone is ready to condemn him—late-night talk show hosts make crude jokes at his expense, and the media are willing to give anyone an audience and air-time if they can to say they knew Hopper, no matter what they have to say.

The dam of speculation finally broke at 4:45 p.m. on Friday, April 15, 2016, when the following came across the banner of ESPN:

Breaking News: The U.S. Attorney for the District of Columbia has charged Los Angeles Lobos' rookie wide receiver Billy Hopper with first-degree murder in connection with the slaying of an as yet unidentified woman at the Mayflower Hotel on March 20, 2016. Hopper has been in the custody of law enforcement since the incident. He will be arraigned on Monday.

A second banner left little doubt as to the Lobos' reaction:

Billy Hopper's contract has been terminated, and he has been released from the team. The Lobos will have no further comment.

FRIDAY

April 15, 2016

1

PHILANTHROPY IS TRULY a good and wonderful thing, and I am fortunate to be a part of the Margaret and Walter Matthews Foundation. I mean that. But just now, sitting at my desk in DC, I must admit to playing with pencils. I was bored. I'm a lawyer, both by training and profession—administration just doesn't float my boat. The insistent rumblings of my cell phone interrupted my inner grumblings.

"Senator Robinson asks that you join her for cocktails this evening at her home. Please arrive promptly at seven." Nothing else. I was left staring at the phone as it went dead.

The cool invitation by the Senator's administrative assistant caught me completely off guard. How did she have my cell number? I hadn't heard from or seen Lucy Robinson in almost two years. Her assistant's assumption that I would drop everything on less than four hours' notice didn't surprise me—Lucy's arrogance was legend. But the invitation itself did. The last time I'd seen Lucy, she'd taken me to the woodshed for a well-deserved tongue-lashing.

After her husband, Senator Russell Robinson, was murdered, Lucy was appointed to fill her husband's unexpired term as U.S. Senator from Arkansas. She took to the job like a duck to water, quickly becoming a rock star in a city full of politicians who craved the limelight. A wealthy, attractive, and savvy woman in a world still dominated by men, she is a media darling and frequent Sunday talk show guest. It didn't hurt that after an appropriate period of mourning Lucy was spotted at Georgetown's Café Milano on the arm of Charles "Red" Shaw, former Marine colonel, billionaire government contractor, and owner of the new Los Angeles Lobos football team.

I was tempted to bag it. Lucy and I had never been close. Her late husband and I hadn't seen eye to eye in college—in fact, I couldn't stand the bastard. But my late wife Angie and Lucy remained friends even after we left Arkansas, and Lucy had supported Angie in her own way as Angie battled ovarian cancer. I was sure the invitation signaled payback time for my having represented the man charged with her husband's murder. I might as well find out what price she would exact.

The invitation also meant I had to go home and change into a coat and tie, a tired uniform I tried to avoid whenever possible. Traffic was always a pain from my office in downtown DC to Chevy Chase, and traffic back to Lucy's Georgetown home would be just as bad, if not worse. At least I had somewhere to go on a Friday night. I usually began my weekend at Pete's on Connecticut Avenue for Greek food before going home to a bad movie or worse TV. A Saturday morning golf game with my usual foursome at Columbia Country Club was almost always the highlight of my weekend.

My playing partner, Walter Matthews, and his wife Maggie were in Tuscany, so tomorrow's game was off. It was just as well—an old friend from Little Rock, Judge Marshall Fitzgerald, had flown in for a short-notice visit, and we were meeting for lunch.

I decided to catch a ride to Lucy's, figuring I would need several martinis to endure the evening. Thanks to an eager cabbie I arrived at seven on the dot. Lucy's household staff was surprised by my timely arrival and didn't bother to hide their displeasure. I ought to have known better. In DC, it's a matter of pride to be late, a clear indication of your importance elsewhere. The well-trained butler escorted me into the large living room without a glance, leaving me to peruse the art and décor of Lucy's stylish Georgetown townhouse in solitude.

Lucy's choice of art was fairly catholic—Motherwell, Lichtenstein, and a small Stella, but the inclusion of a Gursky photograph came as a surprise. The furnishings were a comfortable mix of antique and contemporary. Everything was in its place, the bookshelves lined with first editions interspersed with objects d'art. I looked for reminders of her deceased husband, Russell, but found none. There were plenty of photographs in silver frames of Lucy with her children, Lucy with

President Obama, and Lucy with Red, but Russell was nowhere to be found. Guess she'd moved on.

I was admiring the Lichtenstein over the fireplace when the waiter brought me a martini, and I heard from across the room, "Dear Jack, I'm so glad you could come."

Lucy wore a shimmering full-length blue dress that emphasized her natural attributes almost as well as the elegant strand of diamonds around her neck. She smiled like we were old high school sweethearts, which we definitely were not. She crossed the room arm-in-arm with Red Shaw—the stocky build, strong jaw, and military haircut were easily recognizable. Lucy held out her cheek, and I managed the obligatory air kiss. Red—he insisted I call him that—extended his hand for a vigorous shake.

"Lucy has told me so much about you. I hope we'll have time tonight for a real talk." His voice was a bit raspy, but his tone was genial enough.

The doorbell rang before I could respond, and Lucy and Red turned to greet their guests.

The living room quickly filled with men in tailored suits and women in expensive cocktail dresses. I was just about the only man without an attractive woman at my elbow, but I was used to being the odd man out at social events. I recognized a lot of the guests— senators from both political parties, former members of Congress who were now highly paid lobbyists, and a careful assortment of the mainstream media. Tonight was about access and being seen—a DC power event.

I had to hand it to Lucy—she'd learned the protocol. No one had to wait more than a few seconds for a refilled glass or another tiny hors d'oeuvre. Rather than the expected chatter about the presidential primaries, the conversation centered on Billy Hopper. Everyone had an opinion. The latest scandal at the Pentagon created a second buzz—apparently the Navy had paid billions for the design and construction of a stealth submarine that had sunk somewhat further than expected. Fortunately, the skeleton crew had been able to escape. Red's company had just been awarded a multi-million dollar contract to recover the wreckage.

The ringing of a silver spoon against expensive crystal caught our attention, and all eyes turned to Lucy and Red, who were now standing at the bottom of the stairs.

Lucy smiled warmly and spoke, "I want to thank all of my closest friends for coming on such short notice. It means the world to Red and me that you're here." Red was beaming ear to ear. Lucy slipped her hand into his.

She continued, "When my late husband Russell was tragically murdered, I thought my world had come to an end. But thanks to so many of you in this room, I've been able to continue his important work."

Lucy paused to emphasize the drama. "But something in my life was missing."

She waited for the room to go absolutely still, then turned to Red and gave him a look that would have thawed Antarctica. She returned to the crowd blushing. I have to hand it to Lucy—she was a natural.

"Then Red charged into my life, and once again I'm a complete woman. I won't share the details of his proposal—Red can really be quite romantic," she grinned. "But he's asked me to marry him, and I've accepted. We wanted to share this moment with you, our closest and dearest friends, before you read it in the *Post*. So thank you all for coming and, of course, you will all be invited to the wedding."

Immediately an army of waiters bearing crystal champagne flutes entered the room, toasts were given, and Red and Lucy graciously accepted congratulations from all.

I watched the unfolding scene from the back of the room, sipping on champagne and wondering why in the world I was here.

I also observed a woman in a deep red dress detach herself from a nearby group and walk directly toward me. I saw that she was quite attractive with full, dark hair, but it was the dress that first caught my eye. Black is the color of choice for most all Washington women—for some reason color is almost unheard of in the posher circles. The dress and her jewelry were understated in a manner that evokes both class and money. She wasn't bone thin either, another anomaly.

"You have to hand it to Lucy. Once she set her sights on Red, he didn't stand a chance," she whispered as we raised our glasses for another toast.

I smiled, knowing exactly what she meant. Her first husband, Russell, had experienced a similar assault in college.

She turned to me, "I don't think we've met. I'm Carol Madison."

Her smile was warm and contagious, her eyes bright, and she had a distinct southern accent.

"Jack Patterson." I extended my hand.

"I'll bet I'm not the only one tonight who wonders why you're here. After all, you did represent her husband's killer."

I couldn't think of a reason either.

She rescued my silence with an easy laugh. Her hand slid down my arm and hooked into my elbow.

"Come on. Let me introduce you to a few people. They won't bite, and I promise you have nothing to fear from me. Let's mingle."

She worked the room with me as her attachment, and I tried to follow the conversations as I wondered about my new companion.

Actually, I knew a few people myself, which seemed to surprise her. In fact, it surprised me. But Carol seemed to know everyone, and they clearly knew her. We chatted with a few members of Congress and a couple of cabinet secretaries. They seemed to be comfortable, so I concluded she couldn't be with the press. She never let go of my elbow and fed my ego by introducing me as "the famous attorney."

We spent the next hour making small talk. I'm not a big fan of large cocktail parties. I usually find a corner to shrink into and drink more than I should, but this time I found myself enjoying the evening. Several martinis and Carol's company didn't hurt. I lost track of time until I realized most everyone else had left. I was about to get up the nerve to ask Carol out to dinner, when Lucy approached.

"I am so glad you two met. I had a feeling you'd get along. Red would like a few minutes, Jack. I hope you don't mind, Carol?"

Maybe it was wishful thinking, but I thought I detected disappointment in Carol's eyes. Dinner with Carol sounded much more appealing than a few minutes with Red Shaw, but we both understood Lucy wasn't really asking.

If Carol was disappointed she quickly let it go. "Of course. I really need to go anyway; my workday is far from over. And again—congratulations, Lucy. Let's plan on lunch soon." She kissed Lucy on the cheek, and as Lucy turned away, Carol pulled me close and dropped something into my coat pocket.

"Be careful tonight." She gave me a peck on the cheek and slipped through the front door before I could respond.

"'Be careful.' What was that about?" I wondered as I followed Lucy into her study.

2

THE STRAIGHTFORWARD MASCULINITY of Lucy's study caught me by surprise, but I remembered that the townhouse had originally belonged to Lucy and her former husband. The desk was enormous and all the chairs in the room were covered in dark leather. Bookshelves adorned the walls, filled artfully with designer books and what appeared to be first editions. Photographs of Red and various sports figures had been cozied up in every vacant niche. The wall inside the bookshelf directly across from the desk supported a new, curved Samsung Smart TV. A talking head spouted financial news, but the sound had been muted. The TV remote held a place of honor on the desk. Clearly Red had taken over this part of Lucy's house.

A uniformed waiter handed me a generously filled brandy snifter and silently left the room. Red sat behind the desk chomping on a cigar and twirling his own brandy. Two other men stood off to the side. Red offered me one of the wingbacks in front of the desk and introduced the men.

"Jack, meet Lynn and Guy. They're my good friends and financial advisors. I don't take an important meeting without them. I hope you don't mind?"

Lynn and Guy looked more like professional hit men in dark suits than financial advisors, but who was I to judge.

"Of course not—nice brandy," I responded, sinking into the leather.

"I'd offer you a Cuban, but Lucy won't let me smoke in the house. I import the brandy from France, glad you like it. Lynn, make sure Jack gets a couple of bottles."

Lynn grunted.

Interesting instruction and reaction to and from a financial advisor.

Red leaned forward across the desk.

"Lucy says you're a whiz-bang antitrust lawyer, the best of the best. Well, I've also made a few calls, learned the hard way to do my own research. Turns out she's right—when it comes to antitrust you're the man."

Lovely, thanks—what next?

"Lucy also tells me you owe her a big favor, and I'm free to call on it. I expect you know what she's talking about. I didn't ask." Red managed a grin even as the gnawed cigar moved up and down.

No reaction called for: first the compliment, then the reminder of an obligation. Red was following the playbook. I waited for the ask.

"Jack, let me get right to the point. The NFL pays lobbyists a bloody fortune to make sure the NFL's antitrust exemption remains the law of the land. They pay attorneys even more to fight nuisance lawsuits trying to get around our exemption."

Here it comes.

"The real danger lies with the Department of Justice and the FTC. Our exemption drives them nuts. I'm worried they might ferret out a weak link in the law or manage to get some liberal judge to side with them. The League may be happy with its lawyers, but I want my own. I want you on the Lobos' payroll to monitor everything we do with an eye to antitrust exposure. Two hundred and fifty thousand a year sound about right?"

Well, shit, I wasn't expecting this. If I were twenty years younger I'd have said yes before Red could whistle Dixie, but I wasn't.

"Well—Red, I'm tremendously flattered, but I have a fairly good law practice, and I'm also heavily involved with the Matthews Foundation. I can't simply abandon the Foundation and my clients. I'm honored and thank you, but I'm not quite ready to become an employee, much less move to LA. But I'm happy to recommend a few highly qualified lawyers who might be willing to move for that amount...."

I spoke firmly, hoping to end the conversation, but Red interrupted with a growl.

"Oh, hell, Jack. I didn't mean coming to work for the Lobos

full-time or moving to LA. I own the damn team, and I'm not about to move out to la-la land. I don't expect you to either. I'm talking about …well I guess it would be a retainer, I want you on retainer as our antitrust guy. You can represent whomever else you want as long as it isn't another team, one of my players, or the damn union. I'll have the team lawyers draw up a contract and deliver it to your office next week. You go over it, clean it up however you want, and sign it. I won't take no for an answer."

I didn't know what to say, but my lawyer's caution told me to go slow. It was one hell of an offer, but straight out of the blue. Why? Lucy Robinson, a lifelong adversary for most of my life, has me over for cocktails to witness her wedding announcement. After dinner her future husband offers me a lucrative retainer agreement with the Lobos, the NFL's newest franchise. Retainers are highly sought after by law firms because they lock the client into a relationship. They usually provide for additional sums to be paid if the client is sued or the hours spent exceed a specified number. Most lawyers or law firms would kill for such an arrangement, especially when the client's an NFL franchise worth roughly, oh, say two billion dollars.

Red wasn't finished.

"I'll make sure the lawyers include provisions that entitle you to get the same perks as other Lobos' executives—skybox seats, away game tickets, Super Bowl tickets, et cetera. Hell, Jack you'll be howling at the moon like the rest of us before you know it."

"Howling at the moon" referenced the Lobos' fans unique pre-game call and cheer. It reminded me of the Arkansas Razorback's famous "Hog Call." Not as good, but the LA fans loved it.

I didn't answer.

"What's wrong, Jack? You're too damn quiet. I don't like that. Tell me it's not about that Hopper kid. Hell, he's already cost me millions and probably millions more when that woman's family dredges up some ambulance chaser and sues the team, but it's not the end of the world. All the bad publicity will die down soon enough once he pleads guilty. If it's about the money, tell me what it will take. I want you on board before I turn to the next draft. I've got a winning team to build."

"Nothing's wrong with your offer—the amount is very generous."

"Great." Red smiled, stood up, and extended his hand across the table. I remained seated.

"I'm overwhelmed. I don't know quite what to say. Your guys can draw up the contract, but I want to think about my other commitments, be sure I can do the work you expect of me. Give me the weekend, but unless I have a complete change of heart, I look forward to becoming the Lobos' second biggest fan."

I rose and took his hand. Red seemed genuinely pleased.

As if on cue, Lucy came into the room, took me by the arm, and said, "Jack, I'm so excited. I wish we could talk a while, but…" I wondered why I was now getting the bum's rush, but shrugged it off. They were bound to have dinner plans. She gave me a quick, dry kiss, and I was quickly out the door, wondering what rabbit hole I'd fallen into.

Before I'd made it down the steps, I noticed a black Lincoln town car parked in front. The back door swung open, and inside I saw the smiling face of Carol Madison.

"Those little pastries weren't enough—I'm hungry. How about you buy me dinner?"

3

RED SHAW PULLED back the drapery and watched from the window as Jack stepped into Carol's town car. He smiled and murmured, "Perfect." Lucy wasn't so pleased.

"He didn't agree on the spot?"

"No, my dear, he didn't. He's a lawyer. Caution is second nature. He'd have been skittish as a cat if I'd given him a contract all ready to go. I'll up the ante and add a few perks. Don't worry. I'll have his signature before the end of the week. Let's go to dinner, I'm starving. How about Joe's for some crab?"

Lucy frowned, "But make sure it's happens. We can't afford to screw this up."

She asked the nearest maid to bring her a wrap, kissed Red on cheek, reached down to his groin, and gave him a seductive rub.

He took her hand and said, "No worries, Lucy. You'll see."

*****

I climbed into Carol's car knowing I would wake up from this dream any second now. A very wealthy, very cocksure client had just dropped into my lap, and now I was on my way to dinner with a woman I hoped to get to know a whole lot better. And, let's face it—I didn't have anything better to do.

"Jack, say hello to Pat—he's my regular driver." Pat nodded at me in the rear view mirror, and I returned the gesture. "DeCarlo's okay? I understand it's one of your favorites."

DeCarlo's, a neighborhood restaurant in northwest DC, is one of my favorites, although I wondered briefly how she knew. DeCarlo's serves maybe the best pasta Bolognese in the city. But I come back time and again because I can hear my companions talk and myself think. The service is excellent, Sinatra still croons in the background, and people leave you alone unless they know you—even then they're pretty discreet.

I was taken aback to find Carol busy texting. She looked up long enough to say, "I hope you don't mind. I have to get this off. Sit back and enjoy the ride while Pat manages the traffic. We have the rest of the night, I promise." I tried not to read too much into her slow smile.

I had reverted to my normal skepticism before we turned the first corner. The car pulled up to a dark red awning beneath the door. Lucy DeCarlo greeted me warmly, but embraced Carol like they were family. She had the "perfect" table for the two of us. Carol slipped her arm into mine.

"I usually sit up front so I can see and be seen, but not tonight. Cell phone is off, and it's time I properly introduced myself."

We quickly agreed to share a Caesar salad and soft shell crabs. A New Zealand Sauvignon Blanc was the perfect crisp foil to the rich crabs.

"Jack, you look nervous. I'm not stalking you if that's what you're worried about. Surely you know how tough DC can be on marriages, what with lots of single women hovering, hoping for a break. Trust me—you did me a huge favor by letting me escort you around the room tonight like we were an item. So, let me tell you what I do to pay the bills. Let's get that out of the way so we can enjoy ourselves and maybe put a lie to tonight's charade."

I leaned forward, ready to listen.

"I'm in the information and observation business. I maintain a select number of clients who pay me large annual fees to feed them information about anything and everything that goes on in DC, particularly with the current administration and Congress. I don't lobby—never have, never will. My clients have armies of lobbyists.

"I merely feed the clients information and my personal observations—some public, most not so public. What they do with it isn't my concern. Most of the time, I'd rather not know.

"I make friends with people from both parties. On occasion I'm able to help a cabinet officer get through the confirmation process, or make sure someone in trouble get the right lawyer or banker. But mostly I keep my eyes and ears open and report to my clients by way of confidential reports and emails. I am very good at what I do." Her slow smile revealed both her charm and confidence.

I believed her. I had heard of people who did exactly what she described, but had never known one personally. At my old law firm, Banks and Tuohey, I'd been the beneficiary of information from such a source. My antitrust client was fighting the merger of two rivals without much success at the Federal Trade Commission. Then a source spilled the beans—the two rivals had no real interest in merging: it was all a sham. They were using the merger process to manipulate their own stock prices, while causing my client to spend millions to fight the merger. Relying on this tip, we quickly withdrew our objection to the merger, and my client's rivals had to do some fast backtracking. I wondered whether that source could have been Carol.

I asked reluctantly, pretty sure I knew the answer, "I expect I'm in for a disappointment, but is this dinner part of your information gathering?"

"Wow, you really are jaded. I've got my work cut out for me tonight. Of course not, silly. I admit I'm curious why you were at Lucy's this evening, but my meter stopped running when we entered the restaurant. For the first time in a long while, I'm here to enjoy the company of a handsome man, talk about anything but politics, and eat some good food.

"Red Shaw's companies are clients, but, honestly, I have no idea what he wanted with you. As for Lucy, lots of people would like to know what makes her tick, and I bet you know more about her than anyone else in this town. But I'm not about to risk a nice evening by quizzing you about that stuck-up bitch."

Blunt talk from someone who makes her bread and butter from politicians. Frankly, I didn't care if she was lying. As far as I knew, I didn't have any information worth sharing.

I raised my hand with a shrug, ready to talk about something other than Red or Lucy. She seemed pleased, and soon we were exploring each other's interests. It turned out Carol loved the Washington

Nationals, so most of the rest of the evening was spent talking baseball. I hadn't met many women who knew so much about the game, much less an individual team.

We drifted on to families. She seemed to know quite a bit about mine, including the fact that I'd lost my wife Angie and that my daughter Beth was teaching at a wonderful school in New Orleans while her constant companion, Jeff, was doing his residency at Touro Infirmary in New Orleans.

She'd grown up in Charlotte, NC, graduated from UNC Chapel Hill, and received a Masters in Public Affairs at Harvard. She moved to Washington, DC to work for Senator Moynihan, but when the Senator declined to run again, she started her own "information" business, inspired by the success of others. I was surprised to learn she had never been married, but figured correctly that it was none of my business.

We lingered over coffee, turning the conversation back to baseball. Our waiter was hovering somewhat anxiously, and I realized we were the last party remaining, so I asked for the check. Carol's driver was waiting out front—in fact, we caught him snoozing. When the car pulled up to my house I said something awkward about having really enjoyed the evening and hoping to see her again. *I was so out of practice.*

Carol reached behind my head and pulled me to her, gave me a soft kiss on the lips, and whispered in my ear, "You forgot to invite me in for a nightcap."

She took one look at my face, laughed, and pushed me out the door. "You should at least ask, Jack."

SATURDAY

April 16, 2016

4

I SLEPT LIKE a log, waking with a start to find my dog Sophie staring intently at me. As we went on her morning walk, I wondered if I could bribe my daughter Beth to take Sophie with her to New Orleans. Then again, New Orleans's heat and humidity would be too much for a Bernese Mountain Dog. DC summers were bad enough.

I also let my thoughts wander to last night—Lucy's invitation, Red Shaw's offer, and Carol Madison. Each presented a bit of a mystery. Back in college we used to describe Lucy as "a piece of work." Ambitious, aggressive and attractive, Lucy was a force to be reckoned with even then, and the last thirty years hadn't changed anyone's opinion, certainly not mine.

Red came across as blunt, gruff, and forceful—didn't bother me in the least, especially when I remembered he was originally from west Texas. I had worked with clients like Red all my life. They were usually difficult, but you always knew where you stood. I was at a loss to understand his offer, almost too good to be true. I suspected once his lawyer's put the deal in writing it wouldn't look so attractive.

Every NFL team needs antitrust advice. In 1961, Congress granted the league an antitrust exemption, an event that has driven the antitrust lawyers at the Department of Justice crazy for decades. But why on earth had Lucy Robinson recommended me?

Carol was even more puzzling. Classy and intelligent—why had she singled me out? I was flattered, but my radar was up. Had Red asked her to entertain me? Had Lucy? Maybe I just looked lonely and available.

I showered and decided to opt for a real breakfast, not my usual Grape-Nuts. DC doesn't have any true breakfast places where they don't serve granola and the smells take you back to your grandmother's kitchen. Bethesda has a few places that come close, but on a Saturday morning they're packed. I opted for the grill at Columbia Country Club even though I wasn't going to play golf that morning. The eggs were cooked well, sausage was well-seasoned, and the hash browns were nice and crisp. Besides, I could read the newspapers in peace.

The *Washington Post* covered the Billy Hopper story as if he had murdered the President—sidebars interviewing former teammates and friends and lots of commentary on the violence of the game. Everyone was "shocked," but at the same time assumed he was guilty. The prosecutor announced that he looked forward to locking up Hopper for the rest of his life and again asked for assistance in determining the identity of the victim. They released her details: about 21 years old, 5'6'' tall, weight 110 pounds, natural auburn hair cut extremely short. An artist's sketch accompanied the article in *The Post*. She'd worn a blonde wig and had a birthmark on the nape of her neck.

Hopper was in town to attend the NFL Honors banquet the evening of the murder. Gossip at Lucy's party was that the police had private videos of Hopper drinking at the banquet and leaving with three women in a limousine. I knew it was only a matter of time before those videos were leaked, as well as the gruesome pictures of the injuries to the young woman. Hopper was in a world of hurt. At least the District had abolished the death penalty years ago. Hopper would live out the rest of his life in a small prison cell in a super max prison. What a waste and what a shame.

I couldn't help but wonder who would represent Hopper, but no attorney was mentioned in any of the articles. His agent had refused comment. It was common knowledge that Hopper had played last year on an NFL minimum contract. So unless he had family money, attorney's fees would quickly eat up whatever cash he had left after the season. Then again, he wouldn't need much in prison.

Stop thinking that way, Jack. I'm a true believer in the presumption of innocence: give the young man the benefit of the doubt. Don't lock him up and throw away the key before he even enters a plea or goes to trial.

I had plenty of time after breakfast before I was to meet Marshall, so I took the opportunity to go to the practice range and try out the new driver the club pro had convinced me to buy. Golfers are always tinkering with their swing, their putting stroke, or new equipment, hoping against hope that a small change will make a huge difference in their game. It seldom works, but dedicated golfers never quit trying.

As I started to get the feel of the new driver, my mind wandered back to Carol Madison. Should I call her? Should I send flowers? Should I wait a few days before asking her to the Nat's next home game? I thought about asking Beth for advice. I usually call her every Saturday morning, but she was off on a working retreat for teachers this weekend. The other option was my best friend Maggie, but she and Walter were still away.

Maggie had been my assistant, paralegal, and right arm when I practiced antitrust law at Banks and Tuohey. Two years ago she married Walter Matthews, the president of Bridgeport Life. Together they chair the Walter and Margaret Matthews Foundation. I now have a solo practice, and the Foundation is one of my principal clients. Maggie is still my assistant and her husband is my best friend and golf partner. It's complicated, but somehow it all works.

Before I knew it I'd worked up a good sweat. I showered, changed, and left the club to meet Marshall at the restaurant attached to his hotel, the Hay-Adams. The hotel sits right across Lafayette Square from the White House and directly across the street from St. Johns Episcopal Church. It surprised me that Marshall would stay at such an expensive hotel, but when I had suggested an equally nice but less expensive option he politely declined. Clearly, Marshall had his reasons, and who was I to tell him where he should stay or how he should spend his money.

I had also offered for Marshall to stay with me. I rattled around in our old family home, but Marshall explained that my house contained too many memories of my late wife. Marshall was the closest thing Angie had to a brother, maybe even closer if that's possible. I understand how he felt about the memories. On many a sleepless night I thought about selling the house, but it was too much to think about, used up too much energy.

I climbed the marble stairs off the lobby up to the restaurant, where the maître d' nodded his welcome and escorted me to Marshall's table. He stood, and we embraced. Marshall was one of my three best friends both in high school and college. He stands over six feet three inches tall and is as solid as a rock. He was dressed in a dark gray suit, starched white shirt and conservative tie. I felt way underdressed in my golf shirt and slacks.

Marshall is a brilliant judge who chooses to sit on the trial bench in Little Rock, Arkansas rather than accept the Federal appellate judgeship that has been offered on several occasions. He had officiated over the preliminary hearing of Woody Cole's shooting of Senator Russell Robinson, Lucy's husband. Our friendship was tested during that ordeal, but with those issues resolved our friendship has resumed, as close as ever.

We spent the first few minutes catching up on Beth. He wanted to know all about her job in New Orleans and when she and Jeff were going to get engaged. I told him that a father doesn't ask about marriage plans these days. He might not like the answer.

"Nonsense," he bellowed. "It's time that young lady and I had a good talk. Tell her if she doesn't call me soon, I may have to pay her and Jeff a visit. It's time for them to fish or cut bait."

I assured him I'd be pleased to convey the message. I had no doubt that Beth was more likely to confide in Marshall than me. She once told me that her Uncle Marshall was the only one she could talk about "certain things." I knew that one of those things included being "neither black nor white." Washington is a progressive town, and it had never occurred to either her mother or me to raise the issue.

I asked what brought him to town, knowing he would be circumspect. The Attorney General had become a close friend of Marshall's after the Cole case, but they both preferred to keep that friendship private.

"A very sad duty, I'm afraid to say," he answered, and I saw my friend's large brown eyes well with tears.

"I'm sorry, Jack. I'm pretty shaken up about this. Give me a minute."

"Of course." I smiled, wondering what could be bothering him. "It's okay. Today my time is yours."

The waiter approached, and we both looked at our menus, giving Marshall time to collect himself. I was surprised when he asked for a beer. I'd never known Marshall to have alcohol with lunch unless we were eating barbeque at Ben's in Little Rock. When the waiter pointed out the many choices on the menu, Marshall looked confused and finally asked for a Stella.

He caught me watching him and said without a smile, "I suggest you order something strong as well, my friend. This story may take a while."

"Marshall, has something happened back in Little Rock? Is Mrs. Cole okay?"

Helen Cole is Woody's mother—she practically raised Marshall and me during high school, a very special woman.

"Don't worry, Jack. Helen is fine."

"What's wrong then?"

"I'm here to meet with Constance Montgomery, Deputy U.S. Attorney, about a telephone conversation I had."

I felt my throat tighten. "You're not in some kind of trouble, are you?"

"No, nothing like that. William Hopper called me the morning he found that woman in his bed. Ms. Montgomery offered to come to Little Rock to take my statement, but I was already on my way to the airport."

"Good God, Marshall, Billy Hopper? Are you serious? Why would he call you?"

He didn't respond, just looked down at his hands, seemingly surprised to see them shaking. I knew I needed to slow down.

Here's the thing—Marshall is brilliant, but he's very literal and linear in this thinking. I learned a long time ago that his brain needs time to process information to see the broader meaning. Crowds create anxiety, whether it's a parade or a cocktail party. He's shy with strangers, particularly women, slow to form friendships. Compassionate rather than judgmental, he's slow to anger, but sure of his convictions. Marshall's friends learned long ago that pressure in any form just doesn't work. Prepared for stress, he handles it coolly and with intelligence, but put him in a tense situation he's not ready for, and he's likely to act more like an ostrich than a tiger.

Right now Marshall was traveling inside, and it wasn't a healthy place to be.

"Marshall, I've got an idea—you listenin'?

"Of course I'm listening."

"Let's ditch this place. I'll pay for our drinks while you go upstairs and change into real clothes. Meet me out front in ten minutes, and I'll treat you to the best barbeque and coldest beer in DC, a place where we can talk in absolute confidence."

"Jack, how many times have you told me there is no real barbeque in the District?"

"Well, it's not Ben's, but it'll be good enough."

In less than ten minutes, he stepped out of the elevator looking much more comfortable. The cab was waiting, and before long came to a halt in front of an old, slightly seedy house on the Hill—no sign, no name, just a street number above the door. I led him around back to stairs leading to a basement door where we were greeted by a wiry fellow of about seventy with a full head of once dark hair sitting at a desk working the *Times* crossword. An old rotary phone sat on the right corner of the table. I signed us in and introduced him to Marshall.

"Welcome back to Barker's, Mr. Patterson. Haven't seen you in a while." I made polite noises as he buzzed us through another door.

We found ourselves in a room familiar to me—creaky pine floors and paneled walls, a room smelling of cigars, old money, and sweat. The bar was topped with jars of pickled eggs, peanuts, and beer sausages. Nobody ate that stuff, except the peanuts, but the dated trappings somehow made you feel comfortable. I wondered idly how a twenty-something would react to them. The few other diners barely gave us a second glance.

"No craft beers," I said. "Just Bud, Miller, and I think they have Sam Adams now. If you want something stronger, the bar is fully stocked. The wine cellar is the envy of many DC restaurants. I wouldn't suggest a pickled egg or sausage, but that's your call."

The juke box was silent, but I led us to a quiet booth in the corner. The waitress delivered a pitcher of cold beer and two frozen mugs, and I was relieved to see him perk up. I ordered two pulled pork sandwiches and a side order of dry-rubbed ribs. Baked beans, slaw, and collards quickly arrived without having been ordered.

Marshall busied himself with slaw and hot sauce, took a spoonful of beans, and asked, "I trust you when it comes to barbeque, even in DC. But where exactly are we and how come you've never told me about it?"

"Well, Barker's is private club, not a very posh club, but a very private one. Roger knows every member, and no one gets in unless there's a member at his side.

"You won't find any menus at the bar. Every day there's one special and a few staples such as salads, cheeseburgers, barbeque, and a shrimp burger that will break your heart. They've got what you might call a formal dining room upstairs. Barker's is a cozy place to meet and talk over drinks and real food in total confidence. Leak an overheard conversation or disclose who is meeting with whom and your membership is revoked, no excuses, no recourse. If a guest violates the confidentiality rule, they're never allowed to return and the member is fined. Big bucks, not a slap on the wrist. One learns the hard way not to bring a guest with loose lips.

"Members can stay overnight in private rooms upstairs. It's really quite nice —showers, a workout room, everything one would find at a good hotel. Most of the members are male, although a few women have been admitted in the last few years. I'd love to show you, but guests aren't allowed anywhere in the building except for the dining rooms and a few meeting rooms. Mr. Barker makes the rules, and the first rule is—screw up, even once, and you're out. If I ever wanted to disappear for a week or two, Barker's would be the perfect place."

"Why would you want to disappear, Jack?"

Again, so literal.

"Just an expression, Marshall. I thought about it right after Angie died. I got so worn out by well-wishers I just wanted to escape for a few days, but I couldn't do that to Beth."

"How many members are there, and how hard is it to get in? Who decides?"

"No one knows except the Board of Governors and Mr. Barker. You have to be nominated by a member, unanimously voted in by the

Board, and finally interviewed and approved by Mr. Barker. If he says no, there is no appeal."

"Sounds pretty autocratic."

"Barker's rules, he owns the place. He spent several years in England and came to appreciate the value of the exclusive gentlemen's club. He brought the concept back to DC, realizing that the exclusivity alone would appeal to men and women of the city who need a source of good food and drink, privacy, and camaraderie."

"Is it indeed exclusive?" Marshall asked. I knew exactly what he meant.

"No, I'm happy to say, it is not. The membership is very representative of the DC community. The only people who seem to have been excluded are those who are known to care about being seen and written about in the papers. Needless to say, you won't find many members of Congress dining here."

The waiter delivered hot sandwiches and ribs, and we concentrated on pulled pork for a while. I poured us another beer, and he smiled his approval, saying, "I think I could get used to this, Jack. It's not Ben's, but I really like your club."

"I could tell you much more about it, but let's get down to business, so to speak. Marshall, in your position you shouldn't talk to Ms. Montgomery by yourself. Let me go with you."

"That's very kind of you, but totally unnecessary. I'm not worried about me. And that's not why I'm upset or why I'm here." Marshall's head lowered.

"Well, then, what's up?" *Why was this so hard?*

"I've come to help William. He needs a friend, and I'm here to figure out how best I can help."

"What? How in the world do you know Billy Hopper? And why do you want to help him?" I tried unsuccessfully to keep my tone neutral.

"Well, I don't know why I shouldn't.""

5

MARSHALL OFTEN USED the phrase. "I don't know why I shouldn't." He had first used it when I asked him to convince Angie to go out with me, and for that reason alone I enjoyed hearing it every time. The phrase had become expected and somewhat amusing, but this time I sensed an edgy, almost querulous tone. I wanted to jump in with all sorts of warnings and advice, but instinct held me back.

"I have a boatload of reasons why you shouldn't, but before I unload the boat, why don't you tell me why Billy Hopper called you and why in the hell you think you—not his family, not his agent, and not his lawyer—are the person who needs to help."

Marshall seemed to shrink, almost physically. I ordered another pitcher of beer and leaned back in my chair. Patience didn't come easy to me.

"Billy Hopper doesn't have any family, his agent has abandoned him, and he doesn't have a lawyer yet.

"I've known this young man since he was a counselor at Camp Carolina. My boys loved him, and when Jerry Stone—he'd run the camp for about thirty years by then—told my wife about his family situation, the next thing I knew William was a fixture at our house most every holiday or college break. I couldn't have asked for a nicer houseguest, and he was a great influence on the boys. Grace treats him like a son, and I guess I do, too. I know William almost as well as I do my own boys. I simply can't believe he murdered that woman. Now you know why I'm here and why I have no choice but to help. If it were Beth, you'd be doing the same. It took all I have to keep Grace and the boys from coming. Thank goodness for school and exams."

Well, now that I understood the relationship, I knew it would be tough to talk him out of getting involved. But what are friends for other than to keep you from doing stupid things. I was ready to start my sermon, but Marshall beat me to the punch.

"Before you give me a lecture, I want to tell you a little more about the young man you probably only know as a pro football player and supposedly a murderer. William was born in a little town in the hill country of east Tennessee. His father butchered his mother when the boy was just eight years old—literally butchered her with a Bowie knife. I realize that experience doesn't bode well for his defense, and it will come out—everything always does. William's alcoholic father then picked up the child and drove off with him in his pick-up. Fortunately the father didn't go far, exactly as far as the nearest bar. While the father was inside drinking, William climbed out of the truck, walked into the country store across the street and told the owner, 'My Dad just killed my mother.'

"William's father ultimately pled guilty to manslaughter, claiming he was too drunk to know what he was doing. For some reason judges and juries seem to think murdering a stranger is worse than murdering your wife, so he got off with a light sentence. But he never made it out of prison. He attacked another inmate with a knife he'd stolen from the kitchen, and a guard shot him. It's only a matter of time before a reporter or law enforcement discovers William's father's history and tries to link his father's behavior to William."

I said, "A propensity to murder with a knife is hardly part of one's DNA."

Marshall shook his head, "Nor is a father's conduct relevant or admissible in a trial of the son, but let's not be naïve. A good prosecutor will make sure both the public-at-large and the jury know of William's past. You can bank on it."

Marshall waited in silence while the waiter cleared the table and then continued.

"Tennessee Social Services didn't know quite what to do with William, so he began the merry-go-round of one foster home after another. They tried to find a suitable relative to take the boy, but it turned out that the father's family was as bad or worse than the father. The mother's family was another matter. No one had any idea who she was. They found no birth or marriage certificate in the trailer; she didn't have a driver's license or any other form of ID in her purse. No one came to claim her body. The father's family was no help. They said that Zeke Hopper— that was his name—just showed up one day with a young pregnant girl named Donna. Sadly, she ended up in a pauper's grave."

A potter's field—not something you think about often, if ever. Surely everyone deserves some sort of decent burial. I was reminded of a friend in Santa Barbara who memorializes the lives of the homeless in his home overlooking the Pacific.

I shook off a little shiver and said, "Very sad, and very hard to believe in this day and age." I took another sip of beer. "The similarity won't be lost on anyone when it comes out."

Marshall replied, "I'm afraid not. Psychologists on both sides will have a field day."

"Do you think Billy snapped? Maybe he has a shot at a temporary insanity defense?"

"Not a chance. Insanity pleas are seldom successful. You know that from Woody's case. Besides, I have no doubt about William's sanity. He's a very intelligent young man, knows exactly what he's doing. You will meet him one day. But let me continue with his history.

"When he was older, William spent a good deal of time trying to find out about his mother. She seemed to have no history before showing up in the hills of Tennessee with Zeke. There's no proof she was ever married. William's birth certificate lists Donna Hopper as the mother and Zeke as the father. That's it: no birthplace or home address, not even a middle initial. She could have been anyone."

"Jeez," I said, interested despite myself. "So how on earth did Billy turn out to be a Rhodes scholar? For that matter, how did he get into a tough academic school like Sewanee—a football scholarship?"

"No, Sewanee doesn't offer football scholarships. Quit jumping ahead, Jack. It would be easy to say William was lucky, that somehow he found the perfect foster parents who recognized his unique skills. I think a more truthful analysis is that school, church, and sports provided the needed escape from multiple terrible home situations. From a young age, William spent every moment he could in school, in church, in the library, or on the practice fields to avoid going back to houses that weren't homes. Most of his foster parents couldn't care less where he was as long as he was present when social services took a body count for the monthly check. Sometimes genes and brains do win out over environment.

"He also had the occasional teacher, coach, or pastor who saw a special light in the young man. It was a junior high coach who convinced Jerry Stone to take a chance on him at Camp Carolina, although truth be told Jerry doesn't take much convincing when it comes to hard luck stories. It was a teacher who concocted reasons for William to stay after school and recommended books for him to read. It was an Episcopal priest who made sure he had decent clothes, didn't go hungry, and steered him to Sewanee. William touched a lot of lives in the Tennessee mountains. Something about him made people care.

"William was valedictorian of his high school, and he came to be more than just okay on the football field. He has the ability to get open for a pass and an uncanny talent for hanging on to the ball, but that's not worth much if your quarterback can't throw the ball. His high school football coach was still running a version of the wishbone, so William went unnoticed by the college scouts. Sewanee was a perfect fit—great academic school where football is played for the fun of it."

I responded. "Okay, you've convinced me that whatever happened at the Mayflower was out of character and that he deserves your loyalty, but what can you do? You're a judge in Arkansas, not licensed to practice law in DC, and even if I could get you admitted for the limited purpose of representing him, you are even more unqualified to defend a capital case than I am."

"I know that, but I can help him decide who should represent him. I'm not a rich man, but I have a little money put aside that can help pay the lawyer. And I can be present in the courtroom so William knows he isn't alone. He needs someone he trusts. He's bound to be scared to death and probably thinks he doesn't have a friend in the world." Marshall emptied his mug, waving off my offer of a refill. I filled it anyway.

"Well, be careful. Don't let him tell you too much. Unless you're his actual lawyer, whatever you talk about is fair game. I'm sure Ms. Montgomery hopes he confessed when he called you the morning he discovered the body. He didn't, did he?" I had to ask.

"No, he did not. He was scared to death. He told me blood was everywhere. He had no idea what to do—who would? Could he take a shower and put on some clothes before anyone got there? Apparently he was in his birthday suit when he woke up."

"What did you tell him?"

"I told him to call the police immediately, not to touch anything, especially the woman. He told me he'd already thrown the knife across the room. It was on his chest when he woke up. I told him it was okay to put on some clothes. He should just tell the police. Did I do the right thing?"

"Hell if I know. I mean what else could you tell him. Did you tell him not to answer any questions without a lawyer present?"

"I did, but I don't know if he was listening. I could almost hear him shaking. I have no idea what he said to the police or anyone else. I haven't talked to him since that morning. As I said, Ms. Montgomery offered to take my statement in Little Rock, but I told her I would come to DC and asked to see William. She gave me a firm 'no,' but I insisted and she finally gave in, as long as I agreed to be interviewed first. William needs someone, so I agreed."

I'd never seen Marshall this upset—I spoke without thinking.

"Look, they probably won't let me sit in on the interview unless I'm your lawyer, but I can wait right outside the door and provide moral support. I can also help you find him a good lawyer. I know several excellent white-collar defense lawyers in DC—they'll know who can handle this kind of case and who won't take advantage of either you or Billy, at least I hope not. What time is the interview?"

"Nine o'clock Monday morning at the Federal Courthouse. I've got the room number back at the hotel, I believe it's on the third floor."

"What about Billy's arraignment? The papers said it was Monday, but I don't remember the time." I asked.

"It's scheduled for three o'clock in the afternoon. Constance Montgomery said she'd let me see William sometime before the arraignment. I suppose they'll hold him somewhere inside the courthouse."

"Did Billy say anything to you that might be interpreted as a confession?"

"Absolutely not. What he said was that he woke up to find her lying next to him. They were both naked. He said she was dead, and there was blood everywhere. He said he had no idea who she was or not even how he'd gotten back to his room the night before."

"Right… sure he doesn't." I said, earning a really dirty look from my friend.

"Look, Jack—I'm not a fool. I know William is in a world of hurt and that it will take a miracle to get him out of this mess. I'm here because he's a wonderful young man—my wife and children love him like a brother and a son, and he needs someone to believe in him."

"You understand that by going public with your support of Billy you may blow any chance you have of being appointed to the Eighth Circuit Court of Appeals, don't you? Your friend the Attorney General thinks that's where you belong, and so do I. It's a real possibility, and you may be throwing it all away if you do anything more than give your statement and go home." I had to say it.

Marshall finished his beer before he spoke.

"What kind of person would I be if I deserted William now? What would you think of me? What would my family think? William is special. I know it looks bad, but I don't believe he could have done such a thing. The least I can do is do everything possible to help him—the Court of Appeals be damned. I'm well aware that if you get in trouble in DC, your friends disappear like lightning, but I'm not from here. In my book, loyalty and basic kindness trump ambition every time."

6

THERE WASN'T MUCH left to say. We agreed to meet at the Hay-Adams for breakfast on Monday. Apparently Marshall had other plans for the evening. He didn't say what they were, and I didn't ask. We took a cab back to the hotel. He said he needed a nap after "some damned fine barbeque and more beer than was good for me." I retrieved my car and headed home—we both needed a break.

*****

Mr. Kim listened to the report that Patterson and Judge Fitzgerald had met for lunch. He wasn't pleased to hear that Patterson had taken the Judge to Barker's, a place he hadn't yet found a way to infiltrate. The meeting wasn't unexpected. He knew Hopper had called the Judge, and he knew Patterson and Fitzgerald were good friends. Nothing unusual about their having lunch, no reason the Judge shouldn't consult Patterson. He was still anxious about what was discussed. If they had remained at the Hay-Adams he would be listening to a recording of the conversation at this very moment. Nevertheless, he called the client to report.

*****

Even on Saturday, the DC traffic was tough, and I figured I might need a nap, too. When my cell phone vibrated, I almost tapped ignore, but decided to pick it up.

"You up for playing escort again? I think we make a handsome couple, don't you?" Carol's voice was cool and inviting.

"I'd love to play your escort—tell me when and where." I knew I sounded too eager, but who cared?

"How about right now? Pat will pick you up in an hour. Pack casual for a couple of days at my place on the Eastern Shore. I have plenty of tennis rackets, but you'll need to bring swimming trunks. That's about it. I'm having a few clients and their guests up for a weekend at my place and thought I'd see if you were up for a repeat performance."

"Couple of days" was a problem. I'd just committed Monday morning to Marshall. He'd probably tell me to forget it, but I couldn't break the date for a better offer.

"Why don't you give me directions, and I'll drive up. I've got to be at the courthouse Monday morning, but I'd love to spend the rest of the weekend with you."

After an uncomfortably long pause, she finally responded.

"No—Pat is already on his way back to DC to pick you up, should be there in about an hour. If he has to, he'll drive you back tomorrow night, but I hoped we could have some time together after my guests left. Oh well, if you have to leave, you do. I'll take as much of you as I can get. Get your cute butt up here—time's a wastin'!"

My ego was blown way out of proportion, but the flirting was probably just part of her shtick. I thought about the weekend ahead: lots of small talk with a bunch of strangers and probably not much time with Carol, a woman I'd barely met. I knew I should probably put the brakes on, at least make a few calls, but it could wait until next week. Maybe she was exactly what she seemed: attractive, ambitious, successful, and slightly lonely. What could a weekend on the shore hurt?

Once home, I quickly arranged for my neighbor's daughter, Amy, to take care of Sophie. I called on her so often to dog sit, Sophie probably wondered where she really lived. I'd thought about offering to give Sophie to Amy, but knew she'd be crazy to take her. Right now, I was providing Amy enough money in dog sitting income to pay for a college education.

Pat was right on time. I tried to join him in the front seat of the town car, but he insisted I sit in the back, pour myself a gin and tonic, and relax. He said someone sitting beside him was a distraction especially when he needed to push the speed limits. Carol had called and instructed, "Haul ass."

I did as he suggested and enjoyed the scenery as we crossed the Bay Bridge on the way to the Eastern Shore of Maryland. Over the years, I'd occasionally enjoyed a weekend at the home of a friend on the Choptank River, near Easton, Maryland. The hectic and stress-filled life of DC calls out for retreats where exhausted people can escape on the weekend to a beach, the hill country of Virginia, or the peaceful plains of Maryland. The Eastern Shore is filled with the weekend and summer homes of those who can afford it.

It didn't surprise me that Carol had a weekend home she used to entertain DC's influential and powerful—what a perfect atmosphere for gleaning information. I looked forward to seeing her place, but not nearly as much as seeing her again. I felt as giddy as a school boy who had a great first date, but was nervous about whether the girl would ever go out with him again. Carol had not just said yes, but she'd made the call.

I asked Pat if he'd been shuttling guests all day.

"No, most come in by copter or have their own driver," he responded.

Copter? Now I was curious about the other guests, but decided not to distract Pat any more. As fast as he was driving he needed to concentrate.

I thought about Carol's explanation that having someone on her arm helped her accomplish her purposes. The male guests wouldn't try to hit on her, and the female guests weren't as touchy about her spending so much time with their male companions. Her reasoning seemed fairly shallow and not particularly PC, but it did reflect reality. Sexual dynamics seldom turn out to be politically correct.

Another motive occurred to me—I was being asked to play the role of a "beard." Maybe she was involved with one of the guests and my presence would serve to prevent suspicion.

My inferiority complex was clearly alive and well. But Carol had sought me out at Lucy's party, and we had a wonderful dinner afterwards. She had suggested we spend time alone after the guests left. I know I can be pretty naïve, but it all sounded pretty good to me.

How about it Jack? Why don't you just enjoy yourself this weekend, get to know Carol a little bit better, and maybe meet some other people. I have a tendency to get ahead of myself rather than living in the present. At least, that's what Maggie would say.

We made it to Carol's in what had to be record time. As we drove slowly down a long driveway lined with pecan trees, I expected to see something like Tara of *Gone with the Wind* fame. Instead, a contemporary home right out of Frank Lloyd Wright's playbook surprised me. The landscaping reminded me of the Japanese Embassy in DC. The information business must be doing quite well.

I caught sight of Carol on the tennis court, hitting balls with a guy I assumed was a guest. Made me want to take up tennis again. Carol waved, and they both walked off the court. The guy took her racket and walked toward the rear of the house. She greeted me with a kiss flush on the mouth and a lingering hug. I might have thought the greeting was staged, but there were no witnesses except Pat.

"I'm so glad you could come. I can't wait for you to meet everyone."

"Don't stop your game for me," I began to pull away, but she interrupted.

"Really Jack. Ray and I were just hitting balls, waiting on you to get here. He's a great guy, you'll like him a lot.

"Pat, we're going to the back porch; everyone's gathering for cocktails. Put Jack's bag in our room, and please join us. Senator Boudreaux's companion, Claudia, is all about specialty cocktails, and Deputy Secretary Cantwell says you're the only one who knows how she likes her martini. I'm afraid it's going to be a long weekend."

"I can carry my own bag." I said.

"Nonsense," she said as she wrapped her arm around mine and led me toward the house. "You'd get lost. Do you need to freshen up?"

She showed me to a bathroom next to the living room, a massive high-ceilinged room filled with comfortable looking chairs and couches, all facing a fireplace and a huge big screen TV.

"Take all the time you need. I'll change for dinner in a bit, but what you have on is perfect—everyone's casual. I can't tell you how excited I am that you're here."

I splashed some water on my face and checked myself in the mirror, deciding not to ask what she meant by "our bedroom." When

I opened the door, I found her waiting. She took my hand and asked, "What will you say if some one asks how long we've known each other?

I'd thought about that possibility on the drive up.

"I'll just smile, because no one would believe me if I told the truth."

She reached up and kissed me gently, whispering, "Perfect."

Without another word we walked into a large, screened-in porch overlooking the river. The room was unexpectedly filled with vintage 60s metal furniture and old rocking chairs, all covered with contemporary fabric and cushions. Behind the rattan bar in the corner stood Pat, martini shaker in full shake. The casual chatter ceased almost immediately.

"Friends, I want to introduce you to Jack Patterson, the famous lawyer and my special friend." Carol smiled.

With that announcement, she reached up and kissed my cheek. Not a soul in the room would doubt we were lovers except Carol, myself, and maybe Pat who maintained his bland expression. I had noticed the same look when Carol asked him to put my bag in "our room."

7

AFTER A ROUND of introductions, Carol excused herself to change, and I asked for a glass of wine. No telling what my head was going to feel like in the morning—beer, gin, and now wine, but still better than a martini. She returned wearing white pants and a loose fitting pale pink silk blouse. Her dark hair was well cut, stopping just below her shoulders, and large gold loop earrings highlighted her face. She needed no other ornaments.

Carol wasn't a super model or gorgeous in the movie star sense. Instead the force of her personality dominated her appearance. Her smile was broad and engaging, and like last night, her clothes were understated, classy, and perfect. I was drawn to her deep hazel eyes, but others might admire her figure and the way she carried herself. A young female staffer probably wouldn't feel threatened by Carol, but she should.

I handed her a glass of wine and eased back into a corner to watch her work the room. As I said, I'm not particularly good at parties. In fact, I'm usually fairly uncomfortable, but I do enjoy watching the social mechanics. Carol had an easy way about her. Each man was convinced she was hanging on his every word, and if he made a joke, she laughed sincerely, touching his arm ever so gently. I noticed she was careful to give her full attention to women, especially wives. She never looked away and usually nodded in agreement.

DC folks, especially at this level, know how to mix, how to take care of themselves and their agenda. But Carol took the extra step, occasionally pulling one person into a different group or towards a single person, thus furthering her own agenda. No one went more than ten seconds without a full drink. I was tickled to hear her ask Pat to give Secretary Cantwell "a little cover"—meaning a full glass.

Her glance turned toward the newly opened kitchen door, and I saw the cook nod her head, then close the door silently.

"All right, everyone, dinner is served." She had raised her voice just enough to carry through the room. Her guests began to sort themselves out and drift toward the dining room, but she edged her way to my corner.

"Why are you stuck in this corner? Not enjoying my party?"

"Just enjoy watching a professional work. You're good." I meant it as a compliment.

"Years of practice. But I also want you to have a good time. I hoped you might like a few of my guests. Just stay away from Jackie Erskine. She's checking you out."

"Really, which one is Jackie?" I smiled.

"She's the sort of boozy blonde in the navy linen blazer. She's on the Board of the Federal Reserve, one of its newer members, but don't even think about it." She kidded back.

"Didn't she bring her companion, Michael Brooks?"

Carol looked at me in surprise and laughed. "Well, well—full marks to you. But he's not really her companion, and I'm very possessive, so watch out."

Both of us enjoyed the banter, and I enjoyed the fact that she was possessive.

Dinner was casual, too—rich crab cakes served with an avocado and lime sauce, a fluffy corn pudding, sliced heirloom tomatoes marinated with onions and cucumber, followed by peach cobbler topped with homemade ice cream. Throw me in that briar patch any time. We were seated at two square tables, close enough to enjoy either our dinner companion or the whole group, as we preferred. Even I chimed in every now and then.

Carol had seated her guests carefully. I listened as a senior member of the Senate Appropriations committee quietly debated with an executive of a defense contactor about the need for more fighter aircraft rather than drones. Carol had given them the opportunity to discuss their opinions out of the limelight. Nothing confidential or inappropriate was discussed as far as I knew. The Senator and the executive could talk without the intrusion of media or staff and Carol was able to add their opinions and desires to her store of knowledge.

DC hasn't worked very well for quite a long time, but this is how it worked when it did—leaders with differing interests seeking compromise away from the vitriol of partisan ideology and the glare of the media, in a comfortable setting of relative privacy. Of course, this process is open to only a few and flies in the face of open government, but surely it's better than the take no prisoners attitude that seems to worsen every year.

After dessert, Carol announced she had a movie, only recently released, waiting in the living room. She suggested we all get an after dinner drink and find a comfortable chair or couch. She shepherded me to a large recliner, and as soon as I sat down with my glass of port she curled up at my side. Soon, the lights went out and the movie began.

Pat silently kept watch, making sure glasses were never empty. I thought I detected a glower when he refilled my glass, but really didn't care.

Several couples peeled off to their rooms before the movie was over. Muttering thanks, the remaining guests departed as the credits began to roll. Carol took me by the hand and escorted me to a bedroom at the end of a long hall, obviously her own. She turned so we were face-to-face and pulled me to her. We enjoyed a deep and lingering kiss, but she pulled away, flushing slightly.

"I can't tell you how much I'd rather be with you right now, but I can't. I have go to my office and file reports. Please, forgive me. It won't always be like this, but I need to get tonight's observations and insights recorded while they're fresh in my mind. Promise me you aren't upset?"

"Well, I'll get over it, but give me a few minutes." I drew her into the room, and we sat carefully on the side of the bed.

"Why have me stay in your room?"

"My other guests all think we're in bed together at this very moment. Not a soul thinks I'm headed to my office to file reports. They all know what business I'm in, and they expect, even want me to report to my clients what I learned tonight, but they also expect me to be discreet. It would take away from the climate I'm trying to create and the appearance of a social gathering if I were obvious.

"My guests don't mind what I do, but I don't throw it in their face. I never reveal a confidence, and their companions never have a clue, at least not from me. It may sound overblown, but this weekend is important to a functioning government. For example, the Senator has been trying for months to meet in private with Chuck Morrison.

"I'm in the information business, but I'm also in the facilitation business. I facilitate meetings that can't be arranged through normal channels. I also report on such meetings to those who need to know, all with the consent of the participants. It has taken months to put this specific weekend together. The Senator and Chuck trust me, or it wouldn't have happened.

"Part of all this weekend is an elaborate ruse so those two can have very private conversations, but part of it's not. For example, I think our Senator's staffer is learning at this very moment that for a man of his age the Senator has amazing stamina."

Carol gave me a soft kiss before she continued.

"I'm sorry if it sounds like I'm using you. I invited you on a whim because I find you interesting and attractive, but I admit that having you here helps further a sense of normalcy, just an ordinary weekend on the Shore. I'll probably have to work for most of the night, but I can't tell you how much I'd rather climb into this bed with you."

Again she wrapped her arms around my waist and murmured, "We can make this work. I know we can."

I took her face in my hand and kissed her cheek.

"Well, my ego has taken a hit, but go do what you have to do. I'm not going anywhere."

SUNDAY

April 17, 2016

8

"I'M NOT GOING anywhere" wasn't exactly true. She already knew I needed to leave late tomorrow afternoon.

I got ready for bed and was asleep almost before my head hit the pillow. I hoped my dreams would be filled with Carol, but for some reason they were filled with me playing baseball at Yankee stadium, naked as a jaybird. I was disappointed when I woke in the middle of the night and realized she wasn't there. I threw down a couple of Tylenol with a full glass of water, hoping to sleep until morning.

*****

"Wake up, sleepyhead, let's go for a swim."

Carol stood next to the bed, wearing a bathing suit and a filmy cover-up. Light was pouring into the room from the porch doors leading to the pool outside her bedroom. I could have sworn I closed those curtains before I went to bed.

"C'mon. I'll meet you outside. Bloody Mary or Mimosa?"

I squinted in the sun. "You're up early."

"Never went to bed, no time. I'll catch up on my sleep when everyone leaves. Meet you at the pool in ten."

"Mimosa."

"That's my man. It's time we got the party started."

I headed to the bathroom and glanced at the alarm clock—seven-thirty. The party was certainly starting early.

I walked out to the pool in trunks and an old Stafford State t-shirt, still yawning a bit. Clearly no one else was quite ready to party.

Stretched out on a recliner, Carol peered up at me from beneath a broad brimmed straw hat, Bloody Mary in hand. My Mimosa sat on the table beside her.

"Are we the only ones up?" I asked.

"Probably, unless the Senator and his companion are having an eye-opener."

Good grief, the man was at least seventy.

I took a sip of the Mimosa. "Um, nice, but a little early. Think I'll swim a few laps and let the water shrink my head from yesterday's festivities."

"Good idea, it's going to be a long day." I wondered why she was in such a good mood and how she could be so, well, awake. As far as I knew, she hadn't slept a wink.

The April water was cold, but it felt good. I stretched out my body in a long freestyle stroke and began swimming laps. Up and down, up and down, until I was totally awake, and my body had begun to complain.

As I leaned against the wall in the shallow end of the pool to catch my breath, Carol dove into the pool with barely a ripple. When she surfaced she threw her arms around my neck, jumped up slightly and wrapped her legs around my waist.

Her mouth joined mine and while her tongue probed, her hips began to rise and fall slowly. Needless to say I responded with enthusiasm. I didn't know how we were going to make this work in the pool, but I was confident we'd find a way.

I was pulling down the straps of her bathing suit when we both heard.

"Excuse me, madam, but I believe you will want to take this call."

Carol's arms were still around my neck, but her legs fell to the pool floor in a hurry.

"Really. Right now? Mattie, your timing is atrocious."

I turned to see a woman in a maid's uniform, looking very uncomfortable. At least she wasn't Pat.

"I'm really sorry, Ms. Madison."

The moment was gone. Carol climbed out of the pool and wrapped herself in the towel offered by the blushing Mattie, grabbed the cover-up and stalked off toward the kitchen, followed by the embarrassed maid.

I sank into a cushy chaise lounge and sipped my Mimosa, wondering when Carol might return. I realized our fun was over when the Senator from Tennessee and his companion walked out to the pool, Bloody Mary's in hand.

What was his companion's name? Then it came to me—Claudia.

"My God, what happened to you?" Claudia exclaimed.

I realized my shirt was still off; the old scars were hard to miss. I tried to sound nonchalant as I tugged my shirt back on. "A bad night."

"Can't you get that fixed?" she asked.

I was tempted to give her the answer she deserved, but was ready to change the subject.

"I could, but I usually just keep my shirt on. Y'all sleep well?"

Claudia turned bright red, but the Senator rescued her. "Like babies."

He continued, "Carol says you specialize in antitrust law. I don't recall seeing you or any of your clients, for that matter, before my committee."

"I work hard to be sure you don't." I smiled, and he laughed. He started to tell me the sad story about some lawyer who had come before his committee unprepared. It was a long story. Quickly bored, Claudia left to refill our drinks.

He watched her backside as she left, then rumbled, "Carol says you can be discreet. I wouldn't want anything that's said or done this weekend to make its way into the papers or be the subject of rumor. Chuck and I need to meet in private from time to time."

A senior member of the Senate Appropriations Committee meeting in private with an executive of an aerospace company was not something either one of them would want to see on the front page of the *Post*. Carol had probably been very selective in inviting her guests to this casual weekend.

"Senator," I gave him a slow grin, "I have a terrible memory for faces, names, or even what happened yesterday. No one, especially you, Senator, has any reason for concern. Carol Madison is the only subject of my interest this weekend. Anything else is none of my business."

"Good man—speaking of Carol, if I were a younger man...." His returning grin was a bit wolfish. *Old goat.*

Claudia returned, followed by Pat, drink tray in hand. Carol's other guests emerged slowly from within, some ready for a brisk swim, but most content to lounge about, sipping whatever they liked. Mattie brought out a large basket of tiny cinnamon rolls and mini quiches, designed to tide us over before brunch.

They were all chatting happily around the pool—except me. Carol was nowhere to be seen, and I felt like a fish out of water. So after a few hearty "good mornings" I retreated to shower, shave, and change into khakis and a golf shirt.

I gave it about twenty minutes before returning, but still no Carol. With no other option, I asked for another Mimosa and joined the rest of the group. The conversation was centered on—what else but Billy Hopper? Needless to say the group was confident it was only a matter of days before Billy pled guilty and was sent away to prison for life. The women were much tougher on Billy than the men, several suggesting the U.S. Attorney should have sought the death penalty, even though in DC it would be impossible to obtain.

Carol finally joined the group, but she clearly wasn't herself. She played the perfect hostess, greeting everyone with kisses on cheeks and cheery comments. I wondered it I was the only one to see her performance as pantomime.

She came to me at last and spoke softly, "Mattie was right to interrupt. I needed to take the call."

"You okay? You seem out of sorts?'

"No, no. Lack of sleep caught up with me, and I took a little nap."

The lie was obvious. The phone call had clearly shaken her. I figured she would tell me about it when she was ready, but I was worried for her and couldn't let it go.

Carol seemed to bounce back quickly—played tennis, waved a couple off on a boat ride with Pat, even helped one guy try to catch crabs off the deck. But she had hardly a word for me. Left to my own devices I tried to play my escort role, even spelling Pat as the bartender—it gave me something to do. From time-to-time, I thought I saw her glance my way, yet she kept her distance. The hands on my watch moved at a snail's pace. I couldn't wait to leave.

I learned one thing during the afternoon's activities. The Senator's assistant wasn't as naïve as she let on. When she thought she was out of sight she tossed her drink onto some unfortunate plant and then called out for another. She also found unobtrusive ways to listen in to conversations while maintaining her role as the perfect staffer. The Senator was clearly smitten, and she had him eating out of her hand.

Yet, I also felt sorry for Claudia. Here she was, sleeping with a man twenty years older than her father and pretending to be a ditz. To what end? Proximity to power, especially in DC, causes strange behavior.

Claudia approached me before dinner and asked, "Lover's quarrel?"

"I'm sorry?"

"Honey, last night Carol couldn't keep her hands off of you. I was surprised she made it through the movie before y'all got it on, but today she's acting like you're the hired help. It's none of my business of course, but just in case." She handed me a napkin with a phone number on it and turned away with an arch smile.

What was that about? But I kept the napkin.

As the sun was setting, Mattie called us all to the porch for dinner. The tables had been pushed together and covered in newspapers. She poured out dozens of steamed Maryland blue crabs out onto the middle, followed by fresh corn and biscuits. We all hammered away, picking out lumps and bits of crab to our heart's content. Carol continued to ignore me, so I concentrated my attention on Claudia, who was intently following the conversation between Chuck Morrison and the Senator. Her tongue worked in a funny way as she tried to figure out how to deal with her crab. Pat kept filling her glass, and she continued to dispose of its contents without drawing attention.

Before too long the sun faded and folks began to fidget. Out of the blue, assorted limousines and town cars pulled up the long driveway to whisk Carol's guests back to DC or to the copter pad. I'd had about enough of the cold shoulder, so I asked Pat if he was ready to take me home.

"I'll pull the car round front." Nothing overt in his tone, but no sorrow at my departure either.

I found Carol shaking hands with the Senator and waving to

Claudia as they left in a limo.

"Thanks for the weekend. I hope it was successful." I didn't bother to hide my irritation.

She reached up to my shoulder, but dropped her arm just as quickly. "It could have been better. You have every right to be pissed. I'm so sorry."

Not even a kiss on the cheek this time—but what did I expect. This was over.

"Whatever—I hope your problems work out." I stepped into the back of the town car Pat had pulled up. She stepped up to the half-open door.

"You're the problem, Jack, a big damn problem, but I'll work it out."

9

I WAS THE problem? What the hell! Maybe someone didn't think much of my presence—I wasn't part of the circle, obviously a last minute addition. I fumed in silence for a while, but the more I thought about it, it had to have been the phone call. Whatever—her mood swing had pretty much spoiled the weekend for me.

I lost interest in my little snit before too long and noticed that Pat didn't seem to be in much of a hurry. I caught him glancing at me in the rear view mirror. "Does Carol ever give you time off? It can't be easy keeping to her schedule."

"I don't mind. She's a very generous person. Mattie and I are compensated very well, and she helped both my wife and Mattie's husband get good jobs in the government."

His eyes found mine in the mirror again. "You probably could tell I wasn't real thrilled that she invited you this weekend."

I smiled. "I did, but nothing wrong with being protective of your employer. I admire that."

"She told me I was obvious."

"Well, maybe just a little," I kidded.

"I was wrong. She's had a few other guys out to the Shore, and one way or the other they've all tried to take advantage. She's had some bad experiences with men over the years, so I'm pretty protective. You seem to be on the up and up, and she seems to be truly interested in you. Sorry—I probably shouldn't be saying any of this."

"No, it's fine—I appreciate your candor. And maybe you can help. She got an unexpected phone call this morning. After that, the whole

weekend vibe seemed to change, she practically ignored me. Any idea
what happened?"

"Mattie said you two were enjoying a morning dip." I could see his
careful grin. "If I did know who called or what it was about I wouldn't
tell you. But she deals with a lot of big shots who are demanding and
unreasonable most of the time. Trust me, whatever the call was about,
she'll handle it. Don't read too much into one day: this weekend was
a really big deal for her business. You were probably becoming too
much of a distraction."

"Thanks. I admit the sudden freeze was pretty hard on my ego."

"Well, if it makes you feel any better, Ms. Erskine pulled her
aside before dinner and suggested she'd be happy to give you a ride
home. Mr. Brooks had to leave early, and she had plenty of room.
She was hardly out of earshot when Ms. Madison told me to be sure
that didn't happen."

I didn't want to think about Ms. Erskine.

The traffic thickened as we approached DC, and our conversation
faltered. I leaned back to relax and enjoy the view. The city really
sparkles just after sunset. The sky becomes a dark marbled haze to
the west and the monuments light up with a pink glow. It was slow
going on the beltway, but Pat was a master at avoiding the "crazies
from Maryland," and I was soon home.

I'd left my phone at home, a bad habit I constantly tried to correct.
No messages from either Marshall or Beth. I checked my personal
email, but again nothing but the usual commercial solicitations. Work
email could wait. Maggie had left a message on my landline chiding
me for not answering my cell and informing me that she and Walter
would be back in town Wednesday. Would I like to have dinner with
them on Thursday night?

My life story—dinner for three.

Therapists had assured me that these frequent bouts of minor
depression were normal. I knew I could shake it off in time. I had no
idea why I was indulging in such a pity party. After Angie died I had
no desire to socialize. It had been six years now, and only two women
had held much interest for me. My sometime law partner in Little
Rock had turned out to be exactly that, and in the end it was much

better for both of us. Marian South, a high school flame who was now
a college professor in Vermont, turned out to be more attached to
Vermont than to me. I had no intention of moving to Vermont.

It was still early, so I opened a bottle of wine and sat down to stare
at my computer. An antitrust lawyer's work is usually about as lively
as my social life. But if I was going to spend most of tomorrow with
Marshall, I needed to sort out my workweek. I spent a while juggling
various appointments and finally felt pretty good about my schedule.
Angie and I used to spend our Sundays much the same way, relaxing
and coordinating our schedules for the week ahead. The familiar ache
of loss was a bit duller, but thinking about her brought me back to
tomorrow's task—Marshall Fitzgerald.

I'd be left cooling my heels while the deputy U.S. Attorney
interviewed Marshall about the phone call he'd received from Billy
Hopper. I wasn't concerned that Marshall was in any trouble or that
he would lose his cool. But I was concerned that she might broaden
her inquiry beyond the phone call. Marshall had firmly refused my
attempts to intervene. He could handle it and didn't need my services
as his lawyer.

MONDAY

April 18, 2016

10

MARSHALL CUT A handsome and imposing figure at breakfast, He wore a dark suit, perfectly knotted tie, a cuffed white shirt, and dark dress shoes, polished to perfection. I had given in to a sports coat and khakis—at least I hadn't spilled anything on my shirt during breakfast.

"You certainly are dressed to impress." I complimented him.

"I've found that on certain occasions it's best to look one's best. Today is one of those occasions. Besides, I received a call earlier this morning. Agents from the FBI will also take part in the interview."

Well, that changed the ball game. I wondered why the FBI would get involved. Murder was normally a local matter, but the reality was that in DC they don't need much of a reason and frequently intervened in high profile cases. We sipped our coffee and I tried to emulate his nonchalance. I thought I'd set a few ground rules, but Marshall beat me to it.

"I appreciate you coming to the interview, but I don't want you to do anything that will keep me from seeing William—understand?"

"Of course, but I've been thinking about this a great deal. I don't want you to inadvertently say something that puts you at risk. I thought before we begin I'd at least ask them to verify that you are not a target of any investigation. I also want to put some limits on what areas they can question you about. For example, I don't want them to question you about Billy's family background."

"None of that Jack—nothing that will give them an impression that I'm not being cooperative. Besides, why would you think I'm a target?"

"I don't, but don't handcuff me. If it were up to me I probably

wouldn't let you be interviewed at all without working out a complete understanding about the scope of this interview with the U.S.
Attorney's office. We're talking the FBI, remember?"

"I am well aware of the practices and methods of the FBI. You are
not my lawyer. I will simply thank you very much and go by myself
if you attempt to impede this interview in any way." His formal tone
evoked the very image of the judge he was.

"Okay, it's your funeral," I said in frustration.

I insisted we take a cab to the courthouse. I didn't want either of
us to look hot and bothered when we arrived. We cleared security
easily and soon stood outside Room 316. I gave a brief rap, opened
the door and saw four men and one woman sitting silently at a table.
The men were clearly from the FBI, so the poised young black woman
must be with the U.S. Attorney's office.

One of the men looked up and said, "I'm sorry, this is a private
meeting—you've got the wrong room."

Marshall emerged from behind me, and the man backtracked,
"I'm sorry, Judge Fitzgerald, you're in the right place. I didn't know
you were bringing anyone with you. Come on in."

I spoke up, "Jack Patterson. I don't think I've met any of you.
Here's my card." I tossed a few business cards on the table, expecting
everyone to do the same. The exchange of business cards is a
Washington ritual, but no one returned the courtesy. The man who
had originally spoken turned to Marshall.

"Judge Fitzgerald, this is to be a private interview. Is there some
reason you need counsel?"

Marshall responded evenly. "Mr. Patterson is not my lawyer; he is
a long-standing friend. I'm a simple Arkansas trial judge, and thought
I'd be more comfortable having a friend sit in, but if that's not per-
mitted, may he sit outside the door until I'm finished?"

The woman rose to address Marshall. She wore a dress with a
jacket rather than the ubiquitous dark suit of the legal world. Her
voice was kind, but firm.

"I'm sorry, Judge, but we cannot allow Mr. Patterson's presence to
be here unless he's your lawyer. But I see no reason why he can't sit
outside, and you may certainly confer during breaks. Mr. Patterson,

your reputation precedes you. I'm Constance Montgomery, Deputy U.S. Attorney. My colleagues will introduce themselves." She passed two of her cards across the table and the men did likewise. Two of them were with the FBI, Travis Barry and Fred Pitcock. The third was one of her deputies—I didn't catch his name.

Constance continued, "Judge, the FBI will conduct this interview. Mr. Salem and I are here only to observe."

So she would set the rules but pretend to only observe. She spoke to Marshall, but looked me directly in the eye. She didn't expect a challenge, and I didn't give her one.

The others pulled out legal pads, and as soon as I left the room the questioning began. Fortunately, Marshall has a wonderful memory, and he was able to recite most all their questions during the first break.

For the first half hour agent Travis took the lead, asking Marshall to recite his name, address, educational background, marital status, et cetera. Easy information they could have pulled of the Arkansas's Judiciary's website in a couple of minutes. Interview Techniques 101—begin the interview with easy questions to put the prey at ease.

Travis continued. "Judge, thank you for giving us your background information. Let's move foreword to the morning when William Hopper brutally stabbed and killed a woman in his hotel room. Mr. Hopper made three phone calls that morning. One to 911, one to the front desk at the Mayflower asking for security. But the first call was to a number you have identified as your home phone number. Is that correct?" His tone was still very cordial.

"I don't know anything about how many calls William made or what you allege William might have done, but he did call me at my home the morning of March twentieth." Marshall wasn't about to give them an inch.

"Okay, he called you at home. The Mayflower's phone records indicate that the call lasted approximately ten minutes. Does that sound right?"

"I don't know if you have any phone records, or what they show, but if you are asking me how long we spoke, I'd say about ten minutes."

"Judge, why did he call you?" Travis asked.

"I don't have any knowledge of his reason. You will have to ask him."

Marshall said at that point Travis became a little testy. "Judge could you be a little more cooperative? What did Mr. Hopper say when he called?"

"Well, first he apologized for calling so early, then said he needed help."

"What did you say in response?"

"I told him there was no need to apologize and asked how could I help."

"Please, Judge. We'll be here all day if I have to drag this phone call out of you in bits and pieces. Can't you just tell me about your conversation?"

Marshall said he knew it was time to quit playing.

"William told me he had woken up in his hotel room and found a strange woman lying next to him in the bed. He said there was blood everywhere, that he jumped out of the bed and had no idea what to do. I asked him if she was alive, and he said he was pretty sure she was dead—she hadn't moved. So I told him to call 911 and hotel security."

Travis seemed pleased. "Did he mention a knife?"

"He said he's found a bloody knife on his chest when he woke up, and that he'd thrown it across the room."

"He said it was on his chest?"

"That's correct."

"Did he tell you why he threw it across the room?"

"No, of course not. Wouldn't you have done the same thing?"

"Okay, did he tell you anything about the girl?

"Only that he had no idea who she was." That seemed to get Travis's attention.

"Did you ask him anything else?"

"I asked him if he was okay, was he injured, things like that."

"And...?"

"He said that he was okay, that the blood must be hers."

"He said that?" Travis was digging in. "He said the blood was hers?"

"No, he said, 'The blood must be hers.'" Marshall recognized the subtle difference.

"Did he say anything else about his own condition?"

"He said he couldn't remember anything from the night before.

He didn't know who the woman was, and couldn't remember how he got back to the hotel from the banquet."

"So he couldn't remember a thing."

"That is what he said," Marshall answered.

"Anything else about his condition other than he wasn't injured, and he couldn't remember anything?"

"He didn't have any clothes on."

Marshall said that Travis looked surprised, as did the others. "How do you know?"

"Well, I don't know. It's what he told me. He said he was naked when he woke up and that he was covered in blood. He wanted to know if he could take a shower."

"What did you tell him?"

"I told him he couldn't shower until the police arrived. I told him it was okay for him to put on clothes, but to be sure and tell the police he had been naked earlier."

Marshall said that at this point Constance had suggested they take a break, but had a single question first.

"Before you hung up, did you tell Mr. Hopper not to talk to anyone without a lawyer present?"

"No. I told him not to talk to anyone until I got here, but I didn't mention a lawyer. Why?"

11

THE DOOR OPENED and the men filed out. Marshall looked relieved, and I was about to suggest we get coffee in the cafeteria on the first floor when Constance tapped my arm.

"Mr. Patterson?" She nodded at Marshall. "Judge. Can I have a minute before the break, just the three of us?"

I wasn't about to argue, so we returned to the room. She spoke directly to Marshall. "I know you're anxious to speak to Mr. Hopper, and I'm not revealing any confidences when I say he won't talk to anyone without your presence. However, I'd like to finish your interview before you meet with him, and I'm afraid that's going to take a little longer."

Marshall grumbled. "And why is that?"

"Whether you realize it or not, you're a critical witness. You explain why the knife wasn't near the woman's body, why blood was on the inside of Hopper's sweats, and that he told you he didn't remember anything that had happened. His phone call to you answers a lot of questions we've had, and we're only getting started."

"My testimony won't change. It is the truth. How can it hurt for me to see him before you're finished?"

"I know you're telling the truth, and I know you would never lie even if it could save your friend, but your present memory is untainted by any contact with Mr. Hopper. I'd really appreciate it if you would allow us to finish before you speak with him." She spoke carefully, clearly treating him gently.

"Will we have concluded before the arraignment this afternoon?

Will I be able to speak with him before it convenes?"

"I honestly don't know. But certainly you can attend the arraignment. I'll make sure you have the chance to speak at least briefly with him. Mr. Hopper doesn't have a lawyer yet, and as I've said, he refuses to talk to anyone until he talks to you. He has taken your advice literally. He won't even talk to a public defender. Other than to be polite, he refuses to talk at all. I'm as ready to have you see him as you are."

"Can I tell him it's okay to talk to the pubic defender?" Marshall asked.

Constance seemed intrigued for a second.

"Since they haven't yet conferred, today the public defender will simply enter a not-guilty plea for him at the arraignment. I'll be sure the jail lets you spend as much time with him as you need tomorrow. You can tell him anything you like. Right now, get a cup of coffee, and we'll reconvene in—let's say twenty minutes."

I spoke carefully, "Ms. Montgomery, it was only a very brief phone call. May I ask why this interview should take so long?"

"I don't want to go into everything, but you're a good lawyer, Mr. Patterson. What would you like to ask if you were in my shoes? I suspect you already have a good idea."

With that she rose, closing the door gently on her way out. Marshall sat with his head in his hands. I was afraid he was going to cry.

"C'mon. Let's go downstairs and get a cup of coffee. This room is suddenly suffocating."

Marshall rose slowly and followed me out the room. We made our way to the cafeteria in the basement. I ordered two coffees while Marshall snagged a table.

"Jack, the least I can do is get him a lawyer. I need your help. It's already been more than two weeks. I bet he thinks I've abandoned him."

"No way. If he thought you'd abandoned him, he wouldn't be refusing to talk to anyone. He'll be sure when he sees you at the arraignment. Right now let's focus on what they might want to ask you next. Then we can figure out a process to get him a good lawyer quickly."

"How do we do that?"

"I don't know yet, but I'll think of something. Have you ever known me not to figure out a way?"

For the first time today I saw Marshall's pearly whites.

"No, Jack. Your methods are sometimes suspect, but you always find a way."

"All right. Let's get ready for the next set of questions. I bet what you just went through was the easy part. The next session will probably test your patience and really piss you off."

"What do you mean? I don't know anything more than I've already told them. What could they ask?"

I told him, and as I had predicted he was pissed.

1 2

A DIFFERENT AGENT—NEITHER of us could remember his name—wasted a good deal of time reviewing the earlier interview, but Marshall kept his patience. Finally, agent Barry intervened.

"Judge I'm going to show you some photographs. Take your time. Do you recognize the woman in any of these pictures?"

Travis pushed five photographs across the table, all of the same naked woman lying in a pool of blood. I had prepared Marshall for this grisly tactic. He took his time, carefully examining each photograph.

Marshall spoke deliberately. "I do not recognize the woman."

"You took a long time, Judge. You sure you don't have some idea who this woman is?"

"You told me to take my time. I have no idea who the woman is."

"This is the woman who was found in Billy Hopper's bed when the police arrived after he phoned you. Yet you say he wanted to know whether he could take a shower? Don't you think he should have been more concerned about calling an ambulance than getting legal advice about showers and clothing?"

Marshall told me he took his time before answering.

"I am not a practicing lawyer. I don't give legal advice. William is a friend, and he asked me what to do. I told him to call nine-one-one and hotel security, which according to you he did immediately after calling me and even before putting any clothes on."

Travis considered this response before asking, "Judge, why do you think Mr. Hopper called you?"

"William has been a family friend since he was a counselor at Camp Carolina where my sons attended camp."

Marshall said this revelation seemed to surprise the listeners.

"Why would he have called you rather than, say, his parents or a sibling?"

"His parents are deceased. As far as I know, he has no siblings."

"Really. How do you know this?" Travis probed.

"He told me."

"Okay, you said he was a family friend. Has he ever been in your home?"

"Yes."

"More than once?"

"Yes, indeed."

"Judge, you can be a little bit more forthcoming. How often would you say Billy Hopper has been in your home?" Travis let his irritation show.

"I can't tell you how many times he has been in our home. When he was in college he spent breaks and most holidays at our house. He spent some time with us before he went to Oxford, and more after he returned. After he signed with the Lobos he moved to Los Angeles. He didn't come for Christmas this past year, but he spent a long weekend at our home right after the season was over. Is that detailed enough?"

Marshall told me they conferred briefly in whispers before announcing they would break for lunch.

Marshall was irritated by the continual delays, but I was glad to have the extra time. I suggested lunch at one of my favorite restaurants, *701* on Pennsylvania Avenue. While we waited for lobster bisque and salad, Marshall filled me in on the interview and his inquisitors' obvious confusion. I laughed.

"They clearly haven't been able to figure out why Billy called you that morning and why you would care one way or the other. Hopper was born in Tennessee, grew up in Tennessee, and went to college in Tennessee. They're probably going nuts trying to figure out your connection. I'd bet the special agents in Chattanooga and Little Rock have been running ragged. There can never be an innocent explanation—it's just not in their genes."

I tried to avoid quizzing Marshall, letting him unwind and tell me whatever he wanted. Constance had told us before we left that they might or might not finish before the arraignment, but either way Marshall wouldn't have any real time with Billy today.

Regardless of Billy's silence, the public defender needed time to explain the arraignment procedure to Billy. Constance had given him Marshall's cell number, and he had texted that we were to sit in the first row of benches behind the rail, an area usually reserved for family. He had also warned him that the press would probably swarm after the arraignment.

"I hope you're ready, Judge," he texted.

I half expected Marshall to say, "Prepared for what?" But even literal Marshall understood the warning. As soon as the arraignment was concluded, the press would descend on Marshall with shouts and cameras, all trying to land an interview with the only person in the room obviously sitting in support of Billy Hopper.

Before we left *701*, I placed a call to Martin Wells, head of security for Walter Matthews' companies and Foundation, and occasionally for me. He agreed to meet me at the courthouse before the arraignment. I explained to Marshall what I was up to on the way back from lunch.

"I've asked Martin to help us leave the courtroom without being mobbed. I've also employed him to help you get in and out of the courthouse for your visits with Hopper. Don't fight me on this Marshall. You have bailiffs protecting you in Little Rock."

I expected Marshall to pitch a fit, but he was unusually cooperative.

"You really think that's necessary? he asked.

"I do. Listen, they mean no harm, but the press is starving for news in this case. An Arkansas judge shows up out of the blue to hug the accused in the highest profile murder case in the country. They learn from a confidential source that Hopper called you the morning he discovered the body and that Billy won't talk to anybody but you. You are about to become the center of their attention. So let me help you in the few ways I can. Martin can give you some semblance of privacy. I'll also call Clovis, my friend in Little Rock. He can keep your wife and kids from being harassed."

"Of course I know Clovis. Would they really bother Grace and the boys? They're in high school now. Surely…"

"You'd better believe it," I interrupted. "Right now Billy Hopper is the biggest fish in the ocean. I think we have a few hours to set things in motion. While you're finishing up the interview, I'll call Grace and tell her to expect a call from Clovis. Martin will take care of everything at this end. He'll also coordinate with your hotel's security, that is unless you want to bunk in with me."

Marshall smiled. "It bothers you that I am staying at such an expensive hotel doesn't it?"

I nodded.

"I'll tell you a story over dinner one night. Like you said, 'one never thinks there is a simple explanation.'"

Constance was waiting for us outside the interview room when we returned. She told us Marshall could have as long as three hours with Billy, beginning at nine a.m. tomorrow. From then on he would need to set up a schedule for visits with the jail.

"I know the two of you have a lot to discuss, but I hope you can persuade Mr. Hopper to hire a lawyer quickly so we all can put this case behind us. The case against him is cut and dried, and the quicker he pleads guilty and we get his cooperation in discovering the identity of the victim, the better for all of us." This time her voice was hard as nails.

Marshall glowered at "cut and dried" but didn't argue the point.

"Let's get the questioning over. I don't want to miss the arraignment." With that, Marshall walked into the room.

I found a small, unoccupied office across the hall where I could make calls in private. Grace wasn't happy when I told her that Clovis would be coming by within the hour.

"Lord, Jack, what would those people want with me?"

I explained as quickly as I could, cutting her questions short so I could get Clovis on board before the press descended. I hoped Clovis could calm her down.

I was able to reach him on the first try and gave him a quick run down on the events so far. Oddly, he didn't seem surprised.

"Judge Fitzgerald and Billy Hopper," he mused. "Small world."

"It is. Listen, I'll call you again tonight and we can catch up, but for the moment watch out for Grace and the boys—no telling who might show up on her doorstep."

It had been more than a few months since I'd spoken with Clovis. In the last three years I'd returned to Little Rock twice to represent, well, let's just say unlikely clients. Unlikely translates to dangerous, and Clovis had provided me security, saving my life more than once. We've become good friends, and I enjoy his occasional trips to DC. We usually try to catch a Nat's game and I had introduced him to Cantler's, a crab house on Mill Creek just off the Chesapeake Bay— best restaurant crabs in Maryland. He's hooked.

I called Martin again, giving a more detailed explanation and a few instructions. Next, I called my assistant Rose to let her know I wouldn't be in the office today. She said a package had arrived from the law firm of Richards and Sullivan, and a Mr. Shaw had called several times. She gave me his number. I toyed with calling Red, but heard a nearby door close firmly. Red would have to wait.

I walked into the hall to find Constance shaking Marshall's hand and thanking him for his cooperation. The others were already long gone.

She said, "I guess it won't do any good to say I'd prefer that you not speak with Mr. Hopper about this interview."

Marshall was direct. "No. It won't do any good."

"Well... Anyway, Judge, get your friend a lawyer so we can put this case to rest."

Marshall had heard enough about Billy's obvious guilt.

"Has it occurred to you, Ms. Montgomery, that perhaps William is not guilty?"

She looked him straight in the eye and said firmly, "No. It hasn't even crossed my mind. He's guilty as sin."

13

THE COURTROOM WAS already packed. Fortunately, no cameras were allowed. I told the marshal who we were, and he escorted us to the reserved seats up front. The crowd fell silent as all eyes turned to watch our entrance. The press was crowded into a couple of middle rows, but one look at Marshall's countenance silenced even the most jaded reporter.

A harried young man strode in and plopped a group of folders on the appropriate table. His eyes scanned the crowd, and he walked straight up to Marshall.

"Judge Fitzgerald, I'm Rich Slaughter, deputy public defender." He handed Marshall his card. "Mr. Hopper was relieved to hear you're here. He still won't talk to me other than to answer the most basic questions, and he was extremely disappointed you couldn't talk before this arraignment. He knows you'll see him tomorrow morning, and he understands that today is just a formality. I'll waive the reading of the indictment and enter a not guilty plea. Hopefully that will be the extent of my representation. Any questions?"

Marshall shook his head and thanked Rich for his help.

Constance Montgomery, accompanied by at least six or seven other lawyers, took over the prosecution table, opening briefcases and spreading out papers. Constance greeted the public defender, but ignored the two of us. She wouldn't show any part of her hand until she was good and ready.

Billy Hopper was led into the courtroom by two marshals. He wore the expected jumpsuit, hands and ankles chained to a belt around his waist. They made sure he was seated before unfastening the chains. Marshall had risen and was trying to reach out to Billy when we heard, "All rise!" Judge Morris Langston strode into the room in flowing robes. He was modest in size, wore horn-rimmed glasses, and seemed very much at ease.

"Welcome, everyone. We are here for the initial arraignment in the case of the District of Columbia versus Billy Hopper. Who's representing the government?"

"Constance Montgomery, your honor, Deputy U.S. Attorney." Her colleagues seemed disappointed that she didn't introduce them as well, but she didn't even look in their direction. *Interesting.*

"And for the defense?" the judge asked.

"Rich Slaughter, assistant public defender, your honor."

"I take it Mr. Hopper hasn't engaged counsel yet. Should I be thinking about appointing counsel?

"I don't think so, your honor. I believe his lack of counsel is a temporary situation." Rich obviously wanted to distance himself from Billy every way he could.

"Okay, but I want you let me know if he doesn't obtain counsel in the immediate future. I want to move this case off the docket as soon as possible."

Even the judge—why the rush? This was a first-degree murder case, not some routine assault and battery case after a bar fight.

"Okay, Mr. Slaughter. Is the defendant willing to waive the reading of the indictment and enter a plea?"

"Yes, your honor. The defendant enters a plea of not guilty."

A loud murmur from the gallery was met with a loud rap of the gavel.

"All right, that's enough. I've received requests from the press to allow cameras in the courtroom. I will rule on those requests after defense counsel is on board. If there is nothing further, court is adjourned."

We all rose, but before the marshals could get to Billy he was enveloped in Marshall's arms. Neither said a word.

The press exploded with questions: "Why'd you do it, Billy? Anything you want to tell your fans? Who is this man, Billy? How are you being treated? Who was the woman, Billy?"

To some extent, my presence and Martin's blocked them from getting too close to Marshall. The rail kept them away from Billy. Finally the embrace ended. Both men were fighting back tears. The uninformed would have assumed Marshall was the pro football player—he towered over Billy.

The marshals pulled Billy away, and Marshall said, "I'll see you tomorrow. Everything will be okay."

Billy nodded and gave a weak smile as they hurried him out of the courtroom. Now it was just Marshall and the press. Fortunately, Martin was prepared. He grabbed Marshall by the arm and pressed him close behind two large guys who were running interference toward the door. I followed behind.

Martin quickly led us to a bank of elevators where another one of his men had been holding the door. The doors closed, and we had a break from the shouting for at least for a minute or so. I dreaded the mob we would face when we reached the front door to the courthouse, but Martin had a better plan.

The elevator took us to the basement, where Martin led us through a twisting route to a garage where Martin had left a large black Suburban. As we got in he explained.

"I called in a couple of favors and got permission to use the marshal's garage. We'll be out of the building in no time and headed back to the hotel. It won't be so easy tomorrow, but leave it to me, Judge. This is the way the marshals get protected witnesses in and out of the building."

Marshall was in shock. He had been forced to deal with the press during the Cole case, but they had shown him respect. In DC, he was a person of interest and fair game.

"Judge, your hotel's security team will ensure your privacy whenever you're inside their doors. I'll have my people there as well. We'll do our best to get you in and out with as little hassle as possible." He looked at me. "If you need working space, I recommend you use Jack's offices."

"We have plenty of room," I said. "You are welcome to use one of our offices to interview lawyers, make phone calls, or anything else.

Our building has tight security, and either Maggie or Rose can help you with anything you need."

He looked overwhelmed, even a little bewildered.

"Seeing Billy had to be tough, and I know how you hate crowds. Let's go back to your hotel, have a glass of wine and a bite to eat before I go home, and then I'll leave you alone. Just follow Martin's lead tomorrow, okay."

He nodded.

Soon back at the Hay-Adams, we washed up and Marshall checked in with Grace. We were the only ones in the dining room since it wasn't even six o'clock. We ordered drinks, and I tried to keep the conversation away from today by asking about our mutual friends in Little Rock—Sam Pagano, Helen Cole, and Ben, the owner of my favorite barbeque place. But Billy Hopper's ghost was sitting at the table. Marshall was the first to bring today up.

"I don't know what I would have done without you today. I thought I could deal with all this all by myself. Thank you."

"What are friends for? The most difficult thing for you will be the press. They'll keep hounding you until they ferret out your relationship with Billy. We might want to consider giving an interview to a friendly reporter. You can set the ground rules, but once one reporter breaks the story the rest are more likely to leave you alone."

"I'm not so sure that's a good idea—Ms. Montgomery might retaliate. We haven't talked about my last session. She repeated her request that I not talk to William or anyone else about the interview."

"That was to be expected." I said.

"I know, but she also said they there was a chance they might want to interview Grace and the boys."

"A nice implied threat to guarantee your continued cooperation," I noted. And one frequently used by the FBI, I thought to myself, wondering again why they were involved at all.

"Absolutely, subtle but unmistakable. You know, Jack, being a Judge can insulate one from the real world sometimes. This experience has already been an eye-opener. Maybe I should have seen the other side of law enforcement a long time ago."

The server brought cheeseburgers and extra crispy fries that we both devoured with quiet relish. It's amazing how much tension can be diffused by solid comfort food.

"Marshall, I wouldn't wish what you are going through on anyone. A second son charged with murder, an FBI investigation, threats on your family, and who else knows what's next. People counsel 'one-day-at-a-time.' I think you'd be well advised to do just that."

Marshall had begun to relax, at least a little. A second scotch didn't hurt.

"Grace told me that Clovis was at the house fifteen minutes after your call. He's talked to the kids. There's a satellite truck planted outside the house, but it sounds like he's got everything under control."

"Another reason to give an interview. Think about it overnight. For now, we've insulated you as much as we can. Do you want to talk about getting him defense counsel? Do you want me to make some calls?"

Marshall picked up his drink, took a small sip, and appeared to be considering his answer. His mouth took a funny shape like a light bulb had gone off.

Finally he answered, "Hold off on any calls for now. Like you said, one-day-at-a-time. I want to meet with William and talk all this over with him first."

"Be careful. Anything you discuss is not privileged. Make sure you tell him to say nothing about what happened or the FBI will be interviewing you again."

"I'm aware of that, Jack," he said sharply.

Of course he was. He was smart, a lawyer, and a judge. I was stating the obvious, but it never hurt to be reminded.

"Sorry—just being a mother hen. What will you talk about?"

"His agent told me he has very little money left. Apparently the Lobos still owe him money under the old contract and for several incentive bonuses. They never dreamed he would be selected offensive rookie-of-the-year, which carries a quarter of million-dollar bonus. Then again his agent never thought his client would be charged with murder or that the Lobos would invoke the morals clause of the contract to fire him."

"He has to have some money left, even under an NFL minimum contract," I stated.

"He did. But according to his agent he used most of it to pay off his student loans and to pay back every single person who lent him money over the years, including yours truly. I still have every penny he gave me and will use it to hire a lawyer, but I am afraid it won't be nearly enough."

"Will his agent help?"

"To put it in his words, 'Not no, but hell no.' Talk about a rat leaving a sinking ship. He got a large percentage of everything William earned in salary, bonuses, and endorsements, but as soon as the ship took on water, he jumped over the side." His face was the picture of disgust.

"Too bad. He might know the perfect lawyer."

"More to the point, he might know something about that evening. He was at the banquet with William to bask in the glory. I'd bet he even charged the whole weekend at the Mandarin hotel to William's American Express card."

"Can he do that?" I asked.

"Apparently lots of agents put their clients on an allowance and give them an American Express card to pay for all their expenses. Makes for good recordkeeping as long as your agent is honest. Like I said, I want to talk to William."

"Did the agent tell you what he remembered about the evening?"

"No surprise—the FBI asked him not to discuss anything about that evening with anyone, and he wasn't about to argue." Marshall shrugged his shoulders.

"Constance got to him early. The FBI has more than likely talked to everyone sitting at Billy's table that night, waiters, the bellman at the Mayflower, and anyone else who had contact with him. They saved you for last."

I should have anticipated the FBI's strategy—there was nothing surprising about it. They had slow walked Marshall, not allowing him to see Billy until they had all the witness testimony locked up.

Marshall again gave me a peculiar look. He finished his scotch and said, "I'm going to call it a night. I want to call Grace again. I'm exhausted, and want to have all my wits about me tomorrow. I'll come to your office after I meet with Billy."

He refused to let me pick up dinner, insisting serenely that I was his guest whenever we were in the Hay-Adams.

I had hoped to hear his story about the hotel, but it would have to wait. He saw me to the door and for the third time tonight got an odd grin on his face.

"You haven't asked me about Micki," he said casually as we left the restaurant.

Micki Lawrence had been my co-counsel in both the Cole and Stewart cases. She was the outdoorsy type: very tall with short, sun-bleached hair. When she wasn't in the courtroom she was riding or grooming her horses. She was also a very good lawyer, dedicated to a clientele that consisted mostly of criminals and hard luck cases. We worked well together and once talked about a loose law partner-ship. Last time I saw her she was practically engaged to a Little Rock doctor. Another reason for us to work together hadn't come up, and we hadn't spoken in more than six months.

"No, I haven't. She must be married by now." I ducked the com-ment. Micki's probable marriage was not a subject I cared to discuss.

"You might want to check in with her."

There was that grin again. I made a mental note to check in with Micki sometime soon.

14

I UNLOCKED THE front door and was immediately greeted by a tail-wagging Sophie, excited by the prospect of a walk. I was ready to call it a day, but as I hooked on her leash, I realized I hadn't checked my email or voicemail all day. I was ready for Maggie to come home. She was great with both the press and testy clients, most of whom melted at her refined British accent.

Sophie and I returned after a quick round the block, and I settled down at my desk. I knew Rose deserved my first attention.

"Jack, don't ever do that to me again. The phone never stopped ringing and a few reporters even got past security. They all want to know how you're connected to Billy Hopper, and who the black man with you in court today was. I mean, I know who Judge Fitzgerald is, but they don't, and I didn't know what to say. And that was just the beginning—that man Shaw, who called before, was downright rude. He demanded to know where you were and why you weren't returning his calls. He said—well, I didn't like what he said and hung up on him. Jack, I'm just not up to this. What's going on? I need Maggie—it's her job to handle stuff like this."

My sentiments exactly. I had left my old law firm, Banks and Tuohey, a few years ago under difficult circumstances. Both Maggie and Rose had come with me. They had been caught up in my work, both were tired of the large law firm atmosphere, and both had decided to put their trust in me. I owed Rose a lot, but I knew her limitations. This was more than she could handle.

"I'm sorry, Rose, and thank you. I know today was tough, and you did great. Calm down and don't worry. I'll take care of Mr. Shaw. Listen, I'll be in the office early tomorrow. Can you come in early?

"Judge Fitzgerald is going to use one of the spare offices and the conference room for at least the next few days. I'll talk to our security folks about keeping the press out. Better yet, I'll get Martin to take care of it."

I heard her take a deep breath, knew she was trying to regain her poise.

"Of course, you know I will. But what's all this got to do with Billy Hopper? He murdered that girl in cold blood, you know—terrible, terrible thing. He's every women's nightmare, cute and innocent, but underneath another violent jock who thinks he can get away with murder."

I would have to convince to Rose to keep her opinions to herself, but not tonight.

"Get some rest, Rose; tomorrow's going to be a long day."

I knew I should call Red, but I needed to unwind. I didn't want to know what he'd said to Rose, but it was worrisome.

I went through my emails; most of them were from the press. I read each one, then punched delete. Same with the voicemails— delete. I usually tried to keep reporters happy—you never knew when you might need a favor. But I didn't want to saddle Maggie with the mess, and I had no skin in this game.

A few messages were from friends questioning my sanity. Several were rude, almost threatening. But one message caught my attention: a call from an old friend, Cheryl Cole. She wasn't exactly a friend, in fact she was—well, she is Woody Cole's former wife, who managed to parlay her relationship with Woody into a popular evening talk show on Fox News.

"Jack, you owe me. Marshall Fitzgerald and Jack Patterson attending Billy Hopper's arraignment. I smell a really big story; you owe me and you know it. Call me any time day or night." To the point, as usual.

I wasn't about to let Cheryl within a city block of Marshall. Maggie was really going to hate making this call. She didn't think much of Cheryl, but I did owe her a favor for her participation in the Stewart case. Of course, her cooperation had worked to her benefit as well, usually the case with Cheryl.

I sighed and punched in Red's number, really hoping he would be out to dinner.

"Where in the hell have you been?" he answered. So much for dinner.

"Sorry I've been hard to reach. I've been at the courthouse all day."

"Yeah, well I know that. It's all over the news. Don't you have better things to do than being a courthouse groupie? They said you were on the front row. How early did you have to get there to get a front row seat?"

Courthouse groupie—I wondered who gave him that phrase. Sarcasm does not impress me.

"Not early at all—the bailiff had saved me a seat. Marshall Fitzgerald, an old friend of mine from Little Rock came to town on Saturday. It turns out he is close to Billy Hopper. I offered to go to the arraignment with him. Lucy knows him—she can explain the relationship."

There was along pause. I suspected Lucy was standing right there.

"Well, I'll be damned. I guess your presence makes some sense. I was worried I'd put my money on the wrong horse. Did you get the contract from my lawyers?" Red's tone was almost polite.

"I did, but I didn't go into the office today. I'll go over it and get back with you tomorrow."

"Good. You know I liked that kid... Hopper... cost me a lot of money and my people think I should sue him."

Why in the world would Red pile on Billy? "I'd say he has bigger worries than a civil lawsuit from his former team."

Red gave out a boisterous laugh. "I guess you're right. Don't understand it. The kid had the world by the tail and threw it all away for a one-night stand with some hooker. Doesn't make any sense. All of us have spent millions trying to distance football from the issue of violence against women, and now Hopper has undone all that work in one damn night."

I was ready to cut the conversation short.

"I'll call you tomorrow, or should I call your lawyer?"

"If it's something major, call me; if it's wording or whatever other stuff you lawyers worry about, work it out with them. Let's get this

done. Thanks to Hopper, I bet some damn Senator is already planning some sort of hearing to appease the women's rights groups. I
need you on board."

"That Senator wouldn't be having dinner with you right now?" I
joked.

"Nope, not this Senator, I hope! I like you, Patterson. You punch
back." I heard a laugh, and he hung up.

I was ready to dislike Red Shaw, probably for no good reason.
To begin with, I was wary of anyone close to Lucy. He was gruff and
demanding, and from what Marshall told me, had been pretty stingy
with Billy Hopper's contract.

Yet, something told me not to judge so quickly. This latest incident of violence against a woman had created another storm of bad
publicity for the NFL, especially for the Lobos. An indignant Congress
was likely to pile into the fray. They love the free publicity of hearings,
especially if they don't really have to do anything.

I needed to make one last phone call before I called it a night,
but before I could call Clovis my cell phone began to vibrate. I didn't
recognize the number but I answered it nonetheless.

"You miss me?"

15

In spite of myself, my heart jumped when I heard Carol's voice.

"Well, sort of, I guess," I said warily, "but after Sunday..."

"Don't be silly," she interrupted. "I told you I'd work it out, and I have. I can explain later, if you insist. But let's get serious. The Nationals are in town Thursday night, and I look damn good in a baseball jersey and jeans. You can teach me how to keep score."

I bet she looked very good—my ego already felt better. I racked my brain...Thursday, Thursday. Damn. Maggie and Walter.

"I'd like nothing better than to catch a Nationals game with you, but I already have plans."

"Do I have competition?" She was toying with me.

"Not what you think. Maggie and Walter Matthews are getting back from a month in Italy, and I committed to dinner with them. How about Friday night? Strasburg is pitching."

"I have a better offer. Pat will pick you up Friday afternoon, and he'll bring you out to my place. The party won't arrive until Saturday morning, so we'll have some time to ourselves. I promise not to work so hard this weekend. This group is a lot more fun."

I wasn't used to being chased, but I wasn't about to turn down the offer.

"Sounds perfect. Strasburg's arm is sore anyway."

"Bring your bathing suit." She actually giggled and hung up.

Sounded like whatever was bothering Carol had been resolved. I'd miss golf on Saturday with Walter, but he'd understand.

I took a few moments to imagine the upcoming weekend. Good

thing Maggie was coming home. She'd bring me back down to earth.

Clovis filled me in on his efforts with the Fitzgerald family. At first, Grace had resisted, trying to make light of the situation, but when the satellite truck showed up and parked in the middle of the front yard she retreated to the kitchen. Clovis had spoken gravely to all the boys, giving each of them his card and instructing them to keep away from both the truck and the reporters.

"They're all convinced Hopper didn't do it. Amazing."

"You ought to hear Marshall. I guess this is normal. The family is the last to know. The DC prosecutor is convinced he did it, and I don't think she's putting on an act."

Clovis responded. "Of course, he did it. The woman was in his bed, the knife was a room service steak knife, and he left the banquet with three women arm in arm. The videos are all over ESPN and CNN."

So the prosecutor had already begun to leak damaging evidence. It would be drip, drip, and more drip. Both the potential jury pool and the trial judge would be convinced of Hopper's guilt long before the trial. It isn't fair, but the prosecutor holds all the cards and controls the media by way of leaks.

Clovis continued, "Jack, tell the Judge he needs to come home. The more he's associated with Hopper, the worse it's going to be for him back here. Hopper is the new poster child for violence against women. The longer the Judge appears to be befriending him, the more likely the women's groups are going to go after him. I'm not just talking about drumming up an opponent next time he's up for reelection. I'm talking about picketing his courtroom and his house. Folks get riled up and things can get out of control pretty quick."

I had worried Marshall might lose his shot at the Court of Appeals. It hadn't crossed my mind that it could cost him his current job as well.

Marshall had peaked my curiosity, so I asked Clovis, "So, Clovis, how's Micki?"

"Uh, … Why do you ask?" He seemed to have lost his usual sangfroid.

"Well, first Marshall suggests I give her a call, and now you sound like you've choked on a soup bone. What's up?"

"She'll kill me if I tell you."

"Do I need to get on a plane and come down there to find out? What in the hell is going on? You won't have to worry about Micki killing you, I'll do it myself if you don't start talking."

"Okay, calm down. So, Micki and Eric split, and she didn't deal with it very well. Pretty classic story: she came home from a fishing trip a day early and caught him in her bed with some nurse. She didn't much mind him cheating, but in her bed was a bit too much. Then he threw gasoline on the flames by blaming it all on you."

"What?" I asked, astounded.

"Yeah, after she calmed down he accused her of still being in love with you, and that's why he was cheating on her."

"What a crock."

"That's what she said, too," Clovis replied. "At any rate, she threw him out on his ear and started drinking. A lot, a whole lot. Finally, Debbie called Sam and me."

Sam was my friend Sam Pagano, the local prosecutor and her former boss. Debbie was her office manager.

I asked, "Why didn't you call me?"

"After we spent a couple of days sobering her up, she made us swear not to tell you. She said she'd start drinking again if we told you. I told her you would ultimately find out, but she made us swear anyway. I think she had finally convinced herself to marry Eric, and somehow she now blames you."

"Is she okay? Should I call her?"

"Well, she's back at work, and I've seen her out with another guy now and then. I'd let the sleeping cat lie if I were you."

"Why would Marshall suggest I call her? Does he know?"

"I have no idea. I guess he doesn't." Clovis said.

"So my good friends Sam, Debbie, and you knew all this and didn't say a word to me?"

"Well, Jack, her demands were pretty specific. I had no reason to tell you until you asked. You haven't exactly been beating down her door—or even asked about her recently, as far as I know."

"Valid point. I'll leave her alone, but dammit, if she stumbles again, I expect a call—okay?"

"Deal."

TUESDAY

April 19, 2016

16

I DIDN'T SLEEP well. Yesterday had been a whirlwind, and the last two phone calls had been pretty unsettling. I didn't know quite what to think of Carol's renewed interest, couldn't quit wondering what had happened. Was Red somehow behind her call? And Clovis was right: I hadn't spoken to Micki in months, and her love life was none of my business. Still… I never did like Eric, and it wasn't my fault he was having a fling with a nurse in Micki's bed.

I arrived at the office with a sack of warm blueberry muffins, a peace offering for Rose. A fresh pot of coffee was brewing in the kitchen, and for the moment the phones were silent. Martin called to tell me the press still hadn't discovered where Marshall was staying—a miracle. But he worried about getting Marshall inside the courthouse today without getting mobbed.

Better him than me, I thought and then felt guilty. I wasn't the one who didn't do well with reporters.

Rose and I quickly went over my notes from last night. I couldn't help but wonder what Billy would tell Marshall and how Marshall would handle it, but I schooled myself: Billy Hopper wasn't my business. I would help Marshall any way I could, but Hopper was his problem. The contract from Red's lawyers sat on the corner of my desk. I toyed with it for a minute, but left the envelope unopened. Instead, I prepared for a nine-thirty meeting with a client about a merger that had drawn the attention of the Justice Department.

The client arrived right on time, accompanied by an entourage of lawyers who knew nothing about antitrust law. We reviewed his options for the next few hours, finally devising a reasonable plan of action. They were pleased and for a few minutes I enjoyed the warm feeling of having done a good job.

Rose and I were reviewing my calendar when Marshall arrived. Rose took one look at him and quickly excused herself. Apparently his morning hadn't gone as well as mine.

"Does Barker's serve a late lunch?" he asked brusquely. "I think we need to hurry."

"Absolutely. Let's go," I said.

Martin whisked us into his Suburban just as a handful of reporters ran back to their waiting cabs. I knew we wouldn't be able to dodge them much longer.

Despite the hour, Barker's was crowded, but after a few quiet words we were led to a corner table. Marshall sat down abruptly and ordered a beer

"You have one, too, Jack, I don't like to drink alone." I ordered a draft.

"That bad?" I asked.

"That bad."

He jerked his hand up and down impatiently as the waitress delivered the beer and waited for our orders. Today's special was fried catfish, hushpuppies, and slaw. No reason to even look at the menu.

As soon as she left, he began. "At first they put him in what they call the Hinckley cell at the courthouse. Named for John Hinckley, the man who shot Reagan. They were worried he might come to harm if he were put with the general population at the jail.

"But after the arraignment they got a call from the office of a powerful member of Congress complaining about favorable treatment. The marshal told me they had no choice but to move him in with the general population. He said they would do their best to see he wasn't harmed, but couldn't make any guarantees."

"What jerk complained? Don't they have anything better to do."

"Apparently somebody senior enough to put the fear of God into the head of the jail." Marshall was clearly distressed.

"Let me make some calls. I still have a few friends in the Marshal's service."

"Don't waste your breath. I said I would call the Attorney General, and the deputy said, 'Even the AG wouldn't buck this senator. Let it go, Judge.'"

A U.S. Senator intervening to make sure Billy didn't get special treatment. Sounded like Red was right. The congressional wolves were out for blood.

"Okay, so what happened next?"

"Well, I told him that anything he told me wasn't privileged so we couldn't talk about what happened. I had to explain to him what 'privileged' means.

"He spent most of his money paying off student debt and paying back friends. Everyone thought the Lobos would want to negotiate a new contract to lock him in long-term, and he was counting on the incentive bonus to tide him over until next season. Paying off his loans made sense."

"Does he know the woman?"

"I didn't ask. I could tell he really wanted to talk about what happened, but every time he tried, I stopped him."

I said, "I know it must have been tough, but you had no choice. You did the right thing."

"God, Jack, I don't know."

The waitress appeared with our lunch: good, hot, fried catfish. Nothing better, and it provided a nice distraction. We even indulged in lemon icebox pie, hardly saying a word.

Full as a tick, I leaned back, thinking we should probably head back to my office. But Marshall had his own ideas.

"Can we talk, old friend to old friend?"

I kidded, "Do I need a stiff drink?"

Literal Marshall answered. "A nice glass of wine might be in order, but only if I'm buying."

Never, never, had I known Marshall to have more than a beer at lunch. Now he had suggested wine and was offering to buy. Either the world was coming to an end, or we were about to have one damn serious conversation. I told him his money was no good here and ordered a bottle of Cabernet.

We waited, again in silence, as the server delivered the bottle, dealt

with the corkscrew and poured each of us a generous glass. I knew
well enough that Marshall's brain was working overtime.

"Jack, where do I begin? Since high school you have been my best
friend. You were best man at our wedding. Your wife was like a sister
to me, and your daughter is not only my godchild, I think of her as
my daughter. Whenever I need you, you show up, seemingly ready
for anything."

"I could say the same for you." I had no idea where this was going.

"Yes, but you weren't a skinny black kid in an all-white school.
When the football coach tried to run me off, there you were, refusing
to play unless I played. You took a stand that day. What you did made
a difference. It took a while, but things got better because you were
willing to do what was right. And that wasn't the only time."

"Okay, but that was a long time ago, and I knew the team needed a
really good left tackle. You were there for Angie and me—remember?"

"Jack, have you ever been so sure of someone's character, that no
matter what others said about him, what others say he did, you just
knew something wasn't right? That there had to be more to the story?"

"Woody Cole." Didn't need to think about that one.

"Say no more, of course you have. You believed in Woody despite
Sam telling you he had changed, and I was pretty much there myself."

"I remember."

"Well, so you will understand when I tell you I believe William
didn't kill that woman. I know this young man, probably better than
my own sons. A father has a blind spot for his children, but I don't for
William. So he plays football—does that mean he has an uncontrol-
lable mean streak? Surely most football players are regular, nice fel-
lows who engage in a sport they're good at. Yes, it's rough and players
get hurt, but Americans love it—every Saturday, Sunday, Monday,
and now Thursday. William can run fast, and he has an uncanny
ability to catch a football, but he's as gentle a soul as anyone I've ever
encountered. He is polite, respectful, and considerate of everyone,
especially women."

"Marshall, I hear you. I appreciate what you're saying. I'm one
of those guys who watch football on Thursday night. But look at the
facts. Maybe his past caught up with him, or maybe all the new fame

and glory, or maybe he just snapped. I mean, you know, guys just sometimes go off the wall when it comes to booze and women. Maybe they were—oh, I don't know, but look at the evidence."

He took a minute, twirling his glass, thinking about how he would respond.

"Jack, I see cases of domestic violence and violence against women almost every day. This particular virus is epidemic, and no matter how many men I lock up it keeps growing. But I tell you: William Hopper is not a man who would ever abuse a woman, much less murder one. I've seen how he treats women of all ages, from Grace, to the girls my boys have brought home to our house, to the girls at Sewanee he dated. Without exception he was kind and respectful. I've never even heard a cutting remark or a derogatory term come out of his mouth."

"Well, something must have changed him. Maybe his year in LA— maybe unfamiliar circumstances...."

"Not a chance." Marshall's voice had grown chilly.

"Marshall, you won't like it, but I need to point out that the longer you stay here helping Billy, the more likely you are going to be the recipient of some of the anger directed towards him. It could hurt you politically, could even cost you your judgeship."

"Grace and I have discussed that very issue. We saw what the anti-gay marriage folks tried to do to Judge Piazza after he issued his ruling overturning the ban. You want to know what Grace told me?"

"Of course." I said, thinking I probably already knew.

"She said, 'Marshall, Jack Patterson didn't abandon Woody Cole no matter how bad it looked. Right now William doesn't have a friend in this world except for our family. All those hangers-on, LA movie stars, and football groupies have run for cover. The whole world thinks he's a lost cause. Well, lost causes are the one's worth fighting for. So don't come home until your job is done.'"

"I didn't abandon Woody because his mother wouldn't let me."

"Don't give me that. I witnessed your passion for Woody in my courtroom. You may have been a little out of control, but you clearly believed in Woody."

"Okay, so let's get him a lawyer so you can go home."

"Jack, I'm well aware that Billy needs a lawyer, and a damn good one. But I have one more favor to ask of you, and I guess it's one you'll have to think about. You've done a lot of favors for me, but you did them on your own, right?" He gave me a bit of a grin, and I was helpless.

"I haven't much thought about it," I had no idea where this was going, but I was sure I wouldn't like it.

"I want you to see William in the jail."

"Ah, Jeez, why would I want to do that?" I knew the answer as soon as I spoke.

"I don't know why you shouldn't."

17

THIS THOUGHT CLEARLY hadn't just popped into his head, so I waited for him to explain his logic.

"I can't ask Billy about what happened that night, as you have pointed out to me more than once."

I nodded. "The attorney-client privilege doesn't apply to you. Whatever he tells you is just as if he was talking straight to the prosecutor. You can't lie or refuse to relate what he says to you, or you'll end up in an adjoining jail cell. Grace wouldn't be happy."

Marshall chuckled at the image of Grace finding out he was in jail.

"I do know that, Jack. But I also know that a lawyer who is interviewing him to become his attorney can speak with him in confidence. The privilege applies to that conversation, does it not?"

"Yes, it does. But even if we pretended that my interview was in connection with potential employment, I couldn't tell you what he tells me. I would be destroying the privilege by telling you anything. My interviewing him doesn't accomplish anything. You still need to get him his own lawyer."

"You're wrong—it accomplishes a lot."

"What?" I asked.

"You are the only lawyer in DC I can completely trust. If you interview him and say 'Marshall, he did it,' I will help him financially and be supportive, but Grace and I can get on with our lives. If you tell me he's innocent, I'm all in until it's all over."

"I probably can't help you there either. A good lawyer never asks his client if he committed the crime. That knowledge limits his options at trial. Probably the most I could say is that I'm not sure he did it. I can't believe I'll get much out of him anyway."

"But you will at least have a better idea of what kind of lawyer I should be hiring—someone who's a take-no-prisoners type or a negotiator."

"True. But remember: ultimately who Billy hires is up to Billy, not you or me."

"Not true. He's authorized me to hire counsel on his behalf. He said he wouldn't have any idea how to choose a lawyer. Three lawyers have already made appointments to meet with him tomorrow trying to get hired. Boy are they going to be disappointed." He smiled.

"It's unethical to solicit business, although you wouldn't know it from all the billboards across the country." I was appalled.

"I know that, but some folks always manage to find a way around the rules. As far as I'm concerned, all three are out of the running. What I don't like is they have taken up all the visiting hours tomorrow. I can't get you in to see him until Thursday morning."

"You've already made the appointment? I haven't said 'yes' yet."

"Jack, I know this is wrong of me, but please say 'yes,' if not for me, for Grace and my boys."

I took a sip of wine, and my mind went to one night over twenty-five years ago when Marshall had carried Angie several miles to the hospital. No way could I tell this man no.

I smiled. "I don't know why I shouldn't."

We both laughed.

I would learn why I shouldn't very quickly. I still would have given in, but I should have given it a little more thought.

We still had wine to finish, so I asked Marshall to tell me more about Billy Hopper. In fact, I asked him to start at the beginning and not leave anything out. I had no desire to represent Billy, but if I was going to decide in a single interview whether Billy could have murdered this young woman, I needed to know as much as I could.

For the next two hours, I heard a story that made out Billy sound to be too good to be true. I know from experience that we all have a dark side, but if Billy had a dark side it first made an appearance at the Mayflower Hotel.

*****

Mr. Kim had finished reading the transcript of Fitzgerald's meeting with Hopper. He hadn't learned much except the Judge was in charge of hiring a lawyer for the young man. Too bad, the lawyer they wanted Hopper to hire was meeting with him tomorrow, but now that would be a total waste of time. The Judge had more influence over Hopper than they had anticipated.

Worse, Patterson was scheduled to meet with Hopper on Thursday morning. The Judge and Patterson had just walked into Barker's, he assumed for lunch. Damn Barker and his obsession with privacy! In fact, he had no idea what they were doing or what they might be discussing, but he was pretty sure it wasn't Donald Trump. After a moment's thought, he decided to call a colleague in Brazil before he reported to the client.

18

MARSHALL AND I finished our wine and walked outside to find Martin waiting in the Suburban. He looked uneasy.

"The press is camped outside your office. Building security has kept them out of the lobby so far, but Rose is in high panic. Apparently they are under the impression that you're meeting with Billy Hopper on Thursday about legal representation. They've figured out who Marshall is and made the connection."

Marshall apologized, "I'm sorry, Jack. I was naïve. I had to give the jail your name. I should have known better."

"That's okay—these are games you're not used to playing. Martin, let's get Marshall back to the Hay-Adams. I'll tell Rose to close the office and go home for the day."

Marshall knew we'd set up an office for him at the Foundation, but we both agreed that it might be better for him to remain at the hotel until the press lost interest. Martin walked him into the hotel and returned to drive me home. Not a single reporter in sight, thank goodness.

I took Sophie out for a quick walk and then settled in behind my desk to check email and make a few calls. The first was to Maggie. I hated to ruin her last day in Italy, but I also didn't want her to arrive home to a firestorm without warning.

"Oh, Jack. I should have known you'd get into some kind of mischief while I was gone. I'm surprised there's not a women involved. Just don't get shot before I get home. Ciao." She obviously had better things to do than shoot the breeze with me.

My cell phone flashed a message from Beth, asking me to call. For the umpteenth time I wondered why she didn't just call in the first place. Of course, I called.

"Uncle Marshall is in DC, and you didn't tell me?"

"You were at a silent retreat, remember?"

"It was over on Sunday night. Anyway, it's all over the news that you're going to represent Billy Hopper. They're calling you a magician who takes on impossible cases. You know most of my girlfriends will think you're scum." Her throwaway comment got my attention.

"That's real nice, Beth. Don't they understand the right to counsel?"

"They understand, but the thought that you might get a ruthless murderer off with a slap on the wrist is pretty hard to stomach. If I hadn't met him with Uncle Marshall, I'd be right there with them."

"He's facing life in prison, not a slap on the wrist. And don't worry: I'm not his lawyer. You've met him?"

"Yeah. Billy arranged for Uncle Marshall to sit in the owner's box when the Lobos played the Saints last fall, and Uncle Marshall arranged for us to meet him for dinner. He and Jeff really hit it off—at the time my friends were green with envy. He is very good-looking and so sweet. Hard to believe he'd do something so terrible. Jeff thinks he was set up."

"What do you mean?"

"Oh, it's just speculation on the part of his fantasy football buddies. Apparently a lot of high stakes fantasy players lost big bucks because of Billy. His game against New England really burned up a lot of fantasy teams the last week of the regular season. He also upset a lot of high-stakes betting pools. Jeff and his pals think the mob set him up."

"Jeff watches too much TV."

"That's what I told him. Want to know what I think? There's too much violence on the football field, too much emphasis on hitting— it's bound to pour over into the players' lives. Billy should've played soccer." Spoken by a Davidson soccer star.

I knew we could debate this issue all afternoon, so I asked her about the retreat and reminded her that Marshall was expecting a call from her. She gave me a rather lengthy rundown of the retreat; apparently it wasn't exactly silent after all.

We agreed to find a good weekend for me to come to New Orleans soon. We didn't get along nearly as well when she came back to DC for a visit. I thought she'd want to spend all of her time with me, and she thought trips home meant seeing all her old high school classmates and staying up way past my bedtime. Some nights she didn't even go out until after my bedtime.

Our conversation ended abruptly as she said, "Sorry, Dad. My kids are walking into class—gotta go!"

I wasn't really hungry, but I ordered pizza anyway. DC isn't known for good pizza and for good reason: there isn't any. At least nothing like Theo's Pizza in New Orleans. You don't think about New Orleans and pizza, but trust me: Theo's is worth the trip. I'd put it up against Chicago's best.

Rose had emailed me a list of messages. I ignored the ones from reporters, tabled two from friends, but knew I had to return Red's angry call.

"Are you crazy?" he shouted.

"Quite possibly," I answered, stalling for time. If I publicly denied any desire to be Billy's lawyer, the jail probably wouldn't let me see Billy, nor would the privilege attach to our conversation if they did. I had come up with a response I thought might work until a real criminal defense lawyer was hired. Might as well test it out on Red.

My affirmative response to his question had taken him aback, so I jumped in before he could respond.

"Crazy yes, stupid no. Your fiancée can tell you how close I am to Marshall Fitzgerald. He asked that I meet with Hopper, and I agreed because I owe him. She will tell you I owe him at least that. But, Red, I'm not foolish enough to sacrifice a quarter of a million dollar retainer. For my loyalty to Marshall, I'm going to catch hell with the press for a few days, but I expect Billy to have an experienced criminal lawyer in a few days, and you and I can practice howling at the moon by the weekend."

Nothing but silence. I could almost hear him thinking.

"You know if you'd simply sign the contract my lawyers sent over, I'd feel a lot better."

"Sorry, it's on my desk. The press descended on us before I

had time to go over it. I should be able to give it my full attention tomorrow."

"You know, I've never had so much trouble trying to hire somebody." His irritation was obvious.

"I'm worth it." I don't know what gave me so much bravado, but the words came out naturally.

"Damn, I'm beginning to like you, Patterson. I expect the same loyalty you are showing to Fitzgerald, I hope you know that."

"You'll have it." Boy was I walking a tightrope.

The doorbell rang as I put the phone down with relief. I had dodged a bullet. I pulled a twenty out of my wallet and opened the door.

"You ordered pizza, but it's going to cost you."

1 9

CAROL STOOD ON the steps holding a pizza box in one hand and a bottle of red wine in the other. She had caught the pizza guy pulling up and paid him. The wine had always been part of her plan.

My response was totally overwhelmed by Sophie pelting down the stairs barking furiously. Laughing, Carol held the pizza high as I struggled to get Sophie under control.

"What a great dog—you've been holding out on me. And representing Billy Hopper—really?" She pecked me on the cheek and sailed right past me toward the kitchen.

"It's not the way it seems." I managed to get Sophie corralled on the back porch.

I took the pizza from her and put it in the oven to keep warm. While I opened the wine she wandered through the downstairs of the house, stopping to look at pictures of Beth, Angie, and my three best friends from high school: Woody, Sam, and Marshall.

"Good looking daughter, she looks a lot like her mother," she said, as she took the glass of wine I offered.

She was dressed casually in jeans and a white cotton shirt, sleeves rolled up. No fancy jewelry, but small diamond earrings and what looked like a David Yurman link ring on her right hand. I only knew because Walter had recently given one to Maggie. A diamond tennis bracelet seemed natural on her wrist.

"I hope I'm not interrupting."

"You can interrupt anytime you want; as you can tell, I wasn't exactly expecting company. To what do I owe this unexpected pleasure?"

"Billy Hopper. You played innocent last weekend—are you really going to represent him?" She got right to the point.

I didn't want to lie to her so I avoided answering.

"See that picture of four boys with our arms around each other? One is Woody Cole and the tall black man is Marshall Fitzgerald. He's known Billy since his kids were at camp in North Carolina. I'm meeting with Billy at his request." I said.

"I know who he is—the other one is Sam Pagano, the prosecutor in the Cole case, your high school teammate and roommate in college. You forget I'm into information. I know a lot about you; it's my business."

"That's right. It's kind of scary that you know so much."

She came across the room, looked up into my eyes, and then kissed me square on the lips. "Not enough."

I was at a loss for a response, suddenly remembering the washout of last weekend. She rescued me.

"Now feed me, and let's talk. We've got some ground rules to set."

We sat on stools at the bar eating pizza and drinking a very nice Chianti.

"Ground rules?" I asked.

"Ground rules. In case you can't tell, I'm interested in you more than having you as my escort at social events. I like your company, and I'm definitely interested in having an uninterrupted swim together, very soon." She touched my hand.

"Well, in case you haven't noticed, you have my full attention. If getting to know you better means enduring boring DC cocktail parties and discussions about drones and fighter planes, I guess I can manage." I meant every word.

"Okay, so ground rules. I don't want to be in the position of giving clients information I learn from you. I want you to trust me, and I want to be able to trust you.

"For example, half a dozen clients would like very much to know how the DOJ is going to come down on the Simpson-Whitfield merger, not to mention the real story of your involvement with Billy Hopper. So here's the deal. I won't ask, and you won't talk about your business with me. Then I won't have anything to report. However, if you talk about business with others at one of our weekends or at a party, or if you slip up and tell me something without my asking, I'm free to report it to my clients."

"I hate to disappoint you, but I don't talk about my clients or my business with anyone. Is there a reason to worry about all this?" I responded, a little confused about why we needed ground rules at all.

"That's pretty obvious. Not a soul this weekend had any idea that you had a connection with Hopper. Everyone was talking about him, but you were as quiet as a mouse, almost as if you didn't read the papers."

She paused, biting her lower lip, and I waited for whatever was next.

"Jack, the other day at the shore I was not my best. I'd like to explain about the phone call."

This time I reached across and put my finger to her lips.

"Please don't. Ground rules are set. You don't ask me about my business, and I don't want to know about yours. We now have our own version of don't ask, don't tell."

She took my fingers and held them to her cheek. I could almost see the tension in her shoulders relax.

I asked, "Can you stay?"

She smiled sweetly. "If you don't mind, tonight let's enjoy the wine and talk. I want you, Jack Patterson, don't get me wrong, but I'm not sure tonight's the right time or place. You have a lot of memories here. So let's go slow, okay?"

She was right, of course. I had never slept with anyone but Angie in our bed.

We took our wine to the downstairs study and turned on the ball game, which turned out to be mostly white noise for our conversation. She seemed to know quite a lot about my family, so I asked about hers. She told me that her parents still lived in their rambling house in the Dilworth neighborhood in Charlotte. I laughed when she imitated her father asking, "Yes, dear, I'm glad you're doing so well, but what is it exactly that you do?"

She seldom saw her sister who had married a London attorney a dozen years ago and was now "quite British." Her caustic tone made me look forward to introducing her to Maggie.

Her older brother Daniel owned a car dealership in Raleigh. He'd been a star running back at NC State, but had already had both knees replaced.

"Jack, he has constant headaches and sometimes forgets things, important things. His wife had to ask their son to come home to help with the business. It's so hard to know how to help."

I had friends in Arkansas who were going through the same thing. Football had given them early glory, a certain path to success, and then cheated them out of both their joints and their sanity. Somewhere Caesar is laughing.

I opened a second bottle of wine, and we talked about the early days of our careers. I told her how much I had enjoyed my time at Justice, and she spoke of the hurdles she had faced as a young female staffer on the Hill. The hours were long, the pay was paltry, and she had to endure frequent and persistent sexual advances from both Members and senior staff. I was even able to talk about Angie—a little.

We ended up watching the ninth inning in silence; she curled up next to me on the sofa. I hadn't spent such an easy evening with someone in quite a long time.

WEDNESDAY

April 20, 2016

20

I slept like a lamb and woke up the next morning in a great mood. Maggie and Walter would be home today, there were no satellite trucks in my front yard, and I hadn't yet read the papers.

I took Sophie for a long walk after breakfast and decided to take the Metro in to work—easier to slip in the back door without attracting attention. Rose had been delighted to have a day off: the answering service could pick up any calls.

I figured I could work in the morning, meet Marshall for lunch at the Hay-Adams, and maybe get in nine holes of golf. Three hapless lawyers meeting Billy at the jail would occupy the press, and I needed some time to think without really trying, if that makes sense.

I put the coffee on and checked with the answering service for messages. Almost all were from the press, with a select few from people who didn't believe in an accused's right to a lawyer. I took a minute to order flowers for Carol. I couldn't help myself. I reluctantly placed a call to Cheryl Cole—she'd called at least seven times.

"Jack Patterson, have you forgotten that you owe me from the Stewart case? I need you to come on my show. Which night works for you?"

You had to be direct with Cheryl.

"First, if I remember right, that 'favor' resulted in skyrocketing ratings for your program and a nice big contract for you. Second, the answer to when I'm coming on your show the answer is never. That answer has served me well so far, and I intend to stick with it."

"So you are going to represent Billy Hopper?" She was quick.

"I didn't say that. I am going to meet with Billy Hopper tomorrow. We'll see what happens after that."

She heard exactly what she wanted to hear—and Cheryl couldn't keep a secret. She would be on the air tonight saying according to a confidential source it was only a matter of time before I agreed to represent Billy Hopper. It would be a nice diversion while I helped Marshall get Billy a proper criminal attorney.

I hung up before Cheryl could quiz me further. I opened the *Post* and found its piece on Hopper on page three, last paragraph:

> "Jack Patterson is well known for having represented Woody Cole, accused murder of Senator Russell Robinson, and Dr. Doug Stewart, the world-famous chemist. Although he specializes in antitrust law, Patterson has a reputation for occasionally taking on seemingly impossible criminal cases. The case against Billy Hopper certainly belongs in that category."

I took a few minutes to read the comics, a habit inherited from my mother who had always called them the "funnies," then tossed the paper aside.

I hadn't forgotten what Clovis had told me about Micki—it lurked just below the surface of my thoughts. I decided to take the bull by the horns. Her receptionist, Mongo, answered the phone.

"Mongo, this is Jack Patterson. May I speak to Micki?"

"You sure you want to?" *Not a good omen.*

"Well, yes, why wouldn't I?"

No answer. Instead I heard him shout across the room, "Hey, Micki, Jack's on the phone for you." Same old Mongo. I waited patiently, wondering whether she would pick up or choose to ignore me completely. The answer came loud and clear.

"If you think I'm going to help you defend that murdering SOB, you're dead wrong," she shouted into the speakerphone.

"Nice to hear your voice, Micki."

I heard a click and her normal voice off-speaker. "Well, hello there. How are you, Jack?" Her tone was, well, it was sort of uncertain, a little shaky.

"I was calling to ask you that same question. But to respond to

your assumption, I have no intention of representing Billy Hopper."
I tried to keep my voice level.

"Then what in the hell is going on? It's all over the news that you're his lawyer."

"Since when do you believe everything you hear in the press? And what happened to my 'everybody deserves competent counsel' defense lawyer?"

"She's tired of football players treating women like trash and thinking it's okay to beat the shit out of them or worse."

"I'm right with you. But what if Billy's innocent?"

"You don't believe that, do you?" she asked.

"Marshall Fitzgerald does." I responded.

"Marshall Fitzgerald? Our Judge Fitzgerald?"

"The one and the same. Why else would I be involved?" She grew calmer with every give and take, and our conversation became less tense.

"Why in the world does Marshall give two hoots about this guy? And even if he does, I still can't help you, Jack. I've reached my limit when it comes to men taking out their frustrations on women. You have to draw a line somewhere."

"I haven't asked for your help. And, yes, it looks bad for Hopper. But Marshall cares a great deal for this kid, has known him most of his life, and I care a great deal for Marshall—I owe it to him to do what I can. Let me tell you what I know."

I went on to explain the relationship between Marshall and Billy. Micki asked a couple of good questions, but didn't seem to be particularly interested.

"Okay, so now I get it, but let me ask you this—why did you call?"

I lied. "We haven't talked in a while, and this unexpected dip into criminal law made me think of you. So how are you?"

Now she lied. "I'm fine. We stay busy. Debbie is still driving me crazy, but she and Paul are still together, and otherwise Little Rock is pretty much the same."

I decided to leave it be, and we ended with a whimper, promising to stay more in touch, knowing we wouldn't. Micki and I had enjoyed a special relationship during both the Stewart and Cole cases. Too bad we've never found that special case we always hoped for.

*****

My lunch with Marshall at the Hay-Adams wasn't anything to write home about. After fried catfish and a wonderful Cabernet, today's chef's salad and iced tea were a bit of a downer. We tried to chat, but gave up pretty soon. Billy Hopper was the elephant in the room, and he took up all the oxygen.

I suggested a movie tonight, but he declined, citing other plans. He'd only been in town a day—I couldn't help but wonder.

Most days, the DC Metro is a model of efficiency, and today was no exception. It delivered me to Chevy Chase Circle in less than fifteen minutes, and I was home after a ten-minute walk.

After walking Sophie, more to clear my head than to give her exercise, I sat at my desk and tried to prepare for an impossible assignment—interview Billy Hopper for one hour in order to determine whether he had murdered the woman found in his bed. Marshall had given me an untenable task.

I thought I had a pretty good plan for tomorrow. Maggie had texted to say their plane had landed, and they were on their way home, ready for bed. I replied that I wouldn't be in the office tomorrow morning, but I would see them for dinner. I'd bet a dollar to a doughnut she'd call tonight to find out what was going on.

I spent the rest of the afternoon tending to my real job, warmed up the leftover pizza, and went to bed early. Tomorrow would be challenging; little did I know how challenging. If I'd been more attentive to my voice mails I might have returned two phone calls.

One was one from Red Shaw; the other was from one James, "the Wall", Stockdell, the NFL's fiercest linebacker and Billy's teammate.

THURSDAY

April 21, 2016

2 1

I DRESSED CAREFULLY the next morning: charcoal pin stripes and conservative tie. The seldom-worn Allen-Edmonds wingtips were tight, but surely I could deal with them for one morning. Martin's man told me the press had set up their gauntlet of microphones and cameras right in front of the jail; there was no way in besides plowing through. After meeting Billy, I would join Marshall at the office. Martin had the codes to open the office if they beat me there.

We pulled to a stop in front of the jail. As the horde of reporters started to shout questions, I slowed just enough to say, "I will not answer any questions at this time." Of course that didn't stop the ruckus, but I continued my slow progress into the building.

I made it through the door with my life. The waiting jailer was chuckling. I started to get out my driver's license, but he said, "No need for ID, Mr. Patterson. I think your fans out there are identification enough. I will have to search your briefcase though."

I handed it over, and he did a half-hearted search. "Conference room 101, third door on the right. We'll bring him to you." I wondered if the jailer knew the significance of Room 101 in Orwell's *1984*.

The room was empty except for a small table and two metal chairs. A pitcher of water and two empty mugs sat on the table. I saw a couple of gnats floating in the water.

The door opened and Billy walked in. He wasn't nearly as big as I had expected. I'm six-foot-three, but seemed to tower over the young man. Beth was right: he was good looking with a fresh face and golden hair, hardly the image of an NFL star. I was pleased to see that he wasn't shackled or chained.

"Billy, we don't have much time. Did Marshall tell you who I am and that you can be candid with me?"

"I've known about you for a long time, Mr. Patterson. I spent a lot of time with the Fitzgeralds—your name came up all the time. The Judge said that talking to you is like talking to him, nothing but the truth."

"Okay, I want you to keep one thing in mind. I will not ask you if you murdered the woman, and I don't want you to tell me. Okay?" I warned.

"It's okay because I don't know if I did or not," he blurted out.

"I'm not sure if that's what I wanted to hear."

"But it's the truth. I don't remember a thing," he said.

"Let's slow down, Billy. By the way, may I call you Billy? Marshall refers to you as William—maybe you'd prefer I call you by your Christian name"

"Some folks call me Glide, but Billy's fine. That's what Grace and the boys call me. I'm not sure if William is even my real name. My birth certificate says Billy, but the Judge has always called me William. I don't know why."

"Okay. Let me do the asking first. Do you remember going to the NFL Honors banquet?"

"I do."

"Who was at your table?" I asked.

"My agent, Cliff Parker. I met all the others, but I don't remember their names. Corporations purchase tables, and the NFL spaces players at each corporate table."

"Do you remember who sponsored your table?"

"I don't. They had something to do with airplanes, I think. I really didn't pay much attention. Frankly, the guys weren't Presidents or CEOs, they were guys who worked in the corporate headquarters and were thrilled they could spend the night with ball players and bid on sports memorabilia. I remember one of the guys said he was surprised his boss wanted me at their table. Apparently, I'd cost his boss a bundle when I caught that third touchdown pass against New

England. There wasn't much I could say."

Might as well ask. "From what I understand, there were several attractive women at the table as well. Did you know them? Do you remember their names?"

"No, I'd never seen any of them before. One of them was called Ginger—I remember because she had bright red hair. I got the impression they were with the corporate guys. They were like most all the girls at these events: giggly, friendly, and drank a whole lot."

"Speaking of that, the press says you drank a lot that night."

I noticed Billy bow up.

"Mr. Patterson…"

"Call me Jack."

"Mr. P… Jack, I don't drink very much, ever. The Judge said he told you about my background. When your father drinks so much that he carves up your mother, you're not inclined to drink. At least I'm not. I remember sipping on a beer so I wouldn't draw attention to myself. I've learned you can sip on a beer all night, and nobody notices how much you're drinking. But order Perrier, and you get lots of looks and ribbing and end up in trouble."

"True, but ESPN is reporting that the waiter says he filled your wine glass all night."

"The waiter is telling the truth. The young woman sitting next to me drank her own wine and then switched glasses with me. I didn't mind."

"Were any of the women at your table the woman you found in your bed?" Might as well get it out there.

"I've given that question a lot of thought. I don't think so. I was pretty shaken up when I discovered her, but I don't think she was one of the girls at our table. It was definitely not Ginger. I can't guarantee that she wasn't one of the other two, but I don't think so. The woman in the bed that morning was a total stranger to me; of that I'm sure."

"Billy, I've told you I can't ask you whether you murdered the woman or not, and you've told me you don't remember a thing. So let's go about it another way. Tell me why I should believe you didn't kill the woman. You have to be asking yourself that same question or the opposite."

Billy paused before answering. "What you're asking me is what would I like to say to the Judge and Grace about the man they took in and loved like their own, given that I don't remember a thing."

"Yes, I am. But I will also say you don't have to answer that question if you don't want to."

He took a deep breath and closed his eyes.

"I've lived with the image of my father murdering my mother all my life. I was eight years old when it happened, young, but not young enough. I was old enough to remember what alcohol did to my father, but too young to know why Mom and I didn't leave. Too young to ask her about my grandparents, or why they would let her stay with such a man.

"I've tried to find them, you know. At first, it was something I just did on the Internet, but I had a little money after Oxford, so I decided to dig a little deeper. I think I'm getting close. But that's not what you asked.

"I loved my mother, and she drummed into me at a young age to respect everyone, but especially women. I would never strike a woman much less kill one. For me it would mean becoming the man I hated so much. Ask any girl I ever dated. Some of them even made fun of me for being so timid and polite. I'm not a prude, Jack. I'm not celibate, and I'm not gay. I believe in every ounce of my being that I could never murder any woman."

I started to speak, but he interrupted.

"I say all that to you, knowing what I woke up to, and terrified every moment that I am my father after all. I'm not sure I could live with that thought."

The moment called for silence. Here was a young man baring his soul to a stranger. I had been conned before, but damned if I didn't believe him. Yet by his own admission, he could have. He didn't remember a thing, and he could have lashed out in a fit of violence. The silence stretched as I tried to measure my response.

"Billy, I believe you. You are in one hell of a mess, and neither of us knows what happened that night. But you are not your father. Of that I am certain."

He seemed consoled, but exhausted by the exchange. I asked a few basic questions about the morning of the event and tried to get a few more details on his dinner companions. The jailer opened the door, pointing at his watch. I asked him for a few more minutes.

"Is there anything else you want to say?" I asked.

"Thank you for believing me. The Judge said that if you believed me, you would agree to be my lawyer. I sure hope that's true."

2 2

I MANAGED TO smile and shook his hand just before the jailer took him away. I couldn't wait to give Marshall a piece of my mind. Why in the world would Marshall tell him I was going to be his lawyer?

I remained in the room for a few minutes to gather my thoughts before facing the press. I reminded myself I was not a skilled criminal defense attorney. Before I got mad at Marshall, I needed to check my ego at the front door. The entire deck was stacked against this young man. He needed someone to believe in him, someone who could find out what had happened that night. That would take money and talent. Billy didn't have any money, and I certainly wasn't the talent.

I walked straight up to the bank of waiting microphones.

"Those of you who know me understand I don't try a case in the media, so this will be a short session."

"Are you going to represent Billy Hopper?" came the first shout.

"My understanding is that Mr. Hopper is interviewing several lawyers. I met with him today strictly as a favor to a mutual friend."

That wasn't going to satisfy anyone.

"Why did he murder the girl? Does he hate women?" came the next question.

"Next question." I stared coldly at the offending reporter. Did he really expect me to answer such an absurd question?

"Mr. Patterson, you spent almost an hour with Billy Hopper. Can you tell us if you think he did it?"

I stared at the young woman, knowing I shouldn't answer. "You know, I don't think he did."

*****

Maggie rose to give me a hug as I walked into our office. I could see Marshall in our conference room talking to a large man I didn't recognize.

"I told you not to come in." I frowned.

"What happened to 'Welcome back, Maggie, I missed you'?"

I gave her a rueful grin and returned her hug, saying, "I'm sorry. Of course I missed you, and I can't wait to hear about your trip."

"Well, you'll have to wait. It seems you've been busy in my absence. The press all claim you're going to represent a murderer, Marshall is waiting in the conference room, and it looks like we may have a new client by the name of Red Shaw. In my opinion, he could use a lesson in manners." Her sharp tone gave me pause.

"I did warn you not to come in. How bad was the press?" I asked.

"The press doesn't bother me. They don't want to talk to me, and the building manager isn't about to let them block the entrance for the other tenants. Rose could easily get in, but she would probably go crazy with all these phone calls."

She tried to keep a straight face, but we both broke out laughing. I was sure glad to have her back.

"All right, Jack, you go talk to Marshall, and I'll try to bring some organization back to this place."

"To whom is Marshall talking?" I asked.

"He was here when I arrived this morning, said he had been trying to reach you. Name is James Stockdell. I offered to take a message, but he said he'd wait. Apparently they're already acquainted; they've been thick as thieves since Marshall arrived."

"Just what I need—another mystery. Do me a big favor and call Red Shaw. Tell him I'm meeting with Marshall and will call him this afternoon."

"Oh dear, that's what I was afraid of. That man…" She grimaced.

"Welcome back, Maggie." I smiled as I turned toward the conference room. Her reply was a muted "hmph."

I opened the door and extended my hand to a muscular man who was seated next to Marshall. He was at least six-five, built like a Mack truck.

"Jack Patterson. I apologize for not responding to your message. I've been getting a lot of calls these last few days."

Marshall spoke up. "Jack, this is James Stockdell. He's one of William's teammates."

We shook hands, and I sat down across from them, "I know you by reputation, Mr. Stockdell. For the life of me, I will never understand why the Redskins released you to be eligible for the Lobos' supplemental draft. Big mistake."

He smiled. "I was disappointed myself, but then if they hadn't, I wouldn't have gotten to know Billy. I'm here on behalf of a group of his teammates who want to offer our help. We think the world of Billy, and even though the Lobos, the union, and his agent have all abandoned him, we won't."

"That's tremendous, and I'm sure it will mean the world to Billy, but right now there isn't much you can do besides try to see him in jail and be publically supportive. He could use a few friends right now." I wanted to be nice, but I needed to talk to Marshall.

James looked at Marshall and leaned back in his chair.

"Well, Jack, James is here to offer a little more than emotional support," Marshall smiled serenely.

"That's right, Mr. Patterson. My teammates and I want to put our money where our mouth is." He reached in the pocket of his sport coat and pulled out his checkbook.

"Whoa," I said holding out the palm of my hand. "I can't let you write me a check."

"Don't worry, I'll collect from the other guys. I have their word. I'm not worried about the money." James pulled out a pen and began to write.

"That's not it. I am not his lawyer." I said, emphasis on the 'not.'

"Marshall explained that you aren't officially on board yet, that you still think someone else could do a better job for Billy. I'll leave that up to you two, but I'm heading out of the country for a month, and I don't want money to limit your options.

"I'm going to leave you with a check. Put it in your trust account and use it for Billy's defense whether it's you or someone else. We can work out a budget when I return. I'm not going to give you a blank check, but if necessary there's more where this comes from."

I had no idea how much he was talking about, but what he suggested was generous and made sense. I called Maggie into the room, explained what was going on, and asked her to write up a paragraph for him to sign giving me authority to use the money for Billy's defense if both Marshall and I agreed on the expenditure.

I thought—now watch the check be for a thousand bucks. I thought wrong. The check was for a half a million dollars.

He saw my jaw drop and said. "Listen, it's ten teammates at $50,000 a piece, a small price to pay for one of our own. And we're talking about Billy—I bet I can raise twice the amount when I get back. I don't know one guy on the team who won't pitch in, except for maybe the placekicker. He's a different breed of cat. We all know how expensive lawyers are. You're as bad as sports agents and investment advisors," he chuckled.

"I don't know what to say, except thank you. Billy appears to have some very good friends." Marshall nodded in agreement.

"Mr. Patterson, you played baseball. I bet your teammates are still some of your best friends, even now. For football players the ties are even tighter, maybe because of all the pain, misery, and suffering we endure together. Here's the thing: when you play ball with a man, you get to know his heart. Billy Hopper has one of the greatest hearts I've ever encountered. Let me tell you how he saved my career.

"I came to camp last summer with a bad attitude, pissed off that the Redskins had let me go. Nobody wants to end his career with an expansion team. I decided to take the Lobos' money for a year, but not put forth much effort. I let every minor injury send me to the locker room, hoping to be traded.

"One day toward the end of preseason I saw Billy Hopper staring at me in the locker room. I remember it like it was yesterday. I growled, 'What are you lookin' at, rookie?'

"'I'm looking at one of the best players in history and wondering when you quit enjoying the game.'

"'I still love the game, but not with a bunch of losers and rookies. We'll never win a game.' I shot back defensively.

"He respnded by saying, 'Well, that may be true, but with all the glory, all the money, all the pageantry, it's still a game, and games are supposed to be fun. When it stops being fun, it's time to hang 'em up.'

"He headed to the showers, and I fumed about some hotshot rookie talking to me like that. The next day I decided to show him what having fun looked like. He came across the middle to catch a pass, and I barreled into him on his blind side so hard he flipped up in the air and landed hard. I was pretty sure he'd be out cold.

"But he bounced up, handed me the ball he was still holding, gave me a grin and said, 'Nice hit—having fun yet?'

"Every day from then on he'd find just the right time to ask 'Having fun yet, Mr. Stockdell?' Needless to say, we became fast friends.

"I was named to the pro bowl again this year and without a doubt had more fun playing the game than I've had since junior high. Billy's enthusiasm infected us all, and despite our losing record I think most of us would say this was a winning season. I'm telling you that kid has heart to spare.

"If not one teammate had agreed to join in paying for his defense, I'd be here writing the same check. Money is temporary, friendship is forever. Anyone who lets go of a friendship for money's sake has his priorities mixed up."

Maggie had heard all this, and I saw she was about to tear up. James turned to her and said, "Come on, young lady. Let's go sign whatever you need me to sign so I can get out of this town. I have a plane to catch, and your Mr. Patterson has a crime to solve."

23

"AMAZING! NO ONE asked, he simply flew to DC, and wrote a half a million dollar check, all for a friend of less than a year," I said.

"William has that effect on people," Marshall said.

"Talk about effect on people, no part of my agreement with you included me representing Billy. Now that money is available, we can get him a real lawyer."

"I saw you on TV. You told those reporters you didn't think he did it. Did you mean it?"

I paused. I'd only spent an hour with Billy, and most people can be convincing and charming when they want to. But I had to admit it—I didn't think he'd committed the murder.

"Well, yes, I did. But that's a far cry from a jury finding him not guilty. You have to admit the evidence against him is overwhelming, and I suspect the prosecution has a whole lot more."

"I agree with you there. Don't forget that I'm a judge. In over ninety-five of the criminal cases that go to trial, the defendant is found guilty. The scales of justice are heavily weighted toward the prosecution—the defendant is at a huge disadvantage. In a high drama case like this, with the evidence such as it is, I'd say the possibility of a not guilty verdict is less than one percent."

"That's why we need the best of the best." Thank goodness he was coming around to my way of thinking.

"No, my friend, that's why Billy needs you. Hear me out." He held up his hand in a gesture I'd often seen.

"Jack, this came to me the other day. You're not a criminal lawyer.

Your performance in my courtroom in the Cole case wasn't pretty. It was unconventional, outrageous, frustrating, and yet the most effective representation I've ever witnessed. Your passion for your client overcame every advantage the prosecution had. That's why I wanted you to meet William. I'm convinced you will develop that same passion for him."

"But Marshall, you said it. I'm not a criminal lawyer. I represent corporations, not people. I represent money."

"That's why you hired Micki in the Cole case. You have to admit, y'all made a great team. That's why I asked if you'd called her lately."

"I called her yesterday. You don't want to know what she thinks about Billy."

"Micki's been through some rough times in the last few months, sort of lost her center. She needs to work on something she can believe in. I bet you can convince her." He clearly hadn't been listening.

"Jack, I know I've used up my favor when you agreed to visit Billy. But I'm going to ask anyway—I want you to consider taking on Billy's defense. Billy and I went over your strengths and weaknesses the other day. In point of fact, he is a very smart guy. We both think you are his only chance.

"Money is no longer an issue. So listen. I'm leaving this afternoon for home: Grace needs some calming. Take the weekend, but ask yourself this—don't you want to know who killed that young woman and went to all that trouble setting Billy up? You may not be the best criminal defense lawyer in the country, but I do believe you're the only one who's stubborn enough to discover the real answer to who did this and why."

With that he walked out of the conference room, silently closing the door behind him. He had an unerring sense for the dramatic. Aw, hell—I liked Billy well enough and God knows I would always owe Marshall. I did want to know what really happened, but I was ready for a normal life, one that included Carol Madison.

I tried to unload on Maggie, but she cut me short.

"Sounds like you have plenty to tell me, but we'll have to catch up later. You have a lunch appointment at Morton's with Mr. Shaw in fifteen minutes. He was insistent. We can talk at dinner. Walter and I are still on European time so we've got an early reservation at the Bombay Club. I've got an itch for their Tandoori Salmon."

"Morton's, huh?"

"Yes, and by the way who exactly is Carol Madison?"

"Did she call?"

"No, her office called to say she would pick you up at three o'clock tomorrow. You didn't answer my question," she said tartly.

"Okay—call the Bombay and tell them you and I will come for drinks a little earlier. It's been an interesting week."

24

RED SAT AT a choice table toward the rear of Morton's on Connecticut Avenue. He waved me over, slipping his iPhone back into a coat pocket.

"Sit down, Jack. Are you always this difficult to pin down? Have a glass of wine." He motioned to a waiter who brought me a glass and poured from the bottle Red had chosen.

He waved off my words of apology. "I know where you've been. Hell, the whole damn country does.

"Listen, I've had a change of heart about your contract." Just then the waiter came to take our orders. Red asked for a filet with creamed spinach. I opted for the crabmeat appetizer and a chopped salad.

There wasn't much to say. I hadn't been responsive, and just about everyone thought I would be Billy's lawyer. No wonder he was pissed. If I lost the job, well, I lost the job. Not the end of the world. So his next words came as a surprise.

"You'll find a revised retainer agreement waiting on your desk. Before you sign it, I want to tell you what I've been thinking about. I told you the other night you could represent anybody but a ball player, the league, or the union. I've decided I'm not going to hold you to that. If you're crazy enough to represent Billy Hopper, more power to you. It's not like you're his agent, or there's any kind of conflict of interest."

My turn. "In the end, I think Billy will hire someone else, but I'm curious about your change of heart. And before I come on board, I'd also like to know exactly why you've chosen me to be your antitrust counsel."

"Before you think I'm some kind of bleeding heart, I'll set you straight. Pro football is still all about winning, and a big part of player motivation is for the guys to know they have the full and continuing support of the owner as well as the coaches. I'll fight like hell if the commissioner tries to do something silly like suspend or fine one of my ball players, but fighting for Billy is a more difficult matter. We're talking murder, not trash talk or roughing the passer. The commissioner would have had a coronary if I hadn't dropped Hopper."

I said, "The league has a lot invested in trying to distance itself from violence against women, and rightly so. I wish they would let the legal process play out first, but I understand the dilemma."

"Right, but I think in Billy's case my people went overboard in listening to the commissioner's office. I told them, just today, that we're going to pay Billy what we owe him under the old contract, including his rookie-of-the-year bonus. Maybe you can help me with this. His agent has dropped him, right?"

"Yup."

"Good, Hopper won't have to share with that jerk. I don't have a clue how Hopper got hooked up with that weasel. I've never ever heard of him. Where should I send Billy's money? Maybe to your friend, Judge Fitzgerald? Let me know, and I'll have the check cut immediately."

"That's very generous." I couldn't help but wonder—why the about face?

"No, it's just good business. Every one of his teammates will know I lived up to my end of the bargain. Billy earned and deserves his bonuses. My people were fools to penny pinch. Makes us look mean and spiteful."

Our meals arrived, and we ate in silence. After the plates had been cleared and our wine glasses were filled again, Red was back to business.

"Am I right that whatever I tell you is protected by the attorney-client privilege?" he asked.

"Yes, if it's in connection with my potential representation."

"Good. Owning an NFL franchise is a gold mine these days. TV revenues are way up, the union contract is stable, everyone is playing to packed houses, and merchandise sales have grown beyond expectations. Better yet, cities and states are begging to help build our stadiums. Tax credits are a given. The taxpayers pay for over seventy percent of pro football stadiums. The tax savings I've negotiated with LA and the state of California will totally cover the debt service on my new stadium and then some. Heck of a deal, wouldn't you say?"

I agreed. But I was pretty sure it was also a good deal for the city—I'd bet the tax credits were offset by the tourism revenue and the prestige of an NFL team.

"But that's only the tip of the iceberg. Fantasy football is quickly becoming bigger than the game itself, despite a few states trying to shut fantasy sports down. They won't be successful, but they will be a pain in the ass. You would be shocked by how much money is spent on fantasy sports. Many owners are positioning themselves to take advantage of this growing industry. We've been careful not to draw attention to our growing investment in fantasy and video games, but a few of us already have an ownership stake in these markets.

"We're also expanding into world markets, not so much to play ball in foreign countries, but to corner merchandising and the fantasy markets. Fantasy sports, especially fantasy football, is a big deal in the Asian markets. A very big deal."

"When your ownership interests in fantasy websites become public, there will be a backlash," I observed.

"You're absolutely correct. I anticipate a political backlash and a flurry of litigation aimed at removing our antitrust exemption when people realize how much of the merchandising, video game, and fantasy market we already own and hope to control. In what other industry can the top thirty-two companies sit down on a regular basis and set prices for their product from tickets to the cost of beer sold in the stadiums? On top of that, we get to divvy up proceeds from TV, merchandising, videos, and now a growing fantasy market."

"Not such a bad problem to have. But you're inviting litigation and government regulation."

"That's why I want you on board. Jack, I'm not a fool. I know there's no love lost between you and Lucy. She loved your wife and admires your daughter, but you've been on her black list for a while I understand. But our Lucy won't let her personal feelings get in the way of good business. Once Arnot and France gave us an analysis of the top antitrust counsels in the country she said, 'hire the son-of-a-bitch.'"

Lucy's opinion of me came as no surprise. I knew exactly what I thought of Lucy. Her backhanded compliment gave me a little twitch of pleasure.

"Thanks for laying all the cards on the table. Sounds like if I agree, I've got a bit of a learning curve to overcome."

"I'm only giving you quick synopsis so you know what you'll be up against. Most of the owners are comfortable with the law firm hired by the league, but I'm not."

"Why not?"

"First, they put at least five associates on every piddling matter, charging over $500 dollars an hour to do everything from research to making copies. Imagine charging $500 an hour for Xeroxing and having the balls to couch it as document prep on the bill. Second, the antitrust partner is a pompous snob. I'm not sure he's ever been to a ball game in his life. Finally, with thirty-two teams paying outrageous bills, the firm has a huge incentive to drag everything out instead of resolving the matters that should be resolved quickly and cheaply. My share of their bill last year was several million dollars. Jack, you're a bargain at twice the price.

"I did my homework. Even when you were at Banks and Tuohey, your clients never thought you overbilled them or drug out a matter to make a buck. Your small practice has an even better reputation. I'm lucky someone else didn't gobble you up while I was fighting with Lucy over hiring you." He leaned back in his chair, obviously pleased with himself.

"Okay, but speaking of Lucy, won't you have to defend me and my work every other day. Doesn't sound like a positive working arrangement." I was sincere. No sense setting up a client relationship that was destined for failure because of personal differences.

"Listen, Lucy is my problem, not yours. She and I have come to a unique arrangement because our agreements exceed our disagreements. When it comes to my business, whether it's raising a sunken ship or turning the Lobos into a Super Bowl champion, I have the final say. When it comes to politics or Lucy managing her family fortune, that's her business. But she'll surprise you sometimes. She knows how valuable Billy Hopper is to the Lobos. When I told her I'd changed my mind, she said, 'Well, if he could get Woody off, maybe there's a chance for Billy. I can't imagine anyone else who'd touch it with a ten-foot pole.'

"Besides. I think Lucy's dislike is more show than anything else. What is that line from *Hamlet*: 'The lady protests too much, methinks.' Something tells me she isn't nearly as angry at you as she lets on. Witness this."

He handed me what was clearly a very expensive save the date card. I was flabbergasted.

"What if I don't go to work for you? Do I give this back?" I asked, only partly in jest.

"It was her decision, not mine—no strings attached. She knew we were meeting and wanted me to give this to you in person. The invitation list is all hers. Your daughter is invited as well. She'll get her invitation in the mail."

Lucy was indeed full of surprises. While I fingered the posh card, Red finished.

"Okay, I've laid my cards on the table. Go back to your office, read the damn retainer agreement, and sign it. Represent Billy Hopper if you want, and let me know where to send his check." He handed me a card with his private number.

"Again, I think Billy and Marshall will hire a really good criminal lawyer. I'll let you know where to send the check—I can tell you they'll both be very appreciative. And I'll let you know tomorrow if I see any problem with the agreement. You have my word."

"Good. Now before I go out to the patio to smoke a cigar with Lynn and Guy, I want to tell you something. I hope you do represent Billy. He needs someone like you. I saw your press conference, if you can call it that. I thought he was guilty from the get-go, but your words gave me pause. Billy needs someone who believes in him, and I think you might just be that person. Think about it."

Lynn and Guy appeared as if by magic. Apparently they had been in the bar the whole time. He had one last bit of advice for me.

"By the way, Carol Madison is also on the guest list. Maybe you two can come together."

There are no secrets in DC.

25

As I WALKED back to the office, I tried to digest all I had learned from Red. He wasn't a man to do anything out of the goodness of his heart; at least I didn't think so. His explanation for paying Billy the money the Lobos owed made some sense, but I wondered...

It sounded like Lucy hadn't changed much since her days in Arkansas—she was a tough cookie, a strong woman with a take no prisoners attitude. I wondered what was up with the wedding invitation. The fact remained that she didn't like me, and I didn't much care for her either—or maybe we both protested too much. My bet was that Red had more to do with the guest list than he had let on.

I knew the gist of fantasy football, but that was about it. I'd never actually joined a league, but guys talked about their teams and players on the golf course all the time. Basically, there are two types of fantasy football leagues. The older version is similar to the old rotisserie baseball leagues I remembered from college. You and a group of friends (or random strangers thanks to the internet) form a league and put money into a pot. You draft players based on position and form your team. Then each week you play other teams in your league with points awarded for your player stats. For instance, if Peyton Manning is your quarterback and he throws a touchdown your team would get 6 points. Each week your team either wins or loses and after fourteen to sixteen weeks, the league has a winner. The money usually goes out to the first, second, third, and so on.

It's that simple, and now that scoring is managed online, easy to play. The NFL loves fantasy football because it makes fans all over the world interested in every game every week, rather than just their hometown team. It now matters to a Carolina fan what is happening to a player in Kansas City. It's no coincidence that the rise in value of the NFL over the last two decades (as well as the rise in television revenue) corresponds with the rise in fantasy leagues.

In the last couple of years a newer and more controversial form of fantasy football has arrived called weekly fantasy football. Controlled by a couple of large, internet-based companies, this version allows you to change your team on a week-to-week basis, so you aren't stuck with a hurt player or bad team all season. The payouts are weekly rather than at the end of the season, and a lot more money changes hands. There are now professional weekly fantasy players, (not too different from day traders on the stock market) who make thousands of dollars each week playing online. Unlike the stock market, weekly fantasy is unregulated. It's also not considered gambling because some degree of skill is involved in choosing the players. And players can't bet on the outcome of a single game or the performance of a single player. But it's close enough that it is outlawed in a few states like Nevada and Louisiana, and is coming under more and more scrutiny by state attorneys general.

Back in 2006, Congress gave the fantasy betting sites an exemption from gambling laws. So today, no government authority oversees fantasy sports, which still feels like gambling to me. To hear that the NFL was moving into controlling this part of their business didn't surprise me, but it did bother me. Gambling and sports have never been a good mix.

I'm a fan of both college and pro football, especially college. But a lot of the modern game bothers me, and I know I'm part of the problem. The fact is that at least ninety percent of all NFL players will suffer long-term ailments, either physical or cognitive. No statistics are available for NCAA ballplayers, but there's no reason to believe the numbers aren't similar. Is it any more violent than soccer? I don't know. But I admit to watching college ball most Saturdays in the fall, and I occasionally attend Redskins games on Sundays when they're in town, if you can call Landover, MD "in town." My support unconsciously condones a sport in which an untold number of young men end up with permanent physical or brain damage, and I pay good money to watch it happen.

I opened the office door to find Maggie still returning press calls. She rolled her eyes, so I shut myself up in my office, took out the revised retainer agreement, and read it carefully. The deal was basically the same, but Red had added a few sweeteners regarding travel accommodations and expenses. Let's just say NFL executives don't go anywhere second-class. The agreement spelled out liberal provisions should my work exceed twenty hours a month, and if for any reason the contract was terminated by either party, I would be paid the equivalent of a two year retainer for signing a confidentiality agreement.

I should have signed it on the spot, but Maggie and I had an unwritten rule that I wouldn't take on new business without conferring. Maggie no longer needed to work, but neither of us had ever considered otherwise. She enjoyed the challenge, and I needed her. With the Foundation as a full-time client, I could be more selective about choosing other clients. It was a nice arrangement, but I was about to upset the apple cart. We had two pieces of business to discuss—pro football and Billy Hopper.

I spent the rest of the afternoon boning up on the business end of football. Around four o'clock, I poked my head in her office.

"Maggie, I've had enough for one day. Let's go on over to the Bombay while it's still quiet." The colonial Indian restaurant was an easy walk from our offices. Maggie was in good spirits, and why not, after a month in Tuscany.

We chose to sit in the small bar area, and I ordered champagne.

"Maggie, I've hardly had time to say 'welcome home.' I'm sorry you got stuck with the press again, but it's been an interesting week. We need to talk about some potential new business."

"Fine, but let's first talk about Carol Madison. Who is she, and where are you going this weekend?"

I couldn't help but frown. "You know, I'm not a school kid, and you're not my mother."

"Well, sometime you act like one, and considering your recent track record with women you need someone look out for you. So who is Carol Madison?"

Okay—so a few of my adventures into dating land hadn't turned out so well. I'd made a few mistakes in the last couple of years that Maggie wouldn't let me forget.

"I met her at a cocktail party; we had dinner and hit it off. She invited me to her place on the Eastern Shore last weekend along with several other couples. She's invited me back this weekend, and I've accepted. And before you ask, she's in the consulting and information business. I bet Walter has heard of her."

"He has," she smiled.

"What? You already asked him? You already know about her? What did he say?"

"He said you've moved up in class, he was impressed. Tell me Jack, is she real?"

I thought for a minute. "She's fun, she's independent, and she's smart. And so far she seems to like me. I know this is fast, and I know I don't have a very good track record, but, yes, I like her a lot. I want you to meet her."

Her brows shot up. I usually don't say much about a woman I've taken out—usually there isn't much to say. Maggie always seems to know whom I'm seeing, but we seldom talk about it.

I was ready to drop the subject, and she didn't push me any further. So I gave her the basics of Red's proposal and an outline of Billy's problems. Of course, she'd heard about the murder, but had no idea Marshall was involved.

Maggie began, "Let's talk about the easy one first—Red Shaw. He's demanding and rude, but antitrust is what we do and do well. We'd be crazy to turn down the opportunity. Plus I like the fact we'll be playing in the Premier league."

Maggie's reference to the Premier league had something to do with English soccer. I knew about as much about British soccer as she did about American football. But we were both in agreement about Red's business. We weren't so excited about helping him get richer, but that's what antitrust lawyers do. We spent a few minutes mulling over whether we needed to take on another lawyer to help with the growing caseload. It might be good to bring some fresh thinking into the office.

Then we turned to Billy. Maggie was characteristically blunt. "You took on Woody Cole because he was a friend. It was the right thing to do, even though you almost got yourself killed. Dr. Stewart—that was for Angie. You got that right, too, but if you remember you were almost killed again. 'Third time's a charm' sounds a little risky to me."

"You're right. Marshall is certainly as good a friend as Woody, but he's not in any personal risk. More to the point, we just talked about antitrust being our niche. Billy has plenty of money available now to hire the best counsel available. Marshall doesn't know that Red is going to pay Billy what he's owed. Between the Lobos' and Stockdell's generosity, I bet we can find Billy the very best. Besides, I don't think I like that 'third time's a charm' logic either. I'll work with Red to get Billy his money and help Marshall find the right lawyer, but that's enough."

I raised a glass in a casual toast. "Maggie, I'm so glad you're back. Between us, I think we're got this figured out. First thing Monday morning we can work on finding Billy a lawyer he can count on."

My toast was interrupted by a bit of flutter as Walter Matthews strode to the table, kissed Maggie on the cheek, and said, "Jack, it's good to see you. I hear you found a companion while we were gone. Carol Madison's one of the best—my company has her on retainer. And I hear she's a pretty fair golfer."

At the maître d's suggestion, we moved to a table for dinner. Walter steered the conversation to golf. I assured Walter that Carol wouldn't get in the way of our regular golf game, although I wasn't so sure. We spent the next hour enjoying a fine meal and talking about their month in Tuscany. I was more than jealous and more than glad they were back.

I could have stayed at the Bombay and talked the rest of the night, but they were feeling the effects of jet lag, so we called it an early night. As the cab made its way up Connecticut Avenue I felt pretty good about how we had resolved the issues at hand.

I would put everything in place tomorrow morning, ready to enjoy a relaxing evening on the Eastern shore.

FRIDAY

April 22, 2016

2 6

I HAD NO trouble with the press on Friday morning. Thanks to an article in the Post reporting that I would represent Billy, they had moved on. I was tempted to disavow the story, but what good would that do? No need to stir them up again—they'd know soon enough that Marshall had hired a real criminal lawyer

A small but niggling part of my brain was still bothered by the idea of helping an NFL franchise dodge antitrust laws. For a fact, most of my antitrust clients weren't saints. I reminded myself that one could sometimes do more good from the inside than by shouting at the rain on the outside. Lawyers are experts at rationalizing.

I made a few tweaks to the retainer agreement, nothing of substance, just enough to prove I'd actually read it. Red seemed genuinely pleased when I called to tell him that the revised contract was on the way to his lawyers.

"Jack, that's terrific. You can fly out to LA with me in a couple of weeks to meet my management team. I try to spend about half my time out there so the timing should work well."

He asked me to put together a list of whatever issues I might want to review and gave me contact information for Regina Halep, who would be my liaison to the team.

"Gina's as smart as they come; she'll get you whatever you need. I won't be surprised if she becomes president of the franchise one of these days. Puts all the men in my organization to shame."

Maggie and I ordered in sandwiches. We had a lot of work to catch up on after her month-long absence. After about an hour she caught me looking at my watch.

"Jack, go home and pack. Your mind is clearly on the weekend, or should I say your companion for the weekend," she said dryly.

"I apologize. I promise to be back to normal on Monday."

"I hope so—Marshall should be here by early afternoon. I must say I don't envy your discussion. I'll have an office ready for him."

"Thanks Maggie. You and Walter get caught up on your rest. Next week is going to be busy."

Little did I know...

Traffic over the Bay Bridge was typically heavy on Friday afternoons, and today was no exception. I had decided to forego the pleasure of Pat's company, preferring my own thoughts to his awkward silence.

Red had called while I was packing to invite me to join him at the NFL scouting combine, an event that bothers me as much as anything about pro football. Think about it: a bunch of predominately white owners and coaches judging young men, mostly African-American, based on physical prowess. Each player is weighed and measured, tested for physical strength and endurance, and put through a regimen of physical and mental drills. I told him thanks, but no thanks.

He was surprised. "I know members of Congress who would give their eye teeth to attend."

I told him to give one my seat.

"You don't know what you're missing." He sounded legitimately surprised.

Representing the Lobos would indeed be a challenge for my conscience.

Carol must have been watching for me because she threw open the front door almost before I stepped out of the car. Her broad smile made me feel terrific.

"Let's go for a boat ride, have a quiet dinner, and take a swim."

"Sounds like the perfect evening."

And it was. The ever-useful Pat drove the pontoon boat while we sipped Manhattans and talked about nothing in particular, enjoying the sunset. She gave me the low-down on her guests for the evening— this weekend she had included a couple of congresswomen. Not fair for the guys to have all the fun. The breathtaking sunset over the water brought a chill to the air, and we soon turned back.

I gave a low whistle when she told me that the movie star couple who were spending the weekend at The Inn at Perry Cabin in St. Michaels had agreed to drop by before dinner. They'd spent the week in DC trying to get Congress to support their project in Louisiana.

"Don't get any ideas. You belong to me this weekend."

She also told me she hadn't included Senator Boudreaux from Tennessee.

"He makes most of the women uncomfortable, attached or not."

"I'll miss Claudia," I kidded.

"You'll miss her bathing suit. I heard she got a nice promotion. Must have been her knowledge of domestic affairs."

For dinner, Mattie served us fresh grouper grilled and seasoned with something called Anne's Aztec Spice. It was fantastic. We lingered over dinner, both knowing how we wanted this perfect evening to end. Pat and Mattie had magically disappeared.

She suggested we freshen our drinks and meet in the hot tub.

She got no argument from me. I changed quickly and carried a bottle of wine and two glasses to the warm pool tucked in next to the swimming pool. I poured the wine, set the glasses on the ledge, and sunk into the warm water. The jets and bubbling water felt absurdly good. It wasn't long before the lights dimmed and I looked up to see Carol removing her robe. I was overdressed.

She eased herself into the water, wrapped her arms around my neck, and kissed me flush on the mouth. I soon realized that my bathing trunks were superfluous.

"Silly man," she laughed, and they quickly came off.

We were interrupted forcefully by a deafening blast that seemed to come from right behind my head.

27

I REACHED FOR Carol who I thought must have hit her head on the side of the hot tub. Pat appeared almost immediately and, in one swift motion, took her from my uncertain grasp and wrapped her in towels. She didn't appear to have been injured, but was clearly woozy, probably in a state of shock.

"Inside, now!" Pat barked as he gently and quickly guided Carol indoors.

I pulled myself out of the water, grasping ineffectually for my trunks and robe. I tried to get my bearings, but was thrown back by the force of a second blast and the sound of more tile shattering. I've been shot at enough times before to know what a gunshot sounds like. Propriety be damned, I dashed inside buck-naked.

Safe in Carol's living room, I could see that she was sitting up, beginning to shake from the rush of adrenaline. Mattie had brought her a blanket and robe and was holding her tight. Pat threw me a towel.

"What happened?" Carol asked, still groggy. She pulled away from Mattie and reached to the back of her head. "I think I'm bleeding." Mattie handed her a towel and stood up, looking a little pale herself. They seemed to be moving in slow motion.

Pat said, "Carol, you're all right. Something hit the tiles behind your head and exploded. I'm fairly certain it was a bullet. Let me check the back of your neck for tile fragments." He looked at me before continuing, "Probably a stray bullet from a drunk deer hunter."

"Twice?" I asked, coldly. His words had cleared my head. "Not likely. I'd say it came from a sniper's rifle."

"But the shots missed," Pat began. "A professional sniper wouldn't miss…"

"…except on purpose," I finished.

"Mr. Patterson, I can't imagine why anyone would take a pot shot at Carol, it must have been meant for you. But why would someone, I mean who would…" Pat turned to look at Carol. "Maybe it was some kind of a warning."

He stopped to let his words sink in. I knew I needed to take charge.

"I don't think it had to do anything with romance. I'm going to change into some clothes. Mattie!" I turned to her. She was peeking out through the curtains, trying to eye the hot tub. "Stay away from the windows! Find some brandy and put on some coffee. Take care of Carol—I'll be back soon." I walked over to Carol, kissed her on the forehead, and left to change.

Khakis and a clean shirt gave me a renewed sense of control. I dialed Martin, told him where I was and asked him to come pick me up. He agreed immediately, no questions. I also asked him to bring a clean cell phone and someone who could drive my car home.

Mattie handed me a glass of brandy when I returned to the bedroom. Carol collapsed against my chest. She held a mostly empty glass and had stopped shaking. I noticed that both Pat and Mattie had poured themselves a brandy as well. Coffee could wait.

I pulled Carol's chin up. She sniffed a little and spoke.

"I'm so sorry. I just panicked when I heard the explosion. I hit my head and…oh my God, was it really a bullet?" I pulled her close, ignoring Pat.

"It's okay. We're both okay, that's what counts. Do you want to call the police? You should, you know."

"I'd rather not, but I will if you insist. Pat seems to be pretty sure the bullet was meant for you." Her voice was steady again.

"Carol. I'm not sure what happened or why. But I do understand that sirens, a herd of policemen, and yards of yellow tape won't do your business any good. So let's play it cool. Pat, my friend Martin Wells will want to send one of his staff around tomorrow to tour the grounds for poachers. Carol's guests will never know he's here."

"Understood."

"Do you need any help protecting Carol for the next few weeks? Martin can easily put a couple of his best at your disposal."

Pat said, "I think we'll be fine, but I won't hesitate to ask if I need help."

Carol pulled away. "What are you talking about? I don't need any protection."

I put my hands on her shoulders and looked directly into her face.

"Carol, someone knew you and I would be alone together tonight. I'm not sure what this is about, but I have an idea. I need some time and space to think about it. Tonight was very scary—I don't want there to be a next time."

She allowed herself a bit of a think before asking.

"So what do we do next?"

I looked at Pat—he was a smart guy.

"Carol, I think I need to, well, sort of fly beneath the radar for a few weeks."

"Okay—what does that mean, exactly?"

I didn't know how far I could trust Pat and Mattie, but I owed her an explanation.

"We could have been killed, but I think Pat's right. Someone just sent me a warning shot that came within inches of killing us both. I couldn't live with myself knowing you're in danger. If I care about you, which I certainly do, I need to go into hiding. It doesn't mean I'm going to quit doing what I need to do. It just means I have to do it below the radar screen."

"What do you need to do?" She was trying not to cry.

"I think I know why someone sent me the warning shot. Now I have to find out who."

"But do you have to leave right now?"

"Believe me, I'd rather not. I'd rather we fixed the hot tub and jumped right back in." My grin finally produced a smile.

"I'll have the tile man out here tomorrow morning before my guests arrive. Promise me you'll come back." She gave me a sweet kiss.

"Promise."

I turned to Pat, "You and I need to talk about a few things. Mattie, do you think I could have a very early breakfast before Martin gets here. All this excitement has made me hungry. In fact, we should probably all try to eat a little."

Mattie headed to the kitchen.

Carol went back to her room to get presentable, her words not mine. After they left, Pat spoke.

"You're playing a dangerous game. That bullet missed your head by inches."

"That's why they call it a 'a game of inches.'"

SATURDAY

April 23, 2016

2 8

Over a midnight breakfast, I tried to get a little information while assuring Carol that she would be safe, both here and in DC.

"Carol, I'm curious. Who might have known we'd be here tonight. Just off the top of your head."

"Well, let's see—all the weekend guests, my staff, and a few people who couldn't come. I'll make up a list and email it to you. That is, if you give me your email."

"You mean there's something about me you don't know?'

"I can get it if I need to," she said evenly.

"Hold off sending it to me until Monday. I'm going to have our office, computers, and phones checked out. I'll let Pat know when it's safe to send me an email."

"Pat. Why not call me? I might like to at least talk to you."

"For the next two weeks at least, there can be no direct communication between us. I don't like it any more than you do, but a professional sniper means someone is spending a lot of money to warn me off something. For all I know, that something could be you. More importantly, I can't have them thinking that they can get to me by getting to you."

Carol frowned, and I turned to Pat.

"Martin will tell you how to get in touch with me. If you want to have your computers and phones checked, he's got an expert who will do that at no cost to Carol."

Pat asked, "Do you think that's necessary?"

"Never hurts to check," I said.

"Wait a minute. You think it's possible that someone might have hacked my computer or my phone. Confidentiality is critical to what I do." Now Carol was paying attention.

"I hope not, but it's certainly a possibility. Carol, the person I use is really good. Let her check everything out. Even if she doesn't find anything, she might make some recommendations to improve your systems. Take advantage of the situation."

"Okay, but if somebody's hacked into my computer I'm going to be pissed." Funny—she'd gotten over almost losing her life pretty quickly, but the idea of someone messing with her livelihood was another matter.

I had to ask her one more question.

"Carol, any chance you told Red Shaw that I'd be here this weekend?"

"I probably did. I certainly invited him. Now that Lucy is in the picture he seldom comes, but he's got pretty much an open invitation. I told you his companies are very good clients, and he has sent a lot of business my way over the years. You don't think he's behind this, do you?"

"No, I don't. Yesterday, he actually suggested I represent Billy Hopper. I think Billy may be what this little adventure was all about. Somebody wanted to discourage me. If that's it, they've definitely made their point."

Martin was about an hour away, so I excused myself to get the rest of my clothes. I returned to find Mattie and Pat doing dishes and Carol sitting on a couch in her great room. She reached up, and I sat down, wrapping my arms around her.

"Jack, I have to admit—I'm a little scared."

It probably wouldn't do any good, but I said, "You'll be okay. Pat knows what he's doing, and I really don't think that bullet was meant for you. Martin will provide him back-up. Just listen to them when they tell you to do something."

"I'm not talking about me. I'm scared something is going to happen to you."

This time I couldn't think of much to say. Frankly, I was too. It took me a few seconds to manage, "Oh, c'mon, Carol, I'll be fine. You'll see."

"We could go away together. I hear Bali is beautiful. No one would look for us there."

The idea of Carol and I on the beaches of Bali held a lot of appeal.

"You mean do what the person who hired the sniper wants me to do?" I asked.

"Exactly. Walk away. Walk away with me. I want you alive."

"Sounds very tempting. But you know a lot about me. What do you think I'm going to do?"

"You're going to go back to DC and figure out who was behind all this tonight and what it's all about. You'll probably get yourself killed in the process. Damn you, Jack, the more I think about it Bali would be perfect."

"You're right, except I hope you're wrong about the getting myself killed part."

She held my face in her hands and kissed me long and hard. Then she pulled away.

"I hope so, too, but I'm seldom wrong."

29

I HEARD A quiet knock on the front door and rose to let Martin in. I gave his associate the keys to my car, and he left immediately. Martin shook hands with Pat who gave him a brief outline of the night's events. He asked to see the hot tub and check the sniper's line of sight before we left. He told Pat he'd be back tomorrow afternoon with a few men, but they would hardly be noticed. They exchanged contact information, while I gave Carol a goodbye hug, promising to be careful. She didn't believe me.

Once we were in the car, Martin handed me a new phone. "All set up and ready to go. Clovis and Stella will be here first thing tomorrow. He said he'd be up if you wanted to call. He's curious as to why you need Stella. Mr. Matthew's tech guys are going to be thrilled."

I smiled when I thought of Stella—Stella Rice. I had worked with Stella in the Stewart case. She was a computer hacking expert trained by IBM, but sure didn't look the part. She owned a gym and taught high intensity CrossFit workouts, including flipping tractor tires. During the Stewart case she had come to DC to check out our office's computers and had blown away Walter's IT guys. They try to hire her at least once every six months, but she's happy in Little Rock.

She met Clovis on the same case, and they now live together—a very unlikely pair, but it works. I punched in his number.

"Clovis, I appreciate your coming," I began.

"Forget it, Jack. What can you tell me? Do you really think someone's after you? Again?"

"I know, I know. And the answer is I'm not sure. But that shot was real, and it scared the shit out of me. As far as I know the only unconventional thing I've done in more than a year is meet with Billy Hopper. Look, it's complicated, and I'd rather tell everyone at once. First things first—Beth."

"Paul is already on his way to New Orleans. He didn't want to scare her over the phone. Do you think she needs protection? She won't like it."

"I don't know, but if someone wants to get to me, she's on the very top of the list. I can't afford to take any chances. Thank Paul for me—I hope he won't need to be there very long."

"He volunteered. He and Beth have become friends after what they went through in the Cole case. Why do you need Stella?"

"I won't be surprised if she finds our computers and office have been compromised. I also need her to set up a system of communication while I go off grid."

"In other words you need to be on grid while you're off grid?"

"Something like that. Why don't you two stay at my house? Sophie loves Stella more than me. Besides, I won't be there."

"Where are you going to be?" he asked patiently.

"I'll explain everything when you get here. One of Martin's men will pick you up at the airport. Come to think about it, staying at my house might not be a good idea. Let me think on it: we can decide later."

"Does Maggie know what's going on?" He was right to ask.

"Not yet. She just got back from Europe a couple of days ago. Whatever I end up doing, she'll be mad as a wet hen," I said glumly, thinking she'd probably blame Carol for the whole thing.

"You got that right. By the way, Stella wants to know about how long we'll be there."

"No more than two weeks. If we don't have this mystery solved in two weeks, the bad guys will have won."

"Aren't you being a little dramatic?" Clovis asked skeptically.

"Well, maybe, but I don't think so."

We hung up after he gave me a rundown on the situation with Marshall and Grace.

Martin drove in silence for a few minutes before I said, "I hope you don't think it's a reflection on you that I called Clovis?"

"Nah—Clovis and I work well together, and from what I just heard we're going to need more than my boots on the ground. Besides, it's about time Stella checked out our systems again. It works out well."

We drifted into our own thoughts for a while. Martin broke the silence.

"Do you think Mrs. Matthews is at additional risk?"

"Well, I hope not, but she might be. Whoever shot at me clearly had no concern for Carol's safety. I hope that if I disappear whoever's responsible will call off the dogs thinking I've been scared off, that the warning shot worked," I answered.

"What happens when they discover it didn't?"

"Let's hope they don't, at least not before we're ready."

"You know, Mr. Patterson, that bullet came very close to ending your life. The explosion alone could have knocked you cold, and you could have drowned. It could easily have turned into more than a warning."

"Yeah, that thought has crossed my mind. But if I had been killed, the police would have been called. The press and my friends, I hope, would have investigated, and they might have tied it to Billy Hopper. Why take that risk? No, I think the shots were a warning. For whatever reason, someone wants Billy to take the rap and doesn't want me involved."

"Why not kill Hopper? If Billy didn't kill the girl, the person who did had plenty of opportunity to kill Hopper as well. Why not kill Hopper rather than have him locked away for life?"

Good question. Very good question indeed.

3 0

I WAS EXHAUSTED after being up all night, but figured I'd have time to sleep soon enough. Martin waited in the car while I packed for a two-week trip. As soon as the hour was civil, I called my dog sitter, telling her there had been an emergency and I'd be gone for at least two weeks. She was delighted when I told her I'd leave a check on the kitchen ledge. I felt a twinge of guilt, but knew she'd take good care of Sophie. The dog loved staying at her house—good thing her parents didn't mind.

It was Saturday, so only a few of my neighbors were up and outside to see me carrying several bags to Martin's Suburban, but that was enough. My briefcase and laptop completed the subterfuge.

"Make sure we aren't followed, and then take me to Barker's—my new home for the next two weeks. Until we have Stella check for bugs, don't tell anyone, not even your staff, where I am."

I dropped my bags at Barker's—they were expecting me—then Martin dropped me off at the office. Saturday mornings in downtown DC are dead, so I was pretty sure no one had followed us. I asked him where Walter's insurance company put people up when they came to town. I was pleased to find out one of the hotels was the Mayflower. We could kill two birds with two stones.

Martin would book a room for Stella and Clovis in the name of Bridgeport Life. It would appear they were in town to work for Walter's insurance company, something they both did all the time. Clovis could do a little investigative work for me, and no one would be the wiser.

I put on a pot of coffee and made a call to a friend, Susan Sandler, with Evers Real Estate, a well-respected DC brokerage.

"Susan, this is Jack Patterson."

"Jack—I haven't heard from you in a while. What's going on?"

"Well, I think I've decided to sell my house. What do I need to do next? I hear the market's good, but I honestly don't have any idea what it's worth." She didn't answer immediately—she was a seasoned professional.

"We'll have no trouble selling it if it's priced correctly. It's a great house in a wonderful neighborhood. First thing, I'd like to walk through with a couple of colleagues to get their thoughts. Then we should sit down with the paperwork and talk price and timing, et cetera. We might want to discuss making some cosmetic repairs. I won't know until I walk through."

"I'm going to be out of town for a couple of weeks, but my next door neighbor has a key. Their daughter walks Sophie while I'm out of town. Now that I've decided to do this, I'd like to get moving. I trust you: you figure out a price, and email me. I'm sure y'all use Docusign or something like that."

Susan wasn't about to let me be sloppy about such an important decision. "Tell you what—I'll go through the house today. I may ask my partner Ellen to go with me. I'll run the comps over the weekend and get you something by Monday. We should also talk about where you want to land. Your house will move quickly once it's on the market."

"We'll do that. Listen, go ahead and put up one of those signs that says 'coming soon,'—it's fine with me."

"Donna thinks those signs are misleading, so do I. I don't put up a sign until the house is ready to go. Besides, let's make sure the house is priced right and ready for the market. I'll move quickly, don't worry. This is kind of sudden, Jack. Everything okay?"

"Yeah, I've been thinking about making a change for a while. Now I'm just ready to get going."

Shoot—I was kind of hoping for one of those misleading signs. I called my neighbor to tell her Susan Sandler would come by today to get a key.

She had a million questions, which I happily referred to Susan.

I had no doubt that the whole neighborhood would know by the afternoon that I was selling my house. Perfect.

I heard Maggie open the front door. She deposited her stuff on a chair, walked into my office and faced me with a frown. "What's going on? My driver told me that Clovis and Stella are flying in on Walter's plane. You send me a message asking me to come in, after telling me you are spending the weekend with your new girlfriend. What's gone wrong, Jack?"

Walter insisted on routine protection for Maggie because of his wealth, not because she worked for me, and this morning I was glad he did. Where to begin?

I spoke distinctly in case our offices had been compromised. "I'm leaving town for a while. Martin wants Stella to do some work for Bridgeport Life. Clovis is coming with her, he says he needs a few days off." I put my fingers over her lips and pointed to the door.

Always quick on the uptake, she sighed, "I saw that Rose didn't replenish my tea. Mind if we walk to Teaism before we get started?"

We left the building and walked to the Teaism across from Lafayette Park.

"You think the office might be bugged?" She asked as soon as we placed our orders and sat down at an outside table.

"I don't know, but I don't want to take any chances. My plans right now are still a work-in-progress, but I need everyone to believe that I've left town, that I won't be representing Billy Hopper."

"I thought we already agreed you wouldn't, that you would help him get counsel, but that would be the extent of our involvement. Tell me what's going on."

I told her. Well, I told her almost everything. I didn't go into all the details about the hot tub or Carol's suggestion that she and I escape to Bali.

I began to wriggle as Maggie's silence lengthened. She finally heaved a sigh and responded.

"You know this is déjà vu. We've had this conversation before about your apparent death wish. You take on these cases you have no business handling, and you almost get yourself killed. I'm honestly not sure I can take this again."

"Believe me, Maggie, I understand, and I don't know what to say other than I'll explain when Clovis gets here—please hear me out. I know we decided not to represent Billy, and I'm still not sure I'm the right lawyer. But for now, I'm the only one he's got. Maggie, this thing's gotten complicated: it's not just about Billy—or Carol, for that matter. Just hear me out. Okay?"

"In other words, for now our law firm represents Billy Hopper?" she asked.

"I guess for now the answer is yes. That is, of course, if you agree." I gave her my widest smile.

"Don't you flash that big puppy grin of yours at me. You know I'm not happy. You just might get yourself killed this time and then what happens to me."

"You and Walter travel the world without having to worry about me doing something stupid ever again." I could tell she was lightening up.

"And after hearing you out, if I still think we shouldn't represent Mr. Hopper, you'll drop this representation?"

"Of course."

3 1

WE NURSED OUR drinks at Teaism waiting on Clovis and Stella to arrive. I told Maggie about calling Susan Sandlin and my impulse to list the house, explaining it was part of my strategy to convince whomever (I was going to have to come up with a name for the bad guy) that I'd been scared off. Maggie asked if Beth knew what had happened at the Eastern shore. I explained that Paul was probably talking to her right now.

"Your strategy doesn't seem quite fair to Susan," she said tartly. "You know, Beth and I have talked about it a lot. Maybe it is time for you to move."

"Oh, really? You and Beth think I should move? When were you going to tell me?"

"At the right time. You know how special Angie was to me, and I know how many memories that home has for both you and Beth. If you ever get serious about another woman, I'd bet she would have problems spending any time there. Moving might just help you move on."

I wondered if all the family pictures had bothered Carol when she came over the other night. She hadn't said anything, but then again I'm a guy. I don't pick up on clues very well. Maybe that's why she didn't stay that evening.

"Maybe I don't want to get over Angie," I blurted out.

"Jack, how can I put this? You will never get over Angie. None of us will, or even want to; she's a part of our lives. But there is a difference between getting over and moving on. Angie will always be present in your heart, but there's room for someone else. I remember her making you promise to do just that."

This conversation was going nowhere, but at least it took both our minds off Billy Hopper. I knew that Beth and Maggie had my best interests at heart, and I can't say I behaved like I was still in mourning. Maybe it was time to sell the house. But Maggie was right: I'd have to make up my mind. I couldn't leave Susan hanging.

Clovis texted that they were on the ground. I texted back suggesting he meet us at Teaism, while Stella should go straight to the office to set up her equipment so we could talk without being overheard.

Clovis was a big man—I could see him walking toward us from over a block away. We shook hands and he sat down, turning to Maggie.

"You talked any sense into our boy yet?"

"I have failed utterly. Perhaps he'll listen to you." She knew exactly when to use her Mayfair accent

I ignored them.

"Any word from Paul?" I asked.

"As you might have expected, Beth is worried about you, wants to come to DC," he answered.

"I'd love to see her, but she has a job and there's no reason for her to be here—her presence would blow my cover. I'll explain after Stella sweeps the office."

"Paul gave her your new cell number. I'll bet that right now Paul, Jeff, and Beth are enjoying a very expensive breakfast on your nickel."

I wasn't about to protest. A New Orleans brunch would put anyone, including Beth, in a good mood.

Soon Stella texted that the coast was clear, and we joined her at the office. Stella had gone from purple to orange—orange hair, orange nail polish, and orange jeans. If possible, her spike heels were even taller than the last time I'd seen her. At least I didn't see any orange tattoos.

"New look?" I asked casually.

"I knew it would drive you crazy—Texas Longhorn orange, just for you. Clovis isn't thrilled either, but he'll get over it." That was Stella, front and center.

"The set-up in the office is temporary. Your computers have had some uninvited entries in the last few days. I can't be sure yet, but it's similar to the activity we encountered in the Stewart case. But it's safe to talk. Why don't you and Maggie hand me your phones so I can check them while we're talking. Jack, I brought you a new laptop, but I can't transfer anything to it till I make sure your mail or files haven't been hacked. That will take some time."

Maggie handed Stella her phone and said, "I'm sure mine is safe. I've been out of the country, and if Jack is correct, all this just came up recently."

Not bothering to respond, Stella plugged Maggie's phone into her computer.

This seemed like a good time for me to jump in.

"Okay, why don't I fill you in on the events of the last couple of weeks. Let me start from the beginning, then talk about what I see as the only option I have."

I briefly gave them a rundown on the press coverage of the Mayflower incident, my invitation to go to Lucy's and what happened that night, and Marshall's revelations on Saturday. Clovis shook his head in disgust, amazed that I had accepted Lucy's invitation.

I skipped my first weekend at Carol's and told them about Marshall's interview, my visit with Billy, my belief in his innocence, Red's change of heart, and then of course the shooting at the hot tub, absent a few insignificant details.

After I finished, I said I knew this was a lot to digest and offered to get everyone coffee from the nearby Starbucks. Our office coffee wasn't very good.

Clovis spoke. "No way. If you're going to disappear it begins now. I'll get the coffee. You stay here."

Before he could leave, Stella interrupted. "Good idea—whoever is trying to listen to our conversations isn't happy. They've upped the intensity of their surveillance; they can't get in, but I'll have to make sure they haven't come up with something new. If they keep this up, they're going to really piss me off."

"Really?" I teased.

"Really. And by the way, Maggie, your phone is compromised. I don't know yet when it happened, but it looks like we've got to get everyone new equipment. I hope this doesn't go as far as your husband's companies, or I'll be here all month."

3 2

Clovis returned with coffee and after we had all settled, I began again.

"Look, I know my half-ass plan is just that, but it's a beginning. Let me give you the basics. Then I need your input.

"The bugging of the offices and phones may not be related to Billy Hopper at all. We made lots of enemies in both the Cole and Stewart cases. I also have several major antitrust cases pending where the opponents might be trying to gain an advantage by tapping our phones. It's also possible someone doesn't want me to represent the Lobos. But the use of a sniper seems an unlikely antitrust strategy. So far my regular law practice hasn't been deleterious to my health. I have to believe the sniper's warning was an effort to get me to back off representing Billy.

"The way I see it I have three options. First, I can hide until Monday, offer to help Marshall find Billy a lawyer, and hold a press conference to that effect. Back to business as usual."

"Sounds like a good option to me," said Maggie.

"I thought it would, but you promised to hear me out," I reminded her.

She frowned, and I continued.

"I can also tell Marshall I'm all in, effectively telling whomever to go jump in the lake. The problem is I don't think they're bluffing. That sniper could have killed me the other night, and if whoever wants to get nasty, he could make me pay a terrific price for my defiance. Beth and Carol are obvious targets. Maggie, I hate to say this, but you are, too. If something happened to any of you I couldn't live with myself.

"The third option is to behave as though I'm scared shitless: go into hiding, and spend the next two weeks trying to figure out what really happened at the Mayflower that night. I would need your help, especially Stella's when it comes to setting up a communication system. We would all have to be very careful not to give away the game. Stella has to help Walter's company clean up their systems, while Clovis acts like he's on a vacation with his girlfriend. Maggie has to run the office without letting on that she is in constant communication with me."

Clovis said, "I see several problems right off the bat."

"Let's hear them." I meant it.

"To begin with: Marshall. How are you going to convince him this is a doable plan? He's convinced Billy is innocent. Why wouldn't he simply hire a different counsel?"

"I'm pretty sure that when he hears I was almost murdered, he'll try to get me to back off. My job is to convince him otherwise. If he doesn't agree, we go back to Maggie's favorite option." She smiled sweetly.

"Okay, your plan presumes that there's more to that night than the prosecutor knows, that in fact Billy's innocent, and that in just two weeks we can figure out not only who killed that woman but why. Why two weeks, and what makes you think you know more than the prosecutor?" Clovis asked.

"I don't think I can pull off this disappearing act for more than two weeks. No matter how careful we are, whoever is bound to smell something fishy before long. I know that if we haven't made any progress in two weeks, we need to get Billy a different lawyer.'"

"Okay, what about Billy? He's our best source of information, but no one can interview him except a lawyer. Marshall can't help. How are we going to get information from him? Only a lawyer can talk to him in confidence."

I gave him a slow grin and he said, "No way."

"Can you think of a better option?"

Maggie interrupted, "You can't talking about..."

Clovis smiled. "Yup. The wildcat."

Stella asked. "Who are you two talking about?"

Maggie gave me a really dirty look. "Micki. He means Micki."

"She'll hardly speak to you—how are you going to get her to come to DC, much less represent Billy? I know you two were close once, but..." Clovis trailed off, fearing he'd gone too far.

"I'm pretty sure it will involve begging on my part." In fact, I had no idea how I would manage any of this.

Maggie relented a little. "Okay, if you intend to represent Billy, your plan makes some sense, but let's go back to why you would agree to represent him in the first place. From what I can tell, the evidence is pretty compelling, and what he did is frankly quite repulsive. I love Marshall, but at this point his loyalty to this young man is hard to understand.

"Your one-hour conversation with him, when he couldn't even deny committing the murder, is hardly reason enough to take on the case. I know you believed him, but you've been fooled before, remember?"

She was right, of course, but I wasn't ready to give in just yet.

"Your argument makes perfect sense, and frankly he might have done it; every bit of evidence points that way. But if that were the case, why would anyone care if an antitrust lawyer, not known for his criminal expertise, represents him? Why bug this office and our phones? Why hire a sniper to warn me off?

"Come to think of it, why would Lucy's Robinson's fiancé offer me, out of the blue, a lucrative contract to represent his football team almost immediately after the murder and a day before I met with Marshall. I can't exclude the possibility of a connection between Red and the murder."

Maggie interjected, "If you're thinking that way, you have to ask why the sudden interest in you by Ms. Madison. I believe you told me she is on Red Shaw's payroll?"

Maggie had cut right to the bone, and it hurt.

"Can you imagine I haven't asked myself that question? I'm not blind to the fact that she arrived on the scene at Lucy's party. I'm not blind to her relationship with Red Shaw. But she was right there in that water with me—she could easily have been killed. Maybe I'm a fool, but I can tell you that I don't think she's involved."

I stared at her, aware of no one except the two of us.

"I'm sorry, Jack," she said, and the room came back into focus, "That wasn't fair of me. I'm sure there's no connection."

"But there could be. We can't ignore the possibility." Clovis looked miserable, and I let him off the hook.

"It's okay—I know we can't. So I have one more thing for you all to consider—if I go forward, you may all be in danger, not just me. That includes you, Stella. You are going to be thwarting highly skilled hackers who may not take kindly to your expertise. How do you feel about that?"

Clovis just laughed. "I learned two years ago that working for you was dangerous and to expect the unexpected, but Jack, I'll say this: you're never boring. Don't worry, I'm in."

"I've spent a lot of time and effort trying make sure the Matthew's companies and y'all are free from computer espionage. Now some bastard's trying to crack my code. I want to find out who he is and repay the favor. Besides, if Clovis is in danger he needs me to protect him." Stella blew him a kiss.

"Maggie?" I asked.

"I'm not happy, but then again you didn't expect me to be. Of course I'm in. I'm not about to let you go off half-cocked without me. But I'll have to let Walter know."

"Of course. Walter's always a part of any crazy scheme I come up with." My team was assembled save one, a critical one—Micki Lawrence.

Clovis said, "Tell me again how you're going to convince Micki to join up."

"I didn't tell you the first time. Micki's going to take some time to figure out. Let's talk about what we need to learn based on what I know so far."

33

I BEGAN WITH the question no one, not even the prosecutor, could answer: who was the girl in the bedroom? Was she one of the girls at the NFL Honors banquet? Did she have any connection with Billy or was she someone off the streets? Who else might have had a reason to murder her? And what had happened to the girls who left the banquet with Billy? Who were they and what did they remember? There hadn't been word one about them in the press so far. I would have expected at least one of them to have appeared on a talk show by now.

Clovis would take the lead on these issues. Stella would set up a secure line of communications for herself, Clovis, Maggie, myself, and hopefully Micki. She would also try to discover who was trying to listen in on our conversations and hack our computers. Maggie would hold down the fort, acting as our go-between as well as keeping up our subterfuge. I would do my best to disappear.

Disappearing while actually working isn't that easy—we'd all have to be on our toes. I had a plan to get Marshall into Barker's so we could talk in person on Monday. Maggie would talk to Beth once the phones were secure.

I suggested that the three of them should go have a nice lunch while I called Micki. I needed the privacy, and it would help if they were seen in public without me.

Micki picked up on the first ring.

"Twice in one week, you must be horny." Sounded more like the Micki I knew.

"Micki, I need your help," I began.

"Jack, I already told you I won't help you represent that murderer."

"I don't want you to help me. I want you to represent him all on your lonesome."

"Jack, have you been eating Liz Stewart's ginger snaps?"

"No, I'm quite serious."

"Okay, I'll play along. Why in the hell would I represent a man who stabbed a woman multiple times until she bled to death?"

At least she hadn't hung up.

"What if I told you I honestly believe he didn't do it?" I asked.

"Every client I have claims he didn't do it—most of them were shooting baskets with their buddies or babysitting their kid sister. Since when did you become a good judge of character?"

"What if I told you there's a fee in it. The client has money."

"I'd say my docket is full." Now she was having fun.

"What if I said this case will garner national publicity, increase your reputation." I had to admit I was having fun as well.

"You've already involved me in two of the highest profile cases in this decade. I don't need any more publicity."

It was time to get serious.

"What if I tell you someone shot at me with a high profile rifle to warn me off this case? What if I tell you I can't guarantee your safety, and I'm going underground for the next two weeks?"

No quick comeback this time.

"If someone tried to kill you it would be all over the news. How come I haven't read anything about this in the papers or seen anything on TV? If you're making this up, it's not funny."

"I'm not lying, Micki, and it isn't funny. A sniper fired a bullet within three inches of my head. Damn near killed me."

Another long pause. "Where's Clovis?"

"He and Stella arrived this morning on Walter's plane. The same plane can pick you up tomorrow morning."

"What about Beth? Is she safe?"

"Paul was dispatched to New Orleans last night. He's supervising her protection as we speak—ask Debbie."

Micki's office manager, Debbie Petrova, and Paul live together. I could almost hear her thinking.

"Are you leaving the country?"

"No, I'm not even leaving town, but no one other than Maggie, Clovis, and Stella know where I'll be. Everyone else is supposed to think I've left town. I'm even putting my house up for sale."

"You should leave the country, Jack."

"Maggie agrees with you."

"Maggie has good sense; obviously you don't. If I get involved, there will be nothing between us, just partners working on this case, right? No flirting?"

"None. Actually, I'm seeing someone." It felt odd to say that, especially to Micki, but it was the truth—I hoped.

"Wow, I want to meet her. What if I bring someone with me?"

"I'd rather you didn't. He couldn't know anything except that you are representing Billy at Marshall's request."

"His name is Larry. He's an artisan woodworker and carpenter who's been doing some work on the place. He could care a hoot about my day job."

Well, at least she was over Eric.

"That's your call. But you really can't tell him anything. And he needs to understand he could be in danger."

"What about Marshall? What does he think?"

"Well, I haven't actually approached him yet. Didn't want to until I had a plan with you on board. But Marshall suggested you should be my co-counsel just last Thursday, before any of this happened. Apparently I didn't impress him with my knowledge of criminal law during the Cole case."

She laughed. "I guess not."

It was time to fish or cut bait. "Micki, I need you. Can I send Walter's plane to pick you up tomorrow morning."

I could hear the wheels turning.

"Oh, what the hell. You had me at hello."

So, the team was assembled, for exactly what, I wasn't certain. I spent the next hour explaining what had happened over the last few days.

34

MAGGIE, STELLA, AND Clovis had enjoyed flatbread sandwiches at Cosi and returned in a great mood. They were all relieved that Micki had joined our gang of thieves. Maggie called Walter's pilot to make arrangements. We decided that for the time being Micki should stay at the Hay-Adams, despite the expense. It would be the natural choice if she was working with Marshall.

"Stella, why don't you and Clovis have brunch there tomorrow? It's quite a spread. I have a feeling that if someone is spying on me, they've bugged Marshall's room at the Hay-Adams. Hotel security should be cooperative if you tell them you're working for Marshall and a new guest arriving tomorrow."

We spent the rest of the afternoon going over details and logistics. Directing a criminal investigation from Barker's wouldn't be easy, but it was important for our antagonist to think I had fled the coop, so to speak.

Martin returned from Carol's place just before Clovis and Stella left for the Apple store and some other specialty electronics store.

He'd found only a few traces of the sniper, who according to Martin must have been an excellent shot given the distance the bullet had to travel. Great. The hot tub had been totally repaired, and Carol's guests didn't have a clue what had occurred the previous evening. Paul told him that Carol was in good spirits, but would love to hear from me if possible.

It was possible, but not smart. Martin also learned that Red Shaw was a last minute guest. Not Lucy, just Red. That was news I didn't want to know. What did it mean?

Soon I was the only one left in the office except for my driver. Maggie and Walter were attending some charity event for the homeless. Stella and Clovis had planned a trip to Cantler's for fresh crabs after going shopping. But for the sniper, I would be snuggled up with Carol at her place on the Eastern Shore watching a first run movie. I admit to enjoying a little pity party.

I finally talked with Beth. Paul had calmed her down, and she, Jeff, and Paul were enjoying the Crawfish Music Festival at Tulane. Paul must have done his job, because she made no mention of coming to DC. I hung up thinking about crawfish.

After tomorrow's meeting with Micki, all my communication with my team would be by phone or email. I'm a hands-on lawyer, and pulling strings from afar isn't my idea of fun. I was looking at a tough couple of weeks.

To some extent I was allowing the sniper to govern the way I worked, but I couldn't bear it if I put Carol, Beth, or Maggie at further risk. Besides, if this plan didn't work all I had to do was walk out the door.

It was time to leave the office. I had an outline of things to go over with Micki, and had begun to think about what I would say to Marshall. Walter, who also belonged to Barker's, would bring Marshall to meet with me on Monday

Barker's was pretty empty for a Saturday night. I couldn't face the dining room alone, so I sat at the bar. I would need to make good use of their fitness room if I kept this up. I munched on nachos, tried to watch the ball game, listened to two men talk about their fantasy baseball picks, and thought about Carol Madison.

*****

Mr. Kim was more than a little surprised that Patterson had heeded the warning shot. He was a doer, not a quitter. But his source had verified that he'd left Ms. Madison's place, gone directly home, packed his bags, and was now missing in action. He'd even talked to a Realtor about putting his home on the market this morning. Maybe Patterson was finally tired of putting his life on the line for his clients.

Nonetheless, he wasn't taking chances. His contacts were monitoring the man's credit card accounts in the hopes of determining his whereabouts. Patterson was most vulnerable when he felt someone close to him was at risk. He was putting people in place to monitor Patterson's daughter, Mrs. Matthews, and Ms. Madison in case he needed to move quickly.

Carol Madison may have been why Patterson took off. Perhaps he was closer to her than original reports. If Patterson surfaced, Madison might prove to a very interesting chess piece. The client had made it clear—under no circumstances was Patterson to represent Hopper. The sniper had been directed to remain under cover in DC, prepared to terminate Patterson immediately if the client gave the order.

He had yet to deal with one annoying problem. As expected, Clovis Jones's had sent his man Paul to New Orleans to babysit Patterson's daughter. No problem in itself, but underworld activity in New Orleans was still controlled by a syndicate modeled after the days of Nitti and Capone. His operatives would need a "license" to work in New Orleans, and any hits needed to be pre-approved. This was an issue he needed to address quickly.

SUNDAY

April 24, 2016

35

I never sleep well the first night in a strange bed. Around 6:30 I finally quit fighting and headed for my favorite meditation spot—the shower. Barker's showers were roomy and had great water pressure, a luxury most hotels don't appreciate. I donned my lucky golf shirt and slacks, enjoyed a long breakfast over the Sunday *New York Times,* and headed to the office. The garage was empty, as was most of downtown. Except during the Cherry Blossom Festival, everyone but the most dedicated tourists slept in on Sunday mornings.

Maggie was already in; coffee and her pot of hot water waited in the conference room. Clovis was already on his second cup, and Stella was buried in a computer.

"I thought I'd be the first one here."

Clovis said, "Stella got me up at six to run the Mall. We needed to run off last night's dinner."

"Please don't tell me any more about Cantler's. I had nachos at the bar. What time does Micki arrive?"

"I think it will be both Larry and Micki. They should land within the hour," he responded.

"Larry's coming? Good for Micki." Stella said at exactly the same time as Maggie asked, "Who's Larry?"

"Larry Bradford—he's a terrific artisan carpenter. Micki found him when she needed some cabinetwork done at her place. He's a little younger, cute as a button, and hardly ever speaks."

"Micki told me he had great hands," I interjected.

Stella laughed. "Jack, I think she was referring to his woodworking skills. He's really very talented."

"Sure she was," I responded dryly.

Maggie began to squirm a little. "Do Micki and …Larry… understand the risk of their participation?"

"I brought it up, and Micki promised to tell him he could be in real danger. I hope she did, but I'll ask again when they get here," I said.

Stella wasn't finished. "Don't underestimate Larry. His family is old Little Rock, and he was educated at St. Albans and Princeton. He surprised everyone when he didn't return to work in the family financial business after college. Instead he spent eight years in New Hampshire and Vermont as an apprentice to master carpenters and furniture makers.

"He returned to Little Rock after his father died and opened a small woodworking studio. Several of his pieces have been exhibited at the Arts Center and in the decorative arts section of Crystal Bridges, the new museum in Bentonville. He may be a quiet man, but he has brought a measure of calm into Micki's life that she badly needed."

While we waited for Micki, Stella distributed new phones to Maggie and me. She also gave me a new fully loaded Apple laptop.

She said, "I would like to check out the network you'll use at Barker's."

"If the antagonist knows I'm at Barker's, the game's up anyway. Barker is anal about privacy. I bet he has an extremely secure network." Listen to me, acting like I knew what I was talking about.

"Still, after a few days we'll need to figure out how I can check it out."

Maggie asked. "Our phones are safe again, but what about other people's? For example, can I call Walter?"

"I'll check Walter's phone tomorrow as part of our supposed reason for being here. There's no reason not to behave normally. Just don't tell anybody anything about Jack. Maybe we should all act as though Jack's off on an extended vacation. You know, answer the phones as usual, but Jack's not available. Paul has given Beth a new phone by now. Sorry, Jack, phone security isn't cheap. My biggest worry is you might get the urge to call your new girlfriend. Should I be concerned?"

"No, you shouldn't." I frowned, thinking her question was a little cheeky, even for Stella.

"Judge Fitzgerald will have to be schooled after Jack talks to him. He needs to come straight to me after your meeting so I can explain phone and computer security. Clovis had me check out his wife and the boys' phones and computers while we were still in Little Rock. Not a thing. Don't you think it's strange that so far no one seems to be bothering with the Judge?"

"I thought about that this morning. It's as if they don't mind Marshall helping Billy, but they don't want me near him," I said.

"Or all this has nothing to do with Billy Hopper. You've pissed off someone for an entirely different reason," Clovis said.

He had a point.

"It will be interesting to see if there's any reaction to Micki when she enters her appearance. I have to believe it's all connected to Hopper, but I could be dead wrong."

"Speaking of Micki," he continued, "she just texted that they've landed and she's on her way in."

"Before Micki gets here, I want your promise about something," I said seriously. "I thought about this last night and again this morning. You all know that what we are about to embark on entails a fair amount of risk. I want each of you, especially you, Maggie, to tell me when I've crossed the line and you feel uncomfortable."

"I think you crossed that line when you decided to represent Billy Hopper. And it's not the first time." Maggie looked glum.

"You're right, and I'm sorry. But this time it will be different. With both Woody and Doug Stewart, I was out front and center, the target for bullets and speeding cars. This time I'll be sitting in a comfortable chair while each and every one of you are on the front lines. Even Marshall will be at more danger than I am."

For a few seconds the room was silent. I was glad my words had sunk in.

Maggie broke the silence.

"Jack, I promise to let you know if you push the envelope too far. Now here's something I thought about last night. You have great instincts. You believed in Woody Cole when not one other person in the world did. You fought for Doug Stewart when he didn't have a chance in the world. Now your instincts tell you that if you don't step in, Billy Hopper will find himself in jail for the rest of his life. And whoever murdered that poor woman will get off scot-free. So I'm in without reservation.

"However, just because I trust your instincts when it comes to crime, women are another matter."

I deserved that.

"So if you go too far this time, if you follow lust rather than logic, you won't need to worry about any sniper." She didn't smile. Clovis looked uncomfortable. Stella just chuckled.

36

MICKI WAS A sight for sore eyes, she always is. Her plaid shirt, jeans, and cowboy boots reminded me of the first time we met. She was thinner, and her hair was a little longer and darker, but her arrival made me go flush with wonderful memories.

She gave everyone hugs, leaving me for last. Not too long ago she would have kissed me flush on the mouth, but not today. She extended her hand.

"Thanks for sending the plane. Larry now thinks a private jet is the only way to fly."

Not much of a way to greet a former lover and current friend, but if she wanted to keep it professional, I'd go along.

"Where is he? And does he know this could get dangerous?" I blurted out immediately.

She didn't flinch. "I told him, and he said he would come if for no other reason than to protect me. Right now he's somewhere at the Smithsonian, studying a special exhibit of eighteenth century furniture. He wants to learn how to duplicate some of their methods. That man loves wood." She laughed easily.

I didn't know why I felt so testy. I needed Micki, and if that meant getting Larry too, well, we'd deal with Larry. The group spent a little time catching up. It had been a while since Maggie and Micki and seen each other, and I admit it hurt when Maggie suggested that Micki and Larry join her for dinner. The food at Barker's was pretty good, but...

Micki caught me looking at my watch. "Okay, partner, now that I'm here, what's your game plan?"

"Stella will give you a run down on using the phones and computers, and Martin and Clovis will coordinate your security. In a nutshell, the plan is for me to go missing for the next two weeks, while you're out front and center representing Billy Hopper."

"Why go missing? Clovis can protect you, he always has." Micki asked.

"I want whoever sent me that warning shot to believe I'm running scared. If I'm out of the picture there's no reason for whoever to think about going after Beth, Maggie or Carol. Or you, for that matter. By the way, and I guess this sounds silly, but since I have no idea who the bad guy is, we've been calling him whoever or whomever, as grammar dictates. Does that work for you?"

She merely shrugged her shoulder, so I continued. "Clovis can't protect me while he's investigating the murder. He's got a tough enough job pretending he's on vacation while he tries to find out who really murdered the young woman."

"Seems to me you're putting off the inevitable. At some point you'll have to come out of hiding. What happens then? Two weeks isn't very long. It's taken the prosecutor over a month just to bring an indictment, and you think you can solve the crime and convince the prosecutor to drop the charges against Hopper in two weeks. You're dreaming."

I appreciated her blunt assessment. "You're absolutely right, and if either you or Larry become targets, I'll come out of hiding immediately. When I meet with Marshall tomorrow I'll tell him exactly that. I will not put you or anyone else at risk more than you already are. We'll all withdraw and turn over the defense to a seasoned criminal defense lawyer."

"Why not do that now?" Maggie asked again. She hadn't quite given up.

"My gut instinct is that when Marshall came into the picture, whoever realized I might get involved, might start asking questions. Who was the girl? If Billy didn't do it, why was she killed? Why was Billy set up? I admit to having a reputation for being a pain-in-the-ass."

"Anything more than gut instinct?" Micki asked.

"Lucy Robinson invited me to her wedding announcement party,

presumably so her husband could talk me into becoming the Lobos'
antitrust lawyer. Among the conditions of the retainer is one that
prohibits me from representing any NFL player. Our offices and
phones have been bugged, our computers hacked. Then there's the
little incident with the sniper who obviously knew I would be at Carol's
on Friday night before her other guests arrived.

Maggie asked, "Why would Red Shaw implicate his best player
in murder? I hear he's a ruthless businessman, but do you think he
would really have someone killed? And why would he hire a sniper
to scare off his brand new antitrust attorney?"

"Maggie, I honestly don't know. To complicate things further, two
days ago he changed his mind. Told me he'd been too hasty, hoped
I would represent Billy. He even released Billy's money so he could
pay his lawyer. Maybe he found out I'm a terrible criminal attorney. I
don't want to think he's involved, but I can't rule it out," I answered.

"What about your new girlfriend? She shows up out of the blue at
Lucy's party, makes a play for you, and is one of the few people who
knew you were going to be alone with her the other night. Is she on
your list of suspects?" Micki asked.

"Your points are valid. And she also works for Red Shaw. But that
bullet could easily have killed her—we were pretty close at the time.
If she'd known about the sniper, surely she would have kept her
distance."

Maggie intervened. "It's none of our business why she was so close,
but maybe she didn't know what was about to happen. You did say
that Red Shaw was a last minute guest. Maybe he came to reassure
her that the warning shot wasn't meant for her."

"I don't know why he came to the Eastern Shore, and it will be
tough to find out since I can't talk to Carol. Tough to figure out from
my monastery at Barker's."

Micki relaxed and laughed. I asked her what was so funny.

"It's hard to imagine you in a cloistered monastery with no female
companionship. Aren't there any women members?" She put her
hand over her mouth, trying to stop laughing.

I acted offended, but Clovis wasn't having it.

"You've got to admit, Jack, a case without a woman involved is inconsistent with the other cases we've worked on together." That got the whole crew to laughing.

Well, if laughing at my expense improved the atmosphere, it was worth it. Moreover, it was true.

"Okay, okay. Enough."

"How about some marching orders?" Clovis asked.

"Until I talk to Marshall, there aren't any. I need his buy-in for Micki to represent Billy before we can do anything else. Why don't you and Stella use this time to see the sights, enjoy Washington as tourists? Micki, I hope you can find Larry at the Smithsonian. The Hay-Adams is a pretty nice hotel.

"You know, Jack, when we checked in Larry was pretty intimidated. You sure we need to stay at such an expensive place? It might inhibit our sex, doing it on those expensive sheets."

I wished she hadn't said that, but at least she sounded more like the old Micki I knew.

Blushing slightly, Maggie jumped in before I could respond in kind.

"Clovis, why don't you and Stella join us all for dinner. It seems logical for all of us to go out together—and safer. Plus, if we're followed, Jack's absence will be obvious."

"Good idea. May I ask where you're going?" At least I could eat vicariously.

"I'm not quite sure. After a month of Italian food, I know Walter would prefer something different. What about that nice French bistro in Georgetown? I think it's called Bistro Francais. Not too fancy, but quite good. How does that sound to everyone?"

I groaned.

We were about to leave when Micki said, "You haven't talked about Marshall. How are you going to convince him to be a part of your plan? Once he hears about the shooting, you know he'll insist you bow out. He loves you, Jack. He's not going to let you put your life on the line."

"I'm not sure. While y'all are enjoying steak frites and trout almandine, I'll have plenty of time to figure something out."

MONDAY

April 25, 2016

37

MR. KIM SMILED. Micki Lawrence had checked into the Hay-Adams. So Marshall had given up on Patterson. He should have expected Fitzgerald to bring her in, not that Lawrence wasn't good. She was better than good, but she was predictable. Every indication was that Patterson had been scared off. He should know where Patterson was hiding by the end of the day; his tech people were monitoring all the phones. Patterson couldn't go a day without talking to his precious Maggie.

Jones and Rice had dinner with the Matthews, Micki, and her latest paramour, but Patterson was nowhere to be seen. It really looked like he'd fled the District, if not the country. It still bothered Kim that Jones was staying at the Mayflower, but Bridgeport Life regularly put their contractors up at that hotel. After all, it was only a Marriott.

New Orleans was still a problem. They were still insisting on pre-approval for hits. He didn't want risk their wrath if he went against their rules, but at the same time he didn't like telegraphing his intentions. If Patterson was really out of the picture it wouldn't matter.

*****

I ate breakfast in Barker's dining room. Fried eggs, sausage, hash browns, and biscuits that melted in your mouth even before you added butter and honey left me in a good mood. The coffee was dark and strong, and I lingered with the *Post*, knowing there wasn't much to do until Marshall and Walter arrived for lunch. For now, at least the print press had lost interest in both Billy and me.

I spent a while in the small library Barker kept for guests, fascinated by the books others had chosen to leave. Before long I sank
into an old armchair, my thoughts turning to Marshall. He was one
of four black students who had integrated Westside High the day I
started high school in Little Rock. Sam Pagano convinced us both
to try out for football, and we showed up for practice on the same
day. It soon became clear that the coach wanting nothing to do with
Marshall—a story for another time. We quickly became the gang of
four very close friends—Marshall, Sam Pagano, Woody Cole, and me.

Marshall graduated summa cum laude from Stafford State, went
to Yale Law, and got his masters in law at NYU. The four high school
friends have remained close during college and beyond, although time,
distance, and circumstances put a strain on our friendships on occasion.

At 12:30 precisely, I was informed that Marshall and Walter were
waiting for me in the main dining room.

I gave Marshall a hug, and Walter spoke. "It's been great to spend
a little time with Marshall, but I assume I've done my duty, and you
would like me to leave."

"On the contrary. If someone were watching and you left immediately, they would guess Marshall and I were meeting. No attorney-
client privilege is involved, nothing you can't tell Maggie later."

I trusted Walter Matthews, both personally and professionally,
more than anyone in the world, except perhaps his wife. I welcomed
his perspective and his advice.

"Let's order lunch and then talk."

Marshall quickly ordered a Cobb salad, hardly looking at the
menu. He was clearly nervous, not uncomfortable, but nervous.

"Something bothering you?"

"When we arrived the man at the front door said you were staying
here. I remember you said Barker's would be the perfect place to
hide. Why are you hiding, Jack?"

So much for my carefully calibrated explanation.

"Marshall, last Friday night at a friend's house on the Eastern
Shore, a sniper shot a high powered bullet within a few inches of my
head. I wasn't hurt, neither was my friend. I think whoever took the
shot was trying to warn me off representing Billy Hopper."

His brows shot up and his mouth and eyes twisted into a deep frown.

"I saw Micki in the lobby. I assume you've sent her home by now."

"No, if you agree, you are going to introduce her to Billy, and she will enter her appearance as Billy's lawyer soon thereafter."

"Why would you be willing to put her at risk, when you are clearly running scared?" That hurt, but it was exactly the conclusion I hoped others would come to.

"Because we both believe the warning shot was specific to me. Marshall, I believe Billy Hopper is innocent, and if we don't screw this up, I hope to represent him, too."

I had thoroughly confused my logical friend. I signaled for our server and asked her to bring Marshall a cold Sam Adams. He sighed in relief.

"Sit back and relax, my friend. Let me tell you how I think Micki and I can best help Billy."

I went over our plan in as much detail as I could, considering details were sorely lacking. Micki would be the public face of Billy's defense, learning what she could from the prosecutor and Billy. I would orchestrate Clovis and Stella's investigations.

I was glad to have Walter at the table; his presence provided both a buffer and a kind of affirmation. If Walter was in on the plan, I couldn't be entirely nuts. Moreover, I'd taken it for granted that Bridgeport would provide the front for Clovis and Stella, not to mention the protection and investigative help Martin and his men could provide. Fortunately, he had no problem with my assumptions.

"Whatever you need. The sooner you figure this out, the sooner I'll get my wife back, and the sooner I can quit worrying about her safety and yours." No smiles, he was dead serious.

I could tell Marshall was still bothered.

"Jack, think about it. Someone tried to shoot you. You're actually in hiding, and your family and colleagues may be in danger as well. I can't let you do this. I'm sorry I ever got you involved. It's time for me to find a different lawyer."

"I appreciate your concern, but I'm not sure hiring a different lawyer will end anything. Maybe that shot was meant for my friend Carol, or maybe it had nothing at all to do with Billy Hopper. In that case, my involvement won't change a thing. Two days ago you asked if I could sit by idly, watching as an innocent man was convicted of a crime he didn't do. Well, I can't. I listened to Billy, and I believe him. Not much makes sense so far, but that shot does. If Billy's guilty, why would someone want to warn me off?

"That sniper may go after me again regardless of who you hire. Let's make a deal. We'll all do our best for the next two weeks. I promise to shut the whole thing down if anything goes wrong. I really will drop out of sight for a while."

"I don't like it, but I know how stubborn you can be, Jack Patterson. I really don't think I have a choice, do I?"

"No, you don't."

I spent the next half-hour making sure Marshall knew the role he was to play. He was to work with Micki on Billy's defense, but under no circumstances was he to tell a soul where I was or that I was even involved, not even Grace or Billy. I knew both Micki and Stella would watch him like a hawk.

It would have been nice to linger, but I didn't want to arouse suspicion. I signed the bill and was about to rise, but Marshall had another question.

"Why are you doing this, Jack? Billy Hopper means nothing to you. Don't tell me this is about injustice. There's plenty of injustice to fight that won't get you shot."

I thought about it for a minute. What causes a man to take unreasonable risks? I hoped it wasn't ego. My friendship with Marshall? Maybe. Billy Hopper? I'd spent less than an hour with him. If I my "gut" was right, people I loved could be in real danger. Maybe I should play it safe, disappear for real, taking Carol with me.

I had tried not to think about Carol, but the box was opening. Was she real or was she a puppet of Red Shaw, or maybe some other client I didn't even know?

The brain is an amazing organ. It was less than ten seconds before I responded to Marshall.

"Well the truth is I don't like being shot at."

3 8

AFTER THEY LEFT, I wandered back into the library. Barker's boasted a nice outdoor garden and patio, but I felt less exposed, safer, in the empty library. I picked up a novel and tried to read, determined not to check my mail for at least an hour. I gave up after forty-five minutes. Stella had emailed to say Marshall was a quick study, had easily figured out the phones and computers. Micki's message said that she and Marshall were about to review both the logistics of meeting with Billy and the paperwork that would formalize her representation of Billy. Micki had been admitted to the DC bar several years ago as part of our plans to work major cases together. So far, our plan hasn't worked out, but now we were ready.

I needed to hear a voice, so I called Clovis.

"Strap on the pads, buddy, it's time for action."

"Put me in the game, coach."

We both knew the sports banter was corny, but what can I say? It was our shtick. It had gotten us through more than a few tough moments.

"I want you to focus on three things—the girl, the hotel, and Billy's past. The girl didn't just appear out of thin air. Somebody has to know who she is, has to miss her. And try to find the three girls who were at the banquet. Did they come back to the hotel? Micki will try to get the prosecutor's file, but let's face it: so far we know shit."

"Jack, if the law can't figure out who she was, we're pretty much up a creek. And how can I play tourist while I'm doing all this?"

"Use Martin's people. Walter said not to hesitate, and you know they're reliable. That reminds me—I told Carol's assistant Pat that Martin could provide him backup if he needed it. I'd like to put a couple of guys in place now. If Pat won't agree, do it anyway."

"You think she's still in danger now you've been warned off?" Clovis asked.

"No, not while I'm in hiding. But if they get wind I haven't backed off, she's a likely target."

"More than Beth?" he asked.

"Not more, but close."

I knew he was thinking I was closer to this woman than I had let on. He was right.

"The hotel—I want to know the layout, especially the floor with Billy's room. Does security have any video footage from that night? The prosecutor probably has any physical evidence, but check it out. Also, we know Billy called Marshall, 911, and hotel security that morning. Check his hotel phone records, and also ask Stella if she can find out who Billy called from his cell phone during the preceding few days."

"I've already started down that road. It's tough to do, but you'd be surprised how people like to talk in this town."

"Good," I said. "Billy's past is indeed a tough one. Ask Marshall to give you as much background as he can. Billy told me he was trying to find his birth family. It's a long shot, but they could have some bearing. That's enough for now, but remember we're already on the clock."

"Aren't you forgetting one other thing?" Clovis asked.

"Am I? What?"

"Carol Madison," he replied.

"What about her? I already told you to talk to Martin about her security."

"That's not what I'm talking about. You said, yourself, you couldn't rule out her involvement."

I knew I had to face the possibility.

"You're right. Check her out, but do me a favor."

"Anything."

"If you uncover anything that's not relevant to this case—old boy-friends, financial problems, anything personal like that–don't tell me.

I don't want to know. You have to promise me."

Clovis understood. "You have my word."

"She can never know you're doing this," I pleaded, knowing that in the end she'd find out.

"You really like this woman, don't you?"

"Yeah, Clovis. I do."

*****

I carefully returned the timeworn novel to the shelf, couldn't remember I word I'd read. I needed Maggie, but it was too risky to bring her to Barker's. So I punched in her cell number, hoping that Stella had gotten rid of any bugs.

"Maggie, do you have time to talk? I've got so much…" She didn't let me finish.

"Of course I do—you're my boss, remember?"

I laughed. "Well sometimes it doesn't… Okay, first thing: I need you to call Red Shaw. Give him the wiring instructions for our trust account. Let it slip that Micki has agreed to represent Billy. Tell him we're collecting the funds due Billy to help pay her fee."

I sensed her hesitation, but she agreed, adding, "Marshall and Micki have gone to the jail, and Stella has gone to the Hay-Adams. Apparently our office, phones, and computers are bug free now, but she says it's only a matter of time before the hackers realize they've been discovered."

"Time is our worst enemy right now. Normally we'd have a year to do what we need to do in two weeks," I said.

"I'm sorry to ask again, but why not turn everything over to another lawyer, one who'll have the time to do it right?"

"Because I'd be looking over my shoulder every time I walk down the street, worried about you, Beth, and Carol so much I couldn't do any work. I think whoever is behind this knows a lot about me, and I won't rest easy until I know just as much about him."

"Or her," Maggie pointed out.

"Or her." I kept an even tone.

"What do you want me to do while everyone else is feeding you information?"

"You and I are going to focus on Red Shaw. He's the only actual suspect I have right now. He said that Billy Hopper cost him millions. How can a rookie sensation cost an NFL owner that kind of money? He pays Hopper a rookie minimum contract, and Billy brings in thousands of fans and merchandise sales. Seems to me that Billy should have made Red a small fortune. I have to wonder if Red was gambling or betting against his own ballplayer in some kind of big stakes fantasy game."

"Even if he had, why would he set Billy up for murder? Maybe he had a different reason," Maggie responded.

"Well, maybe—I hadn't thought about that. We need to learn as much as we can about Red's past, how he came to be the owner of the Lobos, and the financial operation of the Lobos. Red gave me the name of my contact person with the Lobos, a Regina Halep. Tell her you need all the financial information on the team and any subsidiaries. You know the drill—ask the same questions you ask any new antitrust client: financials, economic analyses, and market studies. Don't ask for anything that will raise a red flag.

"And call David Dickey. Ask him to find out as much as he can about Red Shaw's companies."

David was one of Walter's favorite investment advisors. I had enjoyed his good advice many times over the years, both for the Foundation and for my own clients.

"Won't he be just a little curious?" Maggie asked.

"David never talks out of school. Besides, we have the perfect reason to call David. Remember, as of today we work on retainer for the Lobos. When you talk to Regina, ask her where we should send our first bill?"

"That's a bit cheeky, don't you think?"

"It signals that I am out of the criminal defense business and back to being an antitrust lawyer."

"What if Red or Regina ask where you are?"

"Tell them I had to go out of town on family business, but I'm keeping up through texts and email. Stella gave me a secure phone which can't be traced. I'll call them back. The more we act like its business as usual, the better off we are."

"How are you doing at Barker's?" Maggie asked.

"The accommodations are fantastic, but I really miss not being right in the middle of the action. It's no fun working through email and phone calls. I know it's only been one day, but it's going to take all I've got to stay put."

"By the way, Susan Sandler called. She's anxious to move forward with the house sale and wants to meet with you. She says word is getting out that your house is going on the market. Several agents have already called to preview."

"Tell her to send the paperwork to you."

"She says she needs to meet with you in person. Apparently she wants to show you the comps for similar homes in your neighborhood before you and she can agree on a price. Jack, she's bound to wonder what's going on—I'm glad to know she's so ethical."

"Okay—tell her fine, I'm happy to meet her at the house, but I won't be back for at least a week. And no previews of the house before we meet."

I didn't want to think about the house or Susan, but knew I would have to at some point. I'd acted quickly, almost on a whim, but I shouldn't let the pressure of the situation control my judgment. I let it go, knowing I could trust her.

"How's the press?" I asked.

"Disappeared, for the most part, thank goodness. As soon as Micki enters her appearance, I'm sure she'll get all their attention. Fortunately, the hotel will serve as a haven as long as they're inside. By the way, Rose won't buy the family business story. She knows the only family you have is Beth," Maggie warned.

"I'll tell her I'm in Memphis. She knows I have cousins in Memphis."

"You're not a very good liar, Jack. You'll tell her how nice the weather is right before she asks about the tornado." Maggie was right.

"I'll think of something."

"I'd feel better if you really were staying at the Peabody in Memphis rather than here in DC. Secrets don't last very long in this town, and you know it. If one person lets it slip you're at Barker's, the whole jig is up."

"I know that. Guess we'll have to trust in a little luck."

TUESDAY

April 26, 2016

39

I woke up Tuesday morning with a dull headache, probably the result of one more glass of cabernet than was good for me. I'd spent the rest of Monday night trying to become an expert in fantasy sports. The more I learned about fantasy, the more the integrity of the actual game seemed to be in danger. A phenomenal amount of money was being bet on the individual performances of the athletes who were supposed to be playing a team game. The potential for abuse and corruption was pretty obvious. The impact on sportsmanship, including running up the score or risking injury to pump up statistics, was subtler but just as real. Use of inside information by athletes, owners, and team employees was an obvious area of concern.

I hoped a good breakfast would take care of my hangover—as good a cure as any. I'd just had time to glance at *The Post* before my phone beeped the arrival of emails. Stella had discovered that Marshall's room was being monitored, as was his usual table in the dining room. Hotel security was most apologetic. They asked no questions and agreed to cooperate fully. I wondered if Stella might gain another client. Micki's room hadn't been bugged, much to her relief. Stella would spend the morning working with Martin on Bridgeport Life's security to further our story line. I hoped she'd have time later in the day to work on the few ideas I'd given her.

Clovis had zero luck with the Mayflower's management—they'd been told by the prosecutor not to say anything to anyone. He had been able to get a blueprint of the floor plan for Billy's floor. He hoped he would have better luck with the hotel employees. I suggested he try to find out if anything unusual had occurred at the hotel during the few days before or after the murder.

Clovis hoped Micki would soon be able to get the dead girl's autopsy and photographs. No one even vaguely fitting her description had been reported missing in the area. He'd come up with a good cover to check out the Mandarin Hotel: he and Stella were looking for a place for their wedding reception.

He had to wait on Micki and Marshall to begin the investigation of Billy's background. I didn't ask him about Carol, except to verify that Martin's men were backing up Pat. He had accepted the help, but didn't want to alarm her with the extra security. For my part, I wondered why she felt safer at the Shore than in DC. Our phones were supposed to be secure, so I thought about calling her, but my better judgment kicked in.

Maggie reported that Red Shaw had been most cordial: the money had already been wired. The money from James Stockdell had already cleared the bank. I was impressed—not many people can write a check for half a million dollars. Red was a little surprised to hear Micki had been hired, remarking, "Jack must have his reasons." He reinforced that Maggie could get anything I needed from Regina Halep. She was waiting for "Gina" to get into the Lobos' office in LA to make that call. She said Red had closed with an offer to contribute to Billy's defense fund.

After reading all the reports and responding to each with suggestions, I called Micki.

"I'm damn glad my room wasn't bugged last night. Larry and I were a little enthusiastic on these fancy sheets." Enough of their sex life, she'd made her point.

"Well good for you. I'm glad you're comfortable, but I'm not interested in the details. Let's stick to business. When do you meet with Marshall and Billy?" I asked.

"You're no fun this morning. You sure you don't want to know…"

"Micki, stop it. I'm quite sure."

"Okay, okay. I'm meeting with a deputy US attorney at one o'clock and with Billy at two-thirty. I had breakfast with Marshall this morning. He was pretty upset to learn his room had been bugged—the possibility had never occurred to him. Grace called to tell him the press had left which I could tell was a relief. He and Larry have gone to see the American History Museum and the World War II Monument. I'm glad to have them out of my hair."

"What can I do to help?" I asked.

"I'd love for you to be out front with the press. You know how irritated I get with them. In fact, I'd love to have you in charge of this whole damn thing. I still can't believe you convinced me to represent a woman killer. I'm only doing this for you, you know." She sounded serious.

"I know, and I apologize for asking you to go against your principles. But I'll challenge you the same way Marshall challenged me. If you still believe Billy did it after you've met with him, I'll find another way to do this. I respect you too much to ask you to go against your principles." I meant it.

"What happened to 'everybody is entitled to a lawyer'?" she asked.

"I believe I already asked you that same question. Don't worry; Billy can afford the very best. We can always get another lawyer," I answered.

"Then why me? You could stay in hiding and still have a damn good defense lawyer taking the lead."

I took a moment—I wanted to get this right.

"Because you're not just another lawyer. Micki, when you and I work together we are the best. All the flirtations and other baggage we bring to each other aside, when we are in the courtroom we are a formidable team. If Billy has a chance in hell, it's because we're working together. Neither of us can do this alone. We need each other, but more importantly Billy needs us. But if you don't believe in him, it won't work.

"Talk to him. Ask him hard questions. If you don't believe in his innocence, we'll both walk away."

She spoke quietly, "So you really do believe in him. And I guess in all that other stuff."

"Yes, I do."

"For the record, we were good in bed together, too." I could envision her smiling.

"Better than good," I responded.

"Larry is very good for me. Do you understand?"

I didn't, so I kept quiet. It was time to end any conversation about our past.

"You do know that some sociopaths can convince the most hardened prosecutors of their innocence?"

"Billy's not a sociopath, and the prosecutor is sure he did it," I said.

"I'll call you as soon as I've seen him this afternoon. You know I wish we could talk together in person—I miss that."

"Me, too." It was the truth, but given the conversation maybe it was best we weren't together. Maggie would call our complicated history a distraction.

I spent the rest of the morning on the phone. I called Rose, thanked her for covering for me, and managed to dodge every question she asked about where I was. Maggie later told me she suspected I was somewhere with that "Carol Madison woman," and I was embarrassed to tell her. Perfect.

I called Walter to thank him for giving me Martin's help. He wondered how long I could stand being cooped up at Barker's. We agreed to have lunch tomorrow. As a Barker's member he could come and go without drawing attention.

If time weren't such an issue, I'd feel good about the progress we had made in our first real morning, but the clock was running way too fast for my taste.

The pressure of time led me to call a man I had been forced to deal with in the Stewart case—Alexander Novak. He was an outlier, a Russian gangster who ran his own organization. I had a grudging respect for the man—without his help Micki would surely be dead.

40

NOVAK WAS PART of the Russian mafia. At one time he controlled gambling and prostitution in the South from Atlanta to Dallas. He ran his business out of Little Rock for many years, but had moved to Dallas last year. Novak claims he's gone legit, but I have my doubts. We crossed paths two years ago in Little Rock, each doing the other a favor. Micki couldn't stand him and would have my hide if she knew I was making this call.

"Alex—Jack Patterson. I hope you are well."

"Jack!" he said in surprise. "A voice from my past. I am fine. To what do I owe this pleasure?"

"I need some information." No need for niceties with Novak.

"Information doesn't usually come cheap, my friend."

"I understand. Alex, I need to know how I would go about hiring three or four attractive women for a night in DC. They'd need to be fairly intelligent, presentable in public."

"Jack, the reason for your inquiry is none of my business, but I have to admit I'm surprised."

"I'm not actually trying to hire anyone. I just want to know how I would go about doing so." I knew I sounded irritated.

"Jack, as I have said, I am no longer in the business, but I might know someone you could call. But I need more information, and I must have your word that you are not helping the government set up some type of sting operation. I am well aware of your feelings toward my former business."

I had hoped he would just give me a name, but I understood his caution. Walter and Maggie's Foundation was devoting a lot of money to organizations that try to rescue young women from sex traffickers, and I was an integral part of that effort.

"In turn, I need your word that you won't use my name without my permission or tell a soul about this conversation," I said. Caution worked both ways.

"Hmm—intriguing. You have my word." Novak may have been a crook, but I had learned that when he gave his word, he meant it.

"Micki has agreed to represent Billy Hopper." Word or no word, I couldn't reveal my own involvement directly. "He attended a banquet with three attractive women who returned to a hotel with him. Later ...."

Alex interrupted. "I've read a few news accounts, say no more. You think it is possible that the women in the limousine and the woman in his bed were not friends, but girls for hire?"

"I don't know. What I do know is that the identity of the woman found in the bed remains a mystery, even to the prosecutor. The three women at the banquet haven't surfaced either. The prosecutor could have them under wraps, but I don't think so. Billy swears he didn't know the victim, and I believe him. I think she might have been working for someone. Why else wouldn't a friend or family member have claimed the body by now?"

"There are many reasons why women disappear and many reasons why no one claims a body, reasons that have nothing to do with prostitution." Of course he was right.

"True, but if three or four of your colleague's best girls suddenly went missing, he wouldn't run to the police."

"No, particularly if he saw a picture of one of those girls in *The Washington Post.* If he were brave, he might try to go after the person who had hired them. More likely, he would have been frightened and simply disappeared," Alex said.

"Why would he have been frightened?"

"People in the business don't murder their goods. Assume for a minute that Micki's client didn't do it. I think he did, by the way, but let's assume he didn't. The person who murdered that woman could just as easily murder her protector. Why take that risk? Maybe he took the other three girls with him."

Alex's use of the word "goods" made my skin crawl. For him it was strictly business.

"Why do you think Billy did it?" Alex was a smart guy; I wanted to hear his reasoning.

"Sex can make a man crazy, even turn him into a cold-blooded, sadistic killer. Powerful men have been ruined, mild-mannered men have become violent—before, during, and afterwards. In my former business we saw this pattern many times. Billy Hopper fits the mold. He'd been drinking all night, he couldn't get it up, and he took it out on the girl. Sadly, it doesn't just happen in brothels; it happens in thousands of homes. I'm sorry, Jack. Micki's client is a poster boy for violence against women in America.

"It doesn't matter whether she was an old girlfriend or a working girl. He likely snapped when he couldn't get it up or prematurely ejaculated. The stupid girl probably ridiculed him, and he exploded. Micki's best bet is to claim temporary insanity, but I doubt that defense will play well in today's atmosphere. May I ask why you're involved?"

Of course he had seen through my subterfuge, but I kept to the game plan. "Micki asked for my help and, naturally, I agreed. She was reluctant to call you directly."

"Ah, of course. That explains your interest. I, too, would like to be of help, if I can. Perhaps I can place a few calls. May I call this number if I find anything useful?"

"Yes—we would both be most appreciative. Thank you."

Novak certainly didn't fit any mold—he was an intelligent and complicated person. During the Stewart case, we developed a level of trust I would never have imagined possible. His reaction today contained equal amounts of bluntness and finesse, insolence and civility. I knew he was right about men taking out their frustrations, sexual or otherwise, against women. I've never understood it, can't imagine such brutality. But it happens day after day, every single day.

I don't know why I thought the girls at the banquet might have been hired. Pro athletes attract women like picnics attract ants, and it was just as likely they'd bought or been given their tickets just like everyone else. Rock stars have groupies, and so do pro athletes. All the professional leagues educate their athletes on the subject. Whether those classes do any good is an open question. Another possibility was that the women came with other men at the table and helped a drunken Billy get back to the hotel. Good Samaritans, so to speak.

*****

Mr. Kim was not pleased that Patterson's whereabouts were still unknown. Patterson was not sophisticated enough to know how to go underground beyond detection, but so far he'd been successful. He did know that Patterson had gone to several ATM's in DC before he left town. Considering his appetite for good food and wine, the cash couldn't last long.

He had to believe that someone with the Matthews' companies, probably Stella Rice, had discovered his entry into Patterson's phone and computers. He was no longer getting any information, not even meaningless chatter. His technicians assured him they would gain entry again within a few days.

Jones was difficult to follow, but from all appearances he was in town as a tourist. He had even met with several hotels about a possible wedding reception. Marshall and Micki were meeting with Hopper this afternoon. He hoped to have a full report immediately after.

His thoughts went back to Patterson. If he didn't surface soon, he would have to be flushed out like a quail.

41

I DON'T KNOW why I felt so isolated. It had only been a couple of days, and I wasn't exactly marooned on a desert island. But I did—I felt all fidgety, just couldn't relax. The worst was waiting for email and phone calls from the team. What were they doing? My mind was absorbed with theories and outcomes; I could hardly think about anything else. I went down to the bar for lunch. When I saw the special was chicken and dumplings, I gave up. I knew the price would be many hours at the gym—assuming I survived.

I finished my lunch and took my laptop to an empty table in a corner. Finally, an email from Clovis.

"Logan Aerospace purchased a table for the NFL's Honors banquet for $10,000, paid an extra $15,000 to have Hopper sit at their table. Details to follow. No information on names of attendees. Ten-person table. Guests included Hopper's agent and female guest, three attractive women, four guys in suits, too young to be high-level executives. Guys bought autographed Lobos' football for $4500. Lots of alcohol served, agent passed waiter $200 to keep drinks coming. Waiter pretty sure agent's guest was not his wife. Agent occupied a suite at the Mandarin for three days, big food and alcohol tab."

I responded with some follow-up questions. I also sent Maggie a message asking her to ask David Dickey to provide a report on Logan Aerospace. We had all agreed that despite Stella's assurances of security, we should keep calls to a minimum, using email as much as possible.

Stella's email was next:

"Bastards already trying to hack into my new system. They won't get in, but they're pissing me off. Hacking is slowing down process of trying to find source, but maybe they will make a mistake."

I wouldn't want to piss Stella off.

Maggie responded to my email:

"David is on it. Says Congress is already looking into fantasy football, but NFL and NBA lobbyists and lawyers will make sure investigation goes nowhere. His company has already done an analysis. Fantasy sports are a gold mine for owners, millions they don't have to share with players or TV networks. Report will be in next delivery to your location.

Interesting development. Hopper's agent showed up at the office. Says he's here to help in any way he can."

I sent this email back to her:

"Must have gotten wind that Red paid what was due, wants his cut. Ask for a copy of his contract. Tell him Micki is representing Billy and schedule meeting between the two. Make sure Clovis talks to Micki before meeting. Need to know what he remembers about the evening, but need to tread lightly. Agent probably ripping Billy off. Don't let on that we are anything but grateful for his help."

This felt more like practicing law. But I couldn't help but be amused—our emails had begun to resemble telegraphs.

The bartender brought me another glass of iced tea. She must be new—I hadn't noticed her Saturday or Sunday. I could tell she had something on her mind and waited for her to speak.

"Mr. Patterson, this might be none of my business, but you might want to stay downstairs for a while. There's a large meeting upstairs with a lot of non-members. One of the guests was asking if any of the staff had seen you lately. We've reported him to Mr. Barker, but don't worry: no one said a word. Just as a precaution, you might want to work from down here. It should be pretty quiet."

My stomach gave a bit of a lurch. The staff is well known for its discretion—their jobs depend on it. But there was always the chance…

I wondered who was hosting the meeting, but knew better than to ask. I thanked her sincerely, adding, "What happened to Wally? I mean you're doing a great job, but … um, sorry, I don't know your name."

She was quick to respond. "It's Barb, Barb Patton. Wally's fine, but his uncle had a stroke, and I'm filling in for a couple of weeks. There's not much family left, you know." She allowed her hand brush mine as she removed the old glass.

Okay, Jack. Don't read anything into that, I scolded myself. I was here to work, not to flirt with the wait staff.

I tried a little research of my own on Logan Aerospace, a multi-billion dollar military contractor. They built components for fighter aircraft. That triggered a memory, and sure enough Chuck Morrison was in their listing of senior executives, the same Morrison who had met with Tennessee Senator Boudreaux that first weekend at Carol's.

Probably a coincidence, but intriguing nonetheless. Maybe I should call Carol to ask her about Chuck. No way, Jack. Forget about it.

I hoped to hear from Micki soon. If she didn't buy into Billy, I'd have to rethink the whole effort. I couldn't do this without her. I'd be in way over my head. I felt almost queasy knowing that someone had asked about me, here, at Barker's. Whoever was suspicious, clearly didn't think I'd left town. Maybe he was just being careful. Either way, I felt uneasy.

Maggie had been able to scan David's report on fantasy sports and email it to me.

Officially, the NFL has long held the position of opposing sports gambling, but the league has done nothing to stop individual team owners from investing in fantasy football. Fantasy sports operate under an exemption to a 2006 federal law that prohibits games like online poker, but permits fantasy sports play with respect to professional sports leagues. The games are legal in all but five states. A handful of other states are also trying to shut them down, but David speculated their efforts would be unsuccessful. Too many voters were playing fantasy sports. A move to shut it all down could be political suicide.

Fans pay entry fees to a website—anywhere from twenty-five cents to thousands of dollars—to assemble a roster of real football players with multimillion dollar prize pools that can pay millions to the winner. One site alone says it pays out over seventy-five million dollars a week and over two billion dollars in a year. No telling how much it takes in: the industry is totally unregulated. No wonder Red says fantasy football is bigger than the sports itself.

People called Red Shaw a fool for paying the NFL over two billion dollars for the new LA football franchise. If David's economic analysis was correct, the franchise would be worth at least four billion in ten years. No, Red was not a fool.

If Red was involved in setting up Billy—and the more I thought about it, the more I found it hard to believe—I had to wonder what role Lucy might have played. Lucy always had an agenda. Her engagement to Red insured big bucks for her campaign coffers. For his part, Red gained a strong ally in the Senate for his businesses and the NFL. I admit my individual prejudice wanted to think that somehow Lucy was involved, but I'd be damned if I could see how. I was lost in my imagination when my cell buzzed. It was Novak.

4²

I HADN'T EXPECTED to hear back from him so soon, if at all, so I
assumed he had bad news. As usual there were no preliminaries.

"One day I will learn to trust your instincts," he said.

"What do you mean?"

"A former colleague in the DC area is missing three girls and their
bodyguard. For obvious reasons, he does not wish to be involved in
your case, and he is pretty sure that the woman found murdered was
not one of his. But he thinks he knows who she was."

I tried to keep my voice neutral. "Does he have a name, a family,
someone who can identify her?"

"Her papers, birth certificate, and immigration documents will
be delivered to your office. She came from Bulgaria and worked
independently."

"Wait a minute—does he know who hired her that night? What
about her bodyguard and the other girls? Did she have any friends
Micki can interview?" My voice had lots its cool, and Novak laughed.

"Calm down, Jack. My former colleague wasn't involved in the
bodyguard's day-to-day operations, much less those of the dead
woman. As I said, the bodyguard has gone missing, as well as the three
other girls. My former colleague has called out the dogs to find them."

Novak's command of English was excellent, but intriguing. For
example, he always referred to a pimp as a bodyguard. Who were
the dogs?

"Can I speak with him?"

"No way. Your reputation precedes you, my friend. He thinks your client—sorry, Micki's client—probably met the dead woman at the Mayflower bar and took her upstairs where he murdered her. She worked that bar regularly—independent, classy, and expensive. He thinks the bodyguard took the other girls out of town to prevent them from getting mixed up with the police. They are probably holed up in a motel somewhere, shooting up heroin.

"He also said that unless you can prove Billy didn't kill the girl, Hopper's life in prison isn't worth a plug nickel. He's dead on arrival."

"Why?" I asked. "Prisons are full of ageing murderers."

"Men who murder professional women don't last long in prison. No one in the business can afford to have his girls murdered without reacting in kind. It is the one thing an organization offers—protection. Even though the dead woman was working on her own, the business has to respond to her murder. I could not prevent that from happening even if I wanted to."

"What if Billy didn't kill the girl? What if the bodyguard and the other girls are still in danger?"

"I told him you didn't think Billy did it. He thinks you're dreaming. But he agreed to keep an open mind about the possibility that both he and the girls are still in danger."

"If he finds the bodyguard or the other girls, may I speak with them?"

"Probably not."

"How can I prove the papers coming to my office are those of the dead girl?"

"The birthmark the press keeps talking about is actually a brand she tried unsuccessfully to have removed. The information about the attempt to remove it will be included in the same delivery."

"I take it that this information is not coming from your former colleague."

"You are correct."

It would have been unwise to press him further. For some reason Novak had taken an interest, that was enough. I wasn't quite sure why and wasn't sure I wanted to know.

"Thank you for your help. How can I repay you?"

"Jack, you have good instincts. But be very careful your instincts do not betray you. That young woman may have been a professional, but she did not deserve such a brutal end. Her murderer must be made to pay for his actions. Keep digging, and you may discover some information you will be willing to share with me. Let's just say we are both running a tab, and we will keep in touch."

I was dancing with the devil, but if it meant saving Billy's life it might be worth it. I just had to make sure that Micki didn't discover my dancing partner.

I emailed Clovis the information that the deceased was a working girl who frequented the Mayflower Bar. He could figure out my source on his own. I also told him the other three might have been for hire as well and were currently missing, along with their bodyguard. Details to follow. He called immediately.

"I'm not going to ask where you got that information. Don't let Micki find out, that's all I've got to say. Here's the question: If she frequented the Mayflower Bar why has no one come forward to identify her? The bartender had to have known her at a minimum."

"That's what you have to find out."

"Don't worry, I'm on it, but don't get too optimistic," Clovis cautioned.

"Why not? It could blow the case wide open. Somebody hired a woman to set Billy up."

"Or Billy hired her after one too many drinks at the bar." Clovis repeated the same assumption Novak had made.

"Or maybe somebody did hire her to set Billy up for blackmail or for a tabloid story, and things went terribly wrong. She might have agreed to blackmail Billy after a night of sex, but I doubt if she agreed to be murdered. You still have Billy in bed with a murdered woman. It's just as much a crime to murder a hooker as a cheerleader." Clovis rightfully admonished me.

Of course, he was right. I had fallen into that trap of presuming a call girl asked for whatever she received. I had learned during the Stewart case how often working girls were victims of terrible abuse. I ought to have my butt kicked.

"Let's assume all the girls were hired to set Billy up," Clovis continued. "Maybe to get him kicked out of football, or to blackmail him or the Lobos, or a million other possibilities. So far nothing explains why or how that girl came to be found dead in Billy's bed. No self-respecting pimp is going to let one of his girls get killed, no matter how much he is paid. I'm afraid the news that she was a working girl at the Mayflower Bar only makes it worse for Billy, not better."

So much for any optimism.

"Nevertheless, let's find out all we can about who she was. I'll have a name pretty soon. And you're right, why has no one come forward to identify her? The Mayflower Bar is a classy place; a lady of the evening had to stand out." I said.

"She probably dressed carefully and wore a wig. Don't be fooled, Jack: classy bars are where girls find the best customers."

Clovis changed subjects.

"I'll have a full report to you tonight on the Mandarin visit. Seems that Billy's agent had a high old time over the weekend. I'm running down his girlfriend. She works on the Hill, so she'll be easy to find. Turns out the four corporate types went to the bar after the banquet and continued to drink. I'll have their names tomorrow. The bartender says three women joined them later, and they almost closed the bar down. They could be the same three. Wouldn't that be interesting?"

"Yup, most certainly would be."

My mind was racing, and I fed Clovis a list of things to find out, even though I knew he was probably two steps ahead of me, listening just to humor me. I closed my instructions with one last one.

"Be sure to tell Micki what you discovered."

"Micki isn't back yet, but I will when she arrives. We're having dinner tonight at Johnny's. It's better than meeting every afternoon at the office. It would look too much like I was working for her."

"Good thinking." I said, and hung up thinking that Micki should have been back from the jail by now. A chill went up my back.

Where was Micki?

43

{ornamental divider}

IT WASN'T THAT late for Micki not to have checked in, but Micki had gone missing once before, and it hadn't ended well. Naturally I was a little nervous. I also was curious to know if I had a partner or not. I resisted the urge to call—no news was probably good news.

While I waited on her, I gave myself a little lecture. In the Stewart case, I had learned more than I wanted to know about sex trafficking in America. Walter and Maggie's Foundation spends a great deal of money funding non-profits which are dedicated to education, prevention, and helping the victims of this national tragedy. How could I have just assumed these women were trying to frame Billy? They were probably victims of someone else's plot, pawns controlled by some master using heroin and fear to ensure their cooperation. If I needed any further evidence of this, the woman's body in Billy's bed was proof enough.

I also had to curb my enthusiasm about the woman's identity and occupation. If she had been working the Mayflower, the logical conclusion was that she and Billy met in the bar and headed upstairs. Her occupation in fact would probably work against Billy. Everyone would presume he had been sexually frustrated or they had argued about her fee and he lost it. The prosecutor would have a field day with me if I argued she was there to frame Billy.

The phone buzzed again. I was relieved to recognize Micki's number. She didn't waste any time.

"I just talked to Clovis, and you tell Novak I still think he's pond scum."

"He told you I talked to Novak?"

"No, he told me he didn't know your source, but I'm no fool. Where else would you find what you did about the victim?" She didn't sound that angry.

"So go ahead and get the lecture out of the way." I was ready to take a verbal beating. Good thing this was a phone call.

"What are you talking about? I don't care who you talk to as long as you get the information you need. Your source is questionable and an asshole, but we can't bother with niceties if we're going to save Billy from a life in prison or worse. Frankly, Jack, I don't think he'll last a week in prison before someone kills him."

"That's what Novak said," I reported.

"I hate to agree with him on anything, but this time he's right."

"I take it we're partners once again?" I asked.

I could feel her smiling into the phone. "Of course. You knew once I met the prosecutor, talked to Marshall, and met with Hopper I couldn't walk away."

"Tell me about it." I was tickled pink to have her back.

"First, the prosecutor, Constance Montgomery, is one cool customer. She said all the right things, agreed to turn over her entire file immediately, but you and I both know that won't happen. She'll give me her file, all right, but not all of what she has. She'll be free to leak the remaining info however she likes, piece by piece. Since she's given me her file, she can claim to a Judge that I must be the source of any leaks. Meanwhile, the press prints her leaks day by day, piece by piece, tainting the jury pool before even one juror is called to the box."

"I'll try to find out what I can about her. I have to admit I was impressed the one time I met her; she seemed very confident. Her confidence shook Marshall."

"You were impressed with her legs." Micki was back to her old self.

She did have good legs, I admit. But as Micki once said about my friend Sam Pagano after he was elected prosecutor, "He's a prosecutor now, and a girl has to have some standards." I felt the same way about female prosecutors, with a few exceptions.

"Marshall gave me everything I think you already know regarding

Billy's background and lack of family. Just in case he left something out I'll send everything over after I write it up in the morning. I don't think it will be of much use. Too bad—the violence and abuse Billy endured during his childhood will work against him. What a tough story!"

I wanted to ask her if Billy had told her what he had learned about his real family, but I didn't want to break her train of thought.

"Billy was everything you and Marshall represented him to be. If it weren't for his fingerprints all over the knife, the girl beside him in the bed when he woke up, and the doors locked from the inside, I'd say we might have a chance because he comes across as honest and innocent."

"Doors locked on the inside?"

"A little nugget from Constance in our 'candid' conversation."

"That's not good." I responded. Then it occurred to me that all hotel doors lock when you leave the room. We needed some clarification on this.

"No, nor is the fact that Billy doesn't remember a thing despite no evidence of drugs in his system."

"Another nugget from Constance." I asked.

"Yes, and there's one more—his semen."

"What semen?" I asked.

"Billy's semen. It was found on the sheets and on the girl's legs, but none was found in her vagina. Constance said it was a sign that Billy had prematurely ejaculated. Apparently the autopsy found no evidence she and Billy had intercourse, at least as it is commonly understood."

"None of this works to Billy's advantage." I said.

"Yeah, and now that she's given me these tidbits, I bet the damaging details will be in the media in the next couple of days, if not tonight."

"I won't bet against that." Prosecutors hold all the cards in dealing with the media during a high profile case. I wouldn't be surprised if they held seminars on how to manipulate the press.

"With all the bad news, what convinced you to represent Billy? Nothing you learned today points to his innocence." I didn't want to talk her out of representing Billy, but I was curious.

"True, I didn't hear a thing today that makes me think Hopper isn't a Ted Bundy. The only thing he has going for him is that both you and Marshall firmly believe in his innocence. I can understand Marshall, he's Billy's surrogate father. He has to believe in Billy. It's you I had to figure out."

"And what did you conclude?" I asked.

"It's what you taught me before. It's too perfect. Airtight. All the clues point to Hopper; not one thing is out of place. There has to be something in the physical evidence we're missing. We have to find the loose end." She had learned, and I smiled.

"Exactly."

"What's next, partner?"

"You go to dinner with Clovis and Stella—get a full report on their day. Make sure Maggie's in the loop as well. I've got lots to read and even more to think about. Let's both get a good night's sleep and be ready to hit the ground running tomorrow morning. Hopefully, I'll have come up with a working game plan by then."

"Wish you could join us," she said.

"Me, too, but Barker's makes a pretty good crab cake. It's not Johnny's, but it'll do."

"If I know you I bet there is a long shower in your future." Micki knew a great deal about my shower thoughts.

"It's a possibility, but it's not the same when I'm by myself," I shot back.

She laughed. "Goodnight, Jack."

Larry was a lucky man.

WEDNESDAY

April 27, 2016

44

THE NEXT MORNING, I actually took advantage of the exercise room at Barker's. I had a lot of energy to work off. I built up a sweat using the rowing machine, elliptical, and stationary bicycle and enjoyed the luxury of the shower attached to the gym. I thought about relaxing in the large hot tub, but I still had my sights on someone else's tub and companionship. A bunch of sweaty guys was not what I had in mind.

I say the luxury of a gym shower and I mean it. My attitude comes from many years of playing sports, especially baseball. Lingering in a high-pressure, hot shower after an exhausting practice—it didn't get much better, and had become the origin of my "shower thoughts."

Over a breakfast omelet, I thought about the upcoming day. Micki was going to enter her appearance as counsel to Billy Hopper. Last night I had emailed her a list of questions I thought the press might ask. I had additional thoughts for Clovis, Maggie, and Stella, and I'd called each of them, taking care not to get them so busy that whoever got suspicious.

Walter was coming to Barker's for lunch, and I looked forward to his company. Barb the bartender was cute, but becoming a bit too friendly. Hopefully, I would receive the packages from Novak this morning. It was a huge relief that Micki didn't mind my reaching out to him. Well, maybe "didn't mind" was a bit too strong.

Except for the loneliness, staying at Barker's wasn't such a bad deal. Maybe I should go ahead and sell my house, live permanently at Barker's like those old clubmen in England. Then again Carol couldn't drop in with pizza and watch a ball game, and where would

Beth stay when she came home. I decided to give Susan a call today and ask her to send me some information on what might be available inside the beltway.

I called Maggie first.

"Miss me?" I asked.

"Not really. Without you, the press are no longer interested, a nice change of pace."

"Don't expect that to last. Micki will be grilled this morning. Once they find out she's working out of our offices, they'll be back."

"They don't normally camp out in front of lawyer's offices."

"I hope you're right, but you can't count on it. I'm not as worried about the press as someone catching on that Clovis and Stella are coming by every day. I hope they are being careful."

"Oh, they are. In fact, I have no idea how they are getting in the building. They go in and out without leaving a trace. It's driving Rose crazy."

"Speaking of Rose, the phones are likely to ring off the walls after Micki enters her appearance this morning," I warned.

"I've already warned her and told her to simply transfer them to me. I'm pretty sure she'd quit if I weren't here," she laughed.

"If you weren't there, I'd quit," I responded.

"That's tempting."

I ignored her. "Have we received anything from Gina with the Lobos?"

"Yes, we spoke by phone yesterday. She was very pleasant and most cooperative. It will take her a few days to get all the information together. I told her it would be fine to send it in stages. The first package should arrive this afternoon, and I'll get it to Barker's."

"Take care my name isn't on the package. And did you ask her about billing?" I thought she would balk at paying us before we did any work.

"Don't worry—no identifying marks! And she beat me to it. She asked for wiring instructions for the first quarter's retainer. The first three months fee hit our account this morning. Quite a refreshing reaction from a new client."

Surely she wouldn't have been so cooperative if Red was part of the plot. Nothing added up.

Maggie told me that Micki had just texted that she had entered
her appearance with no problems and would hold a brief press conference at ten a.m. Apparently it would be covered live on ESPN. I
snickered at the reality of a sports network covering a high profile
criminal case. On further consideration, I realized they do it all the
time. Sports figures were celebrities, and ESPN covered their sins and
misdeeds both on an off the field. I went back to my room to watch,
saying a silent prayer that Micki had read the questions I sent over.

"Ms. Lawrence, isn't a bit unusual for an Arkansas lawyer to be
hired to represent a sports figure like Billy Hopper? What is your
connection to the accused?"

I had to admit Micki looked fantastic in a royal blue jacket and
slim skirt.

"Mr. Hopper is very close to Little Rock's Fitzgerald family. Judge
Fitzgerald asked me to come to DC and meet with the accused. I met
with him yesterday, and as a result, I am now his counsel. I entered
my appearance today and met with the lead prosecutor yesterday."

"What happened to Jack Patterson? He met with Billy and led us
to believe he would represent the accused. You usually work together.
Is he going to be involved?"

This was the delicate question I worried about. Micki shouldn't
lie to the press. At the same time she needed to convince whomever
that I was not working with her.

"I understand that Jack did meet with the accused last week as an
accommodation to Judge Fitzgerald. You are right that we worked
on two cases together in Arkansas, and we remain friends. But as you
know his practice in DC is limited to antitrust law. He has been kind
enough to offer me office space during this case, but he is dealing
with a family matter and has a full caseload at the moment."

I shouldn't have worried. Perfect. Now hopefully they would let
follow up questions drop. I gave a little sigh of relief as the reporters
turned to the case at hand.

"Are you going for temporary insanity?" came the next question.

Micki flashed a smile and began in her best southern accent.

"Listen people, y'all don't know me. I practice criminal law every
day in Little Rock and have one unbendable rule. I don't talk about

any case with the press until the case is over, and usually not even then. If I were representing any one of you, that's the way you'd want it. You can ask me questions about my strategy till the cows come home, but I won't break that rule."

"Billy Hopper was found in his room with a brutally murdered woman in his bed. The door was locked from the inside. How do you defend that?"

Good question, and I worried that Micki's temper might flare at the leak by the prosecutor's office of the detail of the locked door. I shouldn't have worried.

"As I said, I don't talk about the details of any case with the press. I save my answers for the courtroom. But I would like to say something about the information you just casually threw out."

The reporter shrugged, signaling to go ahead.

"Here in DC, people leak information 'off the record' and 'on the condition of anonymity' every single day. It's become such common practice that reporters take such information as gospel, never questioning why someone isn't willing to stand behind their own words.

"You seem to be a professional, so I assume you have independently verified the information you were given. But to others who aren't so diligent, I caution you to do your homework before you go about reporting information from confidential sources. It might save you from looking, shall we say, unprofessional."

The reporter had been called to task, and Micki had at least planted a seed of doubt in the other reporters' minds. They should have left well enough alone, but a guy from the *Post* immediately called out.

"Are you saying that the room wasn't locked from the inside and the prosecutor's office was wrong to put forth that detail?"

Micki paused and stared down the reporter for a minute. The questioner was starting to fidget, when Micki turned on the charm again.

"You know I've been on this case officially for less than an hour. If the prosecutor leaked the information as you suggest, whether it is right or wrong is a question for her, not me. I have no independent verification of your source, so I'm not inclined to worry much about it."

Micki paused and then continued.

"Here's what I will say. I don't leak details of a case. Once I assemble a team, they won't either—if they do, they'll be fired, that simple. We will present our case in a court of law, not in the press," she said with emphasis and then softened.

"Sorry to disappoint, folks—it's just the way I roll." She turned and walked away.

Micki had been impressive without saying much of anything. If I were Constance Montgomery I'd be pissed. Someone in her office had leaked the fact that the door had been locked from the inside, and in order to confirm their story, the reporters had betrayed their source.

I waited to give Micki time to get away and then called.

"You're a natural. Why were you nervous?"

"Thanks, it was your list of twenty questions that made me nervous," she replied.

"Constance Montgomery has to be upset. The reporter fingered her for the leak."

She brought me back to earth. "I'd feel better if we had a good explanation for how the doors got locked."

"I agree, but as you said, you've only been on the case for an hour. We'll deal with the locks later."

"Yes, and my partner is holed up in a hotel watching TV. I don't need a TV critic, I need facts." She was definitely on the case and on mine.

45

Mr. Kim was getting nervous. His people had yet to discover Patterson's whereabouts. Lawrence's performance with the press had been flawless; maybe he needed to revaluate his opinion of her. Jones and Rice were still acting like starry-eyed lovers when she wasn't working for Matthews, but she had proven a worthy advisory to his hacker. The information flow coming from Patterson's office had never been this low. To top it off, his listening devices at the Hay-Adams had been discovered.

He had finally gotten someone into Barker's, but even that had proved to be useless. No one had seen Patterson. The case against Hopper was still airtight, and the client was happy, but Kim still worried where Patterson might be. Perhaps the time had come to act.

*****

Walter walked into the dining room, and I breathed a sigh of relief. I wished we were meeting at Columbia for a round of golf and the nineteenth hole. Good friends like Walter and Maggie make up for a lot of the sucker punches life brings. Goodness knows I needed the company of a friend.

He gave my hand a warm shake. "We need to get you out of here. It's just been three days, and you're already turning pale."

"And a whole lot heavier," I laughed. "The skin color will return as soon as we hit the golf course. I'm not sure about the pounds."

"If you don't return soon, we may need to get a new addition to our foursome," he kidded.

"Don't think I'm not worried. The stir crazies are setting in."

Walter sat down and said seriously, "I've never seen you quite like this. You really are worried this time, aren't you?"

I nodded my head. "A bullet whizzing within inches of your head will do that. I'm even more worried about Beth and Maggie. My love and concern for them is well known."

"And now, Carol?" he asked.

"Yes, and now Carol, but don't tell Maggie."

"She already knows. She can read you like a book," he smiled.

"Let's order." On cue Barb sidled up to the table, put her hand on my shoulder and said with a flirt, "What can I get you, Jack?"

Walter raised his eyebrow, but said nothing. I wondered why she was working the dining room. We both ordered, ignoring her smiles. She left looking a little crestfallen.

"What do you know about Red Shaw?" I asked Walter.

I knew Maggie had told him the Lobos were a new client. Maggie knew she could share whatever she learned at the office with her husband. It was a violation of the attorney-client privilege, but I was realistic about conversations between husbands and wives, and besides I'd trust Walter to go to the grave with anything Maggie told him.

"I've never had any personal dealings with him, except when he was putting together his syndicate to purchase the Lobos. Everything I've heard is that he's a straight shooter, makes money for his investors, and is as honest as the day is long. He's a little rough around the edges, but that's to be expected. As I remember, he grew up somewhere in the middle of rural Texas."

"So you almost invested in the Lobos?"

"Came very close," he said.

"What caused you to back out? According to David Dickey, it's a gold mine." I really was interested.

"It wasn't anything to do with Red or the deal. It's player safety, the brain injuries. A report was released last year about football players and what they call CTE, chronic traumatic encephalopathy. The study said that ninety-six percent of now deceased players in the study tested positive for CTE. The NFL is doing what it can to reduce concussions and develop better equipment, and the ball players are at least aware of the risk and are paid well. But for some players the price to pay for fleeting glory is still tragic."

"If it isn't the NFL, what bothers you?"

"It's high school and college ball, the farm system for pro football. This study determined that the incidence of CTE for college athletes isn't much less than those who play in the pros. These are kids who don't make a penny. They get a questionable education in exchange for a shot at the big time—the NFL. Fewer than two percent of the ball players are ever drafted, many of them never actually play a down. At some point the colleges and high schools are going to get nervous about their liability for destroying kids' brains to fatten their endowments, and start shutting down programs. I'm surprised it hasn't already happened." Walter was always a straight shooter.

"Well– but don't you think some of them play because they enjoy the game? Baseball was my real game, but I played football for a while in high school. Nobody made me play—it was fun. Girls could never understand getting hit and falling down over and over, but, I don't know, it was just fun.

"And don't forget sports is the only way some of these kids can ever go to any college." I don't know why I felt the need to defend the game. I hoped it wasn't the result of my new position with the Lobos.

"All true, Jack. And I think most folks would agree with you. I enjoy watching the game as much as anyone, especially the pageantry of the college game. But the fact remains that if you had played college ball, odds are that you would have sustained an injury that you'd still be dealing with today. I don't see how schools will be able to afford the liability now that the risk of permanent injury is so well documented.

"Don't get me wrong. It would be fun to be an owner of an NFL franchise, as well as a good investment. I talked to Red about the concerns I have, and privately he has similar concerns. I believed him when he said he is doing everything he can to reform tackling techniques, improve equipment, and reduce helmet-to-helmet collisions. But in the end I turned him down. All the efforts in the world can't change the game itself."

"So what's the answer?"

"I think we'll see changes sooner rather than later. As insurance companies become more concerned, liability insurance premiums will begin go through the roof. High school sports will be the first to be affected. At some point neither public nor private high schools will be able to afford the insurance premiums for football programs. It won't happen overnight—there's too much money at both the college and pro level for the game to go quietly into the night.

"In my business—life insurance—we're beginning to have underwriting discussions about premiums associated with former ball players. We already ask if the potential insured is a former smoker or has a family history of heart disease. I suspect it won't be too long before we start asking about whether he played football and for how long. When that happens the NFL is going to cry foul, but it will be forced to do more especially when the public-at-large understands that former ball players have a significantly reduced life span."

"I hadn't really thought about the insurance ramifications. Do you know anything about Red's other businesses? Government contracting, for example?"

"I checked him out pretty thoroughly. He makes most of money cleaning up other people's messes—airplanes that don't fly, boats that don't float, and tanks that fall apart. There are plenty of all three. I have a report I can give you if it would be helpful, but I'll tell you it doesn't contain a lot of negatives.

"He's made his share of enemies. Most government contractors make their fortunes through change orders and by taking advantage of delays in decision-making. If the government can contract with Red to fix a problem rather than being stuck with the original contractor, then that contractor loses a lot of his money."

"Anybody in particular?" I asked.

"I remember one pretty well–Logan Aerospace. Red has been called in to clean up a lot of their mistakes."

46

LOGAN AEROSPACE—THE SPONSORS of the table at the NFL Honors banquet who paid extra for Billy Hopper to sit with their four young executives. I don't believe in coincidences. Walter said he would send me the report that afternoon. I was tempted to call Red about Logan, but he was still a suspect, and I sure didn't want to blow my cover.

Both our moods and conversation lightened when our food arrived. He treated me to some good stories about their trip to Italy. I had hoped we'd have time to talk about Carol, but he grew pensive over coffee, idly playing with the sugar spoon. Finally he said, "You've been in danger before, Jack, but I worry that at some point your luck is going to run out. Micki is a good enough lawyer to represent Hopper. If you think you're in real danger, I think this time you should consider walking away. This isn't about Maggie, it's about you. It's time you learned there are times to walk away."

We both rose and shook hands, no smiles this time. He had made a good point, and I had no good response. Maybe he was right.

The dining room was almost empty, so I sat alone for a few minutes before calling Maggie to remind her to get a report on Logan Aerospace from Dickey. She replied somewhat tartly that she had already asked, but couldn't make it appear like magic. Stella was still at Walter's office cleaning up their computers; Clovis had dropped by for only a few minutes for a cup of coffee. She had no idea where he was going. Micki was back at the jail with Billy. She added that she had just sent several packages to Barker's, and not to worry because Martin's men were being careful with deliveries.

Almost as soon as I got off the phone three packages of documents were brought to me by one of the bellmen. I carried them to my room—time for some serious work. The first package I opened was the one from Novak. It consisted of one small manila folder that had seen better days and a second folder that seemed more current. The tab on the outside of the first contained a single name, "Nadia." Inside the folder I found a Bulgarian passport and other immigration documents for one fifteen-year-old girl named Nadia Nikolov. One of the documents written in a language I assumed was Bulgarian contained her fingerprints. The only photograph of her was the one in her passport. Nadia had entered the country in 2001, just before September 11th.

The second file was also labeled "Nadia," and it contained a treasure trove of information. He found a copy of her Virginia driver's license issued in 2015 that revealed both a picture of her face and a residence address on Chain Bridge Road in McLean, Virginia. The name on the driver's license was Carla Diaz. The file also included several professionally taken photographs of Carla. There was no doubt that the woman found in Billy's bed was Carla/Nadia Diaz. The file also contained other photographs of Carla that appeared to have been taken without her knowledge—photographs of her exiting a condominium, at a bar talking to a man, of her getting into a limousine.

The pictures seemed to be in sequence, rather like someone was keeping tabs on her, nothing pornographic. Her confirmed age came as a surprise—according to the license she was almost thirty years old rather than the early twenties reported by the press. Something was amiss here—either her license or the coroner's determination was inaccurate. She certainly wore nice clothes, and the file had a car registration for a 2012 Mercedes. Clovis and Stella had their work cut out for them.

Micki informed me through email that any information we obtained about the deceased was considered our work product; we weren't required to give it to the prosecutor. I felt a stab of conscience—surely Nadia had a family somewhere who would be worried about her. Then again, our duty lay with Billy.

I texted Micki to ask when we would get the autopsy report. I also texted Novak a very brief thank you. I didn't want to know how or from whom he had obtained the files. I was more concerned about what he would expect in return.

The second file also held copies of Nadia's medical records regarding her attempt to have the brand removed. I didn't recognize the name of the surgeon. I made a mental note to check him out with my friend Jim French, a local plastic surgeon. I wondered why neither the surgeon nor any of his staff hadn't already notified the authorities. Surely murder takes precedence over HIPPA.

I tried to call Clovis to tell him about the latest developments, but he didn't pick up. So I dove into the first batch of information on the Lobos. For a while, I felt like an antitrust lawyer. I reviewed the team's financial projections, profit and loss statements, as well as their organizational chart. An NFL Team is comprised of a lot more than just the coaches and players on the field; both income and expenses came from multiple sources. I was about to open the collective bargaining agreement between the player's union and the owners, when I remembered that I still hadn't heard from Clovis.

I punched in his number, but again got voicemail. I called Maggie, who hadn't heard from him either. I felt a twinge of unease. Clovis and I work well together—I respect his judgment and intuition, and he always has my back. More than that, we're friends. I knew my unease was premature and tried to put it out of my mind.

I returned to the collective bargaining agreement, but couldn't concentrate; my thoughts turned to Nadia. Clearly she had broken away from her original handlers, who had branded her and taken her immigration papers.

She seemed to have freed herself from bondage, yet she had stayed in the business. Very few women were able to earn a living without the protection of a pimp.

My phone finally vibrated—Clovis, thank goodness.

"Where've you been? I was beginning to think you'd been kidnapped or something."

No answer. "Sorry, Clovis, I was only kidding."

"I know you were—I just can't believe you said it."

"No—sorry, I really was concerned." This conversation was taking a strange turn.

"You sitting down?" He asked.

Something wasn't right. "What's happened? Tell me."

"Someone tried to snatch Carol Madison."

47

I ASKED THE only question that mattered.

"Is she safe? Is she okay?"

"She is safe, and she will be okay. She tried to fight her attackers, and they roughed her up. She's pretty bruised, gonna have a shiner for sure. A local doctor is checking her out, but I'm pretty sure she'll be fine."

I took a deep breath, willing myself to remain calm. "Tell me what happened."

"Whoever must have staked out her place at the Eastern Shore for a couple of days. Pat had gone into town for groceries when they stormed the complex. Carol was outside by the pool."

"How many?"

"Two guys and the driver, all wearing camouflage stocking masks. There was probably a spotter in the woods, as well. Carol heard the sound of a strange car coming up the driveway. She tried to call for help, but they were on her too quickly. She fought hard, but there wasn't much she could do. They had wrestled her halfway to the car when Martin's men arrived and broke things up. They got the two attackers, but the driver sped off at the first sign of danger, probably the spotter too. In the confusion, Carol managed to get back into her house. Martin's guys found her hiding in the wine closet, cold and beat up, but alive."

"Anyone else hurt?" I couldn't talk about Carol just yet.

"Well, Pat got back from town in the middle of the fracas and went after one of the bad guys. Gave him at least a broken nose before Martin's men rescued him."

"Good for him. And it sounds like Martin's men did a good job."

"They did. Martin called me as soon as he learned what had happened, and we drove up together to help. I guess the local authorities don't get too many attempted kidnappings in their back yard. I was afraid the Feds would already be on the scene, but Carol had already brushed them off."

"I don't understand. What…"

"Apparently she knows the local sheriff. She asked him to change the charges to assault and battery in order to avoid the Feds."

I sat drumming my fingers against the top of the table. The more I thought about it, keeping the Feds out was the right thing to do. But Carol—how could I help from here?

Clovis let me stew for a few minutes before continuing. "Calm down, Jack. I know you. You're trying to figure out how to get your ass up here. After meeting Carol, I can understand why. She is one cool customer and really easy on the eyes. But she gave me a message for you, so hear me out before you go off half-cocked.

"Carol told the sheriff she was leaving the country 'for a vacation,' and didn't want to get bogged down in some long and complex investigation. The sheriff got the picture and told her she ought to hurry.

"The bad guys won't talk and have demanded access to their lawyer. They clearly already had one on board. The sheriff is looking for the driver, but I bet he's long gone. We're not going to get anything out of these guys." I had to agree. I told him to let me know who the lawyer was.

"Carol says she'll leave as soon as she gets medically cleared and can get packed. She says you'll think you know where she is going. Is that right?"

"Bali. She was telling me where to find her."

"She also said you shouldn't even think about coming until your work is completed. Apparently, during the scuffle by the pool, one of the men referred to her as 'bait.' She thinks, and so do I, that they were going to kidnap her so you would come out of hiding. She said that only Pat will know exactly where she is and how to reach her, and that you aren't welcome until this business is finished."

I wasn't happy with that, and was becoming more inclined to go after her before she left town. Clovis continued before I could react.

"Listen to me, friend. Carol seems to know you pretty well. Listen to what she said. 'Please tell Jack to stay in hiding. Someone is convinced that Jack is going to upset his or her plans. I don't know who or why, but that someone is not going to stop until Jack is out of the picture. I know people, I work with people who are ruthless in business dealings, and I believe this someone will stop at nothing. No one, not me, not Jack, not anyone he cares about is safe until Jack finishes this business one way or the other.'"

"Is that it?" I asked.

"No."

"Well, go on," I said, frustrated.

"Okay, but I'm not sure what it means. She said she'd found a place better than Bali, someplace with a very private pool. That make sense to you?"

Clovis could probably hear me smile.

"Jack, you found a gem in that one. Don't let them scare you away, but we need to be smart about this."

"First thing, let's get Beth out of New Orleans for the next week or so. It won't be easy, but I sure don't want her to be next."

"Already in the works. The Matthews plane is on its way to pick her up. Paul will come with her. Maggie has asked them to stay at her house. It will be both easier and safer than having her at your place. And I can sure use Paul here in DC."

"I wish I could figure out a way to get you into Barker's. I've tracked down some info on both the dead woman and Logan Aerospace. I thought about asking Walter to bring you to lunch, but it's just too risky." My mind was churning.

Clovis said, "Not to worry–I'll knock on your door around 11 o'clock tomorrow morning. I promise no one will see me go in or out. I'd come out right now, but I need to help Martin clean up here and get Carol back to DC so she can leave town. Can you get the kitchen to bring us some sandwiches?"

"Yeah, I think I can arrange that. Won't be as good as Ben's barbecue, but it'll do. The food here is actually pretty good. Thanks, Clovis."

*****

Mr. Kim threw his cell phone across the room, totally frustrated. How in the hell had his men been arrested, the kidnapping foiled, and Patterson still nowhere to be found? He'd sent a lawyer to the Eastern Shore to make sure the men made bail and disappeared. The Feds hadn't been called in yet, but he worried it was only a matter of time. The driver and spotter were on their way to Central America, but the two who had been captured wouldn't be so fortunate. Failure couldn't be tolerated.

Maybe he should just accept that Patterson was out of the picture and move on. But where could he be? As far as he could tell the man hadn't used a single credit card in the last three days. Nobody can go anywhere without using a credit card. He couldn't have just disappeared. The sniper was bound to know Patterson's whereabouts, but he didn't want to risk the gunman's cover by attempting to make contact.

Patterson had got the best of him twice before. Why take chances? He placed a phone call to New Orleans. Syndicate or no syndicate, if Patterson had an Achilles heel it was his daughter. Her funeral would bring Patterson out into the open.

THURSDAY

April 28, 2016

48

AFTER A NIGHT of bizarre dreams and little sleep, I decided to reward myself with a breakfast of oatmeal-banana pancakes with a side of bacon. No paper this morning, just thoughts. Of course, I wished I could see Beth, but there was no way she could come to Barker's. Clovis had made the right decision to have her stay at Maggie's. She could also help Maggie and Micki. Maggie's car had deeply tinted windows, and her driver always let her off in the parking garage, so I wasn't too worried Beth would be seen. The loss of freedom would be hard on her, but surely it wouldn't last longer than a week.

The little library was deserted, so I sunk into an old chair and called Micki. She was already at the office, and Maggie and Beth were on the way in. I cut right to the chase.

"I know who the dead woman is. Her name is Nadia Nikolov, about thirty years old—she worked independently."

I didn't want to call her a hooker, or a prostitute, or worse. Most of the women who sold their bodies were victims, refugees from another life.

"It appears she was branded when she entered the country, but recently tried to have it removed. I'll give Clovis the medical record today. He'll check out her home, see the doctor, talk to neighbors, all the usual stuff."

"Jack, let me handle this. You're trying to orchestrate everything and whoever is going to figure it out. Give Clovis the files you got from Novak and we'll run with it. You've got enough on your plate and I know you must be worried sick about Carol Madison—I'm sorry."

I appreciated her sympathy and told her so, but I didn't like turning anything over, not that I didn't trust Micki or Clovis. Delegation never came easy for me.

"Okay, but there's more—I have a new suspect. The company that bought the table where Billy sat at the NFL Honors banquet is Red's competitor, Logan Aerospace. Maggie has asked David Dickey to look into the company and its financials. One of their executives is Chuck Morrison, a guy I met that first weekend at Carol's. He was lobbying Senator Boudreaux from Tennessee pretty hard. Something about fighters and drones."

"Hard to believe a government contractor would care about Billy Hopper or the future of the Lobos, but it's an interesting development. You sure you aren't just seeing suspects around every corner? Lots of corporations give money to attend banquets like the NFL Honors."

I had to agree. "You're probably right. Still, why buy a table at the dinner, pay extra to have Billy at your table, and then send low level management with a company credit card? Doesn't make sense. Besides, when I talked to Billy he said one of the guys at the table said his boss lost a lot of money because Billy busted one of his fantasy pools."

"Let me look into that one, too. It makes sense for Billy's lawyer to check out everyone who was at the banquet that night. It shouldn't raise any red flags with whomever. But, corporate executives don't set up athletes for murder because they lost money on fantasy sports. That theory is more than a little far-fetched."

"I know it is, but it's all I've got right now. Look, just be careful." I was suddenly worried.

"Don't I always have to be careful when we're partners? It's the price of working with your fantastic ass." Micki and Larry must have had a good night.

"I thought flirting was off-limits?"

"That rule applies only to you. My flirting is the price of my coming on board."

"And I'm not supposed to reciprocate?" I asked.

"Correct. And let's not forget about Carol."

Time to get back to work.

"What did you learn from Billy about his family's background?"

"He tried to hire a private investigator. He'd received a couple of anonymous notes from Bibb, Tennessee while he was playing ball saying the family was real proud of him."

"Does he still have a copy of those notes?" This could be a real breakthrough.

"No. That's the confusing part. He gave them to his agent who hired the investigator. The agent gave this guy the notes and five thousand dollars, didn't think to make copies. The man promptly disappeared, and neither Billy nor the agent can find him."

"Billy's agent seems to be very careless with his client's money."

"I've got a meeting with him this afternoon. I've asked to see his contract and a complete accounting. The name of the PI, and the whereabouts of the notes are on the top of my list."

"Maybe we should find another investigator," I suggested.

"Jack, it's Bibb, Tennessee. About all that's left in Bibb are a post office, a gas station, a feed store, and the bar where Billy's father was arrested. It's in the mountains of east Tennessee. Billy said the investigator was from Knoxville.

"By the way, I've sent Marshall home for a few days. Billy is gaining confidence in me, and Marshall really is a fish out of water at the office. Clovis still has people watching his house. Should we move out of the Hay-Adams? It's so expensive. I don't know why Marshall is so wed to the place."

"Marshall promised he would tell me 'in due time.' He must have a logical explanation. I thought it was probably time for him to go home. You were ahead of me, good job. I know the Hay-Adams is expensive, but I think you should stay. People will assume you're just gouging your client like most every other lawyer. Besides, your room is currently bug free, and the hotel has promised Stella to keep it that way. I need her elsewhere."

Micki wanted to meet with Billy again before meeting with the agent, so she gave the phone to Beth who had just walked in with fresh coffee.

"Hey, baby. Sorry to interfere with your life again."

"Dad, it's not a problem. Paul, Clovis, and Maggie explained everything last night. When do I get to meet your new girlfriend?"

Well, no beating around the bush. I paused before I answered.

"Truth be told, I do want you to meet her, but she's left the country for a while. I hope she can return soon."

"Wow—she must be something. Sounds like you are really into this woman. Actually, I'm sort of excited about being here—I've already asked Micki how I can help."

"Beth, Clovis brought you here because we thought you were in danger. Please listen to what they have to say, and don't take any risks."

"Dad, it's okay. They've already explained everything, but I do have one question."

"Okay, shoot."

"Billy Hopper? What he did was terrible. How can you try to get him off? Especially with what happened all those years ago?"

Some lawyers have no problem representing clients who have been accused of heinous acts. Yes, everyone deserves counsel, but there are some cases I just couldn't take on. Billy Hopper had almost fallen into that category.

"Beth, three people you love very much and respect, Marshall, Micki, and I, don't believe he did it. I don't think any of us would be involved if we believed he was guilty of such a brutal crime. We're not just trying to get him off, we're trying to gather enough evidence to prove someone else murdered that woman."

"Isn't that a job for the police?"

"Yes, but in this case all the evidence points to Billy. Those in authority tend to take the simple way out. We believe someone went to a lot of trouble to make it look like Billy murdered the woman."

"So, you honestly don't think Billy Hopper murdered that poor woman?

"No Beth, I don't. I don't know yet who did it or why, but I believe Billy is innocent."

"That's all I needed to hear. Now—put me to work."

"Just do whatever Micki or Maggie asks. I have some ideas, but Micki's running the show. And use your common sense: don't go out on the town or even to Starbucks. Please."

"Can you and I at least have coffee or lunch or something?"

Beth and I had always been close, but after Angie's death we'd became even closer. It was hard to be in the same town and not get to be with her.

"No, Beth, we can't, at least not now. But I promise I won't let you go back to New Orleans without us spending time together. I miss you."

"I miss you too, Dad." I could hear her voice crack a little.

Beth passed the phone to Maggie.

"Micki has gone to the jail. Anything else you need before Clovis arrives at Barker's?" she asked.

"Yes. If I'm right, we are going to need to borrow Walter's jet on Saturday. Can you check to see if it's available?"

"Sure. Are you going after your girlfriend?" I wasn't sure if she was teasing.

"No. I'm not going anywhere at all. If I'm right, Micki and Paul are going away for the weekend."

"Do they know yet, and may I tell the pilot where they're going?"

"No, and Knoxville, Tennessee. They're going to spend a nice weekend in the mountains of Tennessee."

49

I RETURNED TO my room to wait for Clovis, hoping he could get in. The pieces of the puzzle were starting to turn over in the box, but I had a long way to go before they were all visible. The work of putting them together to form the correct image usually required some skill, more than a little luck, and a lot of perseverance. I felt confident we were right about Billy, but I couldn't help but feel the occasional niggle of doubt.

The quiet rap on the door about made me jump out of my skin, but I quickly opened the door to let Clovis in. I can't tell you how good it was to see him. We took the first few minutes just catching up. Carol had come home, packed her bags, rented a Net Jet, and left the country, whereabouts known only to Pat. A lawyer had arrived at the Eastern Shore and arranged bail for the two assailants. Clovis said dryly that they might be out of jail, but he bet they weren't out of the woods. The lawyer was with the multi-national law firm of Bird and Starling. I didn't know him, but I could easily check him out.

I decided to take the risk, and we walked down to the bar for lunch. Clovis had barbeque ribs and a pulled pork sandwich with slaw. For me the daily special was too tempting to resist—an enormous, hot corned beef and pastrami on rye. A cold beer was the perfect accompaniment. Barb wasn't as warm and friendly as normal, probably hurt I because I'd chosen to eat in my room last night. Her attention to Clovis was another matter. I'd never seen him in a suit before. His custom tailored suit fit his All-American linebacker physique to a tee. He could be an announcer on ESPN. Barb couldn't keep her eyes off him.

"Nice suit," I kidded him.

"I didn't know if there was a dress code and decided to be safe rather than sorry."

"You look good." He really did.

"Stella likes me better in jeans. She is more than a little jealous if you haven't noticed."

"If Barb's reaction is any indication, she is right to be worried."

Clovis shrugged my kidding off, but seemed unsettled by Barb's presence. Until Stella came around, he'd always been nervous around any woman who showed him the slightest interest. He pulled out some drawings from the documents he brought. They were the floor plans of the hotel floor where Billy's room was located. It showed a door between the adjoining room and Billy's, but if the press was correct, the door had been locked from Billy's side.

Clovis had been able to get the guest list for each of the rooms on the floor for the night of the murder and one week before and after, but nothing seemed out of the ordinary to him. He said every day more and more of the staff were opening up to him. It was a phenomenon I was relying on. Regulars at a restaurant, bar, or even a hotel become part of the family, and often a confidence slips out. So far Clovis hadn't discovered anything to contradict the story in the papers of what had happened that night. He'd had no luck obtaining any surveillance tapes.

I gave Clovis the files Novak had sent. He and Micki had decided to send Paul to Nadia's residence. Stella would search the public records, and at some point Clovis would visit the doctor. He told me Micki had been pretty adamant that she should take the lead, and I didn't disagree. We did have a lively discussion about Nadia. He was amazed that a regular at the Mayflower Bar wouldn't have been recognized when her face appeared all over *The Post* as the victim. Maybe Novak's source had gotten it wrong.

"You know, Jack, we were lucky before, but Novak isn't the most reliable of sources."

"I agree, but if the fingerprints match and the dead woman is Nadia, it is one hell of a break."

"That it would be, and that's why Paul needs to check out her

apartment before someone else stumbles on her ID. Micki is supposed
to get the autopsy results this afternoon," he answered.

We had fun imagining Micki's meeting with the sports agent—was
he in for a surprise. I told him what little I'd learned about Logan
and what we needed to learn from the four men who'd been at the
banquet, along with the girl who had been the agent's date.

I was a jealous wreck to hear that Clovis and Stella had gone to
last night's ball game where Bryce Harper had hit a grand slam in
the ninth to win the game. I wasn't so excited about their plan to
have Beth work with Paul. On the other hand, Beth had proven her
worth during the Cole case and would be in the way if she didn't have
something to do. This way, Beth wouldn't go anywhere without Paul
being by her side.

I'd first met Paul during the Cole case. With his slight frame
and owlish glasses, Paul didn't fit one's image of an investigator or
bodyguard, but looks can be deceiving. He'd been a champion wel-
terweight wrestler in college and is an expert in martial arts. Clovis
had told me in the Cole case, "If I had a child, I'd rather have Paul
protecting her than anyone else I know." His opinion had proven to
be accurate.

Over a second beer, I told Clovis how I thought the puzzle pieces
might come together. I was convinced the key to the case was hidden
somewhere in the mountains of Tennessee.

"And I think you're crazy," was his deadpan response.

We both laughed, but I stuck to my guns, and so did he. This
type of give and take sharpened my thinking. I missed the input and
perspective Micki and Maggie also provided.

Clovis concluded our long debate with a reality check.

"Jack, you're off worrying why Billy's family abandoned him and
trying to figure out why a defense contractor wanted to sponsor a
table at a football banquet. We have absolutely nothing that links
Billy's past to the murder of a prostitute. Furthermore, the few clues
you've uncovered about the deceased do nothing to negate the fact
that she was found with Billy in his locked bedroom, her blood and
his semen everywhere, his fingerprints on the murder weapon. To
top it off, he isn't sure he didn't do it.

"Any criminal lawyer worth his salt would be trying to develop a temporary insanity defense to negotiate a sentence of less than life without parole, and your mind is wandering in the Tennessee Mountains. Maybe you should chase after Carol Madison and let Micki do what she does best?" Strong words from someone I employed and trusted.

"Well, I appreciate your confidence. Nothing you've said explains why someone wants me off this case. Why did a sniper fire a bullet inches from my head? Why did two men tried to kidnap Carol? No one seems to care a fig that Micki is representing Billy, not bothered in the least. I have to believe that somehow I learned something that concerns someone enough to make sure I'm not part of Billy's defense. Think about that."

"Jack, if I didn't have confidence in you, I wouldn't be here. But if someone wanted you off the case that badly, why didn't the sniper shoot you outright?"

"I've thought about that, believe you me. I think it's because if he'd taken me out in the hot tub, every authority from the locals to the Feds would feel the need to know why someone wanted to murder Billy Hopper's lawyer. It might force them to rethink what happened in the hotel room that night. They want to see Billy go to prison, and they want this investigation over. I haven't figured it out yet, but I'm getting closer.

"I need your honest assessment on another matter first. Don't tell me what you think I want to hear, okay."

"Never have, at least not yet," he smiled.

"I know you haven't. That's why I can ask." I paused because I worried how to phrase the question and what Clovis might say.

"On occasion I've shown very bad judgment when it comes to the women I've found attractive. I cannot rule out Red and Lucy as potential suspects, but I'd like to think Carol has nothing to do with any of this. Yet she did come on to me at Red's, Red and Logan are both clients of hers, and she did know I was going to be alone with her at the Eastern Shore. Am I once again being played for a fool? Give it to me straight, tell me whether I'm being stupid again."

I'd laid my self-doubts out on the table, face up. He hesitated.

"My first reaction would be to tell you to never rule out anything.

You can't ignore your concerns. But I've met her. Martin told me how hard she fought her kidnappers, and I've seen her injuries—she could easily have been killed. She wasn't worried about herself—she was worried about you, how you would react, what you would do. She was right to leave. We may both be wrong, we've both been wrong before. But I think if she's involved, she's being manipulated.

"You asked why someone wants you out of the picture. I don't think it's Carol, but consider this—is it possible that while you were with her you heard or observed something you shouldn't have? It sounds to me like you were pretty focused on her, but could you have overheard something damaging to someone else?

"You told me the weekend was about information, and that you promised Carol that you wouldn't breathe a word about anything you overheard or observed. No one else knew about your understanding, did they? Did any of the other guests seem nervous or worried?" he asked.

"The senator from Tennessee was worried I might say something about him sleeping with his young staffer, but I assured him I had a poor memory."

Clovis responded with disdain, "I'm not talking about who was sleeping with whom. Think about it. Anything else?"

I thought about it as I finished off my beer, and then it hit me like a lead balloon.

"Clovis, that's why I've got to get out of this place. This discussion is exactly what I need. Thank you for reassuring me about Carol, for forcing me to focus on that weekend. I've got one more question."

"Shoot," he answered.

"The young woman who was with Billy's agent that night—was her name Claudia?"

"Claudia Ellis, yes. How on earth did you know?"

"Claudia spent that weekend with Senator Boudreaux. She's the staffer he was with that weekend."

"Coincidence?" he asked.

"I don't think so."

"Do I need to ask what you want Micki to do with this information?" Clovis asked with a smile.

My immediate reaction was Micki should interview her as quickly as possible, but then I thought the better of it.

"Hold off for now. If Micki barges in asking her about the Senator, it won't take much to realize I'm involved and our cover is in tatters. Tell Micki what I just told you, but tell her to save Claudia for last. Have Micki interview the guys first, appearing to be more interested in the other three girls. Let Claudia be more of a casual throw away. Meanwhile, let's find out as much as we can about Miss Claudia Ellis. I bet you can find a couple of her office cohorts who don't appreciate her getting promoted."

I was tempted to call Micki with suggestions, but I'd probably get an ear full. Clovis simply needed to give her the information and subtly pass on my suggestion. Micki would probably handle the interviews better anyway.

Clovis brought me back to reality one more time.

"We may find there is something funny going on, or Miss Claudia may just enjoy sucking up to her boss. I know how you feel about coincidences, but we're still no closer to coming up with a defense for Billy. Locked doors, bloody knife, his semen, and her blood. What do they have to do with a philandering member of Congress? We could probably dig up dirt on a hundred Congressmen, but it won't help Billy."

"You're right, but my gut says there's a connection. We have to work this puzzle one piece at a time. The prosecution has had over a month to develop its case. We've discovered who the victim is in less than a week, and we're learning more about the other characters. We have to be patient and follow the clues wherever they take us."

"Okay, boss—anything else?" he asked.

"No, you've got enough on your plate. I'm still fascinated that Nadia was a regular at the Mayflower Bar, yet no one has come forward to identify her. Answer that my question, my friend, and we'll have made real progress."

"Paul will have been to her apartment this afternoon, so I should have an answer for you tomorrow, how about that?" he smiled.

He rose to leave and said, "What are you going to be doing? I know sitting in this place all day is driving you crazy."

He was right, but I still didn't see a better alternative.

"I think it's time I hit the books. I need to study up on Senator Boudreaux, Logan Aerospace, and Red Shaw. I've also decided I need to know a lot more about our client, Billy Hopper."

"Billy? What don't you know about him? He's been all over the newspapers for over a month."

"You know, when I take on a new antitrust client, I research the company, its financials, and its corporate philosophy. I haven't done that with Billy. I've relied on his press and what little Marshall has told me. I need to do my own research."

"Billy Hopper?" Clovis asked.

"Billy Hopper."

50

━━━━━━━

WHILE CLOVIS WAS learning more about Nadia, Paul was checking out her apartment, and Micki was meeting with Billy's agent, I retreated to my room and pored over documents that Maggie had obtained about the Lobos, Red's other companies, and a report on Logan Aerospace from David Dickey. Billy would be my homework for the night.

My cell phone buzzed, and I picked it up.

"Novak here."

I was equally abrupt. For some reason all our conversations began this way.

"Thank you for the information. The girl found dead at the Mayflower is most certainly Nadia. I will be able to compare finger-prints as soon as we get the autopsy. I'm no expert, but the photographs you sent were almost identical to those in the press."

I expected an immediate response, but he said nothing.

"Alex?" I asked.

"I was afraid that would be the case. Tell me—do you still believe your client didn't do this?"

I responded without hesitation.

"More than ever. Who is this girl, Alex? Why are you so interested?"

"Information for information. I answer your questions and you tell me who did this?"

"I don't know who committed the murder yet, but I'm convinced it wasn't Billy. Anything you tell me may help me find out who killed her, or maybe who ordered her killed. The actual killer may be long gone. I can't provide you what I don't have. But I won't hold back on you, as long as you don't hold back on me. Who's the girl?"

"She was my niece," he said heavily. "She was recruited to this country by a piece of shit who is no longer relevant. Her parents finally contacted me after they hadn't heard from her in several years. I tracked her down, paid for her release, and sent her to a clinic to get cleaned up."

"But she was still in the business. Did she work for you?" I asked.

Novak exploded, "Absolutely not. I would never use a relative. Her father is my baby brother. I tried to reason with her, but her, shall we say 'work life,' had changed her, turned her to stone. She was appreciative, but told me she was going independent. She adamantly refused to get out of the business. The only thing I could do was make sure no one hurt her. She was working in DC under my protection, but that was it."

"Thus the surveillance photographs," I asked.

"Yes. I can't tell you how many times I tried to get her to quit, but she laughed in my face, calling me a hypocrite. I believe she developed a very high paying clientele. She lived very well."

"Do you know the identity of any of her clients?"

"No. She was very private. She was willing to go to their apartments, meet them for drinks, and arrange hotel rooms, that sort of thing. But as far as I know she never allowed a client to come into her home."

"You said she frequented the Mayflower."

"Information from my sources. I have no personal knowledge of where she worked."

"Anything else you can tell me?" I asked.

"Yes, and this is why I called, why I must know who is responsible. She called me the day before she was murdered to say she was about to retire. She asked where she could go that no one could follow her. It was the first time I'd spoken with her in months. I promised her I would get back to her, asked if she needed money in the interim. She laughed, saying money wasn't the issue. She had only one more night's work, then she would be ready to retire."

"One more night's work – did you ask what that meant?"

"No, I assumed she was meeting with a high roller. After you called I tried to get in touch with her but got no response. Fearing the worst, I called some associates in DC and put two and two together: she was talking about a rendezvous with Billy. Do you realize how much the tabloids would pay for such a story? I'm telling you that Nadia was a cold-hearted woman—she would have sold her soul for that kind of money."

"Alex, the problem with that theory is that it assumes she knew Billy beforehand. Billy swears he'd never seen her before and had no idea who she was. If she were somehow counting on seducing Billy when he came into the bar, surely someone would have seen her that night. How could she even know Billy would come to the bar after the banquet? According to the papers he was drunk and left with three girls on his arm. Hardly an ideal opportunity for a first meeting."

"You're reasoning rings true, and what you describe is not consistent with her cocky attitude. The way she talked, she was meeting a regular." He sounded frustrated.

"Maybe someone arranged for her to be in Billy's room, perhaps a bodyguard?"

"Not possible. She worked alone—no pimps, no bodyguards. I am certain of that."

"Then how in the hell did she end up in Billy's room?" I tried to keep an even tone.

"I'm sorry to say I have no idea, unless your client's lying. Men do lie about such things, you know."

He was right, of course. Billy would find it difficult to admit to either me or Marshall that he knew Nadia. If he had arranged to meet her in his room after the banquet, we might as well close up shop.

"Alex, I don't know how she ended up in his room, but I hope you won't do anything rash. I don't believe Billy committed this crime, and you have to give me time to establish who did." I was suddenly worried that Novak might seek some kind of retribution before I had a chance to prove Billy didn't do it.

"I can be a patient man; you have proven to be very successful so far. But if you discover who murdered my niece, you must tell me. Do I have your word?"

No easy answers. I decided to hedge.

"I will let you know what I discover, you have my word. My job is to establish that Billy didn't do this, not necessarily to discover who did."

I continued before he could object. "Did Nadia have any friends she might have confided in, someone who knew her clients, a girl-friend possibly?

"Not that I know of. She was very much the loner. Not once in any report was there mention of a girlfriend. She told me all along that she intended to make enough money to live comfortably on an island somewhere. She wanted to go somewhere that would let her forget her years in this country. She came close, only a day away. One more reason to regret that she was murdered. Jack, I must go, but let us both remember to what we have agreed."

It wouldn't do any good to remind him that he was also a man who had destroyed young girls dreams. Nadia had been right when she called him a hypocrite. Anyway, the line went dead.

I sat pondering our conversation, wondering how far I could trust the man. With a start, I realized he might be thinking the same thing about me. A strange bedfellow to be sure—I remembered thinking the same thing about Red. I wondered how many… I shook off my musings as a beep alerted me to an email—Paul.

Someone had removed everything that might connect Nadia to her residence—clothes, photos, files, shoes, and make-up, anything vaguely personal. The place was nicely furnished, but every closet was empty, the refrigerator and bookshelves were empty, no photographs or pictures on the walls. The apartment had been wiped clean of fingerprints, as had her car, which was parked in the complex. The property manager said Carla kept to herself, paid her rent on time, didn't participate in any building meetings or social events, and never complained. From his perspective she was a perfect resident. The few neighbors who agreed to talk gave the same picture of a quiet and very private person.

Stella was trying to run down the ownership records for the unit, as well as any bank accounts she might have had. I called Novak back to tell him what Paul had found, or rather what he hadn't found.

"Who would do such a thing, and why?" he asked.

"Well, it wasn't Billy—he's in jail. It's as if someone doesn't want Nadia to ever have even existed."

I was glad to have been able to share easy information with him and hoped he would keep to his side of the bargain.

I phoned Micki to tell her about Paul's discovery, but she didn't pick up. She must still be with Billy's agent. I had the same frustrating result when I called Clovis.

I fidgeted with the pens on the desk, frustrated that I couldn't reach my colleagues. Micki finally returned my call, and I filled her in on my conversation with Novak and Paul's discovery.

She brought me back down to earth.

"You may trust Alexander Novak, but I don't. I don't believe a word he says, certainly no judge or jury would. As far as her house being empty, did it occur to you she might be moving? According to your questionable source she was retiring, going away to an island. What do you do when you move? You empty the closets and give everything away."

I decided not to argue with her.

"You're probably right. How'd it go with Billy's agent?"

She laughed, "I just got out of the shower."

"That bad, huh," I smiled.

"I can't wait to ask Billy how he ended up with this jerk. The first thing he wanted to make clear was that he was entitled to twenty percent of any monies Billy receives from the Lobos. I reminded him that he had been widely quoted as having said he had already dropped Billy as a client, but it didn't faze him. He said, and I quote, 'So what? He still owes me my cut, that's the way it works.' What a sleaze."

"Let's hope one day you and I get to defend that lawsuit." I would enjoy that kind of case right now.

"He brought an accounting ledger, but initially refused to let me see it, saying it was between Billy and him. He sang a different tune after I showed him a Power of Attorney from Billy giving Marshall control over his assets and Marshall's notarized letter directing him to turn over all Billy's records to me. He backed off real quick, said he was just being careful, and wanted to cooperate anyway he could," she snickered.

"Sure he does."

"I've hired an accountant to do an audit of the account and told the agent his failure to cooperate would be reported to the NFL

Player's Association. He was gone before I could say shoo."

"What about the banquet?" I asked.

"He swears it was Billy's idea that he come and that he'd assumed Billy was staying at the Mandarin when he booked his room. That story doesn't wash because Marshall says it was the agent's office that booked Billy in at the Mayflower. The agent also claims that his date for the evening was an old family friend, sort of a favor. I didn't buy it for a minute—his eyes were all over the room. He claims he'd never met Claudia before that night. That might be true, but from what Clovis got from the staff at the Mandarin, the two of them hit it off for more than one night."

"That's not surprising. She's very attractive, Beth would call her hot, and has already demonstrated bad judgment in her choice of men," I said.

"Attractive like a snake, I suspect." Micki came back. "If I believed in fantasies, I'd bet your Claudia was hired to distract Billy's agent so he didn't even think about his client that evening."

"You could be spot on with that one. Anyway, Ms. Claudia is becoming more and more interesting."

"Don't even go there, Jack Patterson. I'll handle the interview when the time is right. You'd end up in her bed, and try to convince us she has some fine qualities. By the way, where do you come up with these women?"

I declined to answer. Micki was scheduled to meet with the team late in the afternoon and would send me a report before she and Larry went to dinner. I felt fairly useless—didn't much like Micki taking the lead, but it was a necessary evil.

I was bored with reading so I went downstairs to the gym and worked out hard; maybe a good sweat would get me thinking straight. As I worked out, I was bothered more and more by questions for which I had no answers and less and less by the bit players. For example, what was Nadia doing at the Mayflower that night if she wasn't meeting Billy? And how did she get in the room. Where were the three girls and their pimp? What really happened in Billy's room?

I showered and headed to the bar. I chose a table so I could read without the distraction of Barb's constant chatter. I noticed a hurt look on her face, but honestly didn't care. I tried to make it up to her by being friendly when she took my order.

I followed pro football and knew a little bit about Billy's career from ESPN highlights, a few articles about him after the murder, and of course a little bit of his background from Marshall, but while I sipped on my martini I began to read.

Honors graduate of the University of the South, Rhodes scholar, and star of the Los Angeles Lobos dominated every article until I came across a tidbit that had nothing to do with football or education.

"Damn," I thought and called Clovis.

IN THE COURSE of an interview, Billy was asked what he ate before each game. Who knows why they asked or who would care, but he answered that he was pescatarian, a vegetarian who eats fish. I also found an article in a California style magazine about his diet, including a few of his favorite recipes.

After learning what a pescatarian was, Clovis asked, "So?"

I smiled before I answered, "Why does someone who only eats vegetables and fish need a steak knife?"

There was a pause on the other line.

Clovis finally responded, "I'm on it."

There could be a million explanations for the presence of a steak knife in Billy's room, and I was sure the prosecution had already developed a chain of custody for the murder weapon, but somehow this small discovery made me feel good. Everyone else was working hard at solving the jigsaw, and I had finally contributed a puzzle piece.

To celebrate I ordered a juicy rib eye and a twice-baked potato, justifying my indulgence by the hour I'd just spent in the gym. I emailed the article about Billy to Maggie and continued to read about my client. For a sports junkie, it was a fascinating read.

Billy had almost been cut the first day of practice because of his slow time in the forty-yard dash, but the Lobos' quarterback pointed out that Billy hadn't dropped a pass the entire practice. What made Billy unique wasn't speed, but his elusiveness and his hands of glue. Each day of the first practice week the coach was prepared to cut Billy when he dropped his first pass or busted an assignment, but neither ever happened. Pretty soon the Lobos' coaching staff knew they had a find, but worried he couldn't stand up to the physical blows an NFL receiver endures. Once again, Billy surprised everybody, using that same elusiveness to avoid receiving direct hits.

His good looks, his slight build, and quiet manner made him an immediate fan favorite. Equally as important, he impressed the opposing coaches, sportswriters, and even the referees by not engaging in trash talk with opponents. When Billy scored a touchdown he didn't dance; he sought a referee and handed him the football.

I was tickled when I read that the coach for the Patriots got in a heated argument with the refs, demanding that Billy should be penalized and ejected after a fifty-seven yard touchdown catch. He said Billy was guilty of wearing stick-em on his hands, even went so far as to accuse the Lobos of deflating the football to make it easier to catch. He claimed nobody could have held on to that pass without cheating. Of course Billy's hands were found to be perfectly clean and the ball fully inflated. Life is full of ironies.

I pulled up a highlight video of Billy's first season put together by ESPN. Because the Lobos didn't play the Redskins during the regular season, I hadn't followed him that much. Billy was as elusive a receiver as everyone said. He really did seem to glide by the defender, but what impressed me was his ability to catch and hold on to the ball. No matter how vicious the hit on him, he never dropped the ball. Billy wasn't a vicious blocker, but he always managed to be in the perfect position to prevent his man from getting to the ball carrier.

Billy sounded and looked almost too good to be true after an hour's reading and viewing videos, which gave me pause. I mean, nobody's really too good to be true.

I also found no articles detailing any crazy antics on the town or showing him with some blonde draped all over him. In a city like LA, the absence of such stories was puzzling and a little bit disturbing. Once she knew that the victim was a high-priced hooker, a good prosecutor would use Billy's lack of a girlfriend against him.

Most NFL teams go to great lengths to prevent their ball players from fraternizing with the inevitable celebrity hounds who seek out famous people and often get them in trouble. Maybe Maggie could ask Red's people how they dealt with this issue.

I was sipping on a glass of wine when Mr. Barker asked if he could join me.

"We've had several inquiries concerning your presence, Mr. Patterson," he stated, flatly.

I looked Mr. Barker directly, matching his flat tone. "I appreciate Barker's discretion more than I can express."

"Thank you. Of course, I will do everything in my power to ensure no one at Barker's reveals your presence." He smiled a discreet smile and I nodded. "Nevertheless, I feel I must warn you that our employees are human, and at some point your presence will be revealed by omission as much as commission."

He was right. If someone tries hard enough, I thought, they will find out I'm here.

"You would tell us if you were hiding from any government authority?" He was serious, and I replied in kind.

"I would, and I am not. Quite the opposite. Nonetheless, I hope you will appreciate that I can't tell you why I have chosen to stay at Barker's for a few days. And by the way, Barker's is an exceedingly pleasant place to stay."

"Thank you, Mr. Patterson. I appreciate your good opinion. I trust that your presence will not put Barker's, the members, or my staff at any risk."

We both enjoyed our polite wordplay, but I got the point. He excused himself soon thereafter.

I was mulling over his intent when the phone buzzed again— Novak. He didn't parse words.

"Is your daughter safe?" he asked.

A question a father never wants to hear.

"I believe so. She is no longer in New Orleans, if that's why you're asking."

"I am, and I'm much relieved. Let me tell you what I know without revealing my source."

"I'm all ears."

Novak told me that to a large extent a syndicate controls organized crime in New Orleans. No one is supposed to engage in underworld business without paying homage to the syndicate and receiving approval. Almost all the gangs pay a modest annual fee to the syndicate for the right to do business.

"A former associate called me this morning. It seems that the syndicate is upset over an attempt to arrange a hit in New Orleans without prior approval. The target was your daughter," he said soberly.

I felt like I'd been sucker-punched.

"How do you know this?"

"I'm sorry, Jack, but I can't tell you that. I also can't tell you who ordered the hit because I don't know. My contact assured me the syndicate would handle the affront. I called only to make sure your daughter is safe."

"What about the hit man? Where is he now?" I asked, worried he might be on the way to DC.

"He was smart enough not to cross the syndicate. He's the one who told them about his orders, and for his loyalty, he's still alive in New Orleans. The man who placed the order will not be so fortunate."

"Can you tell me anything else?" I asked.

"No. I can't begin to tell you how relieved I am. But, Jack, if someone had the cojones to offend the New Orleans syndicate, he will try surely try again. Be sure she is well protected. You have made one serious enemy. Do you know who could have been so bold?"

"No, but I have a feeling it may be the same person who ordered the murder of your niece." I was pissed.

"Tell me who he is, and he will cease to be a problem for either of us."

God knows, part of me was ready to hop right in that bed. But I knew it wouldn't help Billy, and might put us all in even more danger. Besides—I didn't know. I simply thanked Novak and asked him to keep in touch. I heard his phone click dead and punched in Clovis's number immediately.

He heard the anger and frustration in my voice and said, "Jack, we'll keep your daughter safe. Maggie, too—I promise. Because she's front and center, Micki's a little tougher, but we're doing our best."

I'd tried to keep those I loved safe by pretending to be out of the game. That strategy hadn't worked very well so far. It was time to fish or cut bait, either publicly drop Billy or come out swinging.

If I dropped the case, Micki would be left hanging, not to mention

Billy. And who new if any of us would be truly safe? And there was Marshall to consider, both his safety and his good opinion. I decided to fish.

"Clovis, I'm running out of clean clothes. Can you pick me up tomorrow morning?"

FRIDAY

April 29, 2016

5 2

THE NEXT MORNING, I relaxed under the almost too hot shower and wondered if all mammals were so susceptible to this pleasure. I also wondered if the same hot water that loosens and soothes my muscles also stimulates my brain cells, because this morning I was thinking at breakneck speed.

I needed to decide where to unpack my bags. If I moved back into my house, Beth would want to join me, clearly not a good idea. I could join Micki at the Hay-Adams, or I could remain at Barker's. I reminded myself that the issue was security—I should let the experts figure it out.

Clovis was waiting outside after breakfast. It felt really good to be outdoors, kind of like how you feel when you leave a hospital—relieved and sort of disjointed.

We made the trip into town relatively quickly although nothing is quick in DC any more. Clovis pulled into the garage without incident.

"Oh, my God. What are you doing here?" Maggie cried when I walked casually into our offices.

I was glad no one else was in yet. It gave me time to tell her about the averted danger to Beth and why I had decided to give up my cover. I also asked her to call Rose and suggest she take a long weekend. I needed a tighter ship than Rose could provide.

"Beth will be here any minute now. She's driving in with Paul. She'll be ecstatic. Talking to you on the phone is one thing, but seeing you will be different. She's been worried about you being all alone at Barker's."

"How about you?" I teased.

"Oh, I figured you'd find some cute waitress to make a fool of you."

Maggie was quick with the comebacks and closer to the truth than I cared to admit.

She continued when I didn't respond. "You know Beth is now going to be worried sick about Jeff."

"Already taken care of—one of Martin's men has been dispatched to New Orleans for the next week."

I didn't tell her that I had also called Novak, or that Jeff had been put under the personal protection of the New Orleans syndicate. It was going to cost me, but we had no time to worry about Jeff's safety right now.

I poured a cup of coffee just as Beth came in. She broke into a grin and gave me an enormous hug. I have no idea how the coffee managed to stay in the cup.

"What's up, Dad?" she asked, pulling back as if to assess me. "Why did you come to the office?" She would have continued with twenty questions if I hadn't held up my hand.

"Let's wait for Clovis, Stella, Martin, and Micki. I don't want to repeat myself. Where's Paul?" I asked.

"He's parking the car. Wherever he was last night he's moving very slowly this morning. We all met with Micki late yesterday afternoon, to talk about where we should go from here. We were going to continue this morning. Have the plans changed?"

"That depends on Micki," I answered.

"What depends on Micki?" I heard.

Speak of the devil: she and Clovis came through the door together.

Micki crossed the room and, to my surprise, planted a kiss flush on my mouth. "It's about time you got your cute ass out of that hotel and back to work. We're struggling here to figure out how we're going save Billy from a life in solitary."

Well, as the Duke sang in Rigoletto, "La donna e mobile."

"You're Billy's lawyer, I'm just consulting," I smiled.

"Bull. I didn't come here to be the lead lawyer. I understand criminal procedure and can take the lead in interviewing witnesses, but I have no idea how to get Billy off. If you don't have a clue either, we better start working up an insanity defense."

"Which hasn't got a chance in hell."

"Right, so come on Jack, work that magic."

Boy, did I like working with Micki. Clovis was grinning.

"Let's wait until Martin and Stella get here. Do you know if she's going to Walter's today?" I asked.

Micki answered, "We had decided to all meet here this morning even if it did blow her cover. I admit that yesterday afternoon we were pretty lost despite all your emails."

It wasn't long before Stella, Martin, and Paul joined us in the conference room. Maggie had ordered in some breakfast pastries and a big pot of coffee. Paul looked like death warmed over. I wondered what he'd been up to last night. I waited until everyone got coffee and settled down.

"There's been a change of plans. I have no idea where I'm going to stay, but it's time to come out of hiding. Clovis, I'll leave that up to you and Martin."

"What happened?" Micki asked.

I explained about the hit ordered on Beth, and went over my reasoning to stay in the game.

As Maggie had predicted, Beth blurted, "What about Jeff? I need to get back to New Orleans."

Clovis answered. "Beth, I know you're worried, but we've already got protection in place for Jeff. Don't worry, he'll be fine, and you're safer here. But I'm sure Jeff would love to hear from you."

Beth bolted from the room.

When Maggie suggested that I stay at her house, Martin objected.

"Let's keep Jack at Barker's for the time being. Once whoever realizes he hasn't backed away from the case, all his attention will be focused on Jack. If he's with any of you at night, your exposure increases. We have a good protection plan in place for you and Mr. Matthews at home and for Jack at Barker's. Let's not change anything if we don't need to."

I hadn't looked at it that way, but it made sense.

Beth sauntered back into the room, looking cool as a cucumber. Whatever, she wasn't worried about Jeff anymore.

Micki nodded at Martin. "All right, we've got everybody snug in their beds at night, especially me. Where do we go from here, partner?"

"Well, for me, no more hiding out. It's time to quit pretending. Clovis, as of now you and Stella are not longer tourists. Let's go over what we've been up to in the last couple of days, what we've learned. Micki, you first."

Micki related her conversations with Billy. He still didn't remember anything, including leaving the banquet. He told Micki what he'd told me: that he couldn't have been drunk because he seldom drank more than a single glass of wine or a beer. He did remember the girl to his right changing her empty glass for his full one throughout the evening, which might explain why someone thought he was drinking a lot. He had never met anyone at the table before that night except his agent. He'd also assumed the girls were with the men; they were very friendly.

Micki said it was possible that he had been slipped some form of drug by one of the girls. She was supposed to get the prosecutor's files today; maybe they had done a drug screen on Billy. She was usually only allowed an hour a day with him, so today she wanted to ask him about his family and other friends.

"Anything else you need me to do?"

"Probably, but let's hear from everyone before we go to next steps."

Stella said she'd had no luck unearthing the source of the eaves-dropping, but she was still working on it. Our offices and personal computers had been attacked multiple times unsuccessfully. She remained confident they couldn't break in. Her work at Walter's was almost finished, so she was ready to go full-time on anything I needed.

Beth and Maggie had been maintaining the offices and fielding press calls. Beth had gone with Paul a couple of times to interview Nadia's neighbors. They had learned very little. Nadia seemed to have been a loner, kept totally to herself.

I looked to Paul, whose eyes were still red and puffy. "Paul, you look like something the cat drug in. You okay?"

"I'm fine. I went bar hopping last night, hoping to find someone who knew the elusive Carla/Nadia Diaz. As far as I can tell, the only place she actually frequented was the Mayflower. I met a lot of working

girls last night, but not one recognized her or the other three girls."
He didn't look fine.

"Please don't tell Debbie—okay?"

"Not a word." I repressed a smile. "You said she did frequent the Mayflower?"

"Frequent isn't the right word. I finally met a bartender who decided to talk after a hefty gratuity. He recognized her, but hadn't seen her recently. She used to meet someone he described as an older gentleman for drinks on Thursday nights. They met at the same booth around eight o'clock at night, talked for a while, and left together. He figured they were going to dinner, but didn't really know."

Clovis asked, "Who paid? Can we get receipts?"

"Funny thing. He said she always paid, and paid in cash. He assumed they were actually related, because no self-respecting hooker pays for her drinks. That's why he thought they were meeting for drinks before dinner."

"Anything else?"

"She always wore a blonde wig; she drank a Cosmopolitan, and he drank very good bourbon on the rocks."

"Do you think he would recognize the man if he saw a photograph?"

"For enough cash, yes; otherwise, no," Paul answered.

I said, "Great work, Paul. Take a nap and some Alka-Seltzer—you may need to go out again tonight. Clovis, your turn."

"You know most of what I've found so far. Today's the day to run down the room service orders for Billy's room as well as the identity of the other guests on the floor. Management won't like me poking around, but I'll manage." He looked pretty confident, so I didn't ask how.

Now it was my turn to tell them what I'd learned about Red Shaw's companies and his competitor, Logan Aerospace. This included telling them a little about my weekend at Carol's and meeting Chuck Morrison.

Maggie teased, "Anything else about the weekend you want to tell us?"

I didn't take the bait.

"Now that we all know what everyone's been up to, it's time to develop a game plan to get Billy out of this mess. Any ideas?"

Silence, no one said a word. Finally, Micki drawled, "Shoot, Jack you're supposed to be the coach."

53

Okay, so I didn't have a game plan as such, but I did have a few ideas about getting into the game.

"All right. We have lots to do in a short period of time, and we need to be organized and efficient."

"What's the rush?" Micki asked.

"The rush is that the longer we take to gather information and evidence, the more time whoever is responsible for Nadia's death has to cover his or her tracks. We're already playing catch-up."

"Well, then, where do we start?" Micki asked.

"Stella." I looked at her. She had gone from burnt orange hair to a purple and black mixture, and purple nails.

"I know. Find out who's hacking our computers." She smiled.

"That, too, but I have an idea I want you and Beth to work on. I want you to create a diversion on social media."

Now Beth looked interested. "What do you mean, a diversion?"

"Whoever tried to kidnap Carol and thought about killing you in order to lure me out into the open. I want to borrow his tactic. I want to draw him out, maybe cause him to screw up. Three young women and their pimp are missing, possibly already dead. Why can't we post their pictures on Twitter, asking if anyone's seen them?"

"Twitter, Dad? You?" Beth asked doubtfully.

"I'll have you know I have an account and have actually twit—tweeted on occasion. But you're the expert. So think of ways we can shake up the real murderer. I've got some other ideas, but I have no idea how to get the word out. Maybe the three of us can talk about it after lunch."

"Do you want to call attention to the three girls like that?" Maggie asked.

"Look, I bet whoever is looking for those girls as well, and not to thank them for a job well done. He won't like seeing their faces show up on social media. Neither will they."

I switched horses. "Okay, Beth your turn."

"Didn't you just give me a job?"

"Yes, I did. But I remember that it was your research that broke the Cole case open. According to their financial statements, Logan Aerospace has recently received some very lucrative contracts to build fighter aircraft components. I want to find out about the legislation that enabled those contracts. I'll help you get started. I just hope Lucy Robinson didn't sponsor the legislation."

"Why do I always get the boring stuff?" she glowered.

Her pout betrayed her age, and I ignored it. "Clovis, I've prepared a list of things we need from the Mayflower."

Maggie gave him copies of the list I'd made last night.

Clovis asked, "Okay if I get Stella's help with this?"

"Sure, whatever it takes."

Micki frowned. "Jack, if we obtain information illegally, we won't be able to use it in court."

"I know, but right now we need information more than we need to worry about getting it into evidence. We'll cross that bridge when we come to it."

"Micki, I think it's time for you to interview the Logan guys at the banquet. But I want you to make them think you aren't going to limit your inquiry to the four who were at the table. Let's make a few higher-ups sweat as well."

"What about Claudia?" Micki asked.

"I don't know. I have the feeling that Claudia's up to her ears in all this, but I don't know how. She could be simply a girl on the make—I understand she was recently promoted. But I don't want her to become a target, and I don't want to alert her Senator. What do y'all think?" I looked around the room.

Clovis spoke first. "Well, from my point of view, an interview would put both her and Micki in danger. But I bet she won't talk at all."

I could tell Maggie was upset; her leg was bouncing up and down. I nodded to her.

"Jack, I understand your purpose, but you're supposed to be a lawyer, not a detective. Why can't you just take your suspicions to the property authorities and be done with this? This young woman could be a totally different Claudia. If you believe whoever is behind all this would actually attempt to kill anyone who gets in his way, then you have to turn over your suspicions and any evidence you have to the proper authorities."

As a Brit, she firmly believed in following established procedure. It was hard for her to imagine going out on a limb when the safety of friends was involved.

"Maggie, I understand how you feel, but that strategy won't help Billy Hopper one bit. The government will say thank you very much, and throw Billy in jail for a very long time. They have what appears to be an ironclad case against him, and they aren't going to back off without ironclad proof on our part. Carol has left the country. She specifically asked us to remain silent about the recent trouble at her house. We only have the word of the Russian mafia that a hit was ordered on Beth. To save an innocent man we have to take some risks," I said.

"Are you prepared to live with the consequences of those risks?" Her voice was tight as she tried to control her rising anger. I let out a deep breath.

"I am. I am because I believe Billy didn't murder Nadia. Whoever did also tried to kidnap Carol and ordered a hit on my daughter. That someone will get away with murder and probably murder again if we don't discover who he or she is. Yeah—I want to catch the bastard."

Maggie had no response—she knew she'd reacted too quickly.

After a few long seconds, Clovis broke the silence. "I think wherever Micki goes for these interviews, we need Martin, Paul, or myself with her."

"I don't. In fact, I won't have it." Micki's response was no surprise. "You guys cramp my style."

"Sorry, Micki, but this time you get overruled. You were kidnapped once before, and I was helpless without you. Almost got myself killed, if you remember. Clovis, Martin, please make sure Micki has adequate protection."

"I thought we were partners. Don't I have a say?"

I caught Maggie's eye, and she intervened.

"Please, Micki, give in on this one. Jack is right. He made a complete fool of himself while you were in the hospital in Little Rock. Don't do it for him, do it for the rest of us." Maggie gave her a warm smile.

Micki's anger melted, so I decided to take advantage of the moment.

"Micki, I know this comes out of the blue, but this weekend I want you to go to Tennessee with Paul. Try to find someone who knows about Billy's mother—who she was, where she came from, whatever you can."

"What! Now I know you're crazy. First, I'm not going anywhere without Larry, and, second, what in the hell does it matter who his mother was?"

"Take Larry if you must, but you're not going anywhere without Paul. If Marshall is right about Bibb, Tennessee, it could be dangerous walking up to people's doors asking about Billy Hopper. I don't know what you're going to find, but my every instinct tells me the critical piece of the puzzle lies in Tennessee."

"I'm going, too," Beth spoke up

"No, you're not!" I had reacted as a father and immediately pulled back. "I'm sorry, Beth. Why do you want to go, and why should I let you?"

"Hear me out, Dad. It'll look weird if Micki, Larry, and Paul drive into Bibb and start asking questions. If it looks like we are two couples traveling together, seeing the sites in the Tennessee Mountains, we'll be less threatening. Besides, I'm pretty good at getting people to talk."

"She has a point," Maggie said quietly.

Martin added, "It might be good to have her out of town for a couple of days."

Micki said "I can't wait for you to meet Larry. You're going to love him."

I'd been overruled. At least Micki had now agreed to go.

Maggie spoke, "You've been handing out assignments, what about me?"

"All these sleuths are going bring us back the pieces of the puzzle. It's going to be up to you and me to fit them together. Then we have to figure out how to get the U.S. Attorney to drop the charges."

Micki laughed. "I wondered when you'd bring that up. You think if we present an alternative to Billy being the murderer, she's going to just roll over? Not a chance."

"I hear you. But you bring me the puzzle pieces. Maggie and I will figure out a way to get her attention."

"How are we going to do that?" Maggie asked.

I looked at the woman who had helped me prepare every antitrust case I had ever tried, my right arm and my best friend, and told her the truth.

"I have no idea."

54

MAGGIE AND I went to lunch alone at one of my favorites in the DuPont Circle area, La Tomate. Our thought was that anyone who cared would think I'd just come back to town. If all eight of us were seen together, what was left of our ruse would dissolve. It wouldn't take long for whoever to realize I was back, but no sense pushing it.

Lunch also gave us time to talk about her concerns. In the past, Maggie had accused me of having a death wish, taking on cases outside of my area of expertise that had nearly gotten me killed. Now I'd involved Beth. She had every reason to worry, but I didn't see a way to extradite myself. Maybe I should have gone with Carol to Bali or wherever she was. I wished I knew where she had gone, but I had to respect her decision. I hoped she knew what she was doing.

We lingered over a glass of wine. I knew Maggie was upset because she seldom drank at lunch. If she'd ordered a single malt I'd have known she was really mad.

"Do you really think you know who murdered Nadia and how?" she asked.

"I don't remember saying that. I thought I said I had no idea." I was surprised by her question.

"I know how you think, remember?"

That she did. In our first trial together she was handing me documents while I cross-examined a witness—before I had a chance to ask for them.

"Okay, what am I thinking?" I asked.

"The way you were handing out assignments. You only act that way when you think you see how things are going to unfold. I'd bet you know exactly what Micki is going to learn from the four junior executives and how to push their buttons. I suspect you know what they are going to find in Tennessee, too."

"That I don't. In fact, I think they'll come up empty in Tennessee. What happened back when Billy was a little boy is likely to have been covered up a long time ago, but it's worth a shot."

"What do you see that the rest of us don't? I know you see a connection between Logan Aerospace and Billy. What is it?"

"I do see a connection, but it's murky at best. I have a suspicion, but so far I've been wrong every time. First about Red, and I hope my suspicions about Carol were wrong too. What I do know is that if I tell any of you what I think the connection might be, everyone will try to shape the proof to prove my suspicion right. That's where prosecutors always make mistakes. They think they know who committed the crime and why, and they go out searching for clues to prove their theory right, ignoring clues that would prove their theory wrong. For them, a conviction is more important than a man's guilt or innocence. I don't want that to happen with us; it's too dangerous.

"Let's just gather the information and go where it leads us. Meanwhile, you and I have to figure out how we're going to get the right person to listen to what we discover."

"Isn't the prosecutor, Constance Montgomery, the logical person?"

"Almost certainly, but let's keep our options open."

By the time we got back to the office, Micki had left to meet with Billy, and Clovis had gone to the Mayflower. Beth and Stella were meeting in the conference room, so I joined them.

"How's it going?" I asked.

Stella answered, "I've set up a Facebook account and a Twitter account for 'Free Billy Hopper' that can't be traced back to this office or our computers. What we lack is content. Let Beth explain to you how they both work. Maybe you can give us some content to plug in. I have photographs of the girls, the table at the banquet, some of Billy in his Lobos uniform, that sort of thing."

Beth explained she would also create a "Free Billy Hopper" website where people could comment anonymously. The site was likely to get a lot of kooks and nuts, but Stella had set up some kind of filtering mechanism. I had a seldom-used Facebook account, and my understanding of Twitter was pretty basic. I knew we needed "Friends" and "Followers," but that was about it. I wasn't sure how one got people to visit websites and social media accounts. Beth assured me the sports networks and blogs would find us before morning—we'd see plenty of activity.

I spent some time with them talking about content, first focusing on the girls and how they could exonerate Billy if they would come forward or be identified. I also gave them a few ideas about the tone of the accounts.

"Can it look like these pages were set up by something like 'Friends of Billy' or 'Women Who Want to Free Billy?' Make the 'Friends' sound like women who have a crush on him. You'll know how to phrase it."

"Perfect, Dad. I know what you want now. I can make it sound a little silly, but be sure the site is well done. The bad guys will figure it out pretty quickly. Who knows? We might get some real information."

"Exactly. Let me ask you this. Is it okay to publish disinformation, such as one of the girls has been found? I mean can Facebook or Twitter shut the site down?"

"No way," said Stella. "Most of the information on the Internet is a bunch of junk. We can't use it to harass someone or put up porn or use foul language, but I'll keep you out of trouble."

I gave my computer experts a thumbs up and left them to their fun with social media and "Free Billy." I was still nervous about Beth going to Tennessee, but I was really glad she was here. She promised to have the research project finished before they left tomorrow afternoon.

Clovis returned with a stack of papers.

"What's this?" I asked.

"These are all the room service orders from the night in question. And to satisfy your curiosity I went back a week. It's going to take forever to organize the orders by room," he said.

"Give those to me." Maggie reached for the stack. "I'll organize them for you. I can do it in half the time, and Jack would only make a bigger mess."

"The good news is there were no room service deliveries to Billy's room. Not that night at least," he smiled.

"Good news, indeed. I'm sure Constance Montgomery can find a way around it, but it's a good find. Thanks."

"It'll take a little longer to get the other information you asked for, but I have a friend in the records department."

"What else do you need?" Maggie asked.

"I asked him to get a list of the guests occupying that floor on that particular night. I want to compare that with the room clean up list from the following day. Maybe someone was in a room that should have been empty," I said.

"I can get those lists, but your other request will be a little tougher."

Maggie was clearly curious, so I explained.

"Let's assume that Nadia didn't go to dinner with her gentlemen friend after meeting him in the bar. Instead, she went upstairs to a room. I want to check the records for the last year to see if the hotel had a regular Thursday customer."

Clovis said, "Problem is, Nadia paid cash for their drinks. She probably did that so no one could trace the fellow to the Mayflower. I bet he didn't rent the room in his name either."

"You're probably right, but I doubt that Nadia was paying cash every Thursday for a room either. There are too many different people at the Mayflower's reception desk, too many people checking in. Someone had a standing reservation, probably for the same room. All Nadia had to do was get a keycard from a cooperative bellman or waiter. It was unusual enough for Nadia to use her own money for drinks. Not many people in her business advance the cost of a room at the Mayflower."

"You think she was working with someone. I thought Novak said she worked alone," Clovis pointed out.

"He did, and I believe him. But this arrangement, if it existed, was too sophisticated for her to have set up on her own. Let's see what you can find out before we jump to conclusions."

"Stella can probably get what you want a lot faster than I can, but then again it might not be admissible in a court of law," Clovis warned.

"The quicker the better. I have a feeling we're running out of time."

55

MICKI AND I retreated to my office to go over her notes. She'd had a good session with Billy. He told her what we already knew about hiring a private investigator through his agent and getting the anonymous note from Bibb, Tennessee. He gave her a few more details about the town, including his father's favorite bar and the country store/gas station. He was pleased that Micki was going to his old hometown for the weekend. "I don't know exactly what you're looking for, but whatever happens, it would be good to know if I have any real family."

She told him I was joining her on the case, but didn't go into any details, and he didn't ask any questions. He seemed confused by her questions about any former girlfriends. Of course he dated at Sewanee. He rattled off a few names Micki could call. He confessed to a serious relationship with a fellow student at Oxford. They kept in touch, and he had planned to visit her during the off-season. No, he didn't date much in Los Angeles. The team counseled rookies to be wary of groupies and girls who hung out at hotels during road trips.

The publicity director had encouraged him to let her set him up with some women in the movie business, to let himself be photographed with them going out to dinner or walking holding hands, but he had politely declined, saying he wasn't interested in a "tabloid relationship." He'd had a few dates with a doctor at LA's Children's Hospital. They had enjoyed each other's company, but were both too busy during the season to get serious.

Well, at least the prosecutor couldn't accuse Billy of having some propensity for professionals such as Nadia.

"I tried to contact the first of the young men working for Logan, but was passed on to a lawyer who said that all four of his clients were cooperating with the prosecutor's office and respectfully declined to be interviewed."

"I was afraid of that."

"Yeah, me, too. I expect we're going to run up against a lot of stonewalls. The waiters at the banquet and the employees at the Mayflower will probably respond similarly. But surely they can't all have lawyers! Have any ideas?" she asked.

"Yes, believe it or not I think I do. But first let me brief you about what we're doing on social media and what Clovis has discovered. I want your sign-off."

"You are actually asking my opinion? Where did this Jack Patterson come from?" she kidded.

"First time, we had never worked together. Now we have."

Micki blushed, recognizing the compliment.

She loved our newly minted social media strategy. She had some ideas of her own for the web site, and I encouraged her to give them to Beth and Stella.

She was less excited about Stella hacking into the Mayflower's computers to get the information we needed about reservations. It was probably illegal and definitely wouldn't be admissible. I reminded her that Stella was so good no one would ever know. We weren't using the information for any illegal purpose; we simply needed to know who had rented rooms at the hotel. Moreover, we owed it to both Nadia and Billy.

Micki was still skeptical, but told me as long as I was aware of the consequences, she wouldn't stop me.

"Okay. Now tell me how we're going to get around the fact that the prosecution is stonewalling all the witnesses? All we've been able to gather in the way of exculpatory evidence is probably inadmissible. I know you well enough by now. You've got a plan bubbling up in that brain of yours.

"And please tell me you aren't planning to ask for a preliminary hearing like you did in the Cole case. There isn't a chance in hell Constance Montgomery is going to let you get away with that."

A preliminary hearing is sort of a "trial before the trial." The judge listens to evidence from both the prosecution and the defense and determines whether there is probable cause to bind the defendant over for a trial. The defendant is almost always bound over, but on occasion the defense uses a preliminary hearing to learn about the prosecution's case. We had asked for a preliminary hearing in Woody's case. It was an unusual tactic, but then it was a most unusual case.

"No, a preliminary hearing in this case would be a publicity nightmare, and we wouldn't learn anymore than we already know. But think about it—we could ask for one even though in the end we intend to waive our right to it."

"What would that accomplish?"

"Well, for one it might shake Constance up a little bit. She's bound to know what we did before."

"You've met her. I don't think there's much that shakes her up."

"True, but what else does scheduling a preliminary get us?" I asked.

"Is this a test? You tell me."

"The right to subpoena witnesses—employees of Logan Aerospace, bellmen, perhaps others. I'm not trying to shake up Constance, but I've got a feeling that once subpoenas start to fly, the real villain might finally screw up."

Micki leaned over, put her hands on my shoulders, and gave me a real kiss.

I pulled away abruptly and said, "Look, Micki…"

"Oh, don't get all bent out of shape. I know it's about Carol now. But it's fun to see you squirm, and I do love the way your evil mind works."

"Excuse me—I don't mean to interrupt." Maggie stood in the doorway, giving us both a disapproving look. I supposed she had seen everything.

"Not at all, not at all. What's up?"

"Micki, a courier has just delivered a very large package addressed to you."

"That will be the prosecutor's file," Micki said.

I asked Maggie to make a copy so I could take one back to Barker's tonight. She backed out without a word.

Micki was disappointed by the implied delay, but relented when I said, "I know you're dying to dive in, but let's stick to our schedule. Help Stella and Beth with the social media before you tackle that mess."

Micki left to find Stella and Beth, and I joined Maggie at the copier.

"Everything okay?" I asked.

"No, it is not. Right now Micki Lawrence is spoken for. You need to turn off your charms. Larry is a nice young man, and what happened to Carol Madison?"

"But she kissed me," I said incredulously and turned on my heel, a little miffed myself.

I returned to my office to find Micki and Clovis waiting. "Okay, lets talk about tonight and tomorrow. Clovis, ask Stella to see if she can find out if someone had the same room reserved every Thursday. I think a desk clerk could arrange a vacant room for one night, but not every Thursday. Management would have caught on. Micki, when you see Billy tomorrow morning find out how he ended up at the Mayflower. Did the NFL put him there, did his agent, or did he book the room himself? We have conflicting reports.

"I've studied the layout of the hotel floor. I think Billy was given that room for a specific reason. Clovis—here's one more thing to check out if you can. Billy's room faces DeSales Street. Anyone in an office across the street on the seventh floor or higher would be able to see straight into Billy's room if the curtains were open. Of course, they'd need binoculars or something more sophisticated, but how hard would that be? See if you can find out who occupies the top four floors of the office building opposite the Mayflower."

Clovis raised his brows, and Micki said, "Well, that comes out of left field. Do you think someone was watching Billy's room that night?"

"Anything's possible. Actually I'm more interested in knowing if anyone was watching the room next door to Billy's."

She frowned, but let it go.

"Is Paul ready for another night time mission?" I asked.

"He is. He crashed right after we met this morning, but says he feels better after some sleep." I had forgotten Paul had gone with her to the jail.

"I'd like him to go back to the Mayflower Bar tonight. Make nice with the bartender who told him about Nadia. Maybe one of the regulars remembers something he doesn't. If we find out who she was meeting on a regular basis, we're going to need someone to verify his identity."

"Anything else?" Clovis asked.

Micki spoke up. "I thought I'd try to contact Claudia. It's about time we know if she is going to cooperate or not."

"Let's hold off on Claudia for a little longer. She just might be our ace-in-the-hole. I don't want anyone to know we're interested in her."

Beth poked her head into my office. "Y'all come into the conference room. Stella is fabulous." Maggie had joined them.

"Free Billy" already had over ten thousand followers on Twitter and several hundred friends on Facebook. The website was getting constant hits, and ESPN and CNN were both reporting that the website had been created by "fans of Billy Hopper."

"Perfect," I said.

Beth and Stella took us through the various features of the site including the comment section, which had already gotten some pretty nasty notes. Not everyone was a Billy Hopper or Lobos fan. Stella said she working on a way to get to the real messages without having to manually sift through all the junk. She really was amazing.

"Micki, you can decide when, but I think its time to tell Constance Montgomery I've signed on as your co-counsel and that we want a preliminary hearing."

"I'm going to meet with Billy in the morning. I thought I'd drop by her office before we head to Knoxville. I bet she's working this weekend. I want to see her reaction in person."

Maggie ventured, "Jack, wouldn't you like to come home with Beth and me tonight? Have a nice dinner? Talk about something besides this case?" Beth looked at me anxiously.

"Sounds great, and I'd love to, but I can't put the Knoxville trip at risk. Today I was able to sneak out of Barker's and into the office. Yes, Maggie and I had lunch, but not with any of the rest of the team. I can get back to Barker's and lay low until tomorrow. By the way, Micki, you don't need to tell Constance where I'm staying—the press will find out soon enough. Once our secret is out, whoever's attention will turn to me while you head to Tennessee. Hopefully, Maggie and I can provide enough diversion over the weekend so y'all can discover the secret to Billy's past."

Beth sighed, "I understand, but I miss you. And I need to get back to my job before long."

"By the time you come back from Tennessee we'll have all the clues we need to begin phase two, presenting our version of the case to the right person."

"You sure about that?" Micki asked doubtfully.

"Absolutely."

56

WE BROKE UP soon afterwards. I went back to Barker's with the prosecutor's file. Clovis and Stella were going to stay at the office to try to access the Mayflower's computers, and Micki was headed back to the Hay-Adams to find Larry. They were going to get a good dinner and take in the nightlife of Adams-Morgan. Maggie, Beth, and Walter were going to Arlington to sit outside, enjoy the fresh air, and eat Maryland blue crab at the Quarterdeck. I thought they were torturing me on purpose.

I sat at a table in the bar at Barker's. Barb brought me a glass of wine, and I began to peruse the prosecutor's file. As expected the facts weren't good. The four men at the banquet all gave statements that Billy ordered a lot of drinks at the banquet, appeared to be snockered, and needed the girls' help to get into a town car to go back to the hotel.

There was no mention of the fact the girls had rejoined the men at the Mandarin bar. I made note to find out about the car service and the driver. The doorman at the Mayflower said Billy could hardly stand when they arrived. Billy practically fell into the elevator, and the girls helped him into his room, or so the doorman assumed. All three returned shortly and left in the same town car.

The surveillance cameras in the hall on Billy's floor weren't working, but they did have video footage of Billy getting out of the town car and being helped to the elevator. One thing we knew now for certain was that Nadia was not one of the girls at the banquet. Novak was correct on that point.

A lot of the file concerned Nadia, which reminded me to find out what Clovis had found out about her plastic surgeon. It included an autopsy photograph of her "birthmark," but I couldn't tell from the picture if it covered a brand. Now we had fingerprints from the autopsy, so we could verify that it was indeed Nadia who still lay in a sliding box in the morgue. It was clear from the file that the prosecution didn't have a clue who the dead girl was, nor had they made much effort in finding out.

According to the autopsy the cause of death was hemorrhagic shock caused by loss of blood from multiple stab wounds to the pubic area by the room service knife. The pictures were hard to look at and I went through them fairly quickly, but I did notice some bruising at the wrists and saw that her jaw was fractured and severely bruised. The medical examiner assumed there had been a struggle between the woman and Billy before he stabbed her. A pillow was found on the floor that contained her saliva. The medical examiner concluded that Billy must have held the pillow over her face either before or during the stabbings. There were no drugs in her system and no undigested food. I wasn't quite sure what that meant. It was interesting that she had been found completely naked. A black cocktail dress and heels were found on a chair near the window, along with a black bra and panties. All the clothes were folded neatly. No phone or purse was found, and for some strange reason all of the labels on her clothes had been removed.

I wondered what had happened to her purse. I started to make a list for Clovis and Stella. A working girl such as Nadia had to have a phone, and how in the hell did she get to the hotel with no purse or money. Something wasn't right. The rest of the inventory catalogued from the room was clearly Billy's, including his cell phone. I made a note to have Micki get access to the phone—I wanted to know whom he had called the few days before the tragedy. No sense being surprised in court. I also texted Micki since she would meet with Constance tomorrow. We hadn't thought about checking phone records, at least I hadn't.

I already knew about Billy's call to Marshall, 911, and hotel security. The file had transcripts of the call to 911. It was short and sweet—no surprises. The police verified he was wearing sweats when they arrived and that he had told them he woke up with no clothes on. Nadia's blood was all over the inside of Billy's clothes. All the reports indicated Billy was both distraught and respectful, but refused to say more until he could talk to Marshall.

The bad news was what had been leaked already to the press. The sheets were soaked in blood, and Billy's semen was on the sheets as well. There were no signs of intercourse, no indication of penetration, no semen found in her body. Billy's fingerprints were all over the murder weapon—a room service steak knife. Where had the knife come from?

The worst of the news was that the door had an automatic locking system. Once the door was closed, it was locked, and only a keycard could unlock it. A door led to the adjoining room next door, but that door was locked from Billy's side when the police arrived. I searched the inventory: they hadn't found a keycard either in the room or on Billy's person. Hmmm!

I emailed Micki with questions, hoping she had noticed the same anomalies in the report that I had. After dinner I would go over the file again, as would Micki. The report contained lots of photographs of the room itself, and I wondered if it was still cordoned off or was back in use. Surely the hotel would be sensitive—the publicity was bad enough as it was.

I sat quietly for a while, just thinking. I texted Micki with a new question to ask Billy. Finally, I ordered dinner and packed up the file. Feeling restless, I moved to the bar—at least Barb's soft voice, her cute smile, and the Cav's game could entertain me. I felt the buzz in my pocket and drug out the phone—it was Novak.

"I have bad news, my friend. One girl and her protector have been found dead in a storm drain outside of Cleveland, Ohio. Their throats were cut."

Who in the hell were we dealing with?

"Any sign of the other two?" I asked.

"My colleague has sent several men to Cleveland to try and find them. I will send you a picture of the girl who was murdered. I suspect your man Clovis can get the police file as well."

"Any idea what happened?" I asked.

"What usually happens—the two of them couldn't just lie low. They probably got bored in a cheap hotel and headed to the nearest bar. They were spotted, word was passed, and now they're dead. Such a waste."

"Your business is not for the faint-hearted," I commented.

"Not my business, my former business, as I keep reminding you."

"Yes, you do, yes you do," I replied. I hoped so, I really did. Perhaps he had finally found a way to go legit, but the past has a way of catching up.

"I believe you now—Billy Hopper did not kill Nadia. But I still want to know who did. Do you have any further information?"

"Not yet, but I'm getting closer, and I haven't forgotten my promise. Be patient."

"Patience is my middle name," he lied. I wished I could give him more.

Neither of us had the need for small talk or social niceties, so the conversation ended abruptly, and I was soon lost in thought. Now three people were dead, and to what end? This young woman had gone to a banquet, partied with a bunch of low-level execs, and helped a supposedly drunk Billy into his hotel room. Now she was dead, as was her protector, who was also the only link we had to the man who had hired her.

Barb asked quietly, "You okay? That phone call must have been a tough one."

I wondered how much she'd heard. The hand still holding my phone was clearly shaking. Barb reached out both hands to still it. Her hands were small and remarkably soft.

She squeezed my hands just a little and then let go. "Why don't I join you for a nightcap in a little while?"

I watched her as she walked away to take another order. She was very attractive, and I was very lonely. Maybe… but now Maggie's warnings filled the screen, and I came to my senses.

It wasn't long before she returned.

All men fixate on the idea of women coming on in a rush—they dream of it. But this time I wasn't interested. I didn't see Barb, I saw Carol.

"Barb, you're a very attractive woman, and thank you, but tonight I have work to do." I picked up the file and left before she could respond.

SATURDAY

April 30, 2016

57

LAST NIGHT, I'D opened the door to my room gingerly and was relieved to find everything in order. I poured myself a glass of wine and began a list of questions for the team to dive into the next morning. I didn't look forward to telling them about the dead girl, but they deserved to know.

This morning I enjoyed a breakfast of fried eggs over-easy, bacon, and cheese grits, another Southern delicacy I bet they weren't familiar with at the exclusive clubs in London.

Martin's person, Rick, picked me up and once again we were able to get to my office without detection, at least as far as I could tell. Micki and Beth were waiting in the conference room and Clovis, Stella, and Paul were on their way. We poured coffee from the service Maggie had set up on the credenza and sat down, ready to get started.

"I hate to start the morning this way, but I heard last night that one of the three girls and her bodyguard were murdered outside Cleveland last night."

Maggie gasped—neither Beth nor Micki reacted at all.

"I know this is unsettling. It emphasizes the danger I've put you all in, and also highlights the need to speed up our investigation."

I saw three grim faces, but no one said a word. It felt almost like a moment of respect for the dead. Micki finally broke the silence.

"I have the list of questions you sent me for Billy. I'll email you his answers before I leave for Knoxville, if I don't see you in person. Anything else crop up this morning, besides a cute waitress?"

"A few more questions." I ignored the jab and was handing her the list when the others walked in. I waited for them to get settled, then began with Paul.

"Paul, did you make any headway with our bartender or the regulars?" He looked a little better than he had yesterday.

"Several of the regulars remember Nadia, and one guy claimed he offered to buy her a drink. She politely declined, but none of them think they could recognize the man who joined her. The room is dark, and he always sat with his back to the bar. The bartender is becoming my new best friend, especially with my generous tips, but it will take cash and a photograph to get a definitive make.

"I spent a little extra time last night in a couple of Eastern European bars where the other three other girls might have worked, but no luck."

"That's okay, get some rest. I'm going to need you on full alert with Beth and Micki in Tennessee. I don't think anybody knows y'all are going, but no sense getting lax."

"Don't worry," Paul said firmly.

I looked to Stella next.

"I have several things to report. First, all the occupied rooms in the hotel that were rented by paying customers on the night in question. The cleanup crew didn't clean a room that wasn't supposed to be occupied for the week before or the week afterwards." My heart sank.

"Here's a list of who occupied every room for the night in question. There are several charged to corporate accounts so we have no names, only credit card numbers."

Beth asked, "What do you mean?"

Clovis answered, "Stella and I are a good example. Bridgeport Life rented our room at the Mayflower, using a corporate American Express card. The only record in the computer is to what credit card the room is charged. Bridgeport called the front desk before we checked in to give them our names, but our names weren't in the billing system."

"Were any of the rooms on Billy's floor rented through such an account?"

Stella looked to her computer screen.

"Just one, room 703," she said.

Clovis and I smiled. "Maggie, did anyone order room service on Billy's floor?"

Maggie looked over her records. "Six. Two ordered that evening, and four ordered breakfast the next morning."

"Did either of the two order steak that night?" I asked.

"Both," she sounded disappointed. I was too.

"Which rooms?" I asked, expecting to be disappointed.

Maggie smiled. "708 and 703."

"Hot damn." I asked Stella if she could find out precisely what was ordered for Room 703 that night.

She said she'd have it for me this afternoon and added, "I do have some good news."

"No one rented a room solely on Thursday nights for the last month or so. But I decided to dig a little deeper, and found that one room was rented every Thursday from August through the middle of February using the same account."

"Any idea whose account it was?" Micki asked.

"Not a clue. It's only a number, and not even I can hack American Express's records."

"Well, that doesn't help much!" Micki said with irritation. "And why are you smiling like the Cheshire cat?" She looked at me impatiently.

Beth jumped in immediately, "C'mon, Dad, what do you know? That grin always means you know something the rest of us don't."

"Stella, is the credit card number for the house account that rented a room every Thursday the same as the one that rented room 703 for the night in question?"

She stared at her screen for a moment. "Well, I'll be damned." She looked up at me with a grin, "It sure is, it sure is."

There were a few high-fives before Micki brought us back to reality.

"None of what we've discovered is admissible in evidence. Besides, we still don't know who rented the room. And you know the management of the Mayflower isn't going to give out that information without a fight."

"You're right. But at least we're getting information. Stella, can you find out if room service was delivered to those Thursday rooms? I'd also like to know what was ordered, if you can. One more thing:

find out if the maids noticed anything missing from room 703 the night in question."

Micki had sobered us all up, but Stella wasn't through.

"Jack, starting at midnight tonight I want everyone to stay off the company computers and emails for tonight and Sunday night."

Beth's voice rose in alarm. "No emails? Not even accessing my email using my phone?"

"Not even using your phones. Absolutely no emails for two days. We all can survive without email for two days, especially over the weekend."

Beth was persistent. "Why?"

"You and Jeff can text all you want, but no email. I have a plan."

"Listen, whoever is trying to hack into our system is upping his traffic and the sophistication of his attempts. I want to let him in just for a little while." Stella was clearly tickled with her plan.

"To what end?" Maggie asked.

"Jack wants me to find out who is trying to hack us. Well, I want him to think he has succeeded. He might just get over confident, and I just might have an opportunity to get inside their network. Whether my ruse works or not, I'll have our system protected by Monday morning. Beth, can you survive?"

Beth looked a little sheepish. "Well, yes. But what about our 'Save Billy' website?"

"You're going to be in Tennessee most of the time, so I'll monitor it. It's really just emails that concern me," Stella responded.

"What about our phones?" Maggie asked."

"Don't worry, they're safe—just don't use them for email," she said.

"Good luck," I said. "Clovis, any luck with the plastic surgeon?"

"I have an appointment this afternoon to remove an old football scar," he grinned. "Then I'll get to work on your latest list—it's about enough work to choke a horse. Tell me you've run out of ideas."

I had piled a lot on his plate, but I knew he could handle the load. Micki asked, "And how exactly will you spend your time while we're exploring the mountains of Tennessee? Got a hot date at Barker's?" She was really on a roll this morning. I let it pass, again, but her attitude was beginning to rankle.

"Think about it. You're going to tell the prosecutor I'm back on the case, that we want a preliminary hearing, and that you're leaving town for the weekend. This afternoon, as soon as Clovis verifies that the girl in Cleveland is really dead, Stella and Beth are going to post on the website that a critical witness to the Billy Hopper cover-up has been murdered. The plastic surgeon who botched the removal of Nadia's tattoo will receive a visit from Clovis.

"While the four of you are enjoying a long weekend in the mountains, I'm going to dealing with the consequences of our stirring the pot."

Micki said sarcastically, "Oh, sure, a romantic weekend in Bibb, Tennessee with Beth and Paul."

What was her problem? Beth stared at Micki.

5 8

As EVERYONE QUIETLY gathered his or her various belongings, Beth pulled me aside. "Dad, what's going on with Micki? I've never heard her be so mean."

"Sweetheart, I have no idea. But don't let it get to you, she'll get over whatever it is, she always has." She sighed and walked out with Maggie.

I asked Stella to stay for a few minutes. I warned her to be careful, and then asked her if she could find out whose credit card had been used to pay for the table at the NFL banquet, to purchase the auto-graphed football, and to pay for the guys' drinks and rooms at the Mandarin. I also asked if she could find out what credit card number was used by Billy's agent.

"You think Logan Aerospace may be behind the renting of the room at the Mayflower," she stated.

"I doubt they'd be so careless as to use the same credit card, but it doesn't hurt to check."

"What about the agent? I bet he used Billy's card."

"I do too, but it's worth finding out. I'm bothered that he's reap-peared and wants to be helpful. I know he hasn't had an attack of conscience, and I don't think it's about his commissions.

"One last thing, any luck finding a bank account for Nadia/Carla?"

"Not yet. But I'm still searching," she replied.

"There wasn't a penny on her person or in her home, no purse, no phone, no nothing. Yet she was planning to go away for the rest of her life. I wonder where she kept her money."

"From what I know, most women in her profession deal only in cash," Stella said.

"I know, but she must have had a bank account somewhere. The kind of money she was talking about would need a container bigger than a cigar box. I wonder if..." I mused. She caught on quickly.

"Novak?"

"Yes, Novak."

Stella and Beth retreated to an empty office to sort through all the comments "Free Billy" had received on the website, Facebook, and Twitter. They also drafted a post to go up later that revealed the girl's murder and offered a $10,000 reward for information that led to the arrest of the murderer. I'd already asked Clovis to clear the reward with the Cleveland police.

I found Maggie back in her office.

"What's with Micki? I've never heard her be quite so caustic," she asked.

"I don't know, and I don't want to talk about it. Are you ready to stir the pot some more?" I asked.

"Sure, but are you sure you know what you're doing?"

"I hope so. In fact, for the first time I'm optimistic. Now the hard part—how do we get the right person to listen?"

"Do you really think they're going to learn anything in Tennessee?"

"It's a Hail Mary play, but you run the play the situation calls for."

I was tickled with my football analogy, but Maggie was not. "Should I be able to understand what you just said?"

"It's a long shot—better?" She'd never quite gotten into American football, much less the lingo.

"Maggie, can you prepare these subpoenas for Clovis to serve on Tuesday morning for the preliminary hearing?"

She scanned the list, raising her brows when she came to one name.

"Have you run this list by Micki?"

"Not yet, but I will. Frankly, I don't want to say much of anything to her before she gets back from Tennessee. Maybe by then she'll have gotten over whatever's bothering her. Can you work tomorrow?"

"Of course. What do you have in mind, or are you still flying by the seat of your pants?"

"Check with Stella. See if we can use the computers. We need to write a summary memorandum for our presentation. Hopefully Stella, Clovis, and the rest of the team will be able to provide the exhibits."

"So we're going to write a summary before you know what the proof is?" She looked incredulous.

"Of course." I smiled and left her to preparing the subpoenas.

I went back to my office, closed the door behind me, and phoned Novak.

"Have you discovered the identity of Nadia's killer yet?" he answered.

"Not yet, and, in fact, I need your help," I replied.

"What do you need now?" I could hear the irritation in his voice.

"You may recall that we found Nadia's home totally empty, not a scrap of paper or even a coat hanger in the entire place. If she was as successful as you have said, she had to have either a place where she stored her cash or a bank account. Can you help me access that account?"

"Why should I do that?" Now his tone was downright chilly.

"Because she may have had a customer who didn't pay her in cash, but either sent her a regular check or wired money into her account. I'd like to find out who that customer was."

"I understand. What you ask for is difficult. There are certain banks that, let's say, are favored by people in my former business. They look the other way when cash is deposited or withdrawn, but wouldn't want anyone to reveal their identity. Moreover, if Nadia had such an account I wouldn't want her money to be seized by your government."

He had a point. As money received as part of the commission of a crime, the Feds could indeed seize it. "I don't care what happens to her money after I prove Billy's innocence. I simply need to be able to prove that someone sent her regular checks or wires. After this case is over, if you or the bank decide to distribute it to your brother or her family, that's none of my business. But I need some form of irrefutable proof that these deposits were made."

"Is the source of the money the murderer?" he asked.

I didn't want Novak to go off half-cocked and kill the only person who might be able to exonerate Billy, so I told a half-truth.

"I don't think so, but proof that such a person exists will go a long way to helping me discover the identity of her assassin."

The line went silent for a minute before Novak spoke.

"Again, Jack, what you ask is difficult, but I will see what I can do." Novak didn't sound encouraging.

"Thanks. I have a second request, one that I should have asked earlier."

"You ask a lot." Now his voice was downright cold.

"I'm sorry—this is an easy one, I hope. Nadia's cell phone wasn't in the hotel room or in her home. You have said you talked to her on occasion. Can you give me her phone number?"

"That I can do." He paused for a second before giving me a number.

I wrote it down, then read it back to him.

"That is correct."

"Thanks, Novak. Remember: verifiable proof of the deposits."

"What if there were no regular deposits?" he asked.

"Please let me know regardless. In that case, I think her money should be returned to her family. It is small consolation for the pain they must feel."

Again, a silence before he replied.

"I will call you as soon as I have answers. Jack Patterson, sometimes you surprise me."

I walked to the conference room and handed the phone number to Stella.

"This is Nadia's phone number. Think we can get her phone records?"

"Shouldn't be a problem," she answered.

I reached in a pocket and handed her a napkin. "What about this number?"

"No problem."

59

MAGGIE AND I met Walter at Joe's Stone Crab for lunch—great food, but hard on the bank account. I decided on Joe's because of its visibility. I wanted to be sure anyone who cared knew I had returned to town and was back at work. Lunch with Maggie and Walter at Joe's should do the trick.

We agreed to share oysters Rockefeller and the crab cakes, followed by chopped salads. After days of bar food, I felt the need to be at least a little healthy. When the waiter left, Walter opened with, "I hear I've lost my golf partner and wife for the entire weekend again?"

"I promise to make it up to you by letting you beat me next weekend." I knew how to get Walter's goat.

Before he could reply, I continued. "I have another favor to ask. Your pilot is taking my crew to Knoxville tonight and picking them up Monday night. Do you mind if he picks up Marshall in Little Rock on Monday morning as well?"

"Not a problem. But it'll cost you a couple of tickets when the Lobos play the Redskins."

"You'll have an invitation to Red's box," I said, wondering if I could pull it off.

Maggie asked, "Why are you bringing Marshall back to town? You surely won't have a preliminary hearing for weeks."

"You're right, but I'm not sure we really want a preliminary hearing. I owe it to Marshall to keep him informed. He can comfort Billy and be available for a couple of days if my plan works."

"Care to share your plan?" Maggie asked tartly.

"Of course—tomorrow, when it's just you and me."

Walter interjected, "I can head back to the office if you two need some alone time." Great—I'd managed to irritate them both and embarrass myself to boot. There wasn't anything I wouldn't share with Walter.

"No, Walter, no—please don't think it's about you. At this point, my so-called plan is still in vague outline form. I haven't heard from Micki about her meeting with Billy and Constance, Stella and Clovis have a lot of puzzle pieces to unearth, and our 'Save Billy' website is just starting to have the desired results. I have to stir the pot a little more this afternoon. What we discover in Tennessee, or maybe what we don't discover, will determine how we move forward. Then I'll actually have a plan to share."

"I have a plan as well, one I'm willing to share right now," Walter said.

"What's that?" I asked.

"Tomorrow night I'm grilling steaks and pouring martinis. You've been hunkered down too long; you need to get some fresh air. You're coming to our place for dinner with Clovis and Stella. No excuses and no work talk. While your crew is exploring the Tennessee Mountains, you are going to take the night off." His tone was stern, but he smiled, and I was reminded why I loved this man so much.

I thanked him, and we spent the rest of lunch going over some Foundation business I'd neglected this past week. The discussion served as a welcome reminder that my real life awaited my return to normality.

Walter left for a meeting in Arlington, so Maggie and I decided to walk back to the office, much to frustration of Martin's men. When we got back, I returned Micki's call first thing.

"You're no longer a very popular guy with Constance Montgomery," she began.

"What—she's not happy I'm back?" I laughed.

"Oh, no, she's delighted you've returned, said she always expected you to show up. It's your request for the preliminary hearing that caused her to blow a gasket." Micki sounded giddy.

"My request? I thought we were partners?"

"We are, and I knew you wouldn't mind my blaming you." She let that sink in. "She said she was fully aware of your bent for shenanigans in the courtroom, and if you think you can get away with playing your games here in DC, you are dead wrong."

I admit to being pleased. "I thought we might ruffle her feathers."

"She also sent you another warning. I'm paraphrasing, of course, but this is the gist. 'Tell Jack Patterson I'm already aware of his reputation for going around local prosecutors to Main Justice. Tell him it won't work. My U.S. Attorney has made sure this is our case, and Main Justice is taking a hands off approach. He'll be wasting his time if he tries to get the attention of his pal Peggy Fortson.'"

Peggy and I had joined the Justice department at the same time. I left for private practice after a few years, but she stayed the course and was now the Deputy Assistant Attorney General for the Criminal Division. We have remained good friends and work together on occasion.

I almost laughed at loud. "Anything else from Ms. Montgomery?"

"Oh yeah, she suspects we're responsible for the 'Save Billy' website. She said she's going to get the judge to shut it down."

"Can she do that?"

"Hell if I know," she laughed.

"She's really going to be upset when we post a reward for the girl who was killed in Cleveland." I returned the laugh, but it was time to get serious.

"You coming in to the office?"

"No, the pilot wants to get ahead of the weather. We're meeting at the airport in an hour. I'm on my way to get Larry."

"Is he all right with this? There could be trouble."

"He's excited. He's already found a couple of hardwood mills in the area. Don't worry about Larry. He's tougher than you might think."

"I do. I worry about all of you." I was sincere.

"I appreciate it, Jack, and we all know the risk. I've emailed you the answers to the questions you wanted me to pose to Billy. He's doing okay, but I don't know how long that's going to last."

"I figured. Walter's pilot will pick up Marshall in Memphis Monday morning before he meets you in Knoxville. Maybe seeing Marshall will lift his spirits. Good luck, Micki—bring back a few answers." With that I clicked off, wishing I were going with them.

I found Clovis working in the conference room. He had obtained approval from the Cleveland authorities for the reward and for posting it on the "Free Billy" website. He warned that it probably wouldn't be long before someone with the DC police came around asking how we had learned about the Cleveland murders.

I shrugged off the possibility and told Stella to go live with the post and the reward. Constance Montgomery would just have to get over it.

Clovis was on his way to see the plastic surgeon. I retreated to my office to stir up more trouble. Maggie wouldn't be happy with my next call.

I punched in Cheryl Cole's private cell number. She had been calling the office daily asking for a scoop. I was about to give her one.

"Jack," she said without preliminaries "you still owe me. When are you going to give me the real scoop on Billy Hopper?" No warm hello this time.

"We off the record?" I asked.

"Jack, we're friends." She simpered, giving my name a full two syllables. I don't have much patience for these reporters' games. I usually refused to play, but I needed her help.

"Yes, we are friends, but I still want to hear from your own lips that we're off the record."

"Jack, don't you trust me? Why don't you tell me what you've got? If it's good I promise not to reveal my source." Did she think I was an idiot?

No more games. "Cheryl, better reporters than you will kill for this story. Let me hear the words, or I'm calling one of them. Who's that good looking guy at ESPN?"

She humphed a bit but gave in, though with little grace. "Bastard! Okay, we're off the record."

"Last night I learned that a young woman and her pimp were murdered in Cleveland. Their throats were cut. You can find out more details from the Cleveland police or on the 'Free Billy' website."

"People are murdered in Cleveland every day. What does any of this have to do with Billy Hopper?" she asked.

"The same young woman was sitting next to Billy at the NFL Honors banquet. Her name that night was Ginger. The other two girls at the table have gone missing, who knows where."

"So, what does that all mean?" she asked.

"Do I have to spell it out for you, Cheryl? Isn't that why you're paid the big bucks?"

"Now, Jack—why be mean? Is that it?"

"For now, yes."

"That website—who's behind it?"

"I can't tell you."

"Can't or won't?" she asked.

"Does it matter?"

"I guess not. Will you come on my show tonight?"

"You know I won't," I laughed.

"I expect to hear more, you know."

"That you will." I hung up.

I walked passed Maggie's desk.

"Maggie, can you please record Cheryl's show tonight?"

"Please tell me you haven't been talking to that woman again."

Maggie thought Cheryl was lower than a snake. She was mostly right, but Cheryl could also be useful. I grinned and left to find Stella.

"Stella, I think you should expect attacks on the website."

"Already incoming. Someone is trying to shut the site down. I can't tell if it's the federal government or the Chinese, but, whoever, they're good."

"Can they succeed?"

"I said they were good, but not good enough," she smiled.

"Anything interesting in the way of comments?"

"Not much. Lots of people are after the reward—most of them are cranks, but who knows? Billy has a lot of fans out in California, and the website is gaining traffic as well as the Twitter account."

"Most defendants don't have money enough to hire a decent lawyer, much less use the Internet to help combat all the advantages prosecutors have. There are still two levels of justice in America one for the rich, and one for the rest of the country. Who knows? The Internet has had a huge impact on politics, maybe it will for criminal justice as well. Wouldn't that be something?"

"That it would," she said.

I spent the rest of the afternoon thinking about Micki's conversation with Billy. His agent had made all his DC reservations. He was surprised to have a corner suite at the Mayflower since the banquet was at the Mandarin. All the other ballplayers were at the Mandarin, but his agent had arranged for a car to take him to the banquet, so he didn't think much about it.

When he checked in the clerk didn't ask for a credit card, just his driver's license. His plane had been late, so he barely had time to clean up and change into a suit before the car arrived. No, he hadn't used the phone in the room at any time, not even for room service or housekeeping. The room was fine, nothing was missing that he recalled. He didn't go down to the bar before leaving for the banquet, and he had never been inside the Mayflower before, much less stayed there.

Either Billy was a consummate liar or something was seriously amiss.

I made a note and took it in to Stella. "Can you check this out?"

She looked at it and commented, "No one is that stupid."

Clovis still wasn't back from the plastic surgeon's, so I decided to return to Barker's. Maggie and Walter were attending a function at the Kennedy Center, so she hoped we could close the office a little early. I wished them both a good night. Stella was set to camp out in our offices over the weekend, hoping to catch our hacker. I felt okay, knowing Clovis would assure her safety.

It was a beautiful afternoon, and I wished I could enjoy the long walk through the city, but I carried a banker's box of files, so a cab was in order. After dropping the box off in my room and cleaning up, I walked down to the bar for a drink. The atmosphere felt all wrong; I really didn't want to be here. I thought about taking my wine upstairs, but Barb put a plate of French fries down next to my wine glass, and I gave in.

It was Saturday night and Barker's was busier than usual. I sipped on a very nice Sauvignon Blanc from New Zealand and listened to Barb who seemed to be in a particularly good mood. My thoughts wandered to Constance Montgomery—how on earth could I convince her someone else had murdered Nadia? Once a prosecutor is convinced of an individual's guilt, it's difficult, likely impossible, to convince them otherwise. With a few exceptions, prosecutors are much like baseball managers: they care about their won/lost record, not much else.

I had no hard evidence to present, and they had Billy's fingerprints all over the murder weapon. Nadia was in his bed, naked and dead, and the doors were locked from the inside.

The insistent buzzing of my phone interrupted my thoughts: Clovis wanted to tell me about his visit to the plastic surgeon. The "surgeon" was nothing more than a doctor who provided health care to unsavory characters and the girls under their protection. Clovis would bring Nadia's file to the office. He had photographs of the brand before the surgery. She had paid cash and not made a follow-up appointment. Clovis said the doctor and his office were equally depressing. He was returning to his hotel for a long shower.

"I hate to believe people have to resort to a quack like that. How on earth did he get a license?" he fumed.

He also reminded me that the entrance to the Mayflower on DeSales Street isn't manned by a bellman or covered by any surveillance cameras. Nadia or anyone else could enter the hotel from that entrance without being either noticed or photographed.

This information solved one puzzle—how had Nadia been able to get into the bar without being picked up on surveillance cameras. Once the DeSales Street entrance had opened directly into the bar, but the bar had been relocated a couple of years ago. Even now it would be easy to avoid the cameras in the lobby. I wondered...

"Penny for your thoughts." Barb smiled.

"I'm sorry. I've got a lot on my mind tonight. Why don't you let me have the rest of the bottle and a glass? I'm going to shut it down for the night."

She smiled again. "Would you like room service to bring it upstairs?" She reached back for a bottle.

"Thanks, but no." I took the bottle, idly wondering how much it would cost, and walked up the staircase.

I had an urge to do something I seldom do—take a bath. Maybe it was wounds from a long time ago, but a warm bath, a glass of wine, and being alone with my thoughts sounded just about perfect.

I had just settled in when I heard a knock on the door.

"Room service." Her voice was unmistakable.

I knew where the evening would end if I answered that door, and the prospect simply had no appeal. Was I a fool? Well, maybe, but the hot water felt pretty damn good. I decided to remain in the tub with my dreams rather than face reality at my door.

SUNDAY

May 1, 2016

60

MR. KIM HAD just received a first-class ass chewing from the client. Patterson was back on the case, if he had ever been off. Some damn website called "Free Billy" claimed that Hopper had been set up and that the girl murdered in Cleveland could have exonerated him. Kim was sure that Patterson was behind the website, but so far his people had not been able to shut it down.

Fox News had run a piece posing the possibility that Hopper was innocent, referencing the murders in Cleveland. That bitch Cheryl Cole broke the story; Kim knew Patterson had used her before.

Lawrence had requested a preliminary hearing, refusing a negotiated guilty plea. Jones and his people were nosing around all over town. He'd found the dirty doctor Nadia had used. He should have eliminated that danger before now. Worse, the other two girls hadn't been found.

He had known Patterson would present a problem. Lawrence played things by the book, but Patterson was creative and unpredictable. The only bright light in this gloomy picture was that his tech people were finally having some success penetrating Patterson's computers. It was about time.

He should have given the order to kill Patterson when the sniper had the shot, but the client was worried that an investigation would blow the whole deal. Now the client wouldn't be given the option.

*****

The night seemed to last forever. I dreamed that I was scheduled to pitch in Yankee stadium, but my uniform had disappeared, nowhere to be found. Not such a terrible dream initially, but it returned no matter how many times I tried to shake it off. Maybe I should have opened the door to Barb after all.

Sunday breakfast at Barker's was always a feast, anything you could possibly imagine at an American breakfast. I ordered blueberry pancakes with two fried eggs, and corned beef hash on the side. Possibly a little indulgent, but it made me a happy man. I lingered over coffee, contemplating the day before me. Maggie and I were to meet at nine thirty; Clovis and Stella would join us at eleven. We'd have sandwiches delivered to the conference room and work until about five. Dinner with Maggie and Walter would be a welcome relief.

I arrived at the office to find the conference room in a total state of disorder, Diet Coke cans and crumpled packages from Cheetos and Snickers tossed about carelessly. Stella sat in front of two computers, looking more than a little bleary-eyed. She didn't look up when I came in. After a few minutes of silence, I ventured to ask how she was doing.

"Hey, we're good. The government quit trying to shut down the website around five o'clock yesterday. The other hacker doesn't ever seem to stop, and I've given him a gleam of hope. He made his way to what looks like a crack in our security, right on schedule, but he'll find absolutely nothing. I'll try to infiltrate their system when I think they're the most vulnerable. I'm still trying to track down who paid for the rooms at the Mayflower."

"Sounds good. Can Maggie prepare a memo on her computer?"

"Sure, no problem. Stay off email, but writing a document is perfectly okay.

"By the way, I managed to get a copy of the call log for Nadia's cell phone. I put a list of the numbers for the last three weeks on your desk along with a log from the other number you gave me. Several of Nadia's numbers appear more than once, both incoming and outgoing. Maybe Beth could trace those numbers."

"Any serious response to the website's offer of a reward?" I asked.

"The traffic went through the moon the night of Cheryl's show. Still mostly a lot of sports related junk, but it takes only one. I just hope I recognize it."

I thought to myself how important it was for one of the girls to try and reach out for protection. So I asked Stella if she could post an encrypted email address or phone number someone could use to reach her. I also asked her to include language promising absolute confidentiality for anyone who responded.

Clovis came in with some kind of specialty coffee drink for Stella and black coffee for the two of us. Maggie would put on a kettle for her tea when she arrived. While we waited on Maggie, I went over Nadia's medical file or what little there was of it. Before and after photographs of the brand were helpful, but that was about it. At least we had additional documentation that Nadia and Carla were the same woman, that she had once been branded with a crescent moon and two initials—td. After the surgery the brand looked exactly like the picture in the medical examiner's report; he had referred to it as a birthmark.

Maggie breezed in and as soon as she had her tea in hand we went to work preparing the first draft of an outline report of what I believed had happened. Maggie still took shorthand, a talent which has almost entirely disappeared. Clovis acted as devil's advocate, questioning my assumptions. We spent about two hours going back and forth before I ran out of steam or fresh arguments.

"So, what do you think?"

No answers. Maggie was expanding her notes, and Clovis sat drumming his fingers on the desk.

"Jack, there's more holes in your premise than a doughnut shop. How on earth are you going to sell it to a prosecutor?" Clovis spoke up first.

"Well, you're right and I'm not sure. But I think it has promise, and besides, it's all we've got. So let's make a list of those holes and how we can plug 'em. You first, Clovis."

"The most obvious thing you're missing is motive. We'll never get to the complete story without a motive, one we can prove. To me, that's where your theory story lacks substance. Sure, someone else could have killed Nadia, but why?"

Why did he always have to be right? Such a downer.

Maggie said, "I agree with Clovis, of course, and I can't get past the same question—How are you going to convince the prosecutor to give up what appears to be an ironclad case against Billy to follow your suspicions?"

"Well, since we meet with that lady soon, we need to come up with a plan for her and try to fill as many holes as we can. Maybe our team in Tennessee will provide the motive. We'll have to wait and see. And who knows what else may turn up?"

Maggie reminded me, "You've already said you believe they won't find anything."

"I did, but discovering nothing is also a discovery. Hey, how about a little optimism and enthusiasm around here. We're out to exonerate Billy, not to talk ourselves out of the game." Their negativity had finally gotten to me.

The awkward silence was relieved when Maggie opened the door to the Loeb's delivery man. She handed us each a still-warm corned beef sandwich with a side of pasta salad, and we soon relaxed, remembering why we were here.

We were clearing up when Stella burst in with her news.

"I found out who rented room 703 at the Mayflower. It's a company called L&A Marketing Advisors. Their mailing address is a P.O. Box in Alexandria, Virginia. I'm trying to pin down the ownership, officers, et cetera. The table at the banquet was purchased with a check from Logan Aerospace, and the purchase of the autographed football was paid for with by an American Express owned by Logan Aerospace."

Clovis commented, "It was too much of a stretch to think Logan paid for the room as well as the banquet expenses."

We were all disappointed until I saw that Stella was grinning.

"Okay, Stella out with it. What else did you discover?" All heads turned to the smiling Stella.

"The four corporate executives bought their drinks, meals, and rooms at the Mandarin with an American Express card belonging to Logan Aerospace."

"Anything else."

"Billy's agent's room was not paid for by Logan." Stella said.

I said, "Of course not. He probably used Billy's card."

Stella shook her head. "Nope. Logan didn't pay for his room because he never checked in. He stayed the weekend with Claudia, the Senator's aide. Her room, room service, and a large bar bill were all paid for by L&A Marketing Advisors."

"Wow. Good work Stella. One hole filled, but of course we have another mystery—who is L&A? Is it possible that the L and A stand for Logan Aerospace?"

"I don't know yet, but I'm working on it," answered Stella. "But since Micki isn't here, I want to remind you that my methods haven't been exactly kosher. I'm not sure how useful the information will be in a court of law."

I nodded in agreement, knowing that if we didn't avoid a court of law, Billy was going to need a different lawyer.

"That's okay, keep digging. How we use it is my problem."

She cleared her throat, looking uneasy. "I hate to do this, but I need a break. The hacker is roaming through a bunch of meaningless files, and I won't be ready to launch my counter attack until tomorrow. I need a little rest before we go to Maggie's tonight."

Clovis looked concerned. She'd lasted longer than I could have—she must be exhausted. I nodded to Maggie, who made clucking noises and told her to enjoy a nice, long nap. We agreed to swing by the Mayflower around five p.m. to pick her up. As she left, Maggie turned to Clovis.

"She'll be okay. She's been going non-stop since you got here. You'll notice a world of difference in her this evening."

Clovis was clearly bothered, but the three of us went back to work. At some point I heard a rap on the glass and looked up to see Martin signaling Clovis. They retreated to an empty office, probably to talk security. My cell phone rang about the same time, and I looked down to see Novak's number. I shoved my chair back and excused myself.

"A package will be delivered to your office Tuesday morning. You were right—she did have a bank account, a substantial one. Tell me this: is one of the depositors our murderer?'

"Again, I don't know. Please don't act on an assumption. Let me do my job."

"I will, but only because I know you to be a man of your word. I sense you are getting closer."

"Alex, I truly believe I am. Can you give me the names of the depositors?"

"I cannot. I have not seen these records myself. My source has agreed to deliver the records, but will only concede that the amount in the account is substantial and that there has been more than one depositor."

"More than one?" I asked.

"More than one."

61

MAGGIE AND I spent the better part of the afternoon adding to and preparing my list of subpoenas. Clovis had hired a process server to serve them Tuesday afternoon, and I spent some time thinking how to serve the one that would prove tricky. I'd hoped to hear from Micki by now, but Maggie reminded me that we'd agreed to keep communication to a minimum.

She asked the right question.

"Why Tuesday? The preliminary hearing won't be for weeks."

"I'm worried that Micki's trip to Bibb won't remain a secret for long. When word gets out, I suspect a lot of documents will find their way to the shredder, and a few key witnesses will decide the time is right for an overseas vacation. As soon as I've heard from Micki, I'll call Peggy Fortson. After that we're gonna have to move fast."

"Didn't Constance Montgomery already warn Micki not to try to go over her head?" Maggie asked.

"Yes, she did. And I'd bet a dollar to a doughnut hole that Peggy turns me down flat."

"You know, Jack Patterson, you can be very frustrating at times. Why would you ask for a meeting you know you're not going to get?"

"Because I want my request to be on record when the attorney general calls her into his office and demands answers."

"You sound pretty cocksure, Counselor."

"I may be wrong. I certainly have been before, but I think I know how this town works. Peggy will get the call from the attorney general. Our job is to be ready with proof, not holes."

She raised her brows in doubt, and we went back to work. The holes in our thesis were only too obvious: no clear motive, no proof.

We finally gave up around five o'clock and joined Clovis in the waiting Suburban. He stepped out at the entrance to the Mayflower, looking around for Stella. "I don't see her anywhere. Give me a minute to find her—maybe she's still in the room."

Maggie plucked at his sleeve, looking a little sheepish.

"Clovis, I think she's standing next to the bellman."

I looked up, and finally recognized a very different Stella. Her hair was pulled back, held in place by a large tortoise clip. It was now an attractive dark brown, not a trace of purple. Her make-up was subdued, and her nails shone with stylish slate-gray polish. She wore a deep green dress, a pashmina draping her shoulders. I was oddly happy to see she hadn't abandoned her heels—they were at least four inches high.

A speechless Clovis held the door as she coolly seated herself in the back seat with Maggie and me.

He slipped in behind the wheel, but could only stare at the image in the rear view mirror.

"I told you she'd be a different person," Maggie giggled.

Clovis tried to respond. "What, how, … you look fantastic."

I rescued my friend. "Clovis is right. You look stunning, but I have to ask—what's the occasion."

"Y'all forget—before I started an extreme sports gym and my own computer company I worked for IBM—'Dress for Success' and all that. Walter Matthews is your close friend, and you've been to his home for drinks and dinner many times. But to me he's the owner of Bridgeport Life and my best client. I'm not the type of girl who gets invited to people's homes very often. I was pretty intimidated, and Maggie understood how I felt. She found a hairdresser who came to the hotel, and a friend of hers brought by some clothes she thought might work."

I'd never dreamed she might be nervous. She was so full of self-confidence on the job, it never occurred to me… Now I felt a bit underdressed.

Maggie quickly covered the awkward silence. "I'll change when we get home. It won't take more than a minute. You're going to love

Walter. He's going to be a little surprised himself. The last time he saw you was at the Foundation retreat. I think you were into pink that week."

We pulled into Maggie's driveway and she excused herself, dragging me with her. Clovis walked around the car and offered Stella his arm as they walked to the door. He looked like the football captain escorting the homecoming queen to the fifty-yard line.

Walter was waiting outside on his deck. The weather was ideal, and a table for five was already set. He had a knack for mixing martinis and was busy with the shaker. He poured one and approached Stella who had hung back just a bit.

"Stella, I'm so glad you and Clovis could come tonight. Some folks say I mix a pretty fair martini—I hope you'll join me." She accepted graciously, and he reached back for his own glass.

"Clovis, you and Jack can fend for yourselves for a few minutes. I want to show Stella around the house. Stella, I still can't understand why you haven't come to work for me full-time. How can I make that happen?" He took her arm and they walked back into the house.

I handed Clovis a martini, and we leaned on the rail of the deck, enjoying both the view of the pool and a moment of silence.

"Clovis, you're in for a treat. Walter is truly talented at the art of grilling. He won't tell me the secret of his marinade, but his steaks are pure perfection."

"I've already been treated enough for one evening. Can you believe I actually didn't recognize her? Just when I think I have things figured out, Stella surprises me."

I laughed. "Better get used to it."

"Better get used to what?" Maggie asked as she brought in a tray of hors d'oeuvres.

"I was just reminding Clovis that women are full of surprises."

"If anybody should have learned that lesson by now, Jack Patterson, it should be you."

The rest of the evening was a perfect respite from the days of work that had preceded Walter's invitation. The Suburban dropped me off at Barker's front entrance, and I avoided the bar area. I was asleep before my head hit the pillow, although I dreamed that Barb knocked at the door bringing "room service."

MONDAY

May 2, 2016

62

THE STEEL OF the barrel felt good to Tina as she carefully assembled the weapon on the rooftop of a DC apartment building across from Barker's. The rifle was the one thing that never failed her, the one thing she could trust. DC was a sniper's paradise—no skyscrapers to impede lines of sight. Here on the Hill, few buildings exceeded five stories. She had chosen an almost perfect place to wait, between the edge of building and an old brick smokestack. She expected her target to exit the building within the next half hour. She made the necessary adjustments to her scope and settled in to wait. Not a breath of wind this second day in May—piece of cake.

Did she have any regrets about her current contract? If she did, she put them out of her mind, replacing them with thoughts of the beach in Rio where she'd be relaxing this time tomorrow. She would take the shot as soon as the target was in the doorway. She tensed as the front door opened, but it was only the doorman, so her muscles relaxed. The door began to swing open again, and she could see him just inside. He was a step away from death.

"Better ease off the trigger, young lady. Right now. Put the gun down." A deep voice spoke as she felt the business end of a gun press against her neck. The target was nowhere to be seen, so she obeyed, dropping the weapon to the rooftop. She heard a boot kick it away.

"Thank you. Now hands behind your back, very slowly."

The cuffs were locked around her wrists, and he spoke again. "Don't move an inch, don't even think about it." She felt his hands slide over her body and couldn't help a little shiver.

"Okay, you can sit down now, but be real careful." She slowly turned and dropped to her knees.

Her eyes swept the roof quickly—three men, two with guns extended and one speaking to her. She'd not heard a footstep. How could the setup have gone so wrong?

She heard him speak quietly into his Motorola. "It's okay, we've got the sniper. We'll stay up here until the police arrive. Yeah, me, too."

He gestured at her with his gun. "Get off your knees. Sit down with your legs crossed." Again she did as she was told. The man remained on his feet, but to her relief holstered his weapon. Maybe she could still get out of this mess.

"So who ordered the hit?" He could have been asking about the weather.

She knew if she kept quiet she might live to tell the story. Her contractor would make her bail, and she'd be out of the country in a matter of days. But how had it gone wrong? How had they known where or when? She hadn't even told her contractor where the target was staying.

"Who are you? How'd you get the drop on me? How'd you know today was the day?"

Clovis responded with an easy smile. "The name is Jones. I work for Jack Patterson. We met the other day at Barker's, remember? When you give me your contractor, I'll tell you how you got careless."

Of course. They hadn't actually met, but she remembered him now. Her contractor had mentioned a Clovis Jones—she should have listened more carefully. Now she could do nothing about his smug grin.

Time seemed to stand still. She heard the sirens as if from another world. Within moments a DC swat team surrounded them. She watched as Jones conferred with a police captain.

She saw them nod in agreement, and he returned to help her to her feet.

"We're going to take the elevator downstairs, just you, me, and a few of DC's finest. Last chance to give me the name."

He was laughing at her. She felt the old anger rise, couldn't help it. She spit directly into his face. His grip on her arm tightened, but instead of punching her, he simply pulled a kerchief out of his pocket and mopped his face.

"Aw, gee, Tina—what was that about? I thought you were a professional."

"You have no idea who I am."

Surrounded by DC police, Clovis took her arm firmly.

"Sure I do. You're Tina Lalas, Olympic champion in the Pentathlon, turned expert sniper and hired assassin. Number two on Interpol's most wanted list, nicknamed the Greek Midge."

With just a hint of a smile, she walked into the elevator. When the doors opened the silence of the elevator was shattered as a team from the FBI confronted them. Two guys in suits announced they were taking custody of Tina. Clovis didn't much care what happened to Tina, so he crossed the street to meet Martin and Jack who were watching the proceedings with interest.

*****

"Clovis, Martin told me what almost happened. I know that woman. She works at Barker's. I mean she's the bartender, Barb Patton. She told me she had come over from Greece with her parents when she was a kid. She even tried to talk me into drinks, well, after hours. Now you tell me she's a sniper? Maggie will never let me hear the end of this. Was she the one who took the shot on the Eastern Shore?" I knew I was babbling. Truth be told, I was more than a little unnerved.

"Most certainly," Martin responded as we watched from the lobby. "Think about it, Jack. Not too many people choose this line of work, and those who do are professional—how else could they look in the mirror every morning? Their work is impersonal, almost totally detached from any emotion. Yet most of them have their own trademark, sort of like a calling card: the weapon, or maybe the time of the day, the list goes on and on—some stamp of their personal existence. I worked my sources within the FBI and Interpol as soon as we returned that Saturday. Tina was near the top of known assassins who could have made that shot, and Interpol was pretty sure she had entered the country recently. I have no idea how she landed a job at Barker's. The big break came Thursday when Clovis recognized her in the bar."

I stared at Clovis. "You could have warned me: we could have gotten real friendly."

Clovis interrupted. "Loosen up, Jack. Did you really think we'd let you stay at Barker's all by yourself? You tend to get into mischief when you're left alone too long. You've had protection inside this building since the moment you checked in."

I wanted to be pissed, but thanks to these two, I was alive. Besides, he was right.

"So you know she tried for a hook-up a couple of nights ago?" I asked.

"Jack, I'm proud of the restraint you showed—a little surprised, but still proud." Clovis snickered. I knew I deserved whatever they were willing to dish out.

"I wonder what would have happened if I'd opened the door to her 'room service.'"

"You would have enjoyed the night together, that's all. Her nickname is the 'Greek Midge.' She usually has sex with her targets at some point before she kills them."

Didn't sound like much fun to me.

"Okay, I'll bite—what's a 'midge?'"

"A female midge sucks the blood from the male during copulation, causing his genitals to break off before he dies."

"Well, that's a bummer—sorry I asked." I couldn't help squirming a little. The prospect was particularly off-putting.

"Don't worry, she's not quite that bad. Her usual pattern is to sleep with her victim a few days before he meets an untimely death. She's much too careful to have slept with you and then killed you inside Barker's. She got sloppy this time. One has to wonder why" Clovis said.

"What do you mean sloppy?"

Martin answered, "She got too comfortable at Barker's, never realized we had men there. Once Clovis recognized her it was easy to follow her as she checked out locations for the hit.

"She seemed to settle on the apartment building Sunday morning, so we guessed the order had been given. We had the entire afternoon and evening to set up shop behind the condenser on the roof. Sure, she should have looked, but she'd gotten cocky."

"How'd you get the police to cooperate?"

Martin answered, "I work with them every day; we have a pretty good relationship. The police are well aware of Tina. Remember, DC is a city full of prime targets. They were tickled pink to help put her out of commission without the failure of an assassination. But the locals will have a hard time keeping her in their custody. She's a huge prize in the International Police community. You watch. The FBI will try to take credit for her apprehension, and the FBI almost always gets its way."

"So why didn't you warn me?"

Grinning, Martin responded, "Didn't want to spook either you or Tina. You actually were lonesome, no acting necessary, and she thought she was safe. If she'd gotten suspicious, she would have realized we were onto her and probably would have disappeared or, worse, taken the shot early."

It all made sense, but I still felt like a twelve year-old who doesn't think he needs a babysitter.

I looked across the street. The police had cuffed Barb and were holding her next to their patrol car. The officer in charge was arguing with the FBI.

"Well, I'm glad you were there and sure glad to be alive, so thank you." I gave his arm a friendly punch and grinned. "Mind if I have a little fun?"

Clovis laughed. "The police have already agreed to get your statement later, so do whatever you feel like."

I sauntered across the street and extended my hand to Agent Travis Barry.

"Agent Barry," I smiled. "Jack Patterson. We met a week or so ago when you interviewed Marshall Fitzgerald. Small world isn't it?"

Barry looked away, barely acknowledging my presence. I ignored the snub and turned to the DC policeman who appeared to be in charge. He took my outstretched hand immediately, looking pleased as punch.

"Officer, I understand you and your men have apprehended a dangerous international criminal, saving my life in the process. Thank you. I'll make sure Captain Lanier knows how much I appreciate your efforts and your competence. Would you mind if I had a few words with your detainee?"

Now Barry turned to me and barked, "No, Patterson, you cannot have a few words with that woman. Who do you think…"

I raised a dismissive hand. "Okay, okay—I can see that you and this officer have more important things to manage right now. But before I leave, I have one question: Do you think Tina was involved in what happened last month at the Mayflower?"

Barry stuttered, "Wha…What do you mean, 'what happened at the Mayflower?'"

"You know—Billy Hopper, the unidentified dead woman in his bedroom. Do you think Tina was responsible for her death?" The DC police were all ears.

He reddened and said coldly, "Absolutely not."

I was tempted to push him further, but I'd made my point. Thanking him politely, I walked back across the street where Clovis and Martin were waiting.

"Jack, Agent Barry doesn't seem to like you very much," Martin deadpanned.

"No, Martin, he does not. Tell you what—I could use a Bloody Mary."

63

WE ORDERED DRINKS downstairs at Barker's and settled into a nearby table. I asked if DC had enough clout to hold Tina for trial in District Court. Martin said she would probably be extradited to Europe. Her crime in DC was attempted murder at best; her crimes in Europe were far more numerous and substantial. Moreover, Justice could use her extradition as a significant bargaining chip with Interpol.

"Let's complicate their lives a little bit more. I'll ask Maggie to prepare a subpoena for Tina. Let's serve it with the others." That got a laugh all around.

Fortified by a strong dose of vodka and tomato juice, we decided to get a late breakfast. I'd slept through breakfast this morning, and being a sniper's target had made me hungry. We agreed on Southside 815, a bar in Alexandria that serves chicken fried steak and white gravy equal to any I'd had in Arkansas. I hadn't been in years. I called Maggie from the car, figuring it was better to deal with her wrath over the phone than in person. She cut me short before I could begin.

"It's all right, Jack. Clovis already called; we can talk about it later. Stay away. Stella is throwing things in the conference room, but I think she's making progress. I'm trying to make sense out of your ramblings of yesterday morning and put together what we'll need tomorrow."

"Anything from Micki or Beth?" I asked.

"Not a word. The pilot just landed at Hodges Air Center in Little Rock to pick up Marshall. They'll be in Knoxville sometime this afternoon. Oh, and please tell Martin the press has figured out that you were the target of an international assassin. You might have to sneak in through the garage again. Enjoy your brunch. We have lots to do this afternoon."

"Maybe a spontaneous press conference would loosen things up a little," I mused.

"Jack, I understand your thinking, but you need evidence, you need proof. Give it time." I knew she was right, but time was slipping away.

There was already a crowd at 815, but we found three seats at the bar. I ordered chicken fried steak, gravy, two eggs over easy, and hash browns, more than enough calories for the entire day. In my defense, I almost hadn't lived to enjoy the day. While we ate, Clovis and Martin explained how they had worked with Barker's from day one to ensure my safety. Apparently, Julius Barker had been as anxious to avoid any untoward publicity as he was for my safety. The recent revelation of Barb's identity has shaken him to the core.

He'd been left hanging when Wally had to leave suddenly and was glad to find a quick replacement. In fact, a member who was part of the defense community had recommended her. As of today, the man was no longer a member.

I also learned that Clovis was almost obsessed with the Olympics, particularly the Pentathlon, and had followed Tina's progress over the years. Apparently, a demanding and abusive coach had controlled her entire life. After she took the Silver for Greece, she tried to break away, but the coach went nuts and abused her physically. Rumor had it she snapped and dropped out of sight, turning up later in Europe, hardly recognizable, as the "Greek Midge."

"What happened to the coach?" I asked.

"No one knows. One day he just disappeared," Clovis said bluntly. "Rumors of what might have happened to him are both the subject of Greek legend and the origin of her nickname."

"That's bad." I tried for a laugh, but couldn't help but think of Barb the bartender. She just didn't fit the image.

We tossed around ideas of how to use the morning's events, but in the end decided to do nothing. For one thing, whoever had hired Barb/Tina was bound to know she'd been arrested. I was pretty sure he wasn't sitting on his hands waiting for the next shoe to drop. We didn't need to let our guard down.

We didn't get back to the office until almost one. Both Stella and Maggie were hard at work. I let Clovis and Martin tell the story while I retreated to my office to return a call from Red Shaw. He had texted more than once: "Call ASAP."

I had no idea what to expect. I hadn't written him off my suspect list just yet, so I was more than a little uncomfortable.

Red continued to surprise me.

"Do you think that woman on the rooftop was the one who shot at you and Carol?"

"You know about that?"

"There isn't much I don't know. I make it my business. Carol called me, and I came to her place right after you left."

I knew he'd been added to the guest list that weekend, but I hadn't known that Carol had confided in him. I wasn't quite sure how I felt about that. Red must have sensed my discomfort.

"Listen Jack, Carol and I have been friends for a long time. I set her up in business and have been her biggest client and supporter for years. But my relationship is paternal and professional, nothing more. She confides in me as a daughter would to her father, so yes when you hightailed it out of there, she called me. She had to talk to someone."

I had to take him at his word. "How is she?"

"She's ready for you to join her, wherever the hell she is."

"You don't know?" I was astonished.

"Nope, only Pat knows. She says its better this way, and she's probably right, but we've talked. That's why I'm asking about the sniper. Now that she's been arrested, do you think it's safe for her to come back?"

The thought of Carol's return was very appealing. But she left for a reason, and Barb's arrest hadn't changed that reason. She wasn't the only gun for hire.

"I'd to love to say she'd be safe, but I can't. She needs to stay put for a little while longer." The words seemed to stick in my mouth.

"Exactly what I thought you'd say. Tell me how can I help?"

He was still on my list of suspects, but I needed information. "What can you tell me about Logan Aerospace and Chuck Morrison?"

I could almost hear him thinking.

"Logan is run by an executive committee of faceless, ruthless former Army brass and CIA higher-ups. Morrison is basically a face man, nice guy but a glad-hander. They are my main competitors and did everything in their power to keep me from buying the Lobos. If they're involved, you're out of your league."

Out of my league? What the hell... I took a deep breath.

"Why do you ask?" he continued. "Did Carol tell you about the phone call she got from Logan that first weekend you were together?"

"So that's who called. She tried, but I was miffed, wasn't buying."

"So she said. Apparently they were unhappy with your unexpected appearance. I told her to drop them as a client; she didn't need to be treated like trash."

So it was Logan who had ruined my first weekend with Carol. Things were starting to make sense.

"Know anything about a group called L&A Marketing Advisors in Alexandria, Virginia? I don't have an address, just a P.O. Box." I decided to trust Red, at least for now—I needed information.

"Who are they and why do they matter?"

"I was hoping you might know."

"Never heard of them, but I bet I can find out."

"Thank you. Please tell Carol to be patient," I added.

"Carol would tell you to forget all this, leave town, and join her on her beach. You didn't ask for my opinion, but I'm going to give it to you anyway. She's a keeper, Jack. Don't blow it."

"I know that. But I really do believe Billy Hopper's innocent—I can't just leave, and you know that."

He said nothing, so I continued.

"Red, I have to ask: do you play fantasy football yourself? When you said you lost millions on Billy was it through fantasy sports? I mean, he was Rookie of the Year."

I heard a sigh before he replied. "I knew something was eating at you. When I said I lost millions I was referring to the big money the team spent trying to offset the impression that pro football breeds men who abuse women. Gina can give you an itemized list of the money we spent on donations and commercials."

"She doesn't need to do that, and I'm sorry I had to ask."

"Don't ever hesitate to ask. But while we're on the subject of fantasy football let me tell you that you're right on target. The potential money for owners and athletes is enormous, the potential for abuse clear. A sure-handed receiver or any other hot-shot of the moment drops an easy pass—you've gotta wonder why. The allure for fans is obvious: every wannabe or used-to-be athlete thinks he can win at fantasy football. The reality is few can resist the chance for easy money, but fewer still ever break even.

"I've been privately lobbying the owners to come up with some basic controls. Of course, we'll need to get the Union's consent, but I hope before the start of next season we'll have a hard and fast rule that no ballplayer or employee of a team can own a fantasy account. We need to go further but it's a beginning. Hell, Jack, since you asked I might make you my front man on this issue. You used to play ball. My biggest worry is that some government busybody or aspiring politician, who never played the game, will use fantasy sports as a reason to tell me how to operate my business. Get Billy out of jail; then you and I can talk about it."

I told him I looked forward to it.

I hung up feeling much better about Red. I sure hoped I wasn't misreading him, but I was running out of time and had to trust someone.

In this case, the attempt to set up Billy was too sophisticated to be the work of someone who'd simply lost a pile of money betting on the wrong guy. But I could see how fantasy football could put real players of the game in significant danger from irate gamblers and fantasy game players—owners would have to up the security they already provided. The issues and temptations were even more complicated than I'd realized.

I left my office and found the others clustered around Maggie's desk.

"What's up?"

Stella began, "First, the bad news. Someone broke into the office last night. They didn't take anything as far as we can tell and weren't able to access the computers, but they were looking for something."

"Trash?" I asked.

"I shredded everything last night before we left. The only copy of your memo is still on the computer, no hard copies have been printed yet. Same with the subpoenas," Maggie said.

"Check the printers and copier. They may have planted one of those devices that reads whatever is printed," I suggested.

"That's next on the list," Stella confirmed.

"What about the information from Novak about Nadia?" I asked.

Maggie responded immediately, "It's all in the safe, which hasn't been tampered with as far as we can tell."

"Well, hopefully we learned a lesson. We need to be more careful," I said.

Martin spoke up. "I hate to mention this, but Stella has been working here all alone for several nights. Our hacker is bound to be getting frustrated—he may have come for you."

Clovis began to rumble, but I cut him off.

"Clovis, you're too close. Thanks Martin, and be sure Stella is never here alone. Any of us, for that matter."

I turned to Stella. "Any good news?"

"I'm close to tracing our hacker. Another few hours should do it." She didn't look the least bit concerned.

"Great. Okay, Stella, back to work. I want the rest of us to work on improving our plan, figure out what we need, and how to get it."

"First, I'm going to check the printers and the copier," Stella replied.

The gaps were obvious. We were still waiting for Novak to let me know who was paying Nadia. I told them I hoped to have solid information about L&A by tomorrow. We could only hope that one of the two remaining girls from the banquet appeared, and we still had heard nothing from Tennessee. Lots of minor pieces were missing as well, but I felt those four were critical to bringing the overall picture into focus.

Stella came back grinning from ear to ear, waving a tiny piece of electronic equipment above her head.

"A device that sends our adversary a copy of every document printed on the copier or any printer in the office. Our intruder was here to plant this baby—I have to tell you I feel much better."

We all took a collective sigh of relief. The tiny devise gave me an idea.

"Don't disable it quite yet. Maggie, please prepare two subpoenas, one for Red Shaw and one for Lucy Robinson. Print them out so our adversary thinks they are targets of our investigation. Then you can do whatever you want with the devices."

Everyone but Maggie looked puzzled, but there was method to my madness. If our adversary turned out to be Red after all, I'd get an angry call from him fairly soon. If not, our true adversary might think we were barking up the wrong tree and relax until the real subpoenas went out.

"I'll reinstall the device," Stella said, "but I'd like to leave it active for the rest of today and tonight. I can use it to help me determine who our hacker is. I'll set up a direct connection from Maggie's computer to one printer so no one can read any of the real stuff."

"Okay, but we'll need the copier by tomorrow afternoon," I said.

"Isn't that wishful thinking?" Maggie asked.

"It better not be." I tried to sound confident.

Stella smiled. "With this device and the other work I've been doing, we'll know the identity of our hacker long before tomorrow morning. You can take that to the bank."

I wished I felt as confident.

Martin had left the room to take a call a few minutes earlier. He returned smiling.

Maggie asked, "Who was on the phone?"

"Micki. They won't get in until late tonight, so she wants to go straight to the Hay-Adams. She promises to meet you here by eight o'clock tomorrow morning."

"Is that it?" I asked.

He grinned. "No. Are you ready for this? She said to tell you she'd never doubt your instincts again."

"Of course she will—just give her a couple of days." But I couldn't help feeling a little twitch of anticipation.

Maggie asked, "Anything else?"

"As a matter of fact, yes. She told me they're bringing two extra passengers."

"For Pete's sake, man—who?" I tried not to lose my patience.

"Marshall's wife, Grace, and someone named Anna Crockett." He was still grinning.

TUESDAY

May 3, 2016

6 4

WITH "ANNA CROCKETT" dancing in all our brains, it was tough to concentrate. Maggie and I spent the time tending to the minute details of preparing a memorandum I hoped to use, trying to bolster my theory any way I could. Stella was hard at work going through all the responses the website had received. Most of them were junk, but I still hoped that it might get us closer to the two missing women. Clovis and Martin worked on the logistics of protecting the crew of people who would be staying at the Hay-Adams, now including one Anna Crockett.

We reconvened around five-thirty. I told everyone to take the night off, but my suggestion fell on deaf ears. Martin was determined to be part of the team that went to the airport. Stella planned to work all night, and Clovis wasn't about to let her out of his sight. I admit to feeling a bit concerned that another assassin was already scouting out Barker's. Yes, we were running out of time.

The bar at Barker's on a Sunday night was practically empty except for me and my babysitters at a corner table. Barb had been replaced with Bill, who had the personality of a lamppost. After a plate of Buffalo wings and a couple of beers, I trudged off to bed, hoping sleep would bring peace rather than nightmares.

******

I was at the office by seven the next morning. A warm shower had cleared my head, and I didn't want to miss anything. Someone had shoved a very thin manila envelope under the office door—Red

Shaw's stamp was in the left hand corner. I tore into it while the coffee was brewing.

I couldn't believe what I was reading and called him immediately.

"Did you read what you sent over?" I asked.

"Of course," he answered.

"Are you sure? Who is your source?"

"The information is accurate. What you do with it is up to you, but it is accurate. You know perfectly well why I can't tell you how I obtained it."

He was right. I thanked him and he said, "Be careful, Jack—seems to me you've uncovered a hornet's nest."

"That I have, Red, that I have."

I made a mental note to ask Maggie to prepare a subpoena for all the records belonging to L&A as well as their bank account at Parra Bank in Alexandria.

Stella and Clovis had never left. They looked a bit ragged.

"Y'all get any sleep?" I asked.

"Really, quite a bit. That big sofa in the conference room is actually quite comfy," Stella answered with smirk. "And I managed to pinpoint our hackers. They're here in the District. Clovis is going to visit them this morning."

"Hold off on that. First, it might be dangerous, and, second, I want to serve them with a subpoena when he does. Know anything about them."

"Just that they are very good at what they do. My bet is they're Chinese, but I could be dead wrong. Clovis and I have a bet. My money is on the office is some kind of International headquarters or an Eastern trading company. Clovis thinks they'll be Eastern European."

"Either way, Clovis, don't go alone, and be extremely careful," I said.

Clovis noticed the envelope from Red when he brought me a fresh cup of coffee.

"What's that?" he asked.

"The information on L&A we needed. Take a look," I said.

Clovis turned the pages in silence and looked up. "Is this for real?"

"My reaction precisely. My source is solid. It's for real."

Clovis whistled.

It wasn't long before Maggie, Beth, Paul, and Micki joined us. They had brought coffee, pastries, and a lot of excitement. We congregated in the conference room. After we all got comfortable, I tried to start.

"Where and who is Anna Crockett?" I asked.

"Don't you even dare, Jack Patterson," Micki interrupted. "We have a story to tell, and we spent the plane ride home deciding how we are going to tell it. Sit down and no interruptions."

"It's your show, Ms. Lawrence."

Quickly Micki took us through the boring details of the flight to Knoxville, pulled pork and ribs at Cleveland's Barbeque, and the morning drive to Bibb. I was quickly bored by tales of stopping at several sawmills for Larry on the drive down, but I knew better than to interrupt.

Once in Bibb, Micki went to the local library to scan the newspapers from around the time of Billy's birth. Beth and Paul headed to the bar where Billy's dad had been arrested after murdering his mother, and Larry crossed the street to check out the only gas station/country store that was still in business. They all agreed to tell anyone who asked that they were doing research for a book on Billy Hopper's life.

Micki spoke, "The library was about what you'd think in a small town. One librarian at the front who was friendly and real curious about why I was there. Back copies of the local newspaper were stacked on shelves by year—no microfilm, nothing on computer. The older ones were pretty fragile, and it took forever, but I found the articles about Billy's father's arrest, his conviction, and his death in prison. The library's copy machine was at least ten years old and had been broken for months, so I used my iPhone to get pictures. You can at least see the headlines. If you need actual copies, someone will have to go back with a real copier/scanner.

"Ms. Hicks wouldn't leave my side and started to fidget when she saw I was looking at papers from around the time of Billy's birth. I found plenty of births, deaths, marriages, and divorces recorded in the public announcements, but no reference to a Zeke, Donna, or a

William/Billy Hopper.

"Since that was a dead end, I went back to the papers eight to ten months before Billy was born. One article caught my eye." Micki's eyes sparkled.

"Jack, I bet you can guess. I suspect that's why you sent us there in the first place."

She had me.

Maggie spoke up, "Come on, you two. We don't have time for games."

"About nine months before Billy Hopper was born, the Bibb Gazette ran almost giddy accounts about second term Senator Jason Boudreaux's long weekend at the Happy Valley Mountain Lodge near Bibb, Tennessee. The pictures show him shaking hands with constituents, fishing the mountain streams, and enjoying the local high school basketball game. One of the best photos is of him with one very attractive fifteen year-old student—Donna Crockett."

Clovis blurted out, "Donna was Billy Hopper's mother's first name."

Micki smiled. "They are one in the same, but you're getting ahead of the story. Let's us finish."

It was hard to be patient, but Micki was having fun.

"I was trying to get a few more pictures when a weather-beaten guy in a Sheriff's uniform barged into the library and snatched the newspapers from my hand. The librarian must have called him. He shoved the papers back on the shelf and got all huffy. 'The people of Bibb don't cotton to nosy reporters stickin' their noses in where they don't belong.'

"I assured him I wasn't a reporter, just doing research for a book about Billy Hopper. He didn't care. He said, 'It's a shame that boy lost his daddy, but folks around here don't like busybodies nosing into their private matters. You better git' on out before people get nervous.'"

"Sounds like an implied threat to me," Maggie noted.

"Nothing implied about it. I later found out found out that the deputy, one Zach Hopper, is Zeke Hopper's second cousin. I worried he might try to confiscate our belongings so I left in a hurry and went searching for Larry."

Beth jumped right in. "While Micki was at the library, Paul and I found the bar where Zeke was arrested. We ordered a beer and struck up a conversation with the bartender. The bar was exactly what you'd expect—dark, musty, smelled of old French fries, and had a juke box in the back.

"We told the bartender about the book, and it turned out he was there the day Zeke was arrested.

"He told us that Zeke always was bad news—nasty, drinking all the time, never could hold down a job. Then one day he shows up with this quiet little girl who was pregnant. He only brought her into the bar a couple of times. She never spoke a word, sipped on a Coke in the corner while Zeke played pool. Pretty soon, Zeke showed up without her. Big difference was all of a sudden Zeke had money. Not a lot, but enough to buy beer, order food, and if he lost at pool he paid his debt instead of fighting over it. When people asked about the money, he laughed and said he'd done a rich uncle a favor.

"We had another round, but the bartender didn't have much else to say, so we left pretty quickly," Beth said.

"Aren't you going to tell your father about the guys hitting on you in the bar? Paul said they gave you a pretty rough time." I was surprised by Micki's tone.

"No, Micki, I'm not. I went with you as part of a team. I had a job, and I tried to do it. I'm glad Paul was there, but quit treating me like a child. I've paid my dues."

She was clearly ready for a showdown—this I didn't need.

"Okay, enough—you two simmer down. When do I get to meet Anna Crockett?"

"After you hear about Larry," said Micki.

"Larry?" asked Stella.

"Larry. While we were all busy with research and talking, Larry found the country store where Billy was found as a child, sat down in a rocking chair outside, and started whittling."

"Whittling?" Clovis asked.

"Exactly. He pulled out his pocketknife and a piece of wood and started whittling as if he'd lived in Bibb all his life. Wasn't long before he was joined by a couple of other guys rocking and whittling, and he learned all about the store owner finding Billy that morning, and those 'no good, no count Hoppers.'"

Micki smiled like the Cheshire cat.

"Here's the best part—they told Larry that Donna's mother is still alive and where he could find her. They warned him that the Hoppers still keep close tabs on her. Our presence in town was bound to spook them. They said she had a phone, but it was a four-party line, and the Hopper's were likely to be listening in if we tried to call."

Beth picked up the story. "We decided to spend the night at the Happy Valley Mountain Lodge. It's actually a very nice place—clean, beautiful mountain views, and a good breakfast. Plus it's just far enough away from Bibb that the Hoppers would assume we'd left town. We found Anna's house—it was just up the hill from the lodge. I could see a sheriff's car parked out front. Over dinner we came up with a plan. Larry would call her asking if he could give her an estimate on the work needed to repair her sagging front porch.

"She agreed and we showed up the next morning. She had some tools and spare lumber in her barn so Larry worked on her porch in case anyone drove by. She was overwhelmed at first, but Micki was wonderful about taking time and drawing her into her confidence.

"When Donna learned she was pregnant, she contacted the real father. Two days later, Zeke Hopper was at their door telling them not to tell a soul about the real father. He would marry Donna and raise the child as his own, but Anna and Donna had to keep quiet, otherwise they would be killed. After Zeke killed Donna, Anna was 'visited' by several other Hoppers. They told her to keep quiet and to stay away from Billy, otherwise the boy would end up like his mother. They still drop by on occasion to remind her of their warning."

"What a terrible story. It's hard to believe that could have really happened," Maggie said.

"You haven't been to Bibb, Tennessee," Micki replied grimly.

"Any chance she has any proof about who the real father is?" I asked.

"The real father sent her a hundred dollar bill every month for over the last twenty years," Beth responded.

"One hundred dollars? Every month? Did she keep a record?" I asked.

"Better than that. She kept the envelopes with the money in them. She never spent a dime of his money. Her husband died when Donna was little, and they lived on his pension from the railroad. The envelopes and cash are in a box we brought with us from Bibb." Micki was tickled. "Hopefully the father's fingerprints are on the bills and envelopes."

"And you've left her at the Hay-Adams?" Maggie asked.

"Don't worry—Grace came back with Marshall, and she's with them. They spent the whole plane ride home talking to her about Billy. It was Beth's idea to call Marshall while we were still in Bibb. Anna had never left the county before, but after listening to Marshall she agreed to come with us to DC. She said she couldn't believe Billy had killed anyone, and it wouldn't hurt to see the nation's capital before she died."

I smiled at Beth.

"Good work; she might be just what Billy needs. Anything else?"

"We have copies of the hotel register at the Lodge showing the real father spent four nights there with a 'guest.' We also have several pictures of that very frightened guest with the father. The man had no shame."

Micki handed a picture to Maggie and looked at me.

"You already knew who Billy's Hopper father was."

"I didn't know, but I thought it was a possibility. It's the only way any of this makes sense. Maggie…"

"Yes, I recognize him. Jason Boudreaux, distinguished senator from Tennessee." She tossed the photograph on the desk in disgust.

65

MY HUNCH HAD paid off, and now a lot of what we had discovered about Logan Aerospace and L&A made sense. My bet was that the bartender at the Mayflower would recognize a photo of the Senator as the older man who used to meet Nadia. We had so much more to figure out—Billy's semen on the sheets, the locked doors, who had been paying Nadia—but the story was coming together. Now it was time to make the bad guys nervous.

Maggie left to finalize and organize all the paperwork. Paul and Clovis would try to surprise the hackers with a subpoena. They'd probably pull up shop, but they'd know we were onto them. Beth and Stella were updating "Free Billy." We still hoped we could locate the two girls. I thought about calling Novak, but decided against it. He would call when he was ready. No sense inviting questions I didn't want to answer.

I sat at my desk playing with a pencil. After a few minutes of thought I called out to Beth, asked her if she could spare me a minute.

She came in and asked, "What's up, Dad?"

I decided to be direct. "What was that with you and Micki? Everything okay?"

She took her time. "So I know about you and Micki being friendly during the case with Woody—who didn't know? It was a little unnerving at the time—I mean, really? It's just hard for a daughter to—but I'm over it, long over it. I want you to find someone to care about. But sometimes Micki treats me like I'm like a child, like she's my mother. I'm sorry, sometimes it just goes all over me. She is not my mother!"

"Oh, Beth, I'm sorry. You know that I care for Micki very much, but not in the same way now—she doesn't either. I can understand how..."

"It's okay, Dad. Don't worry; we'll work it out. I should get back to Stella—we're so close to finding...." With that, she practically fled the office. I wondered if sons were so mercurial.

I needed to refocus. It was time to call the one person who could bring matters to a head. I hated to involve her, but I couldn't think of a better strategy. I was way to far out on the limb to chicken out now.

Micki listened as I ran the gamut of aides and assistants. Finally I got to Peggy Fortson.

"Jack, why am I not surprised you're calling. Interpol's most wanted assassin targets you, the FBI saves your life, and now I bet you're calling to ask me to go easy on her because she's cute."

The FBI. Already? I took a deep breath—I had more important things to worry about than who got credit for Barb's capture.

"Well, she is cute, but that's not why I'm calling."

"Seriously, Jack, are you okay? We'll probably send her to France in a few days, but I promise we'll find out who was behind all this. I take this one personally. And what's this I hear about you representing Billy Hopper? Tell me you've come to your senses."

"It's good to hear you're concerned, I appreciate it. In fact, that's why I'm calling. I believe Tina's attempt on my life is directly connected with the Billy Hopper case. I'd like to meet with the Attorney General to explain why they've got the wrong man."

I heard a deep sigh as she considered her response.

"Jack, that's not going to happen, not a chance in hell. The Hopper case is correctly in the hands of the U.S attorney and his deputy, Connie Montgomery. You know we maintain a hands-off policy regarding local crime. This one may be high profile, but it's local nonetheless. Tina has no connection to the Hopper case. She wasn't even in the country when Hopper murdered that poor woman. Sorry, Jack. If you think the government's got the wrong man, take it up with Connie. The AG is not going to give you the time of day."

Peggy was a good friend. I knew it was fruitless to argue. Career lawyers at Justice understand the chain of command as well as any Marine.

"Okay, I understand. Let's have lunch soon." Interesting how the offer of lunch or a drink becomes code for "never mind, love to see you, but don't count on it."

"You're not even going to try to argue, Jack? Tina must have gotten inside your head. I expected at least a little fight."

I probably shouldn't have said anything further, but I was irritated that she had slammed the door in my face.

"No, Peggy, I'm not going to fight, even a little. But remember this call; remember I asked for a meeting." I clicked off before she could respond.

It was time to rally the troops. "Game's on, folks! Let's get the subpoenas out."

I turned to Micki. "Be ready for a call from Constance. She's going to want to meet, and you have to refuse. She's liable to push you pretty hard. For us to have any shot at a meeting with the AG, they have to believe we're about to go public in a very vocal manner. Shoot, I might even call the press."

"You don't think Constance will listen on her own?"

"This case involves much more than Billy Hopper." I handed her the file that Red had slid under the office door.

She looked through it and asked, "What does this mean?"

"I'm not sure yet. We have a couple more clues to nail down, but it means the government will do its best to make sure Billy Hopper is found guilty and sent away for life. Constance couldn't drop the case if she wanted to."

She smiled. "I love working with you, you know that."

I refrained from saying something I'd regret. "I love working with you, too. Thank you for coming here when I really needed you. You had a hundred reasons to say no, but you came."

We sat quietly for a few minutes, neither sure how to react or what to say next. The air was thick with memories from the past. Fortunately, Beth burst into the office, breaking the rising tension.

"We may have a real inquiry on the website. A 'Mary' is asking questions about the reward, how we can guarantee her safety, and can she meet someone?"

I asked, "You don't think it's a prank?"

"No, I've been very careful. I think she may be for real," Beth said excitedly.

Micki spoke up. "Let us handle this, Jack. If she is one of the girls, she'll be afraid of you. I'm used to dealing with victims like her."

"She's all yours, but be careful. Make sure you have plenty of security. Martin has plenty of female employees, so don't do anything without protection. This woman could be the break we need."

"Or very important to the prosecution," Micki said, forever the realist. "If she is one of the two girls at the banquet, she can verify that Billy was drunk and violent, putting a lie to your theories."

"Well, that might happen, but it would mean she's alive and maybe the other girl as well. And, by the way, Billy sure didn't kill the third girl and their pimp."

Micki gave me a frown and left with Beth to try to reach Mary online. Maggie handed me an envelope that had come by courier. It was bound to be Nadia's bank account information, but I didn't open it.

Maggie asked, "What's wrong?"

"Let's go for a walk," I said.

I knew one or two of Martin's men would be following us, but I needed some fresh air.

Once we were outside, I headed for Lafayette Park. We found a bench, and sat down.

Maggie reached for my hand and held it. "What is it? You were on a high this morning, now you look like you just lost your best friend. What's wrong?"

"You and I both live a very good life. We want for little. Beth is happy and doing well, and our Foundation is doing very good work. But every now and then we find out that the world isn't that simple, and I learn things about people and our government I'd rather not know.

"Billy Hopper was cocktail party talk, far removed from my world. Then it turns out Marshall is his surrogate father, he may be wrongfully accused, and people are trying to kill me, my family, and my friends to keep me from finding out the truth. Part of me wants to cry uncle, give this case to someone else, and go back to the old days when my biggest concern was beating your husband at golf."

Maggie squeezed my hand. "Life's never simple, it just sometimes seems that way. Jack, I don't know why these cases seem to find you. If it weren't Billy Hopper it would be something else. Maybe they're the obligation you trade for enjoying 'a very good life.' You're an idealist at heart, Jack. Disillusion comes hard for you, but sometimes you can't avoid it.

"I'm going to give you the same advice you gave me when I started working with you. Get the job done and enjoy what you do. Everything else will take care of itself. It's my understanding that Walter and I won't get to meet this Carol Madison until you get this job done, so let's get on with it. Besides, you can't very well just walk out on Billy now, and you know it."

I gave her a kiss on the cheek, and we walked back to the office enjoying the warmth of the spring sun. Micki texted that she and Beth were on their way to Arlington, and that, yes, Martin's people were with them. I sat down at my desk and opened the envelope from Novak. Nadia had saved quite a bit of money, and her deposits were numerous. She made frequent, regular cash deposits. L&A had made occasional but substantial deposits. Logan Aerospace was a regular, monthly depositor, as were at least ten other individuals

I asked Stella to see if she could find out more about the backgrounds of the other depositors. I would have Maggie prepare subpoenas for them, too. The only good thing about the list of names, all men, was that none of them were my clients. Red Shaw wasn't on the list either, relieving a troubling possibility. How could these guys have been so stupid as to write checks or give their credit cards to Nadia, and think it wouldn't eventually come home to roost?

Clovis and Paul returned from serving the hackers. Paul announced that the sign on their office door read 'P.S. Eastern Trading, LLC, L. Kim Proprietor,' and Clovis silently handed five twenties to Stella. The space consisted of a small reception area, an office with a view of the White House, and not much else. Clovis felt sure Mr. Kim recognized him, but his only reaction to the subpoena was a hint of a smile and a request that they leave.

*****

Mr. Kim's employer was not pleased to learn that Tina had been arrested trying to assassinate Jack Patterson. Shanghai would make sure she was released once she arrived in Paris. Kim had no doubt that Jones was responsible for her apprehension. The fools with the FBI who were taking credit didn't even know she was in the country.

The client had terminated the contract and registered a complaint with Shanghai. The syndicate in New Orleans had taken insult at the proposed hit on Patterson's daughter and was demanding a financial apology. Who were they kidding? It was time for Kim to leave the country; he had made preparations for such a situation long ago.

He'd finally met Jones this morning—a worthy adversary. He knew the subpoena to be what it was—a message from Patterson that he had been discovered and that it was time for him to leave.

Kim took consolation from one thing. Patterson would fail utterly in his attempt to exonerate Hopper. He had learned enough from the client to understand that it was imperative for Hopper to be found responsible for Nadia's death. Nothing Patterson could do would prevent that result.

66

I MANAGED TO find time to meet Walter for a late lunch at The Daily Grill. I eyed the meat loaf, but when Walter ordered a Cobb salad, I settled on the grilled trout. I needed a lunch with my golfing buddy where we could talk about anything except this case. We lingered over coffee. I knew that no news from Micki and Beth was good news. This afternoon would be a waiting game.

We returned to the office to find Maggie holding down the fort. I read through the report Stella had left me on the background of Nadia's clients. I recognized several names—it just didn't do any good to think about. I spent the next hour on the phone with Marshall. He told me all about meeting Anna Crockett and how Grace and Anna had bonded. He couldn't wait to tell Billy about his grandmother.

Marshall understood why we needed to keep Anna's presence a secret, at least until the subpoena for the Senator had been served. Grace and Anna had gone shopping for a new outfit to wear when she met Billy. She'd told Grace she didn't have much use for new clothes back in Bibb. I explained to Marshall that if the press found out that Anna was Billy's grandmother, they would eat her alive. We sure didn't want to let the cat out of the bag about Billy's paternity. I felt strongly this was an issue for Billy to decide how to deal with.

Micki and Beth returned, fairly bursting with their news.

Micki began, "They're real and they're both safe. We're calling them Mary and Ruth, no real names. Martin's people are protecting them in a secure location. I have to hand it to your daughter—she was great. She immediately realized these women were scared to death and took great pains to put them at ease. Beth, I owe you an apology. I've been a bitch, I don't even know why. I hope you will accept it."

I rushed in before Beth could reply, hoping to avoid a scene. "So both women are okay?'

"They're okay, but fragile and need medical attention," Micki answered. "I'll get into their story in a bit, but we've taken on a huge responsibility. Someone wants these two girls dead."

I said, "Don't think I don't understand. I'll do everything in my power to keep them safe, nothing less."

"From anyone?"

"From anyone." I wondered why she asked.

"Good, 'cause you won't like this next part. They don't trust men right now, any man. I think they'll cooperate with Beth and me, but men are verboten at this point. That means you, Jack. You're going to have to trust me to get their complete story and present it to the authorities."

Beth looked uncomfortable. "Dad, this isn't about you. It's just that right now they have no reason to think that good guys actually exist. I can't begin to tell you how frightened these women are. I feel pretty sure we can get their story, but in the end, I hope we can get them the help they need to feel good about themselves again."

"Thanks, Beth. I understand and hope we can, too. Micki, promise me this: if you learn anything that implicates Billy, you need to tell me. Don't let me say he's innocent if they don't corroborate our theory."

Micki smiled. "Oh, I think we'll have an affidavit by tomorrow morning. Beth is right—we couldn't push them at all this afternoon. We needed to build up trust and get them into a doctor's care. If it makes you feel better, both women have said that Billy was drugged at the banquet. He wasn't drunk. That's about all I know now."

I smiled. I had complete faith that Micki knew exactly how to get statements that would hold up under scrutiny. I did worry a bit about another two people who needed protection. Martin's people were already spread thin. I made a mental note to talk to Clovis.

I didn't expect to hear from Peggy for a few days, but I knew I was making a new enemy with every subpoena. The most difficult one to serve would be on the Senator. He was immune from service while in

the U.S. Capitol, so I had swapped favors with Cheryl Cole again. She
and the Senator were having lunch at Sam & Harry's this afternoon.
He couldn't resist her charms or a free lunch. He would be served
with the subpoena in the restaurant, and Cheryl would be right there
to ask him why. I kind of felt sorry for the old man, but then again he
had raped Billy's mom when she was fifteen, abandoned Billy, and
sent her off to an early death at the hands of Zeke Hopper. He didn't
deserve much sympathy.

The first call came to Micki. We all gathered in her office to hear
the story.

"That was Constance Montgomery. She knows we want to meet
with the Attorney General, and although that isn't possible, she's
available for an 'open and frank' discussion about the case. I blamed
you, Jack. I said I would be happy to do so, but you were adamant
about having the AG present. She continued to insist that would
never happen.

"Then she said she'd heard we were issuing subpoenas and what
could I tell her about them. I told her we were simply preparing for
the preliminary hearing, and that after they were all served, I would
provide her with a list. She was clearly unhappy with that response,
gave me a little lecture about ethics and procedure."

I laughed and Micki responded, "Well—but she didn't budge on a
meeting with the AG. You may be counting too much on the Senator
trying to get the subpoena quashed."

"Maybe, but it's the subpoena to L&A that will turn the tide, you
watch," I said, and then realized I had forgotten about one possibility.

"Stella, can we use the copy machine?" I asked.

"Sure—it's no longer a problem."

"Good. Okay, guys all hands on deck. We need to make several
copies of every document we've got on this case. Especially the file on
Nadia, L&A, and Nadia's bank account and phone records."

No questions, no argument: everyone pitched in and within an
hour the job was done. Martin's people delivered the originals to a
safe deposit box, copies to another secure location, and returned
with sandwiches from Cosi.

We were sitting around the table eating when my premonition

came true. I heard a noise in the hall and walked out to see a man in a grey suit trying to open the locked door. When I opened it and smiled, he identified himself as special agent Boerner with the FBI and demanded that we relinquish our computers and all our files. Two rather burly men accompanied him.

"May I see your warrant?" I asked.

"Don't need one, this is a matter of national security. Please step away from the door, Mr. Patterson."

"It may indeed be a matter of national security, agent, but unless you have a warrant you're not welcome, and you may not have my computers or files." I stood firm, feeling better that Clovis and Martin were both standing behind me.

"I'm here on the orders of the deputy director of the FBI himself. You would be wise to cooperate. If you refuse, I can take you into custody."

"For what? You don't have a warrant, and you don't have probable cause for an arrest. You go back to Deputy Director Calhoun. Tell him if he wants my files he can join me when I meet with the Attorney General."

"We can be back in a matter of hours with a warrant." Apparently my offer wasn't acceptable.

"That you can, and I will honor a valid search warrant. But you and the deputy director will have to explain to the Attorney General why you don't want him to see my files."

"I take it you are refusing entry to your offices?" His bluster was fading fast.

"I am."

"Have it your way, but you can be sure we'll be back." He turned to the others. "Come on, let's get out of here."

I had no doubt Agent Boerner would be back. I had no control over the FBI, and I expected them to do whatever was necessary to end my game. My job was to make sure that didn't happen.

"Beth and Micki, you need to see Mary and Ruth this afternoon. I know you think it's too soon, but we have no choice. We have to be prepared to present our case as early as tomorrow morning."

"Tomorrow morning?" Micki exclaimed.

"It's the worst possible case, but by now Logan, L&A, and the Senator are pressuring whoever they can to have those subpoenas quashed. They'll probably try to get a judge to impose some kind of Order that will completely tie our hands, and with a friendly judge they're likely to be successful.

"The rest of us will spend today and tonight getting ready for whatever comes next. You and Beth are in charge of presenting whatever the girls know. Don't forget that whoever might have already hired another sniper. Time works against us, not for us."

I gave Stella some language to put up on the website which was bound to cause a stir. I also asked her to be vigilant for the FBI or the NSA trying to hack into our computers or listen in to our cell phones. I know I must have sounded paranoid, but then again when you stir up a hornet's nest you'd better be ready for an angry reaction.

Everyone nodded soberly and went their separate ways. Maggie and I were left to finish the presentation we hoped to be able to give.

The call came just after six o'clock.

"You son-of-a-bitch, you have your meeting." Peggy Fortson wasn't usually so direct.

"Peggy, such language." I opted for a nonchalant tone.

"What do you expect? You subpoena a U.S. Senator in front of the press. You subpoena and ask for mountains of records from one of the major defense contractors in the country. To top it off you subpoena Tina Lalas, interfering with our negotiations with Interpol. You know damn well Tina had nothing to do with the Hopper matter; she wasn't even in the country. You've gone too far, Jack. You'll get your meeting, but don't expect it to be friendly or for the Attorney General to be cooperative. If I were you I'd bring some comfortable clothes. You just might find yourself locked up after tomorrow's meeting." Peggy was hot. I expect she'd had a rough day.

"May I ask who'll be there?"

"Why not? You might as well know—the Attorney General, myself, plus a couple of members of his immediate staff. Constance Montgomery and the U.S. Attorney for the District, and Deputy Director of the FBI Felix Calhoun along with a couple of agents. I believe you know one of them, Travis Barry. Neither the Senator or

Logan will be represented, despite their requests.

"Who are you bringing?" A fair question.

"Maggie, Micki Lawrence, and myself. Oh, and Marshall Fitzgerald."

"I'm not sure Judge Fitzgerald is appropriate. We both know he is a friend of the Attorney General, plus he is a critical witness." She had a point, but I had one as well.

"Marshall is the closest thing Billy has to a family member right now. He respects the Attorney General too much to expect special treatment in any way. Check with the AG and Constance—I'm sure they won't mind." It was worth a shot. "What time?"

"Ten o'clock," she responded.

"We'll be there, with all the documents. No need for that warrant now."

Peggy paused, sounding confused. "What warrant?"

So the FBI hadn't told the AG or Peggy about this afternoon's attempted raid. Interesting.

"Sorry, I've got two cases going and just got confused." Lame, lame, lame, but I couldn't think of anything else on the spur of the moment. Fortunately, she let it go.

"Don't expect a welcome mat, Jack. You've stepped on too many toes this time."

"Don't worry. My skin is pretty thick."

I called Marshall and Micki to tell them about the conversation. We agreed to meet at eight in the morning at the Hay-Adams to go over any last minute issues. Micki was clearly nervous about her prospects with Ruth and Mary on such short notice. Marshall wanted to know if Anna could come, and I reminded him that might tip our hand. He saw my point immediately and said he'd suggest an outing to the Smithsonian.

Maggie and I worked late into the night, and I felt as prepared as I could be considering I had no idea what to expect or what Micki's interview with Ruth and Mary might uncover.

We turned off the lights, and I took a cab back to Barker's. Hopefully I wouldn't be sleeping in DC's jail tomorrow night. I'd spent a night in jail once before, hadn't been much fun.

WEDNESDAY

May 4, 2016

67

WE ALL ARRIVED at the Hay-Adams promptly at eight. No jokes this morning; we were all business, all clearly nervous. Micki looked terrific in khaki pants, a cream silk blouse, and a black linen blazer. Marshall's character was obvious, even without his judge's robes. Micki murmured that Beth had returned to be with Ruth and Mary. It must have been a difficult evening.

Micki cleared her throat. "I'm ready to present what happened to these two young women. We don't have time now to go through their story, but trust me, Billy Hopper did not murder Nadia."

Exactly what I needed to hear. I knew that a seasoned prosecutor would have a field day cross-examining two working girls, but we weren't in court today. Our audience was one.

All three of us knew our roles, so there wasn't much else to say. Our audience was the Attorney General. We were asking him to interfere with the prosecution of a crime, to meddle in a local case against the will of the US Attorney, and to disregard the demands and influence of a Senator and a well-known defense contractor. The AG would be a tough sell, but I was more worried by Constance Montgomery. She was no slouch, and he would be guided by her position.

We cleared security at main Justice quite easily. The Attorney General's office is on the fifth floor of a magnificent WPA building. A huge table that seats at least thirty people comfortably dominates his conference room. At the far end is a wood-burning fireplace. When Robert Kennedy was Attorney General he used the conference room as his office. He was a family man to the core, and the large oriental carpet still reveals reminders of the exuberance of his children and his dogs. The current Attorney General prefers a smaller office and uses the room for meetings.

His executive assistant invited us to sit at the table. We were left to twiddle our thumbs for several minutes before an army of people filed into the room. The AG took his place at the head of the table. On his left were Peggy, Constance, the U.S. Attorney, and Deputy Director Calhoun. Staff, lots of staff, sat in chairs that lined the walls. I recognized Agent Barry. There were no offers of coffee, no casual conversation. You could have cut the air with a knife. I squeezed Micki's hand quickly, a silent reassurance.

Finally, the Attorney General fluffed up some papers and looked at Micki.

"You must be Ms. Lawrence. I'm sorry to have met you under these circumstances." She remained silent, not betraying even a hint of reaction. He turned to me.

"Mr. Patterson, you asked for this meeting, and I will give you ample opportunity to speak. However, I'd prefer to dispatch this issue quickly, so let me tell you what I think."

I nodded.

"I'm aware that when a lawyer is faced with an impossible case to defend he is tempted to use various tactics to distract and obfuscate. My lawyers face these tactics all the time, and we are perfectly capable of dealing with them. We go into court and seek gag orders, have frivolous subpoenas quashed, prevent irrelevant testimony from being presented, and on rare occasions seek sanctions against the worst abusers of the system. We do this all the time.

"But you take the cake. You have issued subpoenas to a respected U.S. Senator, one of this country's primary defense contractors, and a notorious assassin, thereby interfering with ongoing extradition negotiations. I'd like to know why I shouldn't bring the entire force of the Department of Justice down on your ass. What in the hell do you have to say for yourself?"

If he was trying to make me mad, he'd succeeded. I wanted nothing more than to gather my papers and my partners and walk out in a huff. I looked at Maggie, who knew me well. She smiled and mouthed the word "no."

I relaxed a little and tried to address the big dog in an even tone.

"Thank you. Let me first address the subpoena to Tina Lalas. You surely know that someone hired her to kill me and that she doesn't work of her own volition or for free. I don't know for sure who hired her, but I believe she was hired to kill me because I have discovered not only who did kill the woman at the Mayflower, but why. You may threaten me with sanctions and the weight of the justice department, but any lawyer worth his salt isn't going to let a key witness leave the country without doing everything possible to find out who ordered that hit." I needed to slow down.

"Now. Ms. Fortson rightfully told me Tina wasn't in the country when the young woman was murdered in Billy Hopper's hotel room. But that doesn't mean that Tina's employer didn't hire someone else to kill the woman at the Mayflower. And I think I have a right to ask Tina who ordered the hit on me."

"She's taking the fifth. She's not going to talk to you, Jack," Peggy interrupted.

"You're probably right, but I'm entitled to discover that, am I not?" I asked.

"To what end?" Constance spoke. "She didn't murder the woman, Billy Hopper did."

I looked at the Attorney General and said, "May I explain to Ms. Montgomery why she's wrong."

"Go ahead, it's your hole you're digging."

"Constance, I'm not sure I can convince you that you're wrong. You've put a lot of effort into this case. You're invested in what seems to be obvious. But let me try. First, the murder weapon was a room service steak knife, yet Billy never ordered room service. He checked in, changed clothes for the banquet, and left only to return late that night."

"He could have gotten the knife from anywhere. An empty tray in the hall, for instance," she responded.

"True, but that indicates some kind of premeditation, not the crime of passion you have portrayed to the media and the Court. What was it your office told the press?—'He was drunk, couldn't perform, and took it out on the girl.'"

"Not necessarily. He could have been frustrated—left his room to get a knife, and then stabbed her to death. Or a knife could have been left over from a previous guest." We seemed to be the only people in this room.

"True, but why didn't she scream or try to escape. Her clothes were neatly folded in the corner. Does that indicate a struggle to you?"

"He smothered her with a pillow. That's what the medical examiner concluded. He smothered her, left the room, got a knife, and returned to the room to stab her to death. Sorry, Jack."

"Where'd the pillow come from?" I asked.

"What do you mean? It's a hotel pillow."

"Check the housekeeping record and the inventory of the room after the murder. There's an extra pillow in Billy's room. Do you think he left the room to find a spare pillow like the knife?"

"Bullshit. An extra pillow was probably left in the room from the night before. Let me ask you what kind of animal murders a woman and then goes to sleep in her blood. Your client, that's who." Constance was getting worked up, and I wasn't making any progress. The attorney general stepped in.

"Stop. This kind of crap isn't getting us anywhere. Save it for the courtroom."

I glanced at Micki, and she took over smoothly.

"You're right, except for one thing. Billy Hopper couldn't have murdered anyone that night. We have two witnesses who have sworn under oath to that effect."

I saw just a trace of concern cross Constance's brow. "What witnesses? Who?"

"For purposes of this discussion I will call them Mary and Ruth. They attended the NFL banquet with Billy Hopper, sat at his table, and, along with another girl named Ginger, helped Billy get back to the hotel and into his room."

Agent Barry rose, couldn't help himself. "Those two women have been missing for weeks. Where are they? If you're hiding them somewhere you need to turn them over to us immediately."

Micki ignored him, continuing to address the AG.

"After they heard about the incident at the Mayflower, the three girls who were involved left town with their bodyguard. The bodies of Ginger and her bodyguard were found over a week ago in a storm drain in Cleveland, Ohio. Their throats had been cut. That event was posted on a website called 'Free Billy,' and the story was carried on Fox News. The other girls fled Cleveland and contacted us looking for a safe haven. They are currently under our protection, and that's where they will remain for the time being."

Calhoun mouthed a warning, but Barry couldn't keep his mouth shut.

"Those girls may be in danger. You need to turn them over to the FBI."

Micki turned to him and said coldly, "Not a chance. If you were so concerned about their safety, Agent Barry, how come as of this morning the Cleveland Police Chief says not a single member of the FBI has made contact with his office. A crucial witness to a murder investigation goes missing, turns up dead in Cleveland, and the FBI doesn't even make a phone call? These women are definitely in danger. You really think I'm going to turn them over to you?"

Micki had made her point; it was time to move on. She turned back to the Attorney General.

"Both Mary and Ruth will say that all three girls were hired for the evening to sit with Billy and the four men from Logan Aerospace at the NFL Honors banquet. They had been instructed by their bodyguard, or pimp, if you prefer, to make sure Billy was the one who ordered the drinks, even though he nursed a single beer for the entire evening. Toward the end of the banquet, the now dead girl slipped a knockout drug into Billy's beer. When he could no longer stand, they helped him get back to the Mayflower and into his room."

Constance spoke up, "A convenient story, but totally inconsistent with what the four men say happened that evening." She shouldn't sound so smug.

"Please let me finish. Both girls will say they helped Billy to his room and into his bed. By then he was now completely out of it. It was easy to remove his clothes and leave him alone and totally naked, just as they had been instructed. On the way out they handed the keycard to Billy's room to a man who was waiting outside the door with a camera in hand. They assumed he was going to take pictures of Billy for blackmail purposes."

Constance looked at the attorney general. "I don't believe this cock and bull story for a minute. First, we have no idea who these girls are. Until they have been interviewed their story doesn't pass any credibility test. Second, what about this mystery cameraman? Is there any proof of his existence—any pictures, any evidence there was another man in the room? Finally, if you believe their story, what prevented Billy from waking up, meeting the deceased later on, and then murdering her? How does Ms. Lawrence explain the semen all over the bed? I don't buy these two girls' stories no matter how credible they seem to Ms. Lawrence. They're probably still on the make, looking for their fifteen minutes of fame."

I could tell Micki was pissed, and was relieved that she kept her poise. She glanced at the AG, who merely nodded.

"I'm not sure exactly which 'credibility test' the prosecutor has in mind—is there a standardized form? If so, I don't think it will present much of a problem for either Ruth or Mary. As to the presence of the cameraman, she is correct—you will find no evidence of his presence in the room because the room was wiped clean of prints. The only prints in the entire room are Billy's, and then only in places where he likely went when he woke up. No prints from housekeeping, no prints from the deceased, even though her clothes were stacked neatly in a corner of the room. Not a single print from anyone else, including the three girls who helped him into the room.

"As to the semen, both Mary and Ruth say they were instructed to masturbate Billy once he was completely unconscious. In case you're curious, I have checked with three physicians and, yes, that can easily be done. Mary and Ruth will describe how it was done in minute detail if you wish."

Barry jumped up gleefully. "See, they're nothing but whores. Ha! Some credible witnesses."

Constance and everyone else turned to stare, this time in distaste, giving Micki a chance to continue.

"I prefer to call them victims, Agent Barry, but, yes, they are professional women. Since you interviewed each of the four employees of Logan Aerospace, you probably know that true to their instructions, the three girls returned to the Mandarin, rejoined the four men at the bar, and after several more drinks went upstairs with the men for a night of sex. Or maybe they didn't tell you that part of their story. These four men may have a few credibility issues of their own, as I believe they all have wives and young children."

I could tell the Attorney General had heard enough about sex; Micki sensed it as well. She finished quickly.

"We have unearthed many more holes in the prosecutor's case. For example, the extra pillow in the room matches exactly a pillow missing from the room next door. The guest staying in the room next door ordered steak from room service. The staff will testify that the previous guest left no steak knife in Billy's room. Finally, Ms. Montgomery has suggested that Billy could have woken up, met the deceased elsewhere, perhaps the bar, and later murdered her. I'd like to point out that the medical examiner's time of death is pegged at only thirty minutes after he arrived at his room. Where was she in the brief period of time between when Mary and Ruth left Billy all alone unconscious and when she was dead? Billy certainly couldn't have leapt up from his drunken or drugged state and gone down to the bar to get her."

Constance wasn't going to give up easily.

"Mr. Attorney General, Mr. Patterson and Ms. Lawrence certainly have pointed out some holes in our case that are worth examining, and I assure you that I will be diligent in determining the credibility of their newly-found witnesses as soon as they are made available. But these are matters for our office. There is no need for you to step in at this point. We are here because Mr. Patterson has gone off the deep end, issuing subpoenas that compel testimony and documents from persons who have no relevance to the Hopper case."

Micki and I had anticipated her response. It was exactly the one that would appeal to the Attorney General—promise to evaluate the new evidence, but shut down all the rest. Looking satisfied, he turned to Peggy. It was time for door number three. I cleared my throat and plunged.

"Ms. Montgomery, let me ask you one more question. How did the FBI get involved in this case? It seems to me that this murder investigation would normally be handled by the DC police."

68

I noticed Deputy Director Calhoun begin to squirm and Peggy's eyebrows rise. Sensing Constance's hesitation, the AG looked at her for an answer.

"Well, I guess that's not a state secret. Director Calhoun called me that first morning and offered assistance. He said this would be a high profile case and that he'd be happy to detail a couple of special agents to help. I accepted, and agents Barry and Pitcock quickly arrived on the scene," she said matter-of-factly.

"And have they have taken the lead in interviewing witnesses such as the four men who work for Logan Aerospace, and supervised the assembly of all the physical evidence?"

She assented, and I paused again.

"Okay. And did they also interview everyone who knew the deceased, her family, her friends, and her work associates."

I'd finally gotten under her skin.

"What is this? You know good and well we don't know the identity of the deceased. We have advertised on the air and in the newspapers, but we haven't turned up a clue as to who she is. But I won't rest until I do, I promise you that." She looked to the AG, throwing up her hands in disgust.

I didn't give him a chance to intervene.

"So, neither Agents Barry, Pitcock, nor Director Calhoun told you they know the identity of the deceased? They've had you spinning your wheels, tossing and turning at night, running ads in the paper, and they never said a word? Constance, not only did they know who she was, they knew her personally." I sure as hell hoped I hadn't gone too far.

Constance's face went white. She turned to Barry—the truth was written all over his face. He bit his lip and looked at the floor. No one said a word as the AG turned to Calhoun.

"Can this be true, Felix? Has the FBI known the woman's identity and withheld it from the U.S. Attorney?"

Felix gulped. "I don't think this matter is appropriate for this audience. There is an explanation, but it involves national security and an ongoing investigation."

I wasn't about to let him off the hook.

"Her name is Nadia Nikolov." Maggie handed Constance a copy of the file we had received from Novak.

I spoke directly to her. "I think you will find her immigration fingerprints match those of the deceased." Constance took the file and began to look through it.

I turned to the Attorney General, but Calhoun interrupted.

"I must insist that this is not a forum for a discussion about Ms. Nikolov. We are talking about a sting operation approved by your predecessor that is still ongoing and has national security implications."

The AG looked at Peggy, who spoke.

"Director Calhoun, you called this office and demanded we put a stop to, and I quote, 'that wild man Jack Patterson.' We've just been told the FBI withheld vital information from the prosecutor in a murder investigation. Now you wish to shut down the very meeting you asked to attend.

"Mr. Calhoun, your request to end this meeting gives credence to Mr. Patterson's allegations. Has the FBI in fact known the dead woman's identity all along? Did some of your agents, including agent Barry, know her personally?"

Calhoun knew when to keep quiet. He simply nodded.

Peggy turned to me again. "Mr. Patterson, I take it that if we simply sit back and listen, we will hear why that flurry of subpoenas went out yesterday."

Finally, I turned to Constance Montgomery.

"Let me first say that my team has no desire to interfere with or upset an ongoing investigation of the FBI, except to the extent we can convince all of you that Billy Hopper had nothing to do with the death of Nadia. Billy never met her, never ran into her, and has no idea who she is. Constance, you had no way of knowing any of this because the FBI had no intention of ever letting you find out who she was or helping you discover who in fact did murder her."

The color had returned to Constance's face; she was ready to listen.

"If you had discovered her identity, you would have known that Nadia's story is the same as many young girls who come to America pursuing a dream, only to get caught up in our nation's sex trade. At fifteen, she was branded and sold on a street corner. The mark on her shoulder that your medical examiner referred to as a birthmark was actually a brand she tried to have removed." Maggie passed the medical records over.

"But Nadia was different from most of these girls—she was a fighter. With the help of friends, she managed to break free of the men who controlled her. But by that time she had become permanently scarred, her heart had turned cold. Who can blame her? She decided to stay in the business, but she would handle her own business: no protectors and no pimp. She was very attractive, as the photographs indicate. She kept to herself and over time developed quite a clientele. Many of them may come as a surprise to you. They certainly did to me.

"One client was Senator Jason Boudreaux, who I'm sure the AG has heard from since we subpoenaed him yesterday."

"The Senator certainly did call. You should be very careful. Are you saying he was involved in the murder of that young woman?" The Attorney General looked truly distraught.

"No, I don't think he was, although he may have caused her death indirectly. I know he was surely the catalyst for a series of events that led to her death, but, no, I don't think he killed her," I responded.

"Then what is your point, Jack?" Peggy asked.

"Let me tell you what we do know. Over twenty years ago, the Senator returned to Tennessee to bond with his constituents, met a wide-eyed fifteen year-old girl near Bibb, Tennessee, and got her pregnant."

Stupidly, Barry interrupted. "You don't know that. You're speculating."

Peggy brushed him off. "Agent Barry, please no more interruptions."

"He's right. I haven't asked for DNA tests yet, but I know the Senator believed he was the father because he sent the young girl's mother a hundred dollar bill once a month for over twenty years. And he probably paid a cousin a whole lot more money to marry the girl and keep her quiet."

Constance looked up from her notes. "I assume you have some proof."

I smiled. "I subpoenaed the Senator, so I hope to be able to ask him directly, but, yes, we have some rather graphic pictures. Moreover, the mother kept the money in the individual envelopes—there are piles of them, neatly tied with string by year. She never spent a single dollar. I bet the envelopes will reveal the Senator's fingerprints."

The AG turned to Peggy and said under his breath, "I'd like to meet that woman."

I responded, "You certainly can. She's in town to meet her only grandson who is currently being detained in the DC jail."

Peggy blurted out, "Are you saying Billy Hopper is the illegitimate son of Senator Boudreaux?"

"As I said, I don't have the DNA yet, but I know that at least the Senator thinks that is the case as does the grandmother. Isn't that true, Director Calhoun?"

"I am not about to confirm or deny a word of what you say." His refusal gave lie to his words.

The Attorney General was fed up.

"I don't know what to do here. I'm tempted to shut this meeting down until I can figure out what in the hell the FBI has been doing."

I couldn't let that happen. Nadia's death would be swept under the rug, witnesses would disappear, and Billy would either be convicted or deemed a murderer for the rest of his life. I knew how long internal government investigations take—forever.

"I don't believe the FBI murdered Nadia or set Billy up, so let me speculate a little before we discuss where you should go from here."

The Attorney General turned to Peggy, and she nodded her head.

"Go ahead."

"The Senator holds a very powerful position on the appropriations committee. He is also well known on the Hill for having a voracious sexual appetite. Certainly a lobbyist has occasionally provided an influential member of Congress with a woman for the night in return for a favor. I'm speculating here, but nevertheless at some point the Senator and Nadia made connection.

"What I do know, as fact, is that Logan Aerospace made regular weekly payments into Nadia's bank account during the same time she met the Senator at the Mayflower hotel once a week. The money came in like clockwork. Last year, deposits from a new source showed up. This 'client' made fewer deposits, but the dollar amounts were significant. That client is a front for the FBI—L&A Marketing Advisors. Nadia had decided to work both sides of the street. L&A also provided Nadia a credit card to pay for the room at the Mayflower."

I turned to Calhoun—this time he had nothing to say.

"My speculation is that the FBI is conducting an ongoing investigation into members of the appropriations committee and payments made to them by defense contractors. Nadia was feeding them information."

Calhoun crossed his arms defensively.

Peggy asked. "Why kill Nadia and why frame Billy for the murder? I assume that's where you are going with this."

"Logical question. A couple of events occurred that brought matters to a head. First, Billy hired a private investigator to find out about his mother and her family. It was only a matter of time before he would discover the truth. I think either the Senator got wind of this and told his friends at Logan, or Logan found out directly. As much as they had invested in the Senator, Logan was bound to have known about the rape and Billy. It was another hammer they held over the Senator. If the rape became public knowledge, Logan would lose their golden goose.

"Second, the Senator found a new playmate—Claudia. She is a young, cute staff member and became a very willing sexual partner. Nadia lost her gravy train. Logan had cut her off several months ago, and it was only a matter of time before the FBI dropped her as well.

From her phone records, it looks like she called her contact at Logan to arrange a meeting. She told a former acquaintance she had one big gig left before she could retire. My guess is she threatened to spill the goods unless they paid for her silence. Thus the meeting and why she was at the Mayflower that night in the room next to Billy's—Room 703.

"I think Logan quickly realized they could solve both their problems with one solution—murder Nadia and frame Billy for the murder."

Barry interrupted, "You really believe a major defense contractor would murder someone?" I wondered if he would have a job tomorrow morning.

I used his question to continue. "No, I don't. I think they hired the same group that tried to murder me by hiring Tina Lalas, PS Trading out of Shanghai. I have proof they were monitoring our phones and computers. I suspect Director Calhoun knows all about Mr. Kim and PS Trading, don't you, sir?"

Calhoun looked at the Attorney General. "I must insist, General, we really are getting into sensitive information with national security implications."

I didn't want to get distracted.

"PS and Logan come up with a plan. Logan arranges for a table at the NFL Honors banquet and pays extra to have Hopper sit at the table. Logan is really quite tickled with the idea of framing Hopper. The owner of the Lobos is Red Shaw, one of Logan's biggest competitors. His newest star will now cost Shaw millions, both in hard cash and public relations. They hire three girls to sit with Hopper, drug him, and bring him back to the Mayflower. The girls strip Hopper and leave, handing a cameraman the room key. The girls return to the Mandarin and do what they were hired to do: entertain the boys so they will later say anything to avoid exposure.

"Meanwhile Nadia goes to the room next to Billy's at the Mayflower, thinking she is meeting with Logan to arrange for the final payoff. She's knocked cold, smothered with a pillow and carried to Billy's room where she's stabbed. Our killers made three big mistakes. First, they left the pillow in Billy's room—housekeeping noted a pillow missing from room 703. Second, they didn't realize the inconsistency of the steak knife. Finally, they took the room keycard with them rather than leave it in the room."

Constance said, "No card key in the inventory. I missed that."

"True. The locked doors mean nothing. The killers had the card key—they could come and go as they pleased. The cameras on the floor had been disabled. Billy couldn't have left the room to get a knife or a pillow. He couldn't have gotten back into his room. The girls gave the only keycard to the cameraman. We checked with the front desk: they only issued one keycard to Billy. Moreover, he was heavily drugged the entire time.

"I'm sorry, Constance, but your lead investigators were so busy making sure Nadia's identity remained a secret and trying to cover up the FBI's involvement that I'm not sure you can trust any information you've received from them. For example, did they tell you that the room next to Billy's was paid for with L&A's credit card? I'd bet good money they also cleaned out her house and commandeered her handbag and phone before it could be inventoried that first morning. The FBI had to get her phone before anyone else; it would show phone calls to Agent Barry." I stared at Barry, who for once remained silent. He was caught and he knew it—so did the rest of us.

Calhoun, however, wasn't ready to throw in the towel. "That's enough. I'm tired of your insinuations. My agents were doing their job; they most certainly did nothing wrong," he spouted.

I'd had enough, too.

"Deputy Calhoun, as if withholding Nadia's identity from the prosecutor, interfering with a murder investigation, stealing evidence from the Mayflower and Nadia's home, and even removing the labels from her clothing weren't enough, how about telling the prosecutor that another crucial witness works for you—one Claudia Ellis, who happens to be the Senator's current love interest."

He looked stunned, not by my accusation; he was stunned I knew. Claudia should have never handed me the napkin with her cell phone number on it.

"Yes, Claudia, the young staffer who is the Senator's current paramour. The same woman who was at the table at the banquet and saw Ginger slip Billy a knockout drug. The same woman who slept with Billy's agent that night to find out what he knew about

Billy's father. She is on the FBI's payroll as well as the Senate's. She called Mr. Calhoun, not the Senator, when she received her subpoena. She also called Mr. Calhoun the night of the murder. Deputy Calhoun, perhaps you'd liked to tell the Attorney General about those conversations?"

Peggy turned and got in Calhoun's face.

"Please tell me Jack isn't telling the truth. Tell me the FBI doesn't employ women to sleep with senators. Tell me that a witness who can exonerate Billy Hopper isn't withholding exculpatory evidence on your orders."

Calhoun's tone was derisive. "Ms. Fortson, you are naïve. The FBI does what it has to do. Our national security is involved. That's all that matters. You have no idea what we have uncovered."

National security. That old sacred cow that justifies anything these days—violations of privacy, lies to Congress, and now employment of paramours. I hadn't really known the full extent of Claudia's involvement with the FBI. I'd exaggerated a little, and Calhoun had taken the bait. All in the name of national security, right?

The Attorney General appeared to be in a bit of a fog, so I looked to Peggy. I almost felt bad about dumping this mess in her lap.

"If I may..." Peggy began. He nodded in relief.

"Connie, we've heard a lot today. I'm not going to tell you how to run your case, but I think we've heard enough to give the case a new and fresh look at a minimum. I would suggest that Mr. Hopper be released into the custody of Ms. Lawrence and Mr. Patterson. I would also suggest that the DC Police take over the investigation of the murder of Ms. Nikolov, as well as the attempted murder of Mr. Patterson. If you agree, the FBI will have no involvement in either case for the present time. I will make sure of that. Given the probable existence of an ongoing investigation by the FBI that seems to have relevance to your investigation, all coordination will come through my office. Does that make sense?" Peggy was being very diplomatic, suggesting not ordering.

Peggy continued, "Mr. Patterson, you have assembled quite a bit of evidence. I hope you can work with this office and Ms. Montgomery's office without compromising the defense of your client. I hope you will withdraw your subpoena of the Senator for the time being. He's not going anywhere."

I didn't respond.

Constance finally spoke up. Her jaw was set.

"I'm prepared to go further, Deputy Fortson, if there are no objections. I am going to dismiss the indictment of Mr. Hopper without prejudice. We can always file charges if we find new evidence. He will be released from jail as early as this afternoon, and I will issue a press release saying that we have come across newly discovered evidence that appears to exonerate him completely. To be honest, the FBI has tainted this investigation to such a degree I'm not sure I could obtain a conviction of anyone, much less the real perpetrator, but I'm going to try.

"I hope Mr. Hopper's defense team will cooperate with my investigation and share with me what you can in the way of evidence. To that end, you have in your custody two women who at this point are our only connection to Logan Aerospace and the murderer. I need to speak to them sooner rather than later. If what you say is true, they belong in protective custody."

I looked at Micki, who I knew would refuse. Constance turned to address her directly.

"Ms. Lawrence, I know you have no reason to trust me at this point. The FBI has compromised my office. If I were you I'd be very protective of those two women, but I hope you will check my record: I've been fighting the sex trade my entire career. I know what those two women must be going through right now. I'll let you call the shots. Why don't just the two of us meet this afternoon? I won't let the FBI come close to those two women. If you're satisfied, the DC police have special housing for women who need protective custody. The living quarters are quite nice, and they are bound to need medical care."

Micki was a tough nut to crack. "Two o'clock at your offices. I'll probably bring Jack's daughter with me."

At that point, Peggy announced the meeting was over.

Calhoun and Barry left quickly. Marshall walked directly up to the Attorney General, and before long they left together. Maggie, Constance, and Micki started talking about documents, so I approached my friend Peggy Fortson.

She smiled. "You know one of these days I'm going to learn not to take your calls. The FBI and a major contractor providing call girls to a Senator and no telling what else. What a mess you've handed me."

She was quick to interpret my silence. "What aren't you telling me?"

"When Constance gets our documents she'll see that Logan was not Nadia's only client. She will also receive more information on L&A. You need to receive your own copies. As a friend told me once, "I've not handed you a mess; I've handed you a hornet's nest."

69

WE HAD WON, at least for now. Many questions remained unanswered, but Billy would be a free man. It's almost as hard to get someone released from jail as it is from the hospital. We finally walked out into the fading sunshine around five o'clock. Thank God, the press hadn't been tipped off. Billy Hopper was soon enjoying a quiet dinner with Marshall, Grace, and his newly discovered grandmother, Anna. The Hay-Adams had been happy to provide a private room for their meal, as well as a room for the night. Billy said he never wanted to set foot in the Mayflower again. Who could blame him?

Micki and Beth spent the whole afternoon with Constance working on a plan to turn over custody of Mary and Ruth to the DC police. Martin was called in, and by the early evening things had been resolved. Beth would coordinate the transition. She had become close to the two women, and I could think of no one better. She wouldn't return to New Orleans until Sunday, so she and I would finally have some time together.

Beth and Micki had a long talk about what was eating at Micki. Beth later told me, "Everything's cool," but refused to give me any details. I later asked Maggie if she knew what was going on. She smiled and said the two of them needed to clear the air about me. When I pressed her she shrugged me off saying, "You wouldn't understand."

I heard almost immediately from Red. He was tickled pink to have his wide receiver back and claimed that it was Lucy who had come up with the plan to hire me. She knew that once involved and intrigued, I couldn't walk away from Billy. I didn't know I was that predictable.

She even told him that she had always doubted Billy's guilt. Same old Lucy—she always had perfect hindsight.

Red insisted that my representation of Billy had always been secondary to him—he really did want me to represent the team's interests. In fact, he gave me an added responsibility, for which he was happy to pay extra—make sure the NFL reinstated Billy, and quickly. The job wouldn't be as easy as one might think. The NFL would want to do its own investigation, and Constance would not be inclined to be cooperative while she was trying to find the real perpetrator. Red also warned that other NFL owners would privately encourage the commissioner to slow walk a decision. They'd be much happier if Billy weren't running amok in their backfields.

I still had reservations about working for an NFL team given my concern about the increased violence and injuries, let alone fantasy sports. Typical Red—when I told him about my reservations, he said he had the same concerns, and we would work on them together. We were certainly strange bedfellows. He went on to tell me how Billy was a key element in his desire to change the face of football from violence to one of purely skill and speed. Getting Billy reinstated was key.

Of course, the press, especially the sports press, was caught totally off-guard. We agreed that it would look better if Micki took the lead in dealing with the press. Her presence before the cameras as Billy's lawyer might soften the hearts of those who were still convinced that Billy was capable of violence against women. Micki was great at the initial press conference and during a series of TV interviews scheduled by the Lobos. I could tell she was enjoying herself. She was so good Red tried to hire her, but she demurred. She and Larry were ready to get back to Little Rock.

I read in the *Post* a few days later that Felix Calhoun had resigned from the FBI to work in the private sector. The Attorney General and the FBI director announced that the FBI would undertake a management restructuring process. I didn't read anything about Agent Barry, but I suspected he had been reassigned to Alaska—maybe he could see Russia from his new outpost. Senator Boudreaux surprised a lot of folks by announcing he'd decided not to seek reelection this fall. Who is in line to take his seat on the appropriations committee? You guessed it—Senator Lucy Robinson.

Clovis reported that PS Trading had closed their offices. The attorney for Logan calls me at least once a day asking when I'm going to withdraw my subpoena. He gets very frustrated with my repeated response: "I have to check with Constance Montgomery."

I dreaded the call from Novak, but he seemed to understand that no one knew for sure yet who had actually killed Nadia. He said it was unfortunate that I was no longer involved, but he thought he might have an idea or two that could help. I gave him Constance's number; my job had ended when Billy was exonerated. He told me "off the record" that Nadia's money had found its way to her parents. I think that made him a little more willing to mourn rather than seek revenge.

He told me the Louisiana syndicate was searching for the man who ordered the hit on Beth. He apparently had failed to show the syndicate "proper respect." He told me to not to worry about Beth or Jeff while they were in New Orleans. I wasn't sure how I felt about my daughter being under the protective umbrella of the mob, but I thanked him anyway.

I had intended my association with Novak to end after the Stewart case, but I was glad it hadn't. While a lot of people congratulated me on being such a good lawyer, I knew I'd been very lucky, and so had Billy. If the dead woman had been anyone else but Novak's niece this case would have never been solved, and Billy likely would have been convicted despite all the holes in the prosecution's case.

That reality made me think about all the people who die every year and are never identified and their families never notified. I decided to have the Foundation do some research into this to determine the magnitude of the problem and how it could be addressed. In this day and time of information no one should live or die in total obscurity.

We all went out for dinner at Cantler's before half the team returned to Little Rock. Jeff came up for the occasion, and I thought he might try to corner me to ask for Beth's hand in marriage, but it didn't happen. Apparently their time schedule is between them, or so Beth told me. Next year Jeff is headed to Barnes Hospital in St. Louis to further his residency. No surprise, Beth is moving to St. Louis as well. She'd been thinking for some time about getting her Masters in social work at Washington University. Her work with Mary and Ruth had convinced her that the decision was the right one.

I finally met Larry. I kind of liked him. He clearly adored Micki, and talked very little unless someone asked him about wood or cabinetry. She seemed to be back in good spirits, but I made it a point to ask Maggie again about what had been eating her.

"Jack, for a smart guy, you can sometimes be clueless," she said bluntly. "You and Micki had quite the romance years ago. She thinks her feelings toward you contributed to the breakup with Eric. She doesn't want to lose Larry, too. You're obviously head-over-heels about Carol Madison which complicates things further—no wonder she's been irritable these last couple of weeks. Frankly, I'm surprised she agreed to come at all."

I decided to leave it alone. Micki was happy and that's what mattered.

Maggie told me that Walter's company had made Stella one hell of an offer to run the Matthews companies' IT operation. The offer allowed her to live in Little Rock and continue to run her gym, but it would involve a lot more travel to DC and to the data center in Charlotte, North Carolina. I could tell they were both torn because they were quieter than usual. I pulled Clovis aside and asked if he wanted to talk. He asked if I could come to Arkansas and go fishing next month. We would talk then. He didn't need to twist my arm.

It took over a week to deal with all the details of closing up the case. I did learn one thing of interest. When Marshall joined a New York firm as a young lawyer, his first case involved a ticklish personal matter for the family that had owned the Hay-Adams for many years. He brought the matter to a successful conclusion without the matter getting into the press, and even convinced his firm not to charge them a red cent. The ownership of the hotel has changed, be he is still allowed to stay there for almost nothing whenever he wants. He, of course, has never abused their generosity and still keeps in touch with the family when he's in town.

Billy and his grandmother are almost inseparable. He has arranged for all her belongings to be shipped out to his home in LA. He doesn't want her to ever return to Bibb, nor does he care to meet his biological father. Who could blame him? He hired a new agent, a former ball player who has an excellent reputation with both management and the NFL Player's union. Red told me he hopes to lock Billy into a long-term deal if I would just do "my job" and get the NFL "off their ass." Working for Red was going to be a challenge.

Maggie and Walter were on their way to a wedding in Cannon Beach, Oregon. They'd decided to leave a little early to enjoy the many wineries and incredible scenery between Portland and the coast. They invited me to join them, but I declined. Instead, I called Pat and asked for Carol's phone number. He told me, "not to bother." My heart sunk before he laughed.

"Carol has been calling every day asking if you've called. Don't bother calling her, she's already arranged for Red's plane to be on stand-by to fly you to where she is. Be at the Lobos' hanger this afternoon at four o'clock."

"Should I be ready for sun or snow?" I asked.

"She said to bring your bathing suit."

Acknowledgments

I PLAYED FOOTBALL in high school and for the Arkansas Razorbacks. My teammates remain some of my best and closest friends to this day. There is something about the sport that bonds you with your teammates and when one hears of a teammate in trouble you come to his aid without reservation or judgment. I know about this firsthand. My thanks to every single teammate for your unwavering support and encouragement.

Terry, Walter, and Caroline read the early drafts, giving me valuable insight. Once again, my wife Suzy spent endless hours reading and editing every draft. My children and their spouses gave me input and encouragement. My Charlotte, DC, and Arkansas friends continue to be my biggest supporters and cheerleaders.

My son, Walter, offered advice and tremendous insight into the world of fantasy football. My sister, Terry, keeps me straight when it comes to medical issues. My friends Sonya and David gave me tremendous advice with the issues surrounding the representation of a high-profile client and pre-trial issues.

Beaufort Books has once again my deepest thanks and appreciation. Publisher Eric Kampmann believed in me from day one. Megan Trank, Michael Short, and Felicia Minerva have given me invaluable help in editing, cover design, and publicity. No author has a better or more patient team.

Every day I remain eternally grateful to George and his family.